LOVER CHILD

A Novel

STEPHEN KRONWITH, M.D.

Lover Child is a work of fiction. Although some of the named places, such as cities and states, obviously exist, the events described that occur in each of those places are the imaginings of the author and any events that might coincide with actual events are purely coincidental. Any structures or buildings mentioned may, by chance, resemble true structures or buildings at or near the locations cited, but again, the structures and buildings in this novel, as well as the story itself, are totally fictitious and imaginary.

Finally, any resemblance of the characters in *Lover Child* to real persons, living or dead, is purely coincidental.

Table of Contents

Copyright Page
Table of Contents
Dedication

To All My Readers

PART I–Reunions, Rewards and Regicide

"The pain of parting is nothing to the joy of meeting again."

~Charles Dickens, 'Nicholas Nickleby'

"If you do one good deed your reward usually is to be set to do another and harder and better one."

~C.S. Lewis, 'The Horse and His Boy'

"By the pricking of my thumbs,
Something wicked this way comes."

~William Shakespeare, 'Macbeth'

Chapter 1

Tuesday, December 31, 2019
Henderson, Nevada
6 PM Pacific Standard Time

My internet search was interrupted by a much-too-loudly dropped, thirty-pound bag of dog food on the checkout counter. Looking up, I faced a twenty-something tattooed dude in a wife-beater T-shirt. On it was a drawing of a lit, phallus-shaped candle with the words "BLOW ME!" emblazoned below.

One of Henderson's finest, no doubt, was my unvoiced suspicion.

"Jesus, that's heavy. Now I can see why my wife's always bitchin' about buying this shit." *A real Sir Walter Raleigh, this guy.*

"How come she couldn't come in tonight?" I innocently asked.

"She's got some sort of weird flu."

Okay, I'll bite—"What's so weird about it?"

The Husband of the Year smirked. "It's kept her from yappin' at me for two straight days."

Suspicion confirmed.

"Well," he continued, "no way I'm doing this again. There are better ways of getting a hernia."

My inquiring mind was interested in knowing what one or two of those might be, but I decided, for once, to control myself. I passed the scanner over the bar code.

"That'll be $58.24."

The guy looked at me as if I were an IRS agent who'd just told him condoms were not deductible as a medical expense. Of course, in this cretin's case I'd argue that rubbers, or anything else to keep him from procreating, were gifts to humanity and therefore qualified as charitable deductions. Anyway, I've been doing this long enough to know what was coming next.

"Shit, my fuckin' dog eats better than *I* do." *Yep, certainly haven't heard that line in... oh... two hours.*

"Well, why not ask your wife to switch?"

He stared at me for a moment, and then, "Say what?"

"Why don't *you* eat the dog food, and have the mutt have whatever your wife's serving? If he's eating better than you, that would seem the perfect solution."

Sir Walter was not amused. "Do they actually pay you to be a bitch?—cunt!"

I smiled, though he had just uttered my least favorite word in the English language. I've killed, or at least maimed, for less. "No, it's a perk of the job." The man's blank expression told me "perk" was one of the rare four-letter words he was unfamiliar with. "By the way," I continued, "I'm hoping to win 'Employee of the Month' for December." I handed him a business card preprinted with my name and a web-site for feedback to 7-Eleven Central, or whatever-the-hell the home office is called. I pointed to the web address. "Vote for me, there. As often as you like."

The guy shook his head back and forth, frowning. "Damn, girl. You're a fine piece of ass but you've got some fuckin' mouth on you." The frown quickly morphed into a leer. "If I had the time, I'd put something long and hard in it to shut you up."

My hands tightened into fists. *Oh yes, please,* I contemptuously thought. *Please try.*

Alas, it was not to be.

"Guess what, bitch? I'm going to Target. I'm sure they're cheaper and have prettier check-out girls." *Ouch, that one really hurt.*

"And you can put this fucking bag back by yourself." He turned and started for the door.

"Don't forget to vote!" I shouted to his back.

The automatic door allowed the man to raise both middle fingers as he exited. I would have given him two of my own, but that would have meant I gave a shit.

My name is *Angelica Foster*. Says so right on my nametag—black lettering on a white background. I know, not exactly an *haute couture* accessory, but I was never much into bling. The large green "**7**" plastered across the work uniform went nicely with my emerald eyes, however. I never bothered with colored contact lenses but had dyed my hair black, added purple streaks and grew it to middle-of-the-back length—the only concessions to mask my previous identity.

Until about six months ago I went by the name Angelica *Fortuna,* a professional, but conflicted, assassin for, and non-biologic child of, Don Vito Fortuna of Philadelphia. Both of us, however, had been unaware of that *minor* detail regarding parentage until shortly before then. His newfound knowledge prompted my "father" to send me to kill the legendary 74-year-old hitman retiree, Sammy Vivino, better known as Lover Boy. The Boss had just learned *he wasn't*, and *Vivino was* my true progenitor from a duplicitous nurse to whom my mother had dictated a deathbed letter intended for my eyes only. The angel of mercy had hoped to curry favor with the Don, but instead was rewarded with a bullet to the head, ensuring no one else ever learned Vito Fortuna had been made a cuckold.

Thirty years prior, Fortuna had requested a favor from Vivino's employer. A hit was needed on a district attorney that had to be made to look accidental—Lover Boy's specialty. The Philadelphia Mafia boss left town for an alibi and Sammy, on loan from New York, stayed at our house to plan. My lovely mother, both inside and out, who had grown to detest her husband, remained home, alone with Lover Boy and... well, you can guess the rest.

Luckily, with the Don and me out of town, my mother had entrusted the letter to a friend, and on my way to kill Vivino, the loyal man thrust *Mamma's* written message into my hands at Philadelphia's 30th St. Station. By that act, my mission of murder transformed into one of discovery, and delight in meeting my true father, himself embracing an unknown daughter—with a similar, deadly skill set! Yes, I was so proficient at my job that I had been nicknamed, to my shame, *l'angelo della morte*—The Angel of Death.

Anyway, during the next seven days, Sammy showed me more love and affection than Don Fortuna had in thirty years, four of which the Boss abused by training me to become a killer of men.

You'll notice I said, "seven days," for after that time I entered the Witness Protection Program of the US Marshall's Service (WITSEC).

Within two weeks, I became Angelica Foster and was relocated to Henderson, a backwater, non-glitzy suburb of Las Vegas. Uncle Sam provided about $60,000 over the first three months while I searched for gainful employment and lodging.

I looked at my watch. It was 6:05. Julie, the night-shift girl, was late, as usual. She had no car and depended upon Henderson's anything-but-rapid transit system of buses. I didn't mind; Julie had become my best and only friend during my stay in Nevada. She was herself unattached—an on-again-off-again relationship with an abusive boyfriend, now in the off-again stage. He was residing in state prison for breaking into a liquor store prior to handing out his last drunken beating to my friend. Julie had six months before any possible parole to decide whether she'd remain in Henderson. Like most abused women, Julie often blamed herself for the bastard's fits of rage, but I hoped our many heart-to-hearts would convince her to move away.

We spent many an off-night together talking, Netflix-watching, and bar hopping—she, still looking for love, and me for alcohol and temporary respite from angst about my future. We got each other through many lonely and depressing nights; I owed her my sanity and much more—probably more than I could ever repay. I knew whatever was delaying her was giving my friend more anxiety than it was me since I'd told Julie the significance to this New Year's Eve, above all others.

Before I left New York, I'd said goodbye to a few wonderful acquaintances who had, in a brief period, become almost as dear to me as my beloved departed mother. One, as mentioned, was my *padre*. Another was Dr. Joseph Peck.

My Joe.

My love.

Over thirty years my elder, we had known each other for only seven days before being forced to part. Yet what a week it was as our love germinated, grew, and flourished. Seven days filled with laughter, passion, joy—and absolute terror, as twice in a matter of a few hours I had to employ my deadly skills to not just save *my* life, but those of *Papà*, Joe, and my new friends.

And as I prepared to leave with Agent Dan Simons, my WITSEC handler, I received parting gifts. One was Maverick, a beautiful German Shepard puppy gifted to me by Anna and Jane Franklin, a wonderful married couple. I had helped rescue their adopted daughter, Felicity, from three renegade kidnappers of a New York crime family.

Maverick has been my stalwart companion these past six months. Not only is he a sweet, loyal and loving pet, I've also trained him to be more, if needed. Besides perfect obedience to me alone, by a simple pointing of my hand with the index and middle fingers extended, and the German command, "*Fass!*" (a word not easily mistakenly uttered), my normally staid, tranquil dog would be transformed—and the object of my gesture would soon find his or her throat torn apart. I had purchased used mannequins, both male and female, from a local department store and spent many hours with Maverick in the backyard of my rented house, teaching him to be the perfect pet—and killer.

Why? Well, though I had eschewed my assassin role, I'd lived too many years among too many dangerous people. So I felt, in addition to my skills, another weapon in the arsenal couldn't hurt, right?

My false father had infused a sense of pessimism in me that I'm still trying to unlearn.

A second gift was an AT&T SIM card from my true father, to be placed into my iPhone moments before the ball dropped in Times Square on New Year's Eve. For until then I was forbidden, for my own safety, to have direct contact with anyone from my previous life. We could not risk that Don Fortuna, who believed me dead, would discover he'd been fooled—that it was I, not Lover Boy, who had killed *Il Boa*, the assassin he sent to drag me and my *padre* to a grisly grave. And it was I who had given a treasure trove of information to the FBI on the Philadelphia Mob—my price for WITSEC protection.

Upon parting, *Papà* promised that by the new year, or earlier, he'd figure out a way to eliminate the Don so I could return without fear of discovery. And each day I'd check on-line, multiple times, the Philadelphia Inquirer website. So far, no mention of Don Vito Fortuna's demise. If he had died, it would be front page news in every newspaper in the city where he controlled so much, and so many.

If *Papà's* promise was to come true, then, it would be tonight—and I was terrified. What if the phone did not ring?

For all I knew, my *padre*, skillful as he was, had failed—he was not a young man by any stretch. Maybe he was dead, either by natural or unnatural means. No, Simons would have informed me—or at least that's what I told myself. Obviously, everything was not going strictly to plan. As of just a few minutes ago, there were still no death notices on the Inquirer's site—no breaking news.

The comfort of Maverick's faithfulness, along with Julie's friendship, had sustained me these six months. But now fear had taken over. Fear of *Papà's* possible failure. Fear I could not yet

11

return—maybe ever. Fear of never again seeing my sweet Joe. Fear I rarely experienced, even when performing deadly duties at behest of my malevolent Don. Duties which, as I've already mentioned, I'd sworn never to repeat—though I *was* sorely tempted by that hernia-averse asshole.

I walked around the counter, sighed, and used a dead-man's lift to place the dog food bag across my shoulders—I've had a good deal of practice with that maneuver. Once the bag was returned to its proper location, the electric eye at the entrance notified all that the door had opened once again. I saw Julie enter, frazzled as always when she was tardy.

"I'm so sorry, Angelica. The damn bus was late again. Can you forgive me?" And she truly was distraught at the thought of my not getting home to prepare for the prayed-for call from my father. I had concocted a story of familial estrangement and of a promised ring on New Year's Eve if there was to be a reconciliation. So Julie knew how important tonight was, if not the true reason behind it. She had become almost as anxious as I about receiving "the call," even though if such a communique occurred, she'd lose a friend. But Julie prioritized my happiness over such a loss, and that fact filled my heart with joy.

We hugged, I proffered my forgiveness and tears came to both our eyes, hers a dazzling blue that went well with her short, cropped, light blonde hair—the color of lemonade. "Good luck," she said. I nodded. "Thank you, Julie. I don't know how I could have gotten through all this time without you. Please remember what we discussed about Brett." That was her hopefully permanent *ex*-boyfriend. "When I get back to New York, I'll text you my new number. Call me whenever you need to. Any time, day or night. Promise me you will." Julie nodded. "*Promise* me," I reiterated. "I promise," she said, adding, "Now go home and walk that lovable mutt, and wait for the call, which *I know* will come."

We hugged again before I grabbed my purse and waved as I raced to the door. Just before exiting, though, I decided, *what the hell,* and opened the purse, extracted a dollar and deposited it into one of the store's three *Jacks or Better* poker machines. This is Nevada, after all; they've got slot machines in the public restrooms!—puts a whole new spin on the pay-toilet concept. After pressing *Play,* and receiving a pair of deuces, I drew three cards. Garbage.

Not an auspicious sign, I thought. I sheepishly smiled at Julie, turned, and left.

It was dark in the lot, and my car was parked around the side, outside the view of the security camera at the front door. This was possibly known by the miscreant who now appeared, jumping out between two vehicles, brandishing a very unimpressive, two-inch knife.

I looked up to the heavens—"Really?"

"Let's have the purse, bitch!"

What is it about me and the "b" word? The kid was shaking, obviously somewhat high on whatever. He smelled of cigarette smoke and piss. Las Vegas was replete with drunks and addicts cruising the strip, day and night. This guy was typical.

Vegas—all the glitz couldn't hide the dirty, not-so-little secret that just below the surface of that small city festered all the problems of a modern-day metropolis, in spades—or hearts, diamonds or clubs if you prefer. Those problems, like a toxic chemical spill, slowly seeped into the surrounding towns and Henderson, unfortunately, was not spared.

I observed this pathetic creature standing before me, blocking my path to the car. It would take me precisely two seconds to disarm him and beat the crap out of him. I could easily turn his weapon against him, leaving the would-be thief bleeding to death as I casually drove away. But Angelica *Foster* decided to show this guy a kindness Angelica *Fortuna* never would. I opened my purse, plucked a twenty and stuck my arm out to the thief. "Let me explain. This is all you're getting. I suggest you take it and walk away. I won't warn you again." Then I just stared—and smiled.

I've been told I have a certain stare-smile combo that could make Satan himself turn on his heels and flee—think Norman Bates at the very end of *Psycho*. In the past, it usually preceded my taking of a life. Here it was to serve as a warning. Despite the drug-fueled haze that surrounded this kid, he seemed to decide that $20 was the better part of valor. He grabbed the bill, turned, but then seemed to change his mind. The addict spun and a look of dumb determination flashed across his face—drugs will do that. He outstretched his knife hand once again, but before any further ultimatums could be voiced, I employed one of my favorite lines from one of my favorite films. Joe and I love movies.

"You call that a knife?..." I began.

I was wearing a light jacket which I'd modified by adding a deep, inside pocket for a leather sheath to contain my KA-BAR 7-inch USMC fighting knife. It wasn't my favorite choice of blade, but that and my beloved Beretta had to remain in New York—WITSEC frowns upon firearms and being caught with one would mean immediate expulsion from the program. So I'd settled for a less lethal form of protection; though in my hands, any knife was almost as deadly as a gun. I extracted it within a second of my question, brandishing it in front of the asshole so he could clearly see it.

"... Now, *that's* a knife!" I said, finishing the quote. Crocodile Dundee would have been proud.

The boy's eyes widened, and he lowered his diminutive blade. "One more thing," I said menacingly. "If I *ever* see you within ten blocks of this place, I will use *this* blade to cut your dick off. Understand?"

I had learned just over half a year ago that this particular threat, especially when spoken ominously by yours truly (accompanied by my stare-smile), worked wonders in convincing the male of the species to comply with any demand. He nodded, swallowed hard, and ran.

Julie will never have to worry about his return.

Maverick greeted me at the door. Handsome and silver tan, he stood about a foot-and-a-half tall and weighed fifty pounds. With little else to do these past months, my training of the pooch had been extensive and extremely successful. He was turning out to be more intelligent than the wise-guys I'd dealt with in my previous life. Most of them were as dumb as a boulder—*rock* seeming too insignificant a comparison.

He licked my outstretched hand. "Hey buddy. Ready for your walk?" I turned, and he followed.

There was no need for a leash, as the well-trained canine matched me stride for stride. I had plastic bags in my purse for poop, which he reliably supplied at his favorite corner, and we slowly strolled for what I hoped was the last time through my quiet neighborhood. After a while, my Apple Watch showed me we'd gone a mile, so we spun, retraced our steps and returned to my ranch-style home on Ward Drive. I filled my friend's bowls with fresh water and his favorite dog food, *Instinct Raw Boots with Real Duck*. Hey, I love duck and Maverick was the closest I had, and probably ever would have, to a child of my own to spoil. So he was going to have the best! I'd eaten a late lunch at work and wasn't hungry—too nervous to eat, anyway.

I glanced at my watch: 8 PM—11 PM New York time. One more hour. I sat on my couch and turned on the TV. Dick Clark's (*how many years has this guy been dead now?*) New Year's Rockin' Eve was in full swing and pretty-boy Ryan Seacrest and airhead Jenny McCarthy were having a blast while I sat there biting my nails. I channel-surfed a bit and caught a replay of Queen Elizabeth's New Year's address. It's eight hours ahead in London, after all. Behind her stood Prince Charles—the world's oldest intern, screwed out of his Kingship for yet another year. If you ask me, the look on his face was not one of filial affection.

15

Enough of this, I decided, and switched back to Ryan and Jenny. After thirty more excruciating minutes, I shot up from my chair (Maverick's ears perked), went to the refrigerator, and withdrew the small bottle of champagne I had bought for tonight. I knew it was meant for midnight, but at this point I needed alcohol, so I opened it with the standard "pop" (that excited my dog), poured a glass and returned to the couch.

I tapped my watch and Mickey said, "8:45, PM"—fifteen minutes to midnight in New York. Yeah, I like Apple's Mickey Mouse watch-face—what of it? I opened my purse and withdrew the envelope. In it, since last July, lay my *padre's* SIM card plus the card ejector tool I had added a month ago. I powered down my iPhone, used the tool to remove the present card, and pushed the new one in. "Energize," I solemnly pronounced in my best Captain Picard voice, and turned on the phone. After a few moments, the ATT logo appeared with 4 bars of signal. All set.

I clicked on the Safari browser and then on the bookmark for the Philadelphia Inquirer. There was a report on new airstrikes in Iraq, some local stories of corruption (what else was new?), but nothing concerning Don Vito Fortuna.

Shit.

My hands started to tremble, and I took another swallow. Three minutes to go.

I watched the TV screen but turned down the sound—the happy talk didn't mesh with my mood. I motioned for Maverick to join me, and he jumped onto the couch and nestled in the crook of my left arm. "No matter what, big guy, we'll always have each other, right?" He looked at me and I could swear he smiled and nodded. *Must be the alcohol*, I thought.

The ball started its descent, the clock counting down from sixty. Everyone on screen seemed so happy as I squeezed Maverick tighter. Finally, 5-4-3-2-1, HAPPY NEW YEAR! screamed the on-screen text. Everybody started kissing each other. I looked at my phone. Nothing. I kissed Maverick on his forehead, and he responded by licking my face. Tears formed and even the dog noticed something was amiss and began to softly whine. I glanced at my watch—9:01 PST. I couldn't move as more tears fell, and then—

Here comes the sun, do, do, do, do... My default ringtone! I grabbed the phone. No name, but that wasn't a surprise since I had only Julie in my address book. The screen read LAKE SUCCESS, NY. *Anna and Jane live in Lake Success!*

I swiped the virtual answer button and picked the phone up to my ear.

"*Papà?*" I could barely croak out.

There was a pause, then "*Sì, mia cara. Sono io.*"

I could no longer contain my emotions and began to whimper, tears rolling down my cheek. Maverick increased the volume of his whining.

"It's so good to hear your voice, daddy. It's been... sooo long," I managed to say between sobs.

"*Sì, la mia bellissima angioletta.* It has. But no more."

I gathered up my courage to ask, "What's the word, *Papà?*"

"The *words are*, my dear—*è ora di tornare a casa!*"

And there it was. The dam burst and my soft sobs grew louder as I heard movement at the other end. The phone was being passed to another. Then—

"Angie?"

Joe. My Joe. I sat up straighter and Maverick followed my lead as he raised his head to my face and licked the tears from my cheek. "Joe, is that you?"

"Yes, *amore.* I'm here. I love you."

I gained control of my voice and said, "I love you more..." and then added an affectionate "... old man." He laughed, as I knew he would. Now I just needed confirmation, needed to know for sure. "Is it true, Joe? Is it true what *Papà* said?" I waited and the second that passed seemed an eternity.

"Yes, Angelica, my love," Joe answered—

"Time to come home."

Chapter 2

Friday, December 27, 2019—Four Days Earlier
Lake Success, NY
8 PM

The four friends sat around an exquisite coffee table inlaid with imported Italian marble. The two men relaxed on high back armchairs with cushions as light as air and the women sat opposite them on an Imperfectio sofa by Covet Paris. Its intentionally flawed, hammered brass end-pieces, to the cognoscenti, turned the luxurious and *très* comfortable couch into a $30,000 piece of functional art. But the price-tag amounted to, as Ralph Kramden of the classic 50s TV show, *The Honeymooners,* would often say, "a mere bag of shells." After all, the slightly older of the women, Anna Franklin, had inherited billions upon the death of her late husband, Jonathan, a detestable man who had taken to beating her and abusing his daughter, Felicity. Those, she had told herself, were the main reasons she had him killed, though when being brutally honest about it, Anna had to admit the money, at least to start, was the prime motivator. Money usually is.

The younger woman was Jane Rieger-Franklin, a Nassau County Police homicide detective who was the investigating officer of Franklin's unusual death. While closing in on the perpetrators, the cop fell in love with the wife and *vice versa.* So, after discovering the truth of the matter, Jane ignored her findings and laid the blame for the murder at the feet of Montgomery Fell, another wife beating brute who had just recently taken to abusing his own, almost seven-year-old daughter, Khaleesi. Anna's almost unlimited funds would come in handy to keep Jane's father, suffering from Alzheimer's, out of a nursing facility and in his own room upstairs in their home. And when she too was being frank with herself, Jane admitted that affording around-the-clock nursing care and ungodly expensive, experimental treatments both played significant parts in her decision, as well.

Money, or the lack of it, explained much of human interaction.

But the two (now married) women truly loved each other, and both adopted Felicity as their daughter, whom they treasured dearly. They, in their own ways, had come to terms with their behavior during the entire Franklin affair, especially Jane, who had also meticulously planned Fell's demise. She couldn't bring herself to pull the trigger (so to speak), though. It was, at least up to now, a line she wouldn't cross. That task fell to the older man who sat across from her—Sammy, *Lover Boy*, Vivino.

The celebrated hitman had been introduced to the younger man beside him, Dr. Joseph Peck, by the assassin's ex-Don, Anthony Esposito (*Ace* to his friends) whose life was saved as a teenager by the future physician during an almost lethal schoolyard brawl. The two boys had since become extremely fast friends for over fifty years. So, when Anna had approached Joe with the lure of money and sex (she, one of the most stunning women on the planet, was bisexual), the man couldn't resist. Through his old friend, now a *retired* Don, Joe was introduced to Lover Boy, who emerged from his retirement for one last hit. Make that next to last, as Sammy took care of Monty Fell too, making his death, as of Jonathan Franklin, appear accidental.

Since that time, over a year ago, Joe, Anna and Jane had grown to regret their actions, despite the fiendishness of the two men whom they had conspired to dispatch. To Sammy, though, who detested all who abused women, it was a simple matter of "they had it coming."

Then, two things happened simultaneously. First, Sammy discovered his here-to-fore unknown daughter, also a trained assassin. Second, Felicity was kidnapped by rogue elements of the New York Mob. Fate and providence (Anna believed in the latter) brought all parties together and Angelica, using her skills with gun and blade, bested the kidnappers and then another killer sent from Philadelphia specifically for her and Lover Boy. And during the brief span of only seven days, she and Joe had met and fallen in love.

It was a wild week, to say the least.

Now Sammy had requested a sit-down at the Franklin home to discuss Angelica's fate. She remained removed to an unknown location, courtesy of the Witness Protection Program. Her father had vowed that by New Year's Eve, at the latest, he would deal with the mob boss so she could safely return home. Thus, Sammy had some explaining to do—Don Fortuna still lived and breathed. So after a low-key dinner, Felicity was sent to bed.

The four friends sat, glasses of champagne on the coffee table before them as an after-dinner treat in anticipation of 2020. Despite the pleasant rewards for the senses—Dom Perignon 2010 for taste and Lily of the Valley (both women wore *Chanel Nº5*) for smell— there was an additional sense, foreboding, infusing the air as the others waited for Sammy to begin. Finally, he did.

"As you know," he began in a voice not much louder than a whisper, "I made a promise to Angelica, Joe and you all that I would do everything in my power to deal with Don Fortuna so that my daughter could return." He paused, took a sip of the champagne, and continued, speaking somewhat louder now, "You have all been very patient, never pressing me during this time. I want to tell you what I've been doing these past months.

"To start, I needed to make sure Fortuna kept his word to me when we last met, after Angelica dispatched *Il Boa*. I was convinced he believed our deception that she was dead at the assassin's hands, and I had subsequently killed the man. And, I was also convinced he truly pardoned me after I debased myself, apologizing for my behavior with his wife, producing Angelica. I still shake when thinking of those words. But they served their purpose, and I was convinced the monster believed them. Still, I had to be sure.

"I have, over the years, made many contacts, in New York, obviously, and Chicago, Boston, Baltimore and Philadelphia. Some of these men still live and have children who have followed in their footsteps. Some of these children are members of the Fortuna Family, a few in the Don's inner circle. I contacted the fathers and offered a handsome sum to their sons for informing me about their families' comings and goings. Out of friendship with me, one agreed to speak to his son; and the obedient boy agreed. But he had to be very careful and not ask too many questions all at once for fear of being discovered. It took two months for me to finally get answers, and they were, as I suspected. The Don had, along with sending *Il Boa* our way, hired two outside assassins on perennial contracts, just in case his primary killer failed. With Angelica *dead*, Fortuna had now released them from their assignments. So that's one problem dealt with.

"When I learned this information, I planned. However, as expected, the first indictments of Fortuna Family soldiers and associates, including the Don himself, were announced—a result of Angelica's information, I'm sure. So, I waited because I knew what would follow. Once Fortuna's men faced the reality of many years to decades behind bars, deals would be made. The Feds always want more—the big fish—and any information regarding the other families and their bosses would go a long way to lighten a man's sentence. Soon, those arrests began.

"As long as Don Fortuna and his boys faced the wrath of the Feds alone, the other bosses were not concerned. In fact, I've been told they detest the man and looked forward to splitting his family's assets between them. But now *they* were being attacked—and they knew it was because of Fortuna's men, maybe even the Boss himself. That, they could not stand for. No, these are not men known for their understanding nature.

"I expected them to come at the Don, so I waited. And yes, over the past three months there have been two attempts on his life." He paused and a stricken look came over his face. "And *twice* the *bastardos* have failed! What's the expression, 'it's hard to find good help these days?'" he scoffed. "Yeah, it would seem it is true of the assassin business as well. If I ever were as unsuccessful as these *figli di puttana*, I would be too ashamed to show my face. Does no one take pride in their work anymore?" The others looked furtively at each other, noting the curious sentiment expressed in that question. "But now," the man continued, "their failures have created a large problem.

"My contact tells me Don Fortuna, whose lawyers have done well in keeping him out of jail, has confined himself to his home because of the multiple attempts on his life. As such, his home has become a fortress. All the windowpanes were exchanged for military-grade, bullet-proof glass, the surrounding structures reinforced with steel. The wooden door to the home has also been replaced with one of steel. The security system is upgraded and there are new codes, which my informant is not senior enough to know. Hidden cameras have been placed in all rooms—except in the Don's bedroom." Sammy sneered. "Yeah, he doesn't want anyone seeing what goes on in *there*—as young, much too young, girls continue to parade in and out to satisfy his unnatural, degenerate lust. *Un'infamia!* And unlike before, when I had only to deal with *three* of his soldiers, now I'm told the house is never filled with less than ten. And when the Don must appear in court, these ten surround him like drone bees do their queen." He paused, anticipating the bemused looks on everyone's faces. "I just saw a video of that on the Nat Geo channel." His friends smiled, amused the savvy, high-school dropout had expected their confusion.

"They also consistently check the roofs of any nearby home where a sniper might hide."

The aging assassin sighed and took another sip. "In other words, the man is now better protected than the President of the United States! But still,"—he jumped up from his chair and paced behind it—"I made a vow to my dear Angelica and somehow, some way, I will make good on it. I would gladly sacrifice myself in an attack on his home *if* I knew it would be successful. But if Fortuna survived, which is likely given all of the protection, he would begin to wonder why I, after having apologized and vowed to never bother him again, would strike. He would worry if anything else I told him was untrue. With his many moles placed among law enforcement agencies, I fear he'd soon discover the truth, putting Angelica in great peril.

"If I simply requested a sit-down with him, he would probably agree, but I would certainly be searched thoroughly and probably not allowed alone anywhere close to the man. So, again, there would be little guarantee of success." Sammy shook his head and returned to his seat.

"So, I see three possible avenues. First, I can leave things be, and hope a future assassin is luckier than the others. But I doubt any will now try with the increased security. And waiting any longer would mean breaking my promise to Angelica. Second, I can let him be prosecuted and convicted. But he would be treated royally in prison and could easily run his business from there. If Angelica returned, was seen and Fortuna notified, he could mount his revenge remotely."

The man known as Lover Boy seemed older now to the others, older than they ever remembered seeing him before. He lowered his head into his hands, running them through his now mostly gray hair. His friends had never viewed him in such a dejected pose.

Joe, who had been calmly listening, though inwardly simmering with despair, asked the obvious question. "You said three avenues, Sammy. What's the third?"

The aged assassin looked up. "Yes, there is a third, and one I think has a very good likelihood of success."

It was Anna who spoke next. "Well, don't you think you could have led with *that* one, Sammy?" she asked somewhat sarcastically, but in a joking manner.

Sammy looked at the beautiful woman and chuckled. "Yes, I can see how you might think so. But I have been reluctant, afraid even, to bring it up. For you see... it would involve great danger and... I'm afraid it will be the beginning of a path that might lead to harm to the relationship you two lovely ladies have, and... to..." he looked now to Anna's left, "*your* kind, immortal soul—*Jane.*"

Anna visibly inhaled. Jane just stared. Joe didn't know what to say, so he remained silent. Then the detective spoke.

"I think, Sammy, all your preliminaries have finally come to where you tell us what this meeting is *really* all about, right?"

The man nodded. "*Sì.* But let me first say that if you say 'no' to my proposition, I will feel no less toward you, or your lovely wife, since she will also, I'm sure, need to—no must—agree. What I'm asking is a great deal, an enormous sacrifice; and you have your own daughter to think about, too."

Jane turned to Anna and saw fear in the beautiful woman's face. The younger spouse caressed the other's cheek, then lifted her glass and drained it. She turned to address Sammy.

"My friend, say what you came to say."

And so, he did.

———————————

It took about an hour for Lover Boy to go over his plan, which he did in exquisite detail. Halfway through, Anna grasped Jane's hand and did not let go. In fact, the hold had become so tight that her wife had to release herself from the other to regain feeling in the fingers. She looked at Anna and saw tears in her eyes. The detective had spent the last twenty minutes or so with her own eyes closed as Sammy's explanation went deeper down a serpiginous, darkening path. She now addressed her friend.

"As far as danger is concerned, I'm no stranger to it, which is probably one reason you've chosen me over Anna for this task. After all, every day when I go to work, we both know there's a chance I might not return. Given our financial circumstances, I obviously don't *have* to work, but I feel being a cop is what I was meant to be. What my detective father meant for me to be. I get great satisfaction finding and taking murderers off the streets; I enjoy having those scum-bags get what they deserve." She paused, then, "No offense, Sammy," she added, smiling.

The retired assassin gave her a grin. "None taken, my dear."

Jane continued. "But the rest... " She poured more from the champagne bottle and drank it in a single gulp. "The rest, I don't know... I..." She turned to her lover and her hands started to shake. "How do you feel about this, Anna? I worry you will never again be able to look at me the same. That..." she began to choke on her words, "... you will not be able to... to *love* me as before."

Anna reached over and engulfed her wife with her arms and Jane softly cried, the sounds muffled by the older woman's breasts. The two men looked at each other but knew not to interject any words. Then, after a few beats, Anna gently pushed her wife slightly away and looked into her vivid blue eyes. "Janie, I've told you all about *my* past, all the sordid details, right? Do you love *me* less?" Jane, still whimpering, shook her head vigorously. "Yes," Anna continued, "I have no doubts about that. No doubts..."

It was at a time like this the two women often resorted to words not of their own, which they felt would be inadequate, but of Shakespeare, whose works they cherished and knew as well as most scholars. They would often play games where one would start a quote and the other would finish. Anna paused for a moment and considered her last spoken words. Then—

"Doubt thou the stars are fire;
"Doubt that the sun doth move;

"Doubt truth to be a liar;

"But never *doubt...*

"I love," they both finished, together. *"Hamlet,* Act II, scene II."

They embraced, both now gently sobbing. Another few instants passed until, from behind the men, at the doorway to the living room, came a soft, tiny and pleading voice.

"Please Mama, say yes."

Felicity.

The women separated and Anna turned, wiped her eyes with the back of her hand, and gave the child a wry smirk.

"Just how long have you been listening, you little spy?"

Felicity grinned. She was a beautiful, eleven-year-old child whose smile never failed to melt her parents' hearts. She had bounced back well after her ordeal, being kidnapped along with Marta, the nanny. The parents thought this would be the time to start therapy, which they had decided, pre-abduction, would be useful for the girl in order to face what they believed her father had subjected her to. But Felicity had adjusted so well to life after Jonathan Franklin, they thought, and, yet again, after the abduction, that Anna and Jane were conflicted now and not sure if therapy was the best idea. The girl walked into the room and sat between her parents.

"When you sent me to bed a half-hour earlier than usual, I knew something was up. Sooo, I took off my slippers and tiptoed down the stairs. I've been listening outside the doorway from the beginning." She squeezed her parents' hands in hers. "I don't understand everything Uncle Sammy said, but I do know one thing: *none* of us, *none,* would be here today if it weren't for Angelica." The women nodded in agreement, surprised at the child's acumen—and boldness. "If there's anything Mama and you all can do to bring her back to us, then I say we go for it."

Anna was the first to speak. *"We?* You're quite something, you know that? You must understand, honey, what Uncle Sammy is describing is very dangerous. Your Mama, I and the others could be hurt, maybe badly. Some might even die. You understand?"

Felicity shook her head back and forth forcefully, yet said, "Yes, Mommy. But didn't Angelica say if bad men came again, you and Mama could, and I quote,"—beginning her favorite adult expression—"'kick their asses?' Unquote!"

Everyone had a good laugh at the child's words, remembering the scene well where Angelica had said her goodbyes. Then Jane continued. "Yes, we remember. And we remember Angelica having to put a quarter in the swear jar for that; and now you will have to as well," she said, a wide smile on her face.

"Well, if this is going to cost me allowance money, then let's go for the gold." Felicity had dreams of becoming an Olympic swimmer. She increased her grips on her parents' hands. "I say you go and kick—their—*fucking*—asses!" And an unnerving, Joker-like grin came to her face.

Everyone was shocked—by her words *and* facial expression. This was the first time the mothers had heard *that* word from their sweet, wonderful, and now seemingly precocious and worldly child. *Cursing was to be expected, I guess, sooner or later*, they both thought. *But that look. That look...* Then, each parent glanced at the other and telepathically seemed to agree that yes, maybe therapy was a good idea after all.

But that was for later. Now, there needed to be a decision. Jane continued to stare at Anna and they both nodded. The detective stood.

Jane went to the large mahogany bar behind the men and retrieved another champagne glass. She returned and filled it slightly less than half-way with the sparkling liquid and then fully replenished hers. The mother handed the partially filled flute to Felicity. "Don't get used to this. This is a one-shot deal. Understand?" The child's eyes widened, and she nodded.

Jane lifted her glass into the air. "To Angelica."

The others stood, raised their glasses and, as one, echoed, "To Angelica." And they drank.

After just a moment, Felicity started giggling. "That tickles," she was able to say between chortles. She continued so, as the bubbles gently caressed her nose. Then, just as abruptly, the snickering stopped, and a serious mien crossed over her face, like a sudden cloud obscuring a noon sun. The child raised her now empty glass and firmly repeated—

"*For* Angelica!"

Chapter 3

Monday, December 30, 2019
Philadelphia, Pennsylvania
11:30 PM

The black Lexus LS 500 came to a crawling stop in front of the home of Don Vito Fortuna. Behind the wheel was "Limo Larry," a nickname given by Don Vincent Esposito, Ace's father. His real name was Frankie Martone. Back in the 70s, Frankie, who managed the motor pool for the Family while running a legitimate limousine service, wore the same suits as his favorite video-game character, "Leisure Suit Larry." *Larry* wasn't thrilled with the Boss's decision—but once the Don decreed it, that was that. At least, until six months ago. That was when Frankie, part of the rescue team that freed Felicity and Marta from their captors, forever took his place within the hearts of Anna and Jane.

The elderly, never-married, overweight man had developed a bit of an old-man crush on the former and confessed to her he preferred being called by his given name. Since then, Anna had done just that. And the others, especially Sammy and Ace (who'd known the man by his moniker for decades), in respect of his valor and Anna's wishes, did the same. Now and then, though, they'd inadvertently slip up.

Over the past six months, the two parents had spent much time and money rewarding all of Felicity's rescuers and others who had contributed to the endeavor. Maverick was one such reward, and this fully loaded $100,000 Lexus was another. They had gone to Sammy for advice on what Martone's secret desire might be. Vivino explained despite all those years surrounded by luxury limos and sedans, Frankie could never afford to *own* anything other than a simple Chevy Impala or the like. Anna presumed a Cadillac or Lincoln would be to the driver's taste. But Sammy assured her whenever he asked Larry, er, Frankie, what his preferred car would be, money no object, the answer was always—*Lexus*. Why?

"Because them Japs really know how to make cars," was always his politically incorrect response.

At a dinner party a few months back at their home, with all the rescue party invited (except Ace who lived in Boca Raton with Joe's ex-wife, Linda), Anna presented Frankie with the keyless remotes, registration, one-year's paid insurance card and title to the Lexus. On seeing the vehicle, with a large, bright red ribbon adorned to the roof like in the TV commercials, the big man wept.

Now, Frankie was at the wheel for another mission, which he'd agreed to immediately when Anna called. Martone then phoned his nephew, who'd taken over the limo business (both legitimate and illicit divisions) when Uncle Frankie retired. Within three hours, a fake Pennsylvania license plate was fabricated in the mob-run chop-shop, along with an equally bogus and convincing registration, insurance card and driver's license. All the documentation was in the name of Bobby Falcone, a soldier Sammy knew of in the Maltucci Family, one of Don Fortuna's rivals. If the license plate was seen, or the car stopped for any reason, Sammy hoped the credentials would create a nice misdirection for the authorities, or Fortuna's men, to follow.

In the car with Frankie were Sammy, in the front, and Joe, Jane and Anna in the rear. At Sammy's feet lay a suppressed Heckler and Koch MP7 sub-machine gun and a sawed-off Remington 870 shotgun, Frankie's weapon of choice. Two suppressed Uzi submachine guns lay at the feet of those in the rear. All were courtesy of the two women—Jonathan Franklin, a believer in a coming apocalypse, had kept a veritable arsenal in his home. A few months back, the parents had caught their daughter ogling the weapons, so they installed a biometric lock to the door. Now only their thumbprints would allow admittance.

Yesterday, the team had driven to an isolated farm in Suffolk County where Sammy gave Anna and Joe a crash course on the Uzi. He was already well versed in the MP7, though in his previous, usually one-on-one line of work, excellent aim with his Glock 26 was more than sufficient. With the Uzi, at ten rounds per second, anyone could merely point-and-shoot and, more than likely, hit their target.

After four hours, the two's proficiency was far from expert, and all prayed, especially a terrified Anna, that using the guns would be unnecessary. But if worse came to worst and the goal of the expedition switched to saving Jane, the *civilians* among them would at least know what to expect from their weapons.

"Maybe," Anna quipped, as she labored while simultaneously firing and remaining on her feet, "Fortuna and his men will accommodate us and just die laughing when they see Joe and me with this shit."

Now, Jane wore her wife's long, mink coat for the chilly, December night, plus the dark, to-the-shoulders wig she had used during Felicity's rescue. Anna had also, early this morning, called upon her stylist to spray-tan every inch of Jane's body a few shades darker than her natural, pale-white color. The many video cameras in the house would, when examined, see a woman whose appearance would be quite unlike reality. The detective also sported a pair of Ray-Ban Aviators. As unusual as wearing such an accessory near midnight on a winter night might appear, they gave Jane an added touch of eroticism besides adding to her disguise.

Twenty minutes earlier she had received a text from Felicity—it was a simple GIF with the words: *Hey, girl. You got this.* Each letter flickered on and off in a forever repeating pattern. Jane had messaged back a big thumbs up and reminded the child there would be "texting silence" until further notice; Felicity answered with another GIF—a teenage girl repeatedly slapping her forehead with her palm while the words WELL, DUH! flashed on-and-off below. Jane frowned but quickly reversed to smiling as a simple text immediately followed: "Good luck!!! I love you. Kiss Mommy for me."

And that is exactly what Jane now did—and then exited the car.

Frankie drove away and turned the corner. Sammy's mole, one of whose jobs was to surreptitiously monitor all external cameras in the neighborhood, even those belonging to the city, knew of a blind spot on the block. Frankie parked the car right at that location and turned off the engine. There they waited, Anna clenching Joe's hand.

Jane would enter the lion's den alone.

The soldier at the front door was in his mid-twenties and chilled to the bone. He was a low man in the pecking order and had drawn the outside-the-door position. At first, he thought he might be hallucinating from the cold when he saw the beautiful woman exit the Lexus, exposing a long length of thigh as her coat briefly opened as she stood. But as she proceeded up the path that led straight to the door, he was convinced the woman was real—and needed to be stopped.

"Sorry, miss," he began, putting his right arm straight out, keeping Jane at a distance, "I think you may have the wrong address or something."

Jane smiled. "Oh, I doubt that." She reached into her coat pocket (at which point the guard visibly tensed), and then *slowly* withdrew an envelope. "Please give this to Don Fortuna. I'll wait."

The soldier had his orders—no one was to be admitted at this late hour unless he was informed beforehand.

"As I said, I'm sorry. You'll have to arrange an appointment."

Sammy had expected such an answer, and Jane reluctantly proceeded with the planned response. She slowly untied the sash around her coat and let it slide open, giving the young man a full view. What he saw was that the extremely pretty young woman was dressed only in a pair of simple pink panties and matching bra. His eyes widened and mouth gaped open.

"Let me explain something to you," continued Jane. She placed her right index finger under his jaw and nuzzled it upwards, closing the boy's mouth. Then, with the other hand, she pointed to a tall, white-birch tree on the front lawn. "You see that tree?" she asked. The soldier could only nod. "Well, if you don't present that note to Don Fortuna and force me to leave, when your boss finds out what you did, or, more accurately, *didn't* do tonight, it'll be your *balls* hanging from that very tree. *Capisce?*" She smiled and then abruptly closed her coat.

Now undistracted by Jane's near nudity, the guard quickly weighed her words and decided the girl might have a valid point. "Er... okay, you wait here. I'll be right back."

"Are you fuckin' kidding me? It's freezing out here. At least let me into the vestibule."

The man was confused. "The *whatstabule?*"

Jane shook her head. *Dumb as a rock.* "The foyer, the other side of this door—where it's *warm*. You think the Don wants to have his cock sucked by a pair of ice-cold lips?"

Shocked by the young woman's language, but again reminded of his own threatened manhood, the soldier opened the door and motioned for the woman to wait just inside. He hurried the short distance to the living room, where approximately seven others milled about, some playing cards, some eating. Now all eyes were fixed upon the new arrival.

The guard went right up to the tallest man in the group. He appeared about six feet-four with jet-black hair parted down the middle. He was not happy. If Sammy's information from conversations with Angelica before her exile was correct, this would be Leonardo Franco. He was Fortuna's *number one*—his Riker to the Don's Picard for you Star Trek fans. Leonardo often compared the meticulous way he went about his job, inflicting damage, humiliation and pain, to the techniques of his famous Renaissance namesake whose paintings the man so admired. Therefore, he insisted underlings use his full, given name—"Leo" tolerated *only* coming from his Don, and *maybe* his mother. They talked softly but heatedly, and Jane saw the soldier thrust the envelope into the underboss's hands. He opened it and read. It took only a few moments, then he looked up at the guest, smiled, and approached. But instead of greeting Jane, he turned just a few feet before her and bounded up the staircase of the center-hall colonial. *To the pedophile's bedroom, no doubt*, she thought, shivering. The detective waited, and when she considered the overly heated interior of the house, Jane knew her quivering stemmed not from the ambient temperature. A few moments passed and Leonardo exited the Don's room and descended. "Come with me," he said as he turned his back to her and walked to the living room. Every soldier was now on alert and Jane quickly counted eleven men, some having entered from other rooms after being informed of the beautiful stranger.

"The Don has agreed to see you, miss. Let me see your phone."

Jane reached into her jacket pocket and handed the man her iPhone. He tapped the screen, and it came to life, confirming it was a working phone and not a dummy, carrying explosives or a hidden blade. He returned it, and Jane placed it back into her pocket. "Now," he continued, with a bit of a smirk, "we will have to search you. Take off your coat."

35

Jane knew this was coming, though it didn't make the task any easier. She quickly untied the coat and let it fall to the floor, remaining only in her young-teen styled underwear. She turned 360 degrees, her arms outstretched and cheerfully said, "Now, you don't really think I've got some deadly weapon under my panties, do you?"

Number one laughed. "Girl, one thing I've learned in life is that the deadliest weapon on this Earth is found between a woman's legs."

Jane was surprised and returned the smile. *Quite a philosopher for a thug,* she thought, and then, foolishly, couldn't help but jab, "How profound. You're cleverer than you look." *Shit, Jane. That was stupid. Stick to the script!*

Leo was not amused. He thought he looked quite handsome *and* intelligent. The man frowned, approached, and placed his index finger under the elastic of the underwear's waistband, pulling it way down so Jane's entire crotch was exposed for all to see. As the men all leered and snickered, the thug stared in amazement. *The Don's really going to like this one,* he thought. For last night, in the privacy of their bathroom, Anna had slowly and lovingly lathered up and shaved Jane's entire pubic area. It was the detective's idea, since they all knew Fortuna enjoyed young, preferably teenage girls. Jane's breasts were a convenient 32A, another reason Sammy chose her over the more-endowed Anna. Her feeling was any other way of appearing as young as possible would improve the chances of "getting out of Dodge," as she put it, "alive." So Anna gently, lovingly trimmed her lover's hair and then the razor did the rest. The two found the experience unbearably erotic and when done, were both primed for the torrid, after-shave sex session that followed. For a while, at least, they could enjoy their love together without worrying about what the next day might bring.

Jane had pictured this scenario in her head, but the demeaning reality of it was overwhelming, especially when the brute placed his forefinger onto the pubic bone and, she thought, was preparing to penetrate her. No *man* had ever touched her like that, and, if she had anything to say about it, no *one*, only Anna, was ever going to.

No way, motherfucker, she thought.

"Somehow," she began, placing her hand gently on top of the man's digit, "I don't think Don Fortuna would be pleased with such a close inspection. I doubt he'll be happy to learn he must settle for *sloppy seconds* because of the sweaty finger of an underling. Do you?"

The man stopped, considered the veiled threat—and his Don's likely response—and removed the finger. The panties snapped closed. He proceeded to roughly pull her bra down below her breasts, gave a cursory inspection of the cups, and then motioned for her to put them back in place. Then he reached behind and pulled the back of the underwear down and out for all to see Jane's bare ass and then let them loudly snap back. Jane fumed, but kept smiling, playing the happy, high-priced hooker to the hilt. She believed she could *smell* the testosterone in the room. Then the underboss picked up her coat, began rummaging through the pockets—and found the bottle.

Shit, she inwardly cursed.

"What's this?" he demanded.

What it was, was a pocket-atomizer filled with a mixture of *Chanel Nº5* and cold-pressed gourmet peanut oil. Angelica had told Sammy of the Don's deadly allergy to the nuts, so much so that he kept a syringe with epinephrine, called an Epi-Pen, in the top drawer of his bedside end-table. Since Fortuna considered this a sign of weakness, no one knew of his allergy or of the Epi-Pen's existence except his wife and Angelica. Even Leonardo had been excluded from that loop. Luckily, Dr. Joseph Peck was around for the planning. Everyone else figured they'd just go to the supermarket and buy a bottle of Planters oil. But the doctor knew that such peanut oil as can be purchased by the masses was highly refined—the proteins that cause the allergic reaction were removed. No, one needed a special, unrefined preparation, usually only found in gourmet shops. Naturally, Anna knew of one and all it took was a phone call to the owner, for whom she had personally financed many a vacation via her extravagant purchases. The man went to his store before the normal opening hour the next morning and brought a bottle of his finest, non-refined peanut oil to her home at 8 AM.

The only problem was determining what percentage the mixture should be. Joe had no idea what amount of peanut protein would cause a deadly anaphylactic reaction; he was sure it varied from person to person, anyway. There were cases of those who died just from exposure to the air near someone eating peanuts, which is why the nuts are banned on commercial airline flights. It was decided, therefore, to try a few different combinations, and go with the one allowing the most oil to be present while still permitting the fragrance of the perfume to emerge. Jane watched as Leonardo examined the bottle, her heartbeat doubling. If he confiscated the atomizer, all was lost.

"This," Jane began her prepared explanation, "is my personal perfume, made especially for me and imported from Venice. A unique mixture of scents and oils. Not only does it smell divine..." She paused and gently removed the bottle from the man's hands. She sprayed the contents a few times on her neck, her face, and finally on her gloved finger, which she then proceeded to sensually lick, all to allay any fears poison was involved, "... but it also acts as a sensual lubricant. Applying it to my skilled hands can work wonders when helping my, er... elderly clients *rise* to the occasion, if you get my drift?" There was some snickering from the others, but a quick, icy glare from Leonardo ended it. "And I wouldn't want to have to tell the Don he was denied such a pleasure because of poor decision-making on his *clever* associate's part. Would I?"

The man smirked but silently seethed at the second, not-so-thinly veiled warning. He had to reluctantly agree, however, concerning his Don's reaction to withdrawing the presumed aphrodisiac. Since he felt the perfume posed no danger—*the bitch* had inhaled and ingested it, after all—Leonardo reluctantly placed the bottle into the coat-pocket and handed the fur back to the woman with, "I may be cleverer than I *look,* but that beats someone *looking* cleverer than they be." Jane was again impressed, and the man also seemed proud of his *bon mots* (though the Italian *arguzia* is more proper here). He grinned and motioned for one of his subordinates to accompany "the whore." She dressed, as it were, and followed the new man up the stairs as a crowd gathered below.

Halfway home, Jane thought as she ascended. But the optimism was short-lived—she knew full well the worst was yet to come.

Chapter 4

"*Avanti!*"

The soldier had knocked, and Don Fortuna answered. Jane entered, as ordered, and closed the bedroom door behind her.

The Don sat upright on his bed, shirtless. He had cruel ebony eyes and was a grotesque figure of a man, seriously overweight with an ample potbelly protruding over what appeared to be silk, black pajama bottoms.

Fat men and gravity—never an attractive mix, Jane mused.

The bedsheet and quilt were pulled down to his feet, exposing the bulbous body which, the woman thought, if put to oil-on-canvas might be titled: *Moby Dick, In Repose.*

And Jane hoped to be Ahab, finally triumphant.

Looking at the man, his triple-chin smiling along with his mouth, the thought of nearing Fortuna, let alone allowing physical contact, suddenly made the woman's stomach turn; she was glad she'd opted for a light dinner.

Jane approached slowly, letting her coat remain closed for the moment. *Anticipation always fuels passion*, she firmly believed. In the sweaty folds of the man's lap lay the letter Sammy had composed. Fortuna picked it up and read aloud:

Dear Don Fortuna,

It is now close to the new year and, in gratitude for your accepting our armistizio, I wish you to please accept this present. I think you will find Maria not only extremely pretty but also most skilled in the ways of love. Remarkable for a girl of just 17...

Seventeen. There was much discussion among the friends as to how many years to reverse-age Jane. Though thirty-one years old, with her lithe body, 32A breasts, flawless skin and a purposely minimally made-up face, she could easily pass for early twenties. But they'd decided to go for less, given their adversary's reputation. The power of suggestion in Sammy's words was a psychological ploy never to be underestimated. It would hopefully aid in the deception.

... Please accept her as a token of my esteem and continued friendship. Wishing you a prosperous New Year,

Sammy Vivino

Fortuna placed the letter on his end table. "Come closer, girl, and take off your coat. It must be stifling under there."

Jane smiled and approached the bed. There was a fine, upholstered chair at its foot, and she stopped there, slowly removed her coat and draped it across. She had been wearing thin, faux-lace gloves—an iPhone would respond to the fingers within them—which she now removed and placed on the seat along with her sunglasses. Then she faced her prey. The man leered.

"*Bella. Molto bella.*" Jane noticed a slight stirring in his groin area. "So, Maria is your name?"

Jane wanted to say, "Call me Ishmael," but forwent any more sarcastic banter. She figured the literary reference would only go over the Don's head, anyway, given his reading habits likely began and ended with the Italian language newspaper that lay on his end table. Instead, she nodded. "Yes, daddy, but you can call me any name you want." She tried to speak a breathy octave higher than normal and felt she succeeded. The groin stirred further. "No, no, my dear. Maria is perfect. I remember another Maria, years ago, in Miami. A Cuban girl. Her mother was a whore and had taught her daughter well. Never before, and rarely since, have I experienced so skillful a mouth. I even gave my trusted associate, Leo, whom you've already met, a turn with her. Only twelve years old. Amazing."

Time stopped for Jane. It took the strength of Hercules for her to control herself, biting down on her tongue to distract her from screaming aloud. *Twelve years old?!* she shrieked inwardly. *Only a year older than Felicity! What was God thinking when he agreed to the creation of this monster?*

The detective had wrestled for hours with her conscience about the finality of what she was there to do. It went against everything her father had taught her about being a cop—and being human. It would go one step further than she took with Monty Fell. That one line she had vowed never to cross.

But no longer. She now yearned to take Fortuna by the neck and choke the life out of him. Not only was he responsible for the deaths of scores of men, but he had, for decades, raped countless young girls. Again, she thought of her treasured Felicity and almost sobbed. *Death is too good for you, you fat bastard. Oh, how I hope you suffer tonight*, she thought. Then, as they often did, Shakespeare's words echoed through her mind as it struck Jane that Vito Fortuna made Richard III look like Mother Teresa—*Thou art unfit for any place but Hell.*

But the woman knew the charade needed to continue. Time resumed. "Well, daddy, I do hope you find me satisfactory. I try to be a good girl." And with that, she reached behind and unfastened her bra, letting it fall forward onto the bed. The Don's eyes widened. Then *Maria* turned, bent over, and slowly brought her panties down to her ankles. *Jane's* embarrassment and disgust were overwhelming. She took them off and walked around the bed.

Fortuna spied the barren groin and his eyes widened even further. The underwear was offered to the Don, and the man took his prize and rubbed it over his face. His erection grew. Jane turned and went to her jacket and removed the perfume. She sprayed a good amount on her hands and massaged the liquid into her breasts, slowly tweaking her nipples, persistently smiling at Fortuna as she did. Amazingly, despite her revulsion the nipples hardened and erotically extended—the body's reflex physiology overruling the brain itself. This reaction, though aiding in the seduction, appalled her even further.

"Cos'è quella?" he asked, pointing to the bottle. Jane assumed he was asking for an explanation. "This is an exquisite perfume, prepared by the finest perfumer in Venice. Not only is the fragrance divine, but it *tastes* delicious." And before the man realized it, the *girl* climbed onto the bed, straddling his body, making sure any dripping liquid would fall on his chest, not the mattress sheet. "Here, daddy, enjoy." Lowering herself, she put her hands against the headboard, and leaned forward so Fortuna could reach her breasts without having to move off his pillow. He grasped the left breast and started to lick and suckle. Jane shut her eyes and thought of Anna, Felicity, her father and Angelica—anything to distract from the flood of disgust engulfing her. The brute bit the nipple, but Jane continued to hold steady, absorbing the pain which she perceived, in part, a punishment for her acts to come. Then he went to the right breast and repeated the actions.

Yes, lick it all off, you fucking son-of-a-bitch. Lick it all and die, now! But he didn't.

Finally, releasing Jane's sore right nipple, Fortuna said, "I think it's time to see if your mouth truly bears comparison to my *Cuban Maria.*"

Jane opened her eyes, straightened up, and smiled at the fiend. She was amazed she still could, given her heart was pounding, and she now had thoughts of killing the man and then herself. Anything to avoid the degradation of having to take *this monster's dick in my mouth. God, please let him die now*. But, again, he didn't.

Anna, can you ever forgive me? Dad, I'm so sorry.

Fortuna had made his request just a mere moment ago, but to Jane, it seemed eons. Desperate, she opted for another, slightly less debasing suggestion. "Of course, Don Fortuna. As you wish. But if I may, this perfume, besides its aroma, has a mixture of oils whose lubricating and stimulating properties have amazing results when applied to... well..." she tittered like a seventeen-year-old might do, "... you know. Here, let me show you." Without waiting for the Don to object, she took the bottle and again sprayed her right hand with a generous amount of the liquid. Then she pulled the man's pajamas down with her left. He was semi-erect.

Jane had only once in her life given a man a hand-job. Well, *man* was not quite the word. It was fifteen-year-old Alan Greene. They were studying for a math test at his house when the request was made. The young girl, who was beginning to discover, and question, her sexuality, gave it a try. Right on the living room couch. The boy came in seconds. Alan was a virgin and Jane could have replaced her hand with a Brillo pad to still yield similar results. It repulsed her, and though she had already suspected where her future sexual path would lead, it was cemented that afternoon. And amazingly, now, amid all this current horror, she inwardly laughed, wondering if Mrs. Greene had ever turned over that cushion and discovered the stain.

She grabbed Fortuna's penis with her right hand and started stroking. Occasionally, she and Anna watched porn to get in an extra-frisky mood, and most had a mixture of straight and lesbian scenes. So despite her one-and-done experience with Alan, male-arousal techniques were not entirely unknown to her. *Anyway,* she thought, *how difficult can it be? He's still a guy, after all*. And, as if in confirmation, the erection grew. The Don closed his eyes and moaned. She noticed he was, as suspected, uncircumcised.

44

Joe had taken her aside at the meeting three days before, out of Anna's earshot, to discuss alternate methods of delivering the peanut protein, if necessary. The doctor mentioned if the man were uncircumcised, the glans, the mucous membrane that was the head of the penis, would not have slightly thickened, as it does when the foreskin is removed. It would therefore behave more like other such membranes of the body, and be very permeable to all sorts of material, such as viruses, STDs—and the protein found in peanuts. So, absorption into the bloodstream would augment that due to ingestion, maybe surpass it. Jane continued to stroke, and Fortuna continued to moan. To the woman, it seemed interminable, but only after a minute or two, still seeming in excellent health, the Don said, "Yes, Maria. You're right. Very nice. But I think now it's time for the mouth, no?" Then, ominously, "Don't make me have to ask you again. Don't..." Abruptly, he stopped talking.

Jane had been looking down as she worked, but now stared into the eyes of the monster. His eyelid fissures had widened, and he seemed to have trouble talking, breathing; attempts at both were met with wheezing. His face grew flushed, his skin clammy and suddenly much warmer. Jane continued to rub and added quietly, "Is something wrong, daddy?" The man knew what was happening. He pointed to his end-table. "Top... drawer," he was finally able to say. "Top..." and then the wheezing took over completely. He tried to push Jane aside to get at his Epi-Pen, but the detective grabbed the man's hand with her left. He stared, confused. "I don't think so, *daddy*," she spat, *sotto voce*, into his ear. Fortuna tried to scream, but the little air he was inhaling made it difficult. Jane removed her right hand from his penis and clasped it over his mouth and nose, further diminishing the ability to speak and breathe. His eyes widened in terror as the woman added, again whispering into his ear— "Angelica sends her regards."

The weakened Fortuna tried to buck the woman off his body, but the detective was much younger and stronger, despite her lanky appearance. The bed groaned, and the springs squeaked

45

underneath, so Jane began the next act of this passion play, which was to camouflage any sounds of distress from the room while simultaneously entertaining the throngs gathered below.

Loudly, in her best porno-style voice, she began: "Yes daddy, that's it! Yeah... give it to me, daddy... Oh, fuck me harder... HARDER!" The Don continued to thrash, but was faltering. Meanwhile, the men downstairs were giving high-fives and fist-bumps in honor of their boss's presumed prowess. Even Leonardo was enjoying himself.

"Yes, more, MORE... Yeah daddy, fuck me... Yes... Yes... YESSSS!" And as the last *s* was voiced, the Don gave a final buck, his entire frame lifting off the bed as multiple body systems, already in shock, failed in unison. Then he fell back. Dead.

Presumed dead, at least. Jane believed he was gone—she'd seen many a dead body in her line of work, but never one this fresh. She placed her index finger along his neck, searched for a pulse, and found none. Ahab had prevailed over her white whale. Jane, looking now into the beast's dead eyes, remembered two lines from that wonderful novel the ex-English Literature major re-read every so often. Whispering, so the throng downstairs would not hear, she bid *adieu* to the Don with some of Melville's madman's final words:

"From hell's heart, I stab at thee; for hate's sake, I spit my last breath, at thee."

Jane hadn't a knife to stab with, couldn't spit for fear of leaving DNA, and, hopefully, had many more breaths to come. Nevertheless, the lines seemed appropriate—more importantly, they calmed her. Sweating profusely, Jane took a few deep breaths and managed to get her pulse down to where she didn't imagine her heart about to explode from her chest, like those monsters in *Aliens*. Then, the final phase of the plan began.

She got off the bed and slowly (*no rushing*, she reminded herself—the steps would be heard below) made her way to the bathroom. "I'll go get some water to clean you off, daddy," she said, hoping it was just loud enough for the spectators to appreciate.

46

They would certainly hear the faucet being employed as the water made a definite *whoosh* through the pipes of the nearly hundred-year-old house. Jane wet the washcloth that was hanging, walked back to the bed, and washed the man's genitals and abdomen.

After thoroughly washing, Jane returned to the bathroom, re-wet the material one last time and repeated the process to the man's mouth and oral area where splashes of the oil-perfume mixture could be seen. Sammy knew the authorities, including those on the medical examiner's payroll, were all beholden, to one degree or another, to the various Philadelphia Families. The other dons would get the word out that the autopsy be done expeditiously. They would be overjoyed Fortuna was dead and wanted the FBI and all other federal government agencies out of their city ASAP. If anything but a simple cause of death, like a heart attack, was pronounced, more scrutiny might come to them. So, the M.E. would be *encouraged* to make a quick and simple diagnosis. Both macro and microscopic findings of anaphylactic shock were minimal, at best, and could be easily missed by any doctor not specifically looking for them, especially one endeavoring to hurry and be done with it. Non-medical professionals would have no clue. But if Fortuna were covered in an obvious, oily liquid, ignoring that would be a difficult endeavor. Especially with other witnesses to the autopsy, such as detectives, assistant DAs, and medical technicians. After a few minutes, Jane was content with her cleaning effort and dried the areas with a towel. Then she washed and dried the headboard where her hands had rested. The washcloth went into her right coat pocket.

Returning to the bathroom, the detective placed the towel back on its rack, rinsed her own hands with a generous dollop from the soft-soap container (using her elbow to depress the dispenser) and continued to talk aloud for the benefit of anyone listening—after-sex chit-chat. She went to her phone and brought up a previously created texting-group to message the others.

Done, was the word she sent; the team would arrive in three minutes. Jane then erased the conversation in case her phone was examined once again.

She put on her gloves and glasses, sprayed some of the perfume around her body to cloak the smell of sweat and death, donned the coat and walked toward the door.

Shit. Almost forgot. She went back to the end-table, opened it and retrieved the Epi-Pen and Sammy's letter. If the former were found by the police, anaphylactic shock would jump to the top of the *possible-cause-of-death* list and the M.E. could not avoid making the diagnosis. If the latter were, the police would have Sammy's name. A false pocket was sewn into the fur-coat last night, just deep enough to place the apparatus and the folded letter, which she now did. Jane glanced at her Apple Watch. The message app was open and pre-written with the word "Help." If need be, all she had to do was tap "send," and within seconds all hell would break loose; and if so, heaven help them all.

Okay, Jane. Time to get out of here alive.

The four friends simultaneously received the "Done" text on their phones. Sammy, knowing the final, dangerous moments had arrived, passed the Remington to Frankie and put the MP7 on his lap. Fortuna was gone—and now Lover Boy vowed he would die, if necessary, to save Jane from a similar fate. He would lead any charge.

Anna squeezed Joe's hand, but the two left their weapons at their feet, unable to conceive of defeat at this moment. Joe, anticipating Lover Boy's possible call to arms, nervously smiled and inwardly paraphrased a variation of Star Trek's Dr. McCoy's standard response to unreasonable requests from his captain: *"Dammit, Sammy, I'm a surgeon, not an assassin!"*

And while Joe tried to remain cheerful despite the dire circumstances, Anna was thinking of how best to console her lover. She shuddered to consider what Jane had endured in that house of horrors. The older woman's first words would be critical to beginning the healing process. Anna now closed her eyes and pondered just what those initial words would be.

"OK, daddy, I'll tell him," Jane said as she left the bedroom and closed the door. She'd purposely left her coat unfastened and walked down the stairs. Since she had placed her underwear and bra in the left pocket, along with the atomizer, her nudity was obvious to the gathering below—modesty taking second-place to distraction. "Men are so predictable," Angelica had always said. The detective hoped that aphorism would again prove correct.

Leonardo motioned for all to return to the living room and Jane followed.

She had been with the Don for about forty minutes, which, according to their mole, was just slightly above average for his many late-night trysts. No effort to close her coat was made as she approached the underboss.

"I assume you're the one called Leonardo?" The man nodded, looking, for the moment, into her eyes.

"Well, Don Fortuna told me to tell you he does not wish to be disturbed until 9 AM."

Leonardo's eyebrows lifted. This was unusual. The Boss always wanted to start the day by seven, Angelica had informed Sammy. But the time change was decided upon purposely, for it now allowed Jane to add, "He wishes an extra two hours. Tonight, took a lot out of him," she said with a wink.

Leonardo nodded. There was no way the woman could know of the two-hour difference unless the Don had told her. Still, the underboss was a cautious man. He wanted confirmation from The Boss.

"Well, let me just go check." He turned and Jane's chest constricted. *Remain calm*, she told herself; *we prepared for this.* She smiled nonchalantly, and added, "Suit yourself. But the Don also said, and I quote, 'Tell that *faccia di culo, Leo*, that if anyone, including him, wakes me before then, I'll take my Luger and shoot the *bastardo in his coglioni*.' I hope I pronounced everything correctly." The men nervously tittered.

Jane had emptied all barrels here, spending all the ammunition Angelica's information had provided. Foremost, as already mentioned, no one used "Leo" except the Don. There was no way the woman could know this unless repeating the words of his boss. Also, *faccia di culo*, literally *ass-face*, though it could be considered an insult, between two men who respected one another was actually a compliment (when spoken in the proper tone of voice), describing someone very direct—brazen, even. When together, with no others present, the Don jokingly used the term frequently with his *number one*. The latter was sure no one else, alive, knew of this. Finally, there was the Luger, which Don Fortuna kept in his bedside table drawer, along with the EpiPen. Three years ago, he had heard of an auction of a World War II German Luger that was the personal weapon of Field Marshal Rommel. "The Desert Fox himself!" the Boss had marveled. Leo went to Christie's in New York to procure it for his boss, "no matter the cost." The Don was a collector of weapons and had long desired such a prize. Until the Don's just voiced threat, its existence was known only to the two men and the *late* Angelica Fortuna.

Leonardo stood, thinking; he knew his mercurial Don well enough to take the threat very seriously. Yet, to Jane's dismay, he still hesitated to give her leave to go.

The detective quickly improvised. There was an additional misdirection to be tried—one more fact she now knew that Sammy did not, and could not prepare her for.

"Do you have a pen and paper, Leonardo?" she asked, brushing the two edges of the coat apart to rest her hands on her hips. She purposely used the long form of the man's name, showing respect, and made sure her total nakedness was now revealed as much as possible. The underboss, suddenly diverted from considering his boss's condition by *Maria's* nude body, complied—as Angelica might have predicted. He searched his breast pocket and retrieved a small notepad and pen. A Montblanc. *The thug has taste; I'll give him that.*

Jane wrote down a phone number. If anyone bothered to call, it would ring at a pizza place in Center City. "This is my number. The Don wished me to give it to you and let you know my skills surpass even those of, and I quote again, *'Cuban Maria.'* He said you can call me anytime. It's on him." And she handed Leo the paper.

The newly found barrel emptied. Though the degenerate had thoroughly enjoyed his time with the twelve-year-old, Leonardo knew better than to ever, *ever* discuss it with anyone. Only the Don knew. Not even Angelica. *The bitch speaks the truth,* he concluded, hesitantly.

Jane *didn't* hesitate. She turned to the crowd. "And any friend of the Don's is a friend of mine. Thirty percent discount for any of you who calls and identifies as being at the house tonight. And just so you know, I give group rates." Then she winked and started walking toward the front door, finally closing and tightening the sash around her coat.

"Just a minute." It was Leonardo.

Shit. Jane inhaled, stopped breathing and tapped her watch to wake it. One more tap was all that would be needed—and the gates to perdition would open. She turned, and the man held out his hand.

"My pen, please."

Jane exhaled. She looked and saw the $500 Montblanc still gripped between her fingers. She smiled and handed it to the underboss. "I like a man with good taste. Call me." And then she turned, opened the door and walked out.

The Lexus was just pulling up, and Jane continued to tread slowly and seductively. She so wanted to run but knew eyes would be on her, either through the windows or via the front-door camera. So, she calmly strolled to the car, opened the rear, left-side door, and entered. The interior lights, for today, were programmed not to illuminate.

"*Andiamo*, Larr... er... Frankie," said Sammy. The man drove slowly away and turned the corner. Once again, he pulled into the camera's blind spot. "Be right back." He grabbed a small screwdriver from inside his pocket, opened the door, and made for the car's rear. The false license plate was attached to the true one with four powerful magnets at the corners. There was a small groove in it precisely to fit the edge of the screwdriver. With the tool, Frankie easily pried the two plates apart. He quickly went to the front of the vehicle and similarly removed a magnetic, fake-dealership cover that sat over the genuine NY State license plate. Pennsylvania only requires rear plates. The man immediately went back to the driver's door, entered, threw the two items at Sammy's feet, and drove away.

From the time she had entered until now, Jane had just sat, facing forward. Mute. No one else had yet said a word, and certainly the men knew it was not their place to initiate conversation. Now, as Frankie pulled away, Anna took her lover's hand. Jane turned to her mate and squeezed the hand tightly. For a time like this, unlike any other they had faced together, Anna had decided on two quotes:

"*I love you more than words can wield the matter; dearer than eyesight, space and liberty.*"

Then, bringing Jane's hand up to her mouth, and kissing it, Anna continued:

"*I would not wish any companion in the world but you...*" to which, apologies to the Bard, she added, "*Janie.*" The first quote came from

King Lear and, befitting this turbulent night, the last was from Jane's favorite—*The Tempest*.

The floodgates opened. Tears streamed down Jane's face and she fell into Anna's open arms, bawling like a newborn child. She continued to sob as Anna held her, rocking her back and forth like the two mothers often did for Felicity after a nightmare. "Have no fear, honey. You can tell me anything." And then she proceeded to emphatically repeat, "Nothing will change between us," over and over. "Nothing will change between us." And indeed, Jane would tell Anna everything. But for now, her spouse's embrace and comforting words were what she needed to begin to purge the scars tonight's acts had seared into her soul.

For a full ten minutes, Jane cried and Anna consoled. The men continued to say nothing, Joe looking out the window, the two in front staring ahead. Frankie wouldn't even intrude by gazing into the rear-view mirror. Then a text tone was heard. It was on Anna's phone and by the ring, the two women knew it was Felicity. Jane composed herself, and the two separated and looked at Anna's screen. The message was simple:

"???????????????"

Jane was the first to chuckle, and it warmed Anna's heart to hear. The one Felicity called Mommy texted back a thumbs-up emoji.

The GIFs came in rapid succession. The first was of Lisa Simpson merrily dancing in front of her couch. Then (from *Seinfeld*), George, Jerry and Elaine with their arms raised in ecstatic celebration. Finally, some actress neither woman knew, smiling, with the words, *"WE DID IT!"* flashing underneath.

Jane took her phone and texted, *"We both love you very much. Now, no more screen time - Time for bed."*

The response was swift. *"Yeah, right. LOL. See you tonight! Champagne, anyone?"*

The two moms laughed, deciding no answer would be better at conveying their response to that last question. Jane turned off her phone and nestled back in Anna's arms. Now Sammy felt he could speak. He turned.

"Jane, my dear. I cannot begin to know what you had to endure in there—and I will never ask. Just know..." The aging assassin paused, barely able to contain his emotions, "that I love you like you were my own daughter. And you, Anna, as well." He motioned for Jane's hand, and then Anna's. He kissed them both as a tear ran down his cheek.

Joe then gently took Anna's other hand and nodded his agreement.

The detective now remembered she was naked underneath the coat. There was a change in underwear plus jeans and a flannel shirt in the trunk. She looked out the window and recognized, from the trip down, where they were.

"Anna, honey. If you don't mind, can you please donate this coat to Goodwill? I don't think I could stand looking at it on you ever again."

Anna nodded. "Of course."

"Also, I need to change—now. I can't wait until we get home. I recall there's a 24-hour diner a few miles up ahead." Then, after a pause, "You hungry, Frankie?"

Everyone smiled. As they all had learned over the last six months in conversations with the lovable man, *that* was a question which would always get the same response. And Frankie knew they knew. So, teasingly, he hesitated, just for a moment. But then, as always, answered—

"I could eat."

Chapter 5

Tuesday, December 31, 2019
Port Jefferson, NY

Marlene Fell sat at her kitchen table—and wept.

She'd just gotten off the phone with her oncologist. Despite the coming holiday, the man felt Marlene should know the results of the PET scan and schedule an appointment ASAP.

The news was bad—very bad. The woman, a heavy smoker since high school, was recently diagnosed with squamous cell carcinoma at the base of the tongue. She had foolishly, though not uncommonly, ignored the symptoms—mild pain on swallowing, weight loss and some tongue numbness—for much too long. The CT and MRI scans had shown, and now the PET scan had confirmed that the cancer had spread not only to her liver but also to her lungs and lymph nodes. Given the staging of the biopsy section, the only treatment options were chemotherapy and radiation.

Marlene had asked for a prognosis, and though he hesitated, the doctor finally admitted that, most likely, the best she could hope for, even with treatment, was six months. The doctor had added, optimistically, "But one never knows. It's possible there could be remission." It was spoken with little conviction, and the patient knew it was just *pro forma*—to provide hope.

Yet Marlene, though devastated by the news, cried primarily not for herself, but for her almost nine-year-old daughter, Khaleesi. The woman had no living relatives and no close friends to call upon to care for the child while undergoing treatments, being confined to bed or, finally, when she was gone.

Foster Care.

The thought of her wonderful girl having to deal first with the illness, then her death and finally wind up in foster care, *with strangers*, was too much for the mother to bear. So, she wept.

It just wasn't fair.

A year-and-a-half ago, the two of them had escaped from under the yoke of a tyrant of a husband and father who had beaten his wife often and had started treating his daughter in a sexual manner. But he had drowned in the backyard pool, and though Marlene had no definite proof, she knew the drowning was not an accident, but a gift from a *guardian angel.* After receiving this second chance, she had gotten a good job and started dating a good man, or so she thought. Once the diagnosis came, however, the man bolted. Khaleesi, now reading and doing her math at two grade levels above what was expected, had managed to come through it all and had matured—even flourished.

It just wasn't fair.

Marlene went to the refrigerator and retrieved the business card she'd placed under a magnet the day her husband died. It was the card of the one person who had shown her any kindness and concern prior to the bastard's demise. She would not call today and ruin the holiday. No, she would wait until Monday to give that individual a chance to enjoy the vacation week with family.

And then Marlene would turn to this person—her only hope.

She looked down at the card and managed a smile as she read the name of the woman.

Her *guardian angel*—

Detective Jane Rieger - Nassau County Police Department.

Chapter 6

Wednesday, January 1, 2020
Henderson
9 AM, PST

All packed and ready to go.

Everything I owned fit nicely into one suitcase. It was gifted to me by Linda, who stuffed it with all sorts of hot/cold weather clothing given we hadn't known my destination. She had remembered my size from a shopping jaunt in Boca Raton when we first met. Re-packing all these items was simple and, since the house I'd rented was fully furnished, very little else needed to be acquired during my stay. I hadn't expected—hoped—to stay very long, after all. In fact, all I'd bought since arriving in July were just two bowls for food and water for my dog, some underwear, and lots of sunblock—it had reached 113 degrees in August!

Yeah, I know, I know, it's a dry heat. Well, guess what—when it's 113 degrees in the shade, dry or not, it's like living in a fucking furnace.

I had stayed on the phone last night for two hours, talking mostly to Joe and *Papà*, but mixing in conversations with Anna, Jane, and even Felicity. Everyone seemed so happy to speak with me, though I had sensed something sad in Jane's voice I couldn't quite put my finger on. I don't know, maybe I was wrong.

By 2 AM their time, we called it a night. They all had to prepare for the coming day, and I had to pack, although, as alluded to, it didn't take very long. I also added just enough dog food to get us through a good week or so.

Since it was 11 PM on New Year's Eve in Henderson, I figured my landlord would be awake and preparing to celebrate, so even though I hated to spoil his night, I called to let him know I was moving out. He had two months of advance rent plus a security deposit, so once I told him to keep it all, he didn't seem too upset by my out-of-the-blue decision. He wished me luck and that was that. Then I called the manager of the 7-Eleven and resigned. He also took it well; long-term workers were not the norm in his business.

I tried to sleep—but failed. I was much too excited, much too happy to allow myself to drop off. Maybe I got in a few winks here and there, but deep slumber never came.

Today, a limousine hired by Anna would pick me up at 9:30 AM and, after a quick stop I told her about, the driver would drop me at Henderson's Executive Airport where a private jet would await— *Papà* and Joe aboard. They were leaving Republic Airport in Farmingdale at 8 AM their time and, amazingly, their rented plane (gifted by Anna and Jane, of course) would, a mere four-and-a-half hours later, land in Henderson. Anna, Jane, Felicity and Marta were flying out around 11 AM from Teterboro Airport in New Jersey, destination Boca Raton, as was mine.

The women had procured an appointment with a highly regarded child psychiatrist at 9 AM in Manhattan. On New Year's Day! He was booked months in advance and had told the mothers that when they had called earlier in the week. But these were two women who would not take "no" for an answer. They had done their homework, and this guy seemed to have a ton of experience with children who had undergone not only trauma from an abusive parent but were also victims of at least one other of a few selected terrible crimes, kidnapping among them. How many doctors could there be with *that* sort of expertise? Since Anna and Jane wanted to get their daughter seen ASAP, a half-million-dollar retainer had been offered and, miracle of miracles, a holiday appointment amazingly opened up! I wasn't told why they were in such a rush, so I guess that's another thing I'd learn shortly.

After their flight arrived, they would go directly to Boca and await the three of us at the home of Joe's father, Morris, two doors down from where Joe's ex-wife Linda and his best friend, Ace, had been living in for a while now. The two had recently returned (December 30) from a two-week getaway in Hawaii, a gift from the wealthy ladies—one of the many *thank-yous* for their help in Felicity's rescue. I choked up when Joe told me they had kept their promise and put their wedding on hold until my return. It was scheduled for three days from now, and I was to be the maid of honor! And before I could ask, Joe anticipated the question and informed me an appropriate dress awaited my arrival, courtesy of the Franklins, based on Linda's remembered measurements.

What a delightful whirlwind of information gleaned in just two hours!

After six excruciatingly lonely months in Nevada, thankfully soothed by Maverick and Julie's companionship, I was finally joining my dad, my lover, and wonderful friends—and I trembled with excitement, pacing back and forth while I waited for the car to arrive.

So, after a last walk with Maverick, I needed a distraction. I went to my phone and brought up the Philadelphia Inquirer's website. And there it was:

VITO ESPOSITO DEAD

screamed the headline. I skimmed through the article. No cause of death was apparent, but the autopsy was still in progress. *No apparent cause of death*, I thought. *Sounds like Papà's work.* The police were seeking a woman, about six feet tall, with long black hair who had visited with Esposito the night before. There was a grainy security-cam photo of this *mystery woman*, but it was clear enough, sunglasses notwithstanding, for me to hazard an educated guess—*Jane, in her wig.* I suddenly felt sad. *Is that why you sounded so melancholy? Oh Papà, did she really need to be involved?* The police were also following up on the Pennsylvania license plate of the woman's car, photographed by security cameras. *That'll lead them to a dead end or red herring, for sure.* A ring of the doorbell interrupted my reading. No problem—I'd get a firsthand account soon enough.

I leashed Maverick—I'd be dealing with strangers who might feel intimidated by an untethered German Shepherd—and we exited the house. I didn't look back. The driver took my bag and placed it in the trunk. He had been told about the stop we were to make and followed as I drove my car with the dog beside me.

It took less than five minutes to arrive at Julie's basement apartment a few miles away. I knew she'd be asleep; she always slept first thing after work, which ended at 6 AM. It was just as well—I couldn't face another sad goodbye right now. I parked the car, and Maverick and I went to her private-entrance door. I slipped an envelope under and placed my open hand on the wood, silently thanking her, once again, for the friendship that kept me sane this past half-year. Inside the envelope were the keys to my car, the registration, title, and a letter, which read:

Dear Julie,

Once again, I want to thank you for your loving friendship these past months. I hope I was at least half as good a friend to you as you were to me. As you can figure out, all went well last night and I'm on my way back to NY! I'm so happy. Since I have no need of a car anymore, please accept this gift as a token of my love and appreciation. No more excuses for being late, girl! LOL.

Please remember what we discussed about Brett. Get away from Henderson. You've got a few months, so start looking for jobs elsewhere. If you want to come out to NY, you can stay with me until you find something, but in any event, do not let that son of a bitch back in your life. Please.

I'll get in touch when I get settled and we'll have a long talk, but right now I can't think straight. I just know I'll miss you terribly. Be safe. Be happy. I love you.

Angelica

Turning, tears in my eyes, Maverick and I walked to the limo. I opened the back door, buckled my seatbelt, and the driver began his short ride to the airport as I wiped my eyes.

Goodbye, Julie.

Chapter 7

"Codename, please."

The voice was female. The tone, no-nonsense.

On the way to the airport, I called the solitary number on the business card Agent Simons had given to everyone at my going-away party. If there ever was an urgent need for contact, that number was to be used. All communication had to go through WITSEC.

I smiled at the woman's request. Six months ago, I had chosen the required codename as an *homage* to my father.

"Lover Girl," I emphatically answered. I heard a keyboard clicking.

"Call back number, please."

I still had *Papà's* SIM card in the phone and had checked the number last night, writing it down on a napkin. I repeated it to the woman and again heard the clicks as the digits were entered into her computer.

"Agent Simons or one of his associates will call back within the next 124 seconds." She ended the call.

124? So specific? I guess WITSEC had done a study—God knows how many millions of tax-payer dollars funded it—and came up with an average call-back interval. Probably to show potential, hesitant clients how quickly an emergency call would be returned. I fought the urge to time the response and then, after what seemed less than a minute, the phone rang and I answered, "Hello."

"Angelica? It's Dan Simons. Everything okay?" He sounded worried. He was a good guy.

"Yes, Agent Simons. I'm fine. More than fine. In fact, I was calling to tell you I would not be needing WITSEC protection any longer. I wanted to thank you for all you've done." The man had helped find me lodging, a used car, employment and had called every month to check up on me to see how I was faring. I really looked forward to those calls—the one slim link to my previous life.

Simons was silent for a moment, and then, "Interesting. I was going through my internal newsfeed this morning and learned about Don Fortuna's *unfortunate* passing. There was also this *mystery woman* involved. I happen to recall a tall, thin lady at your going-away party. I assume that's just a coincidence, right?"

"Like I said," answering with a non-answer, "I'm very grateful for all your help. I hope I wasn't a bother."

The man laughed. "Bother? Hah, you've no idea what some of the people I've had to relocate have put me through. One guy wanted both his wife *and* mistress to come along and be provided for, including specific cars for each. You can guess who got the fancier ride. Another guy *just* wanted his mistress to join him! Needless to say, we got the wife out too and then found them a divorce lawyer at their new location. Most of these miscreants, er, sorry, clients, didn't want to work. I had to constantly remind them WITSEC wasn't a fucking welfare program. Finally, there was this one fat slob from Minneapolis with erectile dysfunction, and Viagra just wasn't getting the job done. So, besides everything else, he demanded a penile implant for his testimony. Well, a few months after the operation, he called, complaining the area he had to push for inflation, alongside his bellybutton, was poorly located. Every time he sat down to eat, his humongous gut would bang that site against the table and, well—*pop went the weasel*. He found it embarrassing, often uncomfortable, and wanted another operation paid by Uncle Sam, of course, to move it to a better site."

I chuckled and asked, "What did you do?"

"He had already given his testimony, so I told Minnesota Fats to either lose weight or eat standing up." I burst out laughing. "Anyway," the agent continued, "you've been the perfect client. All your new credentials will remain in place. Be careful, please, Angelica *Foster*. From this moment on, you're an unprotected private citizen again. For good—or bad. Much luck." He sounded sincere in his wish before he ended the call.

One thing I would miss from my Elba in the desert was the occasional amusing billboard. I'd thought none could compete with the hilarious ones seen during my quick trip to Boca, now last year, but now and then there would be one to bring out a smile. During the short trek to the airport, I passed two of my favorites. One, from the myriad of personal injury lawyers, was:

ROLLED SNAKE EYES AT THE CASINO THEN SLIPPED AND FELL ON YOUR WAY OUT?—CALL *1 - 800 ROLL 7 11*: THE LAW FIRM OF SANTINO, BAKER AND COLOMBO. A JACKPOT AWAITS!

The other, cashing in now marijuana was legal in Nevada:

THE SOUTH VEGAS CANNABIS DISPENSARY—FOR ALL OF YOU *HIGH* ROLLERS.

Vegas.

After a few minutes, the driver, who wore a Bluetooth headset, raised his arm and tapped the device with his finger. "Yes?" he said and then listened for about thirty seconds, after which he tapped the instrument again.

"Good news, Miss Foster. Your people have arrived and are waiting on the tarmac. I can drive straight to the jet, and you'll be on your way in minutes."

I was shocked. "Wait. No taking off my shoes? No getting felt-up by TSA agents?"

The man chuckled. "No, Miss. This is a private jet. Henderson Executive caters to a very wealthy clientele and under most circumstances, passengers can board without harassment." And just as he spoke those words, he turned right, onto an unnamed paved road adjacent to the airport. He stopped by a guardhouse, flashed ID of some sort, and was passed through. We continued for about a quarter mile and after another turn, I saw the jet. I'd learn later it was a Citation X+, top speed a touch less than Mach 1—717 mph! It was stopped with mobile boarding stairs in place. Two figures stood at the foot of those steps.

My heart leaped into my mouth, and I had to control every fiber of my being not to weep in front of the driver. We came to a stop about twenty feet away. The man quickly exited and opened my door, after which he proceeded to the trunk to retrieve the luggage. Maverick and I stepped out, and we stood, unmoving, for a moment. Then I bent down to be in my trained dog's face. I pointed to both men, then to my heart and nodded my head, up and down, twice. "Friends," I said. "Friends." That should be enough to let him know these two were not a danger to him or, especially, to me. I was confident now to let go of the leash—and ran to *Papà* and embraced him, sobbing.

We stood for a few moments, hugging, no words needing to be vocalized. I finally kissed his cheek and he mine. Finally, he spoke. "Go," was all he said, nodding to Joe. I smiled and then walked slowly to my love. We just stared at one another. Then, after a good fifteen seconds, huge grins appeared, and we burst out laughing, reached out and kissed, passionately. "Oh, Joe, I've missed you so," I finally said. "As have I, Angie," he responded. Then, hopeless romantic that I am, I yawned.

Joe tried to look aghast. "Tired of me already, huh?" I gave him one of my trademarked light punches to his shoulder.

"I didn't get much sleep last night."

He caressed my cheek. "Neither did I. And I expect even less tonight." We both grinned like horny teenagers, then kissed deeply once more. As our lips finally parted, I wiped my eyes, turned, and saw my father petting Maverick. They both seemed to already have taken a liking to each other. I whistled, and the dog ran to me. "Pet him, Joe. Let him know you're a friend." Joe did just that and Maverick smiled, especially when scratched under the chin, his favorite spot after his belly.

The driver, who had already placed my bag on the jet, now asked if there was anything else I required. I thanked him and said, "No. I've got everything I need—right here."

After a sumptuous brunch, we sat, drank champagne, and each of us summarized the last six months. Both Joe's and my doings over that time were excruciatingly dull. After all, how much trouble can an aging ophthalmologist and a 7-Eleven worker, both vowed to celibacy, get into in half a year? The Pope probably led a more exciting life. I lovingly spoke of Julie, the electrifying daily routine at a convenience store and the scintillating town of Henderson—as perfect a locale as any to play dead in. Joe regaled us with tales of some of his more colorful (I think he used the word "insane"—or was it "inane?") patients. But *Papà* was another story.

"I've disbanded the *Harem*," he announced.

"No way!"

The *Harem* was a group of about twenty ladies of a *certain age* who my father bedded on a rotating and regular basis at QueensGate Towers, three high-rise co-op apartment buildings, one in which his penthouse apartment sat. Each lady knew of the other women and had come to an understanding—if my father's attention was equally apportioned. It was a weird arrangement, but my dad truly cared for the women and provided the companionship and tenderness each lady still craved. Somehow, it all worked. But now, he had informed the members that he was in a monogamous relationship. They were disappointed, and yet all truly wished him well, which said a lot about the way he had treated them over the years.

What was more interesting, however, was the woman who had seemingly stolen my father's heart. She was not a member of *Papà's Harem*, a fact I'm sure secretly pleased every one of those ladies. Each would now not have to face the lucky winner of the Sammy Sweepstakes every day, strolling through the grounds of their common residence. No, the grand-prize winner was an outsider, and a more unusual pairing would be hard to imagine, especially since sex did not, at least yet, factor into the equation.

The woman in question was Helen Mandel, Joe's office manager for over thirty years. She was about five-foot nothing—Dad was a little over six—with an acerbic wit that cowered many a younger, stronger and taller verbal opponent. She was a fierce, loyal keeper of the portal to Joe's office and was instrumental in providing Anna and Jane with information that proved crucial in their quest to free Felicity and Marta.

The two had met six months ago, the same day I met my *padre* for the first time. And for whatever intangible reason, whatever chemical reactions take place in the brain when people meet and talk, they started seeing each other; first on a bi-weekly basis, then more regularly.

But was it Shakespeare who said, "The course of true love never did run smooth?" Probably, but Anna and Jane would know for sure. Anyway, my father, of course, is Italian—Catholic. Helen is Jewish—*orthodox*. She calls herself *modern orthodox,* my father said, which meant she was not as *super*-strict as the traditional kind. But sex outside of marriage was out of the question. Kissing, hugging and holding hands were okay—"I'm not a fucking fanatic!" Helen would admonish. Obviously cursing was on her acceptable activities list as well. As was being alone with a man. I wondered what she might add to that list as time went on. After all, what constitutes "sex" is up for interpretation, right? Just ask Bill Clinton.

Yeah, I admit it—I've got a dirty mind.

Helen was divorced and had a son who'd fled to California years ago with his non-Jewish girlfriend (known, Joe informed me, as a *shiksa*), now his wife. He and his mother had been estranged for a decade over that choice, but recently they both had finally and happily reconciled. That's how Helen learned she was a grandmother. She asked her new boyfriend to accompany her to the West Coast as moral support when visiting her family for the first time. She and he got to use the first of hopefully many free trips via the fractional jet ownership gifted to Helen by the Franklins as a reward for her help and for her prayers. Helen had recited her devotions hourly while Felicity was in peril and Anna was a firm believer in the power of prayer, no matter the religion.

Now that her family had been put together again, Helen's views on intermarriage had softened, but only slightly. She accepted her son's choice and loved her *shiksa* daughter-in-law and grandson. But for herself? No, she sadly explained to Dad, she couldn't. Too many decades of firm beliefs could not be buried for any man. Even for Lover Boy, a name she knew of but had not yet asked him to explain. She and he had discussed her beliefs a lot lately, which is why now, remarkably, *Papà* announced to me and Joe—

"When we get back to New York, I have an appointment with an orthodox rabbi—to discuss conversion. Haven't told Helen yet."

I sat with my mouth agape, and Joe looked like he'd just received an IRS audit—or worse, a Medicare review.

"It's just a first step, but after returning from our trip to Israel, I gained a new appreciation of the Jewish people."

Another shock. "Trip to Israel?"

"Yes. Soon after you left us, Anna and Jane learned that Morris's one unfulfilled dream was to visit Israel before he died. So as the first reward for his help, they arranged for him, Joe, and, since it was Helen's dream as well, for her and me to accompany them. Separate rooms, of course. Two weeks, first-class all the way. What a way to travel!"

I looked at Joe questioningly. "I was going to get to it eventually," he said, sheepishly.

"Anyway," *Papà* continued, "it was a remarkable experience, not just for Morris and Helen, but I too had always wished to see the Holy Land, where Jesus had himself walked. Helen and Morris were so happy, and they were wonderful additions to the official tour guides in providing me with an introduction to Judaism, its people's history and, sadly, their persecution. But it was after hearing the story of and then seeing Masada I began to consider conversion. What a story! Just 960 Jews against a Roman legion of 15,000. Finally, after holding out for a long time, the Jews realized all hope was lost—so they killed one another (suicide was forbidden), preferring death to dishonor, forced conversion, and slavery." He paused for a few moments, again admiring the bravery. He understood such sacrifice.

"Anyway, I'll talk to the rabbi, and we'll see how it goes. Can't hurt, right? What's the saying? 'Nothing ventured, nothing gained?'"

"*Sì,*" I answered as he picked up his glass and finished the champagne. This discussion had left me reeling, and I was having a hard time believing it all. But anything that would bring happiness to my *padre* was a priority for me. I was looking forward to getting to know Helen better.

"Ahem." It was Joe. I looked at him and a devilish smile stretched across his face. He steepled his hands together, fingertips touching, like a Bond villain.

"Sammy, I assume you are *not* circumcised, correct?"

A suspicious look came over my father. "Siiii," he answered, drawing the word out.

Joe's smile widened—I swear if he had a handlebar mustache, he'd be twirling it. "Well," he continued, "you realize, of course, for an orthodox conversion, for it to be strictly kosher, you *will be* required..." He trailed off, not bothering to complete the sentence.

Dad sat, somewhat stunned, understanding Joe's inference perfectly. His head fell and he slumped back in his chair. After a few moments, he slowly shook his head back and forth, sighed loudly, and looked up.

"Well..." he began, picking up his glass and refilling. "... as Helen might say—'*Oy! Vey!*'"

It took a full three minutes for Joe and me to completely stop laughing. I had not laughed so hard or felt so relaxed in six long months.

Finally recovered, I took a long sip of champagne and looked at them both.

"Okay, guys, on a more serious note," though I was still smiling, "it's time to tell me how Don Vito Fortuna was dragged kicking and screaming to the gates of Hell."

The two men in my life looked at each other and nodded. Dad put down his drink.

"*Sì*, Angelica. You should know what sacrifices others have made for your return. The debt we *all* owe."

His voice had turned somber, and it surprised and shook me. My smile quickly melted away—the comedy portion of today's program seemed to be at an end. I'd been slouching in my very comfortable seat, but now sat up straight. "Yes, *Papà*. Please, tell me."

And so, he did.

Chapter 8

Boca Raton, Florida

We pulled up to Morris's home at 2 PM. Almost immediately, the door opened, and Linda appeared. A very attractive woman in her late 50s, I had grown extremely fond of her during the few days we'd spent together six months back, and my heart filled with joy at finally seeing her again.

She and Joe had once been married for a little over three decades. But the woman finally tired of the man's infidelities and split, moving to Boca to what was once the divorced couple's second home (two houses down from Joe's father), where she now cohabitated with Tony, Joe's best and oldest friend. She and her ex-father-in-law were close during the marriage and continued to be. Prior to beginning her relationship with Tony, each time Joe had come down to visit his dad, he and Linda would get together to *reminisce*, as they euphemistically referred to their post-marital sex-capades. Somehow, despite all that occurred during their time together, the two still had loving feelings toward each other. But they also knew living as husband and wife was impossible.

Let's pause a moment. In case you're wondering how I feel concerning Joe's *pussy-hound* reputation, my lover has sworn up and down to me he's a changed man—and I believe him. We're an unconventional pair, especially given our age difference, that's for

71

sure. But his experiences over the last year and a half have sobered him. The love I feel for him is on par with what I feel for my *padre*, unlike anything I've ever felt in my sordid and loveless past. Being with him, I feel so special, like I was the only woman in the world. And I can see Joe's adoration for me in his eyes, and in his sweet tenderness when we make love.

Anyway, Joe has seen what I can do with a gun and a knife, so... no, *Lover Girl* has no worries about his fidelity.

To continue, Tony—*Ace* to his closest friends—had always gotten along beautifully with Linda during the years he, his deceased wife, and the Peck's socialized. It was just about two years ago when he re-entered Linda's life, visiting a few times before he had the courage to tell his friend. And Joe was thrilled for them both, as crazy as it may seem to one just looking in, not knowing the history. So, soon after the *l'affaire Jonathan Franklin*, where Ace introduced Joe to Lover Boy, the former Mafia Don moved to Florida where he and Linda have been an item since. They were already set to get married, but they sweetly postponed the day until I returned from exile. The reason was simple.

Tony, Joe, *Papà*, Jane, Anna, Frankie and I had together stormed the upstate NY hideaway where Felicity and Marta had been held. We rescued the two captives, my assassin skills finally used for a good and noble purpose. Ever since, the bond between us, including Morris and Linda, the latter to whom I had vowed to return Ace alive, was stronger than steel. There was nothing any of us would not do for the other, and Tony and Linda just could not foresee a wedding without me in attendance.

Being involved in a harrowing, life-or-death situation can do that to people.

Maverick was leashed and held by Joe as Linda and I ran to each other and embraced, kissing each other's cheeks, shedding a few tears. We spoke of our joy in reuniting, and then I reached into my pocket and retrieved a doggie treat. I turned to Maverick, pointed to Linda, then to my heart, nodded and said, "Friend." I handed the treat to the woman and motioned to Joe to unleash my dog. He jogged over. "Bend down, Linda, and give him the treat." She did, Maverick gobbled it down and Linda was now a member of the family as far as my pet was concerned.

Tony was right behind her and took me in his arms. "It's great to see you again, Angelica. We missed you terribly."

"Me too," I answered, before calling Maverick over for a similar introduction. Then I then saw Morris appear at the doorway and he and I walked to each other, smiled, and hugged.

"I'm so happy to see you again, Morris. You look well."

"Indeed," the lovable, almost ninety-year-old man said, "I've been sure to get my exercise and eat properly these past months. I didn't want to risk missing your return." My heart melted, and we hugged once more. I then handed him a treat and repeated the introductory regimen with Maverick.

Behind Morris was Marta. We enfolded and then I showed her I still wore the cross she had gifted me—her mother's. "I have never taken it off, not even for a moment," I said. The woman smiled, nodded, and met my dog.

"Angelica!"

I turned. It was Felicity now who came charging out of the doorway into my arms. I squeezed tightly.

"How you doin', kiddo? You miss me?"

"More than anything, Angelica. You miss *me*?"

"Even more, and—"

Suddenly Maverick left Marta and bounded over and before either of us knew what was happening, raised himself on his hind legs, placed his front paws on Felicity's chest—and proceeded to rapidly lick her face.

"Maverick!" I shouted. I'd never seen him act this way, and for a moment I was confused and worried about the girl's safety. But Felicity was giggling uncontrollably as she fell to the ground and started rubbing the dog's well-presented belly.

"He remembers me, Angelica! You remember me, don't you, boy?"

And then *I* remembered and smiled widely. After I had picked up the six-week-old puppy from his box for the first time last July at the Franklin home, Felicity had asked to pet him. So, I sat her down on the floor and she did just that. After a while, the dog began to lick her hand.

Even after all this time, it seems he recalled her smell! I was happily jealous of their bond.

I walked through the doorway, leaving my friends behind, knowing who remained. And then I saw them—Anna and Jane. I smiled and nodded my head toward the bedrooms, and they followed me to the guest room where Joe and I had first made love. I bid them to sit on the edge of the bed, drew up a chair, and extended my arms; each woman grabbed one of my hands with theirs.

I had promised myself I wouldn't cry, but who was I kidding? The tears flowed and through soft sobs I looked at Jane, squeezed her hand, and began:

"*Papà* and Joe have told me everything. I can't..." I continued, simultaneously shaking my head back and forth, "... I can't begin to imagine what you went through... with my false father, the cruel, degenerate bastard he was. The shame. The humiliation." I shivered. "And Leonardo. That man always gave me the creeps. Another sadistic pervert." I had stopped sobbing by now, but some tears still flowed. I looked at Anna. "And you, sweet Anna. It's unfathomable what you must have gone through, not knowing what was happening to Jane in that cursed house." I squeezed her hand harder. "And I know, I *know* she would never have gone in had you not agreed." Looking straight ahead to have both women in my field of view, I continued. "So, I'm here now, reunited with Joe, *Papà*, with you all... because of you two, and what you sacrificed. I can never repay you."

Anna smiled and said, "Well, you should know, Angelica, that Felicity had a say in the matter as well. The little spy overheard the planning and told us, and I quote, "*We*, should go for it!""

Everyone laughed. "We?" I asked. Anna nodded.

"She is something, that little cutie," I added. "And she and Maverick just greeted each other like long-lost friends. Amazing."

The two women looked at each other suspiciously, and then Jane said, "We need to talk to you about Felicity and Maverick. We have a favor to ask."

"Anything," I immediately answered, squeezing both their hands. "There is nothing you could ask I'd refuse." Then I stood, still holding on, which caused each woman to rise, as well. "I had a brother who I loved dearly. Fucking cancer got him way too young; I had no sisters. But if I had, I could not have felt more for them than I do for you two wonderful, wonderful women. *You*, are my sisters. Now, and forever."

I first approached Jane. She knew what was coming and our mouths met in a long, soulful kiss. The same type of kiss she had given to me after I put a bullet through the head of *Il Fucile*, Felicity's kidnapper, thus reuniting the girl with her loving parents. I had been shocked, momentarily, by that caress then, but it was a kiss of love, nothing sexual, as might be thought by someone looking from without. Our lips finally parted, and I and Anna repeated the act. When we were done, the three of us tried to kiss, as one, but it just didn't work—foreheads, noses, and chins getting in the way. We broke out laughing at our ineptitude.

After the giggling ceased, we took our seats, and Anna and Jane discussed some recent history, and then their request. I listened without interruption; the entire conversation took about thirty minutes. When done, I smiled and said, "Of course."

Chapter 9

After our discussion, Anna, Jane, and I joined the others for a marvelous late lunch. The last time I had been in Florida, Linda had served up a meal unlike any I'd ever experienced, strange as it sounds from someone who went to U of P with its diverse student body. It consisted of toasted bagels, cream cheese with chives, and Nova Scotia lox, all topped with a Bermuda onion and a slice of beefsteak tomato. Heaven. She had remembered my reaction then and happily prepared an encore.

Nothing like *that* in fucking Henderson!

Linda then showed me her wedding gown, beige, with a six-foot cathedral train. Keeping that delicate appendage behind and not under her feet would be my primary job as maid of honor, their backyard wedding set for Saturday, three days away. The dress was custom made and fitted at a boutique in Palm Beach, commissioned by Anna. It looked as if made for a movie bride in a Hollywood production; or for a royal wedding. It was Anna and Jane's gift to Linda, as were the caterer and a string quartet. The ladies would never tire of rewarding us all.

As for me? Well, except for my communion when I was eight, I couldn't remember ever wearing a fancy dress. My wardrobe consisted almost entirely of jeans and T-shirts, except for that one time I had to blend into a fancy cocktail party for a contract kill. My dress proved useful, allowing the target to lower his guard as he lowered his hand, slipping it under the flowing garment as we groped each other in the duplex's upstairs bathroom. The man's preoccupation with getting into my panties allowed me to slip my hidden dagger between the third and fourth rib, into his heart before he'd even gotten to third base. I left him slumped over the toilet, finished my champagne, and left a small "Out of Order" sign—brought in my purse—on the door. The body was discovered by the maid the following day.

But I digress.

All I meant to convey was I'm no expert on posh ladieswear. But upon seeing the gown Jane and Anna had chosen and brought from New York, I knew enough to know it was a one-of-a-kind. Pink, it had what they called a cold shoulder and flounce sleeves. The entire top was embroidered in a floral pattern and the back of the bodice was open, leading to the long, chiffon skirt, ankle length. Just gorgeous. A lump formed in my throat as I looked in the full-length mirror upon trying it on. I had a hard time recognizing the girl gazing back at me, mouth open. The measurements were perfect— Linda had remembered them well. But if they had needed last-minute alterations, ever-prepared Anna had a seamstress on emergency call in Boca. I hugged the three ladies *en masse*. "I love you guys. You know that, right?" I said. They all nodded and remarked on how lovely I looked, and I could tell they were sincere.

I admit, I've always been a self-centered little bitch. But I'd worked hard these past months to turn over a new leaf in that regard, especially for my Joe. I wanted him to see what I hoped was the real me, the new me—Angelica Foster—not the old me, Angelica Fortuna, killer of men and narcissistic asshole.

But I couldn't help but agree with my friends. So, my journey of self-reflection from arrogance and conceit to humility and modesty would require a slight detour—because *damn*, I looked fabulous!

Joe announced that he had to drive his father to the Super Target for some items, but I volunteered for the duty—I knew my man was looking forward to humoring Morris's Super Target obsession as much as removing lice from a child's eyelashes, a task needing to be performed about once a year, he'd told me. *Che Schifo!* Anyway, I had never been to one of these super-stores, so might as well see what the man found so intriguing as to warrant the ritual of an almost-daily visit.

Jane and Anna had insisted I drive their rented 2020, white, S-Class 450 sedan—Joe had informed them of my love of all things Mercedes. I found it sweet he'd remembered that fact, gleaned, as it was, from our first *date*.

We were at a pizzeria near his office when, discussing our top-ten movies, I mentioned Scorsese's *Casino*. It was also one of Joe's faves and he laughed when I described what I considered one of the film's best scenes. In it, Ginger (Sharon Stone), maniacally rams her 1975 Mercedes 450SL repeatedly into her husband Sam's (Robert DeNiro) 1981 Cadillac Eldorado, shrieking out a string of obscenities along the way. Shocked that I had recognized the make and model of the barely-on-screen vehicle, I explained cars had been my obsession since my teens. I'd always coveted, but could never financially justify purchasing a Mercedes, even one of the bottom-tier models. As for owning a beauty such as this S450, whose motor purred like a kitten yet could pounce like a hungry cheetah when called upon—fuhgeddaboudit. At $100,000 bare minimum, it would never happen.

The trip, back and forth, took less than an hour and, I must admit, the Super Target was super impressive. However, Morris's habit, I was sure, stemmed more from a desire for a daily activity where he could meet up with the same group of acquaintances. The store, to him, was like the *Cheers* bar in the old TV show—everyone knew his name.

Jane and Anna were strolling hand in hand, near Morris's house, when we returned. The man excused himself for his afternoon nap, and I reluctantly returned the key fob to Anna. "You like it, huh?"

she said, more a statement than a question, nodding toward the Mercedes.

"Are you kidding? Just looking at it makes my nipples hard. If it came with an accessory penis, Joe would be out of luck." The ladies, for the first time since I'd known them, blushed. "Sorry, but a beautiful, perfectly crafted machine like that, with its plush leather, air-conditioned seats custom-made for my perfect ass," *oops, there's the old Angelica peeking through*, "just pushes all my buttons. Also, it'll never need Viagra to get it going on a frosty December morning—not that Joe needs a pill, mind you. Just keep *this* baby on a steady diet of 93-octane and it'll be good to go like it was the first time, every time."

We all had a good laugh, and then my friends gave each other a conspiratorial look. "What?" I tentatively asked.

Anna slipped her hand into her purse and came out with an almost exact copy of the Mercedes's fob. "Happy almost birthday, Angelica. It's January eighth, right?" I nodded, struck momentarily mute. "You'll find it starts a car just like this one, except in black, sitting in our driveway awaiting your *perfect ass* to grace its cushy leather, air-conditioned *and* heated seat." She smiled and handed me the key. "After all, you'll need wheels to come visit us and Felicity often, and in *our* snooty neighborhood, only vehicles like *this* are allowed on the roads—it's a local ordinance."

As you probably have learned by now, I tend to cry at the drop of a hat, but I vowed to keep my shit together, especially in public. I slowly shook my head. "You guys are something else." They stood each to the other side of me and I placed a hand on the nape of each neck. "Cars, clothes, all that stuff is nice, more than nice." I slid my hands around their necks and gently stroked their cheeks. "But what *we* have transcends all of that. We all know the saying 'money doesn't buy happiness' is pure bullshit. Of course, it does. What it *doesn't* buy, though, is love. Or respect. And it doesn't buy what *we* have, what I said, about being sisters. I meant every word and I say it again now and would, Mercedes or no Mercedes—

79

though I am *not* giving back this key," I rapidly added, chuckling. "And Felicity, even though I guess she would now technically be my niece..." they, too, laughed, "is more like a daughter, my own child. I like to think I feel for her much as my *Mamma* felt for me.

"What I did six months ago, for her... for you... I would do it again in a heartbeat. No rewards necessary or expected. And..." I was now fearing my vow would turn hollow, "what you did for me..."

"We would do it again, in a heartbeat," Jane said, completing my thought. "Again... and again."

I nodded and used my already well-placed hands to bring our heads together, barely holding back the tears.

"Sisters," I whispered, kissing each on her cheek.

And they repeated—"*Sisters.*"

Chapter 10

Floral Park, NY

Melinda-Ann Queen (often referred to as MAQ, "pronounced *Mack*, like that *big-ass* truck," she would say) sat at her kitchen table—and rejoiced.

Everything was in place for a very happy new year. She had all the evidence needed—and soon it would be time for the reward.

Three months ago, the tall and attractive woman had won a position on the Board of Directors at QueensGate Towers (the first time she'd run), and became chairwoman of the Finance Committee. She replaced the previous man, Jack Wellman, whose death after thirty years at that position had led to the special election. She had beaten out four other contenders and found herself in the perfect position to gather the data she needed. Unfortunately, to get the plum committee chair she had to sleep with the President of the Board, Peter Plick, or, as Melinda-Ann would often think of him, *Peter Prick*. But it got her what she wanted. Though her first thought after the dirty deed was, *well, I've had worse,* she had almost passed out due to his excessively applied and pungent cologne. *Probably buys it by the gallon at Price Club,* she'd decided, rushing to her 30th-floor balcony for some air.

The woman wasn't surprised at how easy it was to lure the man to her bed. After all, she considered herself *a finely aged piece of ass.*

And Plick was well known in the buildings to be quite the Lothario, openly bragging of his sexual prowess (of which Melinda-Ann discovered not a whit during the brief encounter). Also well known was his love of blowjobs which, *Thank God,* she thought with relief, had not been demanded. *If you had, I'd have bitten it off—if, that is, I could have found your pitiful, puny Plick-prick.*

MAQ chuckled. She so enjoyed a bawdy alliteration every now and then.

Yet, despite her displeasure with the man's odor and sexual performance, Melinda-Ann was way more annoyed that she'd had to resort to bedding him in the first place. Given her background, the finance chair should have been a no-brainer.

I have an MBA from Wharton for fuck's sake! she'd inwardly screamed. In fact, she was also a CPA (with additional certification in forensic accounting), and had been among the army of CPAs to many Fortune 500 companies during much of her career. She had retired at age sixty-seven, just last year. In her mind, the tryst and the Oscar-worthy fake orgasm were humiliations that should never have been necessary.

Unfortunately, all her experience and financial savvy hadn't kept Melinda-Ann from losing much of her lifesavings to "that fucking sonuvabitch!" Bernie Madoff in early 2009. Once her (and many others') bad luck had gone public ("fucking newspapers!"), she found her employment by many of those same corporations slowly dry up. If she couldn't handle her own finances, the theory went, why should they, multi-billion-dollar businesses all, entrust her with their own?

Luckily, Melinda-Ann had gotten suspicious of the enormous returns showing up *on paper* and withdrew a good, but ultimately not good enough, amount before the scandal broke. Now, eleven years later, the Wharton grad's luck had finally run out. Pricey maintenance fees on her corner, four-bedroom Manhattan-facing unit plus equally expensive tastes in life's pleasures were costly enough. Combine that with the reduced income from the meager number of bottom-tier clients she'd been able to keep before retiring, and it was no wonder her financial position had turned dire.

Selling her apartment and buying a smaller one at The Towers was "out of the fucking question." No, if she had to sell, she'd move—the *pity-stares* that would come her way were indignities she could never endure.

She loved living at QGT. After all, she was *The Queen of QueensGate*.

Melinda-Ann Queen had lived at her current residence for fifteen years and during that time had been on virtually every committee, been a member of every club, and had gone to every country club dinner and special event. She was an active golfer and tennis player and enjoyed life there to the fullest. Thus (especially given her surname), the sobriquet.

It didn't take long after moving in for her husband, Jacob, to decide he hated living at The Towers. That, coupled with his inability to satisfy her in bed for the better part of their marriage, created the perfect storm leading to their split-up. The apartment went to the wife in the settlement. The husband died two years later—a heart attack while climbing upon his favorite horse, *NeighSayer*, at a stable in Muttontown.

"Ironic," the ex-wife scornfully quipped upon hearing the news. "He was usually much better at mounting *that fucking horse* than he ever was at mounting *me*." The man was buried with his saddle, and more than one mourner at the funeral commented that the occasion marked the first time they could remember seeing MAQ smile within twenty feet of the deceased. The floral-print dress she'd worn to the service might have also been a clue to her mood.

Since the split, Melinda-Ann had enjoyed sexual dalliances with many of the men found among the three thousand QueensGate residents. But she had to painfully admit, losing Sammy Vivino as one of them a few months back was a huge blow. Of all the clubs she belonged to, being part of his *Harem* (though none of the ladies knew the name Sammy had bestowed upon them), brought her the greatest joy. True, she had to share the man with others, but still no one in her life had made her feel as special and had brought her to as volcanic and vocal an orgasm as Sammy. He would be sorely missed. But *The Queen* was a benevolent sovereign and didn't have it in her heart to be angry with the man. She had, when in his company, been shown the loving attention she felt befit one with her nickname. Knowing his aversion to her favorite four-letter word, she even had made it a point to scrupulously avoid using it in Sammy's presence. So, she truly wished him well with whomever he had chosen. *Who knows*, she mused, *maybe it won't last....*

Anyway, fretting over her sex life had now taken a backseat to distressing over financial difficulties—thus, the goal of chairing the Finance Committee and the minor debasement of sleeping with that "perfidious, peremptory, prick Plick." *Try saying that five times fast*, she considered.

Having lived at QueensGate for so long, she had heard rumors of financial improprieties, downright corruption and other titillating material from her neighbors, *yentas* all—especially the male bedfellows. Gossiping was a high art at The Towers—second only to complaining.

MAQ was always too busy making a living to worry about unsubstantiated rumors or running for the board. But with her personal finances now "turning to shit," a plan was needed.

As the wife and mother of investigative reporters, her *ex* on the Times for three decades and her son, Jason, now muckraking at the NY Post, she had learned a thing or two. Most of the lessons gleaned were about how the rich and powerful manipulate their way to become even richer and more powerful. The key ingredient to success was, without a doubt, greed. "Without greed," Jacob used to say, "nothing could ever get accomplished in this fucking city." And taking that as first principle, MAQ used all his teachings, plus her son's resources at The Post, to explore the co-op's history, stretching back the thirty years of its existence. Now, with her position and access to past financial records, she had added her own expertise to the mix and come up with the mother lode—evidence of massive corruption and theft.

It was time to make lemon-aid out of the lemons of her post-Madoff existence.

Early on, Melinda-Ann had doubted the rumors were true. That was, until just a day after the first unofficial board meeting, which was a meet-and-greet among the eight members that included Building Manager Bill Brown (called *B.B.* by all), and co-op attorney Abe Crowe (known to many as either Abe or *Asshole-Abe*). Crowe's wife, Celine, was the recording secretary. Queen was the only non-incumbent, most of the others having been on the Board *for decades*, as had *B.B.* and Abe in their positions as co-op employees. No such thing as term limits at QueensGate Towers.

There was just one quick piece of old business to vote on and although her views were the opposite, she voted with the majority, including the President. Committee chairmen would be decided upon in a week by Plick, at their first *official* meeting, and she wanted to get on his good side immediately. So she voted "aye" and planned his seduction for two days hence.

She smiled now, remembering the knock on her door the day after the meet-and-greet. It was Jesús, the superintendent of the building, a man whose eyes were so narrow he always appeared to be on the verge of falling asleep. He was accompanied by three porters carrying a 60-inch, plasma, thin-screen, state-of-the-art smart-TV!

"Where do you want this to go, Your Majesty?" Jesús quipped—he always called Melinda-Ann by her unofficial title.

"I didn't order a fuckin' TV, Jesús."

"I know," the man chortled. "This is a gift from Mr. Plick. It's his way of welcoming new members to the board. In the past he's given out furniture, refrigerators, stoves—even totally redid the kitchen for one couple, both elected at the same time. It's his way of thanking you, in advance, for your support... and votes." He winked, or so she thought—it was difficult to tell. "So, where do you want it?"

Melinda-Ann was shocked, though not so much as to interfere with pointing the crew to her old, 32-inch CRT—that's Cathode-Ray-Tube for those of you born after the turn of the century—beast in the living room. They soon went to work and in no time, she was staring at the huge, beautiful screen with Judge Judy, big as life, holding court. She thanked the men and gave them a nice tip. The woman then remembered a conversation at the boardroom table, discussing her imminent cataract surgery, necessitated primarily by trouble viewing computer and TV screens. Plick must have picked up on that, and here was his first, not-so-subtle, bribe to ensure she'd be a good drone and vote his way.

I'm a fucking queen, not a drone, Melinda-Ann bristled.

Any doubts about rumors she'd heard were gone. So, the ex-CPA quickly went to work and now, three months later, had the evidence required for her plan. The President of the Board, the B.M. (unfortunately, Building Manager did not lend itself to polite abbreviation) and the co-op's sole attorney were all knee-deep in corruption, netting them tens to sometimes hundreds of thousands in either dollars or non-monetary kickbacks a year.

One of Plick's non-monetary rewards was a long-time relationship with Emi, who ran the Mall liquor store. In Japanese, Emi means *beautiful smile*—which was the one expression no one had ever noticed cross the woman's face. *Well, look who she must service*, MAQ ruefully considered. Yet Emi seemed to turn a blind eye to her man's philandering, smell, and lack of lovemaking skills. *The Queen* guessed that not being burdened with the customary onus of paying rent on one's establishment (now twelve years running) probably had something to do with that. *The only time she probably smiles is in the privacy of the mailroom, every first-of-the-month, noticing the lack of a bill from QGT.*

Plick had a nice *quid pro blow* policy going with Emi. Through fake receipts and an innovative juggling of the books MAQ couldn't help but admire (thanks to dearly departed Jack Wellman), Tower Liquors's *in arrears* state had been masterfully hidden for more than a decade.

I'd bet Emi provided more than a free bottle of sake to jugglin' Jack now and then, Queen decided with a smile.

The most interesting board member was Tina Thomas. Known as *The Dragon Lady* by the others, she was the mouthpiece of the builder and sponsor of the cooperative agreement. There was no direct proof of involvement in the shady dealings, but *she dresses much too nicely, drives too expensive a car and lives on too high a floor for a single woman on her reported salary*, the financial sleuth deduced.

QueensGate Towers opened as rental apartments in 1980. Out of the fifteen-hundred apartments, there were close to five hundred whose renters, in 1990 when the conversion occurred, decided not to buy. They remained renters, and their units stayed in the hands of the builder. As the tenants moved out or passed on, their apartments automatically were put up for sale and joined the cooperative if sold. As of now, one-hundred-three empty residences remained after the most recent sale that, unusually, was done one-on-one, without going through a real-estate broker. Thomas, certainly with the aid of good ol' Jack, had skillfully made it appear to her employers as a fair-price buy. But the purchaser, a well-known Garden City plastic surgeon, actually paid $100,000 below market-value, unheard of for a builder-controlled unit where *haggling* was always treated as a double-four-letter word.

"So, Tina," Melinda-Ann said to her empty apartment after discovering the sly manipulation, "that explains your disappearance from the social scene,"—for two weeks last July—"and the decades-younger face, flat tummy, tighter ass and gravity defying, teen-age tits when you returned. Brava!"

But I'd bet you didn't report to the IRS—Schedule C—what they might consider bartering income from the good doctor, did you, Tina? Yes, those bloodsuckers might be interested in that.

For thirty years now, the newly rejuvenated woman had been permanently ensconced on the Board (by contract) as the builder's representative. That would continue until she sold all of the remaining apartments. Because of those one-hundred-three units, plus her own, Thomas had tens of thousands more votes to cast in any election than anyone else, votes based upon the number of shares a particular unit was worth. And each was worth thousands.

Therefore, Tina Thomas was probably the most powerful person at QueensGate Towers; yet almost no one would recognize her if they tripped over her in The Mall. Regrettably for the co-op, all that power lessened the woman's incentive to sell those remaining units! Each apartment sold meant financial rewards for QGT in the form of revenue from fees, country club dues, flip taxes, etc. But selling a unit meant that much less influence for Tina. Selling *all* would eliminate the woman's job, salary, and the many fringe benefits.

So, to summarize, here was someone who worked for the builder and was, at best, disinterested in selling apartments in a co-op that was run by a board (on which she permanently sat until all those units were sold) that had, supposedly, the best financial interests of its shareholders as a priority!

Quite the conflict, Melinda-Ann marveled. *Well, time to shove an IRS reality stick up that newly tightened ass of yours, my dear.*

Thomas's votes had single-handedly swayed many a Board election, and the members were to a man, and woman, grateful. She was *the lady behind the curtain*, so to speak, and was instrumental in the hiring of B.B. and Crowe and making them constant stars in the QGT firmament. They knew all-to-well that as she *giveth* she could as easily *taketh away* if not kept happy. She owned them, plain and simple. *Here at QueensGate*, MAQ mused, *board members are mostly selected, not elected.* The Queen was the rare exception.

Two other long-term board members were *Jack and Jill* Ginsburg—yeah, you can't make it up. Running in the same year, the juxtaposition of their names factored big in their winning that and all subsequent elections—so much for voting on the issues. They were also crooked but involved in more penny-ante type deals, just enough for the President to give them a taste and keep them happy. They were the ones Jesús had referred to who had received the new kitchen. Turns out, kitchen remakes were not restricted to just the Ginsburgs and were one of the President's oft-chosen rewards.

Situated on the Mall Level, The *Park Avenue Remodeling* company was the only *recommended* contractor at QueensGate Towers, having been awarded their no-bid deal twenty years earlier. Anyone who wanted any work done on their apartments had to get clearance of their chosen contractor. Unfortunately, QGT made that go-ahead an extremely time-consuming, complex maze of paperwork. However, if you chose *Park Avenue Remodeling*, it was smooth sailing. In addition, all work done to get a just purchased *builder-owned* apartment into shape was automatically tossed to *Park Avenue,* by default. No exceptions. And, if an extra refrigerator, oven, cabinets, flooring or big-screen TV was thrown into the order and somehow found its way to another unit, who was to know?

It took some investigative work by Jason, but it turned out *Park Avenue Remodeling* was owned by *Maspeth Plumbing, Tiling and Flooring,* which was itself owned by *Universal Contractors* of Boston whose CEO just happened to be—wait for it—B.B.'s first cousin! The relative made sure *Park Avenue Remodeling* charged full retail to QGT—plus 20%! Yet only the already high retail amount showed up on the company's balanced books. The other 20%? One needn't be Sherlock Holmes to deduce in whose pocket it wound up. How much B.B. kicked back in cash to his cousin, Plick, Crowe, Thomas, or some combination of all four was unknown.

The other two relatively new board members, Tony and Carla, were totally clueless, left out of the lucrative loop. Their hands were not yet dirtied, except for a simple new dishwasher each received as their "welcome aboard" gift from Plick. *Give them time*, Melinda-Ann mused. *They'd get to wet their beaks soon enough.* She chuckled at the organized crime reference.

Anyway, as much as *The Queen* would love to see the guilty behind bars, she had herself to think about. What she wanted, what she needed, was a piece of the action. To be in on the schemes, the kickbacks and the bribes—all of it. The time for being Miss Goody-Two-Shoes was long gone.

"I will not be fuckin' pity-stared at!" she screamed to her reflection on the enormous TV screen.

So, Monday, January 6 at 4 PM, after the close of the next board meeting's business, she would privately meet with Plick, *B.B.*, *Asshole-Abe Crowe*, Jack, Jill and *Teen-Tits Tina* and present the evidence and the demands for her silence. She'd give them 48 hours to think it over; and by the evening of the eighth, their most certain compliance would be the cherry on the cake to celebrate her return to excellent eyesight—cataract surgery scheduled first thing in the morning that very day with Dr. Joseph Peck. In fact, the woman just remembered a pre-op appointment this coming Monday morning. She needed to discuss a stye forming in the eyelid of the eye to be operated on.

It better not interfere with my surgery.

And by the ninth, *The Queen* would see Judge Judy as clear as day and bask in the knowledge her financial predicament would soon be a distant memory.

The co-op has a sixty-million-dollar budget, she considered. *No one's going to miss a few extra hundred thousand here and there each year.* Which is precisely why the perpetrators had not been caught all these years. It took a desperate, Wharton MBA on the inside, helped by her investigative reporter son on the outside, to figure it all out. The physical hugeness of the place, with its gigantic, hopelessly and purposely non-transparent financial records, easily lent itself to corruption. It seems a few wolves had been feasting at the table for decades.

"Well, make room for one more, motherfuckers!" she cried aloud.

Melinda-Ann walked to her living room and sat down on the couch, a glass of left-over champagne in her hand; time for Judge Judy.

One more week, she thought, *and all my problems will be over.*

The Queen of QueensGate would turn out to be correct about that. Unfortunately for Her Majesty, it would not exactly be in the way she had imagined.

Chapter 11

Boca Raton
10 PM

"I'm pissed at you guys!"

Tony was livid, as expected. The only thing we hadn't known was when the explosion would come. Now, it seemed, was a good time, with Felicity sent with Maverick and Morris to the latter's house. The girl would sleep on Morris's sleeper sofa in the living room, Maverick on the floor beside her. It was the first step in the process I had agreed to after the Franklin's and I had discussed their meeting with the psychiatrist earlier today. More on that later. As far as the other bed arrangements, Anna and Jane would sleep here, in Tony's and Linda's guest room. Marta had been picked up earlier by relatives who lived in Miami. She would stay with them until the wedding. Joe, *Papà* and I would return to Morris's place, to his guest rooms, including the one where Joe and I first made glorious love to each other. And speaking of making love, *I'm getting fucking impatient. Hmm, two ways to interpret that*, I mused.

But first, we had to deal with Tony.

"You should have called. I could have found a way of getting back in time to join you," he continued.

As mentioned before, the soon-to-be-married couple was on an early two-week honeymoon, a gift from the Franklins. They had some lengthy roof repairs scheduled over the following weeks, which could not be postponed. Good roofers were in such demand in South Florida, the couple felt they had no choice but to accept when informed of a cancellation moving them up the waiting list. So instead of the traditional order of things—wedding, then honeymoon—they bucked the thousand-year protocol. Anna and Jane were happy to accommodate the change in plans.

Tony and Linda had been on the last leg of their trip, visiting the island of Kauai, when the Philadelphia gambit had been planned during the December 27th get-together. Yes, it would have been no problem for the wealthy ladies to adjust the return trip. Scheduling was not the reason Anthony Esposito, known as The Choir Boy during his Mafia days, was kept out of the loop despite having taken part in Felicity's rescue mission. He would certainly have been an asset, and he knew it. So, his resentment was understandable. We left it for Joe to explain, at least to start.

"Look, Ace," my lover began, "We—"

"Don't give me that 'Look Ace' bullshit, Pecker."—that was his nickname for Joe—"You guys purposely kept me out of this, and I want to know why."

"Well," interrupted Linda, "if you'd let Joe finish a sentence, you big *jamoke*, maybe you'd find out!"

That rebuke seemed to cause a halt to Tony's tirade, so Joe quickly jumped in.

"First, we felt another person in the mix would not add much to our chances, and—"

"*Not add much?!* You seem to forget there were only two experienced shooters in that car with Jane already in the house, unarmed—Sammy and Frankie and, no offense against the latter, his expertise is cars, not guns. Giving Joe and Anna lessons for a few hours on the Uzi was something, but let's face it, if you needed them in a shootout, they'd wind up being as useful as a dildo made of sandpaper—no offense, Anna."

"None taken," Anna replied. He *was* right, after all—about Anna and Joe's usefulness—*and* the imagined sex-toy. I winced at the thought.

"What about me?" asked Joe.

"You can take that dildo and shove it—"

"Tony! Joe!" It was *Papà*. "I hate to see two such good friends go at it like this, and for no suitable reason. Joe, tell him and be done with it. I'm sure Angelica and you would like to *re-acquaint* yourselves with each other already, so just get to the point. The truth is, Choir Boy, we all agreed with Joe."

Linda gently grasped Tony's hand. "Let's just hear what Joe has to say, okay, *mi amore?*" The man took a deep breath, seemed to gain control of his emotions, and nodded. "Okay. Go ahead."

Joe followed Tony's breath with one of his own. "Sure, Ace. We knew having you there would be a plus if everything went to shit. But with you two deciding to get married, the wedding only a week away, the thought of something happening to you because of any assault, well..." Joe looked down, then up. "I'd never be able to look Linda in the eye again. Ever again." His voice dropped to just above a whisper. "I couldn't bear the thought of it."

"None of us could, Tony," added Anna. "It was a unanimous decision."

"Yes. I agreed as well," added Jane. "It was *my* life, after all, being put on the line, Tony. I knew you might make the difference if another shooter was needed. But I agreed with the rest. So, if you want someone to blame, blame me. My vote counted the most, and I voted to keep you out of it—for Linda's sake."

Dead silence. Linda's eyes had filled with tears, now dripping down her cheeks. Tony put his arm around her, and she buried her head in his chest. I decided it was my turn to speak. I began, quietly.

"Look, Tony... I wasn't involved in the decision, obviously. However, if the plan had succeeded and I was free to return, but it had been at the cost of losing you, I could never have lived with it.

Especially after my vow to Linda to bring you back alive last time. It would have devastated me.

"Yes, tactically, it was a foolish decision. These guys were incredibly lucky. But emotionally, it was the only one to be made so you and Joe," I grew louder here, "should bury the hatchet now and put the blow to your ego behind you because," I raised the volume even further, "Joe and I haven't been *together* for over six months, and we've got some serious, OLYMPIC- CLASS *FUCKING* to attend to!" I turned to my *padre*. "Sorry, *Papà*, I know how you detest that word."

My father smiled. "*Mia cara*, I'm just so happy to have you back, I can overlook your flowery vocabulary... this once." He chuckled. "Anyway, it's the sentiment behind the word that counts, and I couldn't agree with you more. So, Choir Boy, let's shake hands. We're all *amici* here... no?"

Tony was silent for a few moments, seemingly deep in thought, but then smiled. "Oh, sorry. I was just picturing Angelica naked in bed with Joe." Linda gave the man an elbow-poke in the ribs. "Hey, that hurt!" he screamed.

"Jesus, you men are all such pigs!" And then we all heartily laughed and Jane, Anna and I rose to give the woman a group hug.

"Thank you," she said in a hushed tone as we surrounded her with our arms and bodies. "Thank you." And then her tears flowed anew.

I was the first to detach from the mass and looked at Joe. He was hugging Tony and *Papà*. All was forgiven. Then, as Joe separated from the others, I motioned with my head toward the front door. He smiled and nodded in agreement.

Olympic gold awaits chez Morris, I thought.
Let the games begin.

Chapter 12

Thursday, January 2
8 AM

Joe and I lay back, exhausted, after our third love-making session in the last ten hours. The first was animalistic, ripping each other's clothes off, eschewing any foreplay and, within minutes, each basking in the afterglow of an explosive orgasm. It was so unlike our previous encounters, and that uniqueness made it even more enjoyable. Now and then, lovers should remind us all that when the veneer of sophistication and civilization are stripped away, along with our clothes, we're just animals; and as such, our animalistic pleasures, under the right circumstances, take precedence over any of society's efforts to dampen them. Unfortunately, our *undampening*—probably not an actual word—was very loud. I wondered what level the sarcastic remarks would rise to from our elderly housemates.

The second go-around, and this just completed third, were more of the genteel, refined lovemaking we had grown accustomed to. Each glorious, in its own way. The doctor's skill extended way beyond his scalpel. Magic hands are expected from a surgeon—a magic tongue is a bonus.

"So, old man," I said, pulling on my underwear and then staring, hands on hips at Joe, "bet you didn't think you had it in you for that third one, huh?" He was still in bed with a glowing yet engaging, dumb-teenager sort of grin on his face.

"Have to admit," he began, "I was concerned. But looking at you now, I suddenly have an urge to rip those panties off and try again for round four. If I go down in flames, so be it. You're the most beautiful, sexiest woman I have ever met, and that includes a certain billionaire brunette two houses down the block."

The words warmed my soul, and I was tempted to grant Joe's wish, but we had a 9 AM breakfast appointment at Linda's. "Now we both know that's bullshit, but I love you anyway for saying it. Face it, Anna and I are in separate leagues."

Joe beckoned me with a wagging index finger and once I got close enough, pulled me down until I again found myself next to him in bed. "Don't shortchange yourself, kiddo. You two are different, yes. But that's like saying Ruth and Gehrig, baseball gods both, were different." He drew me close for a kiss and reflexively my hand went south. "Jesus, how the hell can you have an erection already? Animal!" I laughed and shot up before *it* shot up any further and things got out of hand.

"Come on, get dressed. We're expected at nine and anyway, I've got to check on Maverick. Strange he hasn't been clawing at the door. I guess he and Felicity are really hitting it off."

Joe climbed naked out of bed and headed for the bathroom. "Yeah," he began, "what's up with that, anyway?"

I had already used the facilities and just needed to pull on my jeans and T-shirt, which I did. "Well, the three Franklins met with a psychiatrist yesterday. You know about that." Joe grunted, a toothbrush in his mouth. "It was just a first visit, and the shrink didn't go into any great detail as to where he'd be going in his sessions. One thing he did initially recommend, though, was giving Felicity some responsibilities, especially interpersonal ones. Make her feel more like an adult. Human interactions would be best. But, since Anna and Jane aren't considering—though Felicity has often dropped hints at—adopting another child she could play big-sister

97

to, the doctor felt a pet to love and care for would be useful. Then the ladies mentioned to him how their friend, that's *moi*, was returning from a six-month sabbatical—how's that for a word to describe my WITSEC days? And *she*, that's me, had a dog. Maybe she would allow the child to care for it.

"Amazingly, the doctor thought it was a good idea, better, in a way, than Felicity having a dog of her own, yet. Then Maverick's visits could be something to look forward to and something to miss when he wasn't around. She also could plan activities for the animal and interact with his owner, who would become an adult mentor. Jesus, me? As someone's mentor! Look, the girls didn't go into detail, and even though I was a psych major, I really don't understand it all. Frankly, I often think this therapy stuff is all bullshit. But I'm willing to try anything I can do to help them with Felicity, even if it means sharing my dog. Once we get back to New York, I'll start showing her how to get him to respond to her commands as well as he does to mine."

Joe was done and emerged, still naked. I was sorely tempted. *Down, girl.*

"Okay," he said, "sounds like it might help." A big smile came to his face. "And this way we have a built-in dog-sitter when we want to get away from it all." He quickly dressed, and we both took each side of the bedsheet and thin quilt, straightened them out, and pulled both up to drape over the pillows.

Already acting like a domesticated couple playing house, I thought.

I loved it.

Next to that oddball oil-on-canvas masterpiece, "Dogs Playing Poker," the tableau that greeted us upon entering the dining room placed a close second in the *peculiar* department; though in the *Bizarro World* that is South Florida, it didn't seem particularly out of whack. Following Maverick's bounding over and rising on his hind legs to lick my face, I witnessed what I guess you could call, "Two Old Men and a Child, Playing Gin." Felicity, Morris, and *Papà* sat at the room's circular table, fully dressed, a pad and pencil at the girl's right hand, and a fanned-out hand of ten playing cards in her left. I later learned they were playing something called Hollywood, a take on Gin Rummy and one of Morris's favorite pastimes along with shopping at Super Target. They'd been at it since 7 AM. Presently, my father was watching, and Joe's dad was the child's opponent. They played one-on-one, the winner taking turns with the other challenger, points being scored via some arcane system I was as interested in understanding as I was in learning to Polka. The child picked up a card, positioned it among her ten, removed one and, placing it face down in front of her, shouted, "I knock with three!" Morris grimaced and lay his cards face-up on the table.

"Okay, let's see..." Felicity said as she stood and excitedly counted aloud, examining the man's cards. "... twenty, twenty-four... thirty! That gets me over the top. Hundred and seven. Game! Now, let's see what you guys owe me," she added greedily.

As she tallied, the child mumbled words like "boxes," "games," "points," and "*schneid,*" whatever the hell that meant. "Okay, at five cents a box, plus a quarter a game, Mr. Peck... you owe me $8.25. But you can make it an even eight—I know you're on... what's it called? Oh yeah, a fixed income. Like me with my allowance."

Joe slightly turned to whisper in my ear. "I bet that kid's *weekly* allowance is more than Dad's *yearly* Social Security take."

"I heard that," countered Felicity, still computing. "And Uncle Sammy, your tab is... twelve dollars. Even."

The men shook their heads, mumbling to themselves, reached into their wallets and paid their debts, which the girl placed into her back pocket. Bowing, she said, "Gentlemen, it has been a privilege playing with you." And then she giggled. "I saw that in some movie."

Joe and I glanced at each other. "*Titanic,*" we said, simultaneously naming the famous disaster flick.

99

Felicity paused, considering. Then, looking at us, she smiled. "Yeah, you're right." Then, back to the men, "Seems sorta appropriate, don't you think?"

My *padre* turned to Morris. "Remind me, whose idea was it to teach this *saccente* to play Gin?"

"Who would have thought she'd pick it up so fast? I figured we had reeled in easy money. Instead," he turned to the precocious child, "we were hustled!" The two men laughed, and Morris tussled Felicity's hair. "Good game, kid. Rematch tonight?"

"You got it. How about we up it to a dime a box? After all, I'll be playing with *house* money." Then she looked at me. "Oh, Angelica, Maverick's already been fed and walked. I'm going over to my moms. See you all soon for eats—cheese omelets!" And with that, she made her way to the door. Just before exiting, though, she turned.

"Oh, B-T-W." Felicity put her hands on her hips and stared directly at me and Joe, a mischievous look on her face. "You realize, of course, your bedroom is only about thirty feet from my bed, right?"

Shit.

"Maverick got really upset at first—thought you were being murdered in there, Angelica. But I've heard enough of those noises from Mommy and Mama's bedroom, so I knew Joe wasn't a serial killer or anything. I gathered Maverick up and he slept in my bed. Tough to get a good sleep, though, with his tail wagging against me all night, soooo... how about this evening you guys try to keep it down a little." And with that, she grinned and left.

I stood, mouth open, embarrassment plastered over my face. Joe, however, was actually beaming—men!

"Was I really that loud?" I sheepishly asked no one in particular.

Papà nodded, not looking me in the eye.

"Even with my hearing aids out," added Morris.

Silence. Then, "How old is that card-shark again?" asked Joe.

I shook my head and frowned. "Eleven... going on twenty-one."

We all just stood, waiting for the awkwardness to dissipate. Finally, after what seemed forever, Morris, bless him, inadvertently ended the discomfiture.

"By the way," the almost nonagenarian began—"what's B-T-W?"

Chapter 13

After a delicious breakfast, the day's plans were discussed. Morris went home for a nap and Anna, Jane, and Felicity left for a meeting with a real estate broker; the ladies were looking for a vacation home in the Palm Beach or Boca area. The child was bursting at the seams with excitement—having a place in South Florida brought her over a thousand miles closer to Disney World, her favorite spot on Earth.

Once they'd left, Tony announced he had a surprise for me; it was a combination welcome home/birthday present.

"Oh no, Tony, not that. Really?" berated Linda.

"I'm telling you," he began, "she'll love it. Bet you. If I'm wrong, you can go to the mall and go crazy. But if I'm right, you stay home, charge-card safely in your purse and just lounge around the pool. How's that?"

Linda frowned. "Okay, go ahead. Let's see. Ask her."

I was intrigued. "Angelica," Tony began, "once you get home, to Sammy's place, what's the first thing you're going to do?"

For a moment, I thought this was some sort of trick question. I didn't know what he wanted me to say, so I decided on the truth. "I guess I'll check up on my Beretta and Needle. That's my dagger, by the way. I had so much free time on my hands in Henderson, I watched the entire eight seasons of *Game of Thrones*. Arya, the kid who was trained to be an assassin, named her dagger Needle, and I sort of liked that. So that's what I named my baby."

Tony smiled from ear to ear and turned to Linda with a *See, I told you so, look*. The exasperated woman shook her head. "Fine, you go ahead." She grabbed her purse and proceeded to the door. "I'm going to the mall, anyway. Gird yourself for some serious bills, *mi amore.*" And with that, she left. Tony's smile vanished.

"She welshed on her bet," I jokingly noted, stating the obvious.

"No shit, Sherlock," the man answered. But he soon recovered and returned to the matter at hand. "Okay, this is what I've arranged. I'm assuming, with Joe's dad, Linda and me living here and soon the Franklins down a good amount of time, you and Joe will visit often. I also assume you don't want to be a *schnorrer,* requesting Anna's free jet service all the time, right?"

"What's a *schnorrer?*"

Joe laughed. "It's a Yiddish word. It describes a person always looking for a handout. Not a poor beggar. A moocher who'd rather have others pay for what he wants. Tony's Yiddish is better than my Italian."

"No," I affirmed. "I'm not a *schnorrer.*"

"As I thought. Now, I'm sure, especially given your answer to my original question, being without your tools-of-the-trade, even having given up the assassin's life, is a difficult transition. You'd feel more comfortable with them on your person, am I right? And I'm sure you'd at least like to go to the range to keep up your skills."

I was ashamed to admit it, but without my Beretta either holstered at my side or in my handbag, my Sig on my ankle, along with Needle strapped to my calf, I felt naked. I knew, once in New York, getting a carry license would be almost impossible unless in a profession that could justify it. But for the present, I figured I'd just have to get used to it, as in Henderson. I nodded as my answer to Tony.

"Here in Florida, we're much more civilized than New York when it comes to the Second Amendment. We're not called 'The Gunshine State' for nothing. It's simple to get a concealed carry, even if you live out of state. The only thing required that, amazingly, New York doesn't, is a three-hour course on gun safety. So," he looked at his watch, "in one hour you have an appointment at a Bass Pro Shops where I signed you up for such a course. They'll also help with the necessary paperwork and fingerprint you—I trust that won't be a problem?"

"Not if the Feds did as good a job as Agent Simon said they did."

"Great. In six weeks or so, your license will be mailed to New York. The only thing remaining is getting a gun for Florida use since you won't be able to bring yours on a commercial flight from New York. Thus, my *schnorrer* question. Since I assumed you're partial to what you're already comfortable with, and you can't legally purchase a gun in Florida without being a legal resident, I've arranged for us to meet with an old colleague of mine. Mel Schwartz. We used to call him Magnum Mel back in the day."

Suddenly, *Papà* grew interested. "Mel is still alive?"

"Yeah, he's still with us," Tony hesitantly said.

"Well, then it's best I don't accompany you. Joe and I will stay back, take care of Maverick, and play cards with Morris. I'm afraid of what I'd do if Mel got within choking range."

Call me intrigued. Tony must have sensed my thoughts and continued. "Mel worked for my dad and then me. He was an expert in procuring and servicing all sorts of firearms for the Family. About seventy now, he retired ten years ago, moved to Florida and bought a Lexus dealership. Now he's expanded to two more brands scattered across the Boca area. He's done well."

"I hope he services his cars better than his ammo!" my father exclaimed. I sensed an explanation coming and Tony didn't disappoint.

"Back about fifteen years ago, Mel provided Sammy with a box of ammo for a job. Trouble was, he forgot to check the lot number. Seems a particular lot of those 9mms was recalled. Sammy had to go through three duds, re-racking the slide to eject the losers before finding a working round. All that extra time almost allowed the target the seconds needed to draw his weapon and fire. It was a very close call. Your father returned with fire in his eyes, and it was only due to my intervention he didn't garotte Mel right then and there."

"Ever since," *Papà* added, "I've had nothing to do with the man—and before you ask, Choir Boy, I do *not* want to bury the hatchet—except in his head. You can go without me."

And so, we did.

The firearms course went as expected—booooring. But I did, after a long hiatus, get to fire off six rounds from the Glock they supplied for the required hands-on training. It felt nice and the instructor, amazed at this *novice's* ability to hit the bull's-eye with minimal spread, jokingly asked me to marry him. At least, I assumed he was joking.

"Okay," Tony began as we drove away, "let me give you some background on Mel—and a warning. I called ahead to make sure he'd be in. Despite the one fuck-up with Sammy, he knows what he's doing, and, though officially out of the weapons business, he still has contacts. He'll get what you want. Mel also was a bit of a celebrity back in the day. Even though he's Jewish, he grew up in Little Italy and then in Bensonhurst. Speaks fluent Italian. At a young age, he acquired the mannerisms and speaking patterns of many wise guys. You know what a malapropism is, right?"

"Of course."

"Well, he was also called *Malaprop Mel*, though never to his face. One day he was sitting in a bar, visiting some friends at a place on Mulberry Street, in Little Italy, expounding on who-knows-what. His monologue was bursting with malapropisms. He was in rare form. Then this guy, sitting at a nearby table, goes up and introduces himself. 'My name is Marty,' the man says. He was a big-time Hollywood director, currently shooting a mob picture, and wanted Mel to consult on the dialogue. The movie was called *Goodfellas*."

I was speechless. Then, "You shitting me?"

"Nope. After that, Mel became *the* one called upon for what, at least by the Hollywood crowd, was considered authentic mob dialogue. His big pay-day came with *The Sopranos*, where he consulted during the entire run of the show. Earned him the cash to buy that first Lexus dealership.

"Anyway, the reason I tell you this is while we all got a good laugh at his murder of the English language, Mel definitely didn't see the humor in it. As far as he was concerned, it was everyone else who didn't speak correctly. He was known to get quite offended, and once even shot a man in the foot who had, at the sudden passing of Mel's first wife, unwisely corrected the widower when he said he was '*prostate* with grief.'"

I, somewhat inappropriately, I suppose, chuckled. *That was a good one.*

"So, even though he's mellowed with age, given your penchant for the wisecrack, please, don't correct, don't laugh, don't make him feel looked down upon. Okay?"

"*Moi*, a wisecracker?" I said in an indignant tone. Tony just stared. "I'm not going to need subtitles, am I?" He shook his head—and continued to stare. "Okay, then." I made a cross with my index finger over my heart. "Cross my heart. I promise to be on my *jest* behavior."

Tony continued to stare—and growled.

"Choir Boy! How the hell are you?"

We met Mel in his office at *MEL'S OF BOCA—LEXUS*. I was told there was a *MEL'S OF BOCA—INFINITY* and a *MEL'S OF BOCA—MERCEDES BENZ* in the man's empire as well. I wondered if the owner realized the subtle reminder of past associations hidden within his establishments' common initials.

Mel was about five-foot-nine, overweight, though not overly, with nary a hair on his head. He was sitting behind his desk but, as we entered, rose for his old boss.

106

"Fine, Mel, just fine. This is Angelica." Mel proffered me his hand, and I shook it. He stared for maybe a second more than appropriate, but given my good looks, I—no, no boasting. This is the new me!

We all sat. "It's been a while, Mel. You certainly have done well for yourself. Three dealerships! Congratulations."

"Thanks. But there's always a fly in the oatmeal." I glanced at Tony, who glared back, gently placing his index finger to his lips. "Take a look out there." The man pointed past the glass windows of his office to another man on the showroom floor. In his late thirties, it seemed, with shoulder-length, black hair, he was gesticulating at a middle-aged couple—obviously a salesman trying to convince them to purchase the very expensive car parked before them. They seemed *very* skeptical, and the Apple AirPods in the salesman's ears didn't exactly help give him a professional appearance either.

"*That* is my idiot son, Lenny. I've been trying to teach him the business for a few years now since he learned nothing at that expensive college I sent him to—except how to drink and *shtup*, if you'll excuse my language, Angelica."

I figured out what the remarkably descriptive Yiddish word meant. "Don't worry on my fucking account," I said.

Mel smiled. "I like her already, Tony. Anyway, he's unmarried and hasn't learned squat about the business. Hasn't made a sale in weeks. Clueless, he sees *himself* as surrounded by assholes—all except the one staring him in the mirror. Listens to jazz most of the day on his fucking *Air-o-pods*. Yet sooner or later I'm going to be checking out of this life—and *that* is what I'm going to leave everything to? Look at his hair. No one wants to buy an expensive car from a fuckin' hippie from the 60s. Take a look at his feet. Loafers—with tassels! Who the fuck wears tassels anymore?" He shook his head back and forth and sighed.

"I tell you, that kid is like an albino around my neck." I put my hand to my mouth, coughing to hide the chuckling. Finally, I just

107

couldn't help myself. I looked at the hirsute son, then the bald father and said, "So that's the *hair* apparent, huh?" I turned to Tony and if his eyes could shoot laser beams, I'd have been reduced to a smoldering pile of ashes by now.

"Exactly!" exclaimed Mel, seemingly unaware of my jest. He gazed at me for a moment and then, "You wouldn't be single now, would you Angelica? My son could use a good, beautiful woman behind him. I can tell just by looking at you you've got a head on your shoulders. You could be the power behind the thong." He smiled, so I wasn't sure if that last statement was one of his malaprops or a clever, purposeful play on words. I assumed the former, but let it slide. *I've tortured Tony enough.*

"Thanks, Mel, but I'm spoken for. I appreciate the offer, though, and after your *glowing* introduction he does seem quite the scat's meow."

Well, maybe not quite tortured enough.

Happily, Mel didn't catch my sarcasm/jazzy-malaprop combo, coming as it did after the disappointing news of my relationship status.

"Yeah, it doesn't surprise me. Think about it, though. Anyway, what can I do for you? Tony said on the phone you were interested in some guns."

"Yes, Mel. I'm looking for a Beretta 71—"

"Ah, The Mossad's favorite."

"Yes, but the European model, not one of those imports with the fake suppressors."

"Fake suppressors?" said Tony.

"In 1962," began Mel, "those fucking crooks in Congress enacted the Gun Control Act which, among a thousand other restrictions, decided the full length of any *imported* semi-automatic gun could not be less than sixteen inches. US manufacturers were exempted, so you know this was a payoff to them for probably millions in campaign contributions. Fucking thieves. Anyway, the Beretta only had a 3.5-inch barrel, so the company affixed a fake suppressor to lengthen it to the required specifications. You could remove the suppressor, but it was difficult since the screw attachment was welded on. You really had to know what you were doing."

I interrupted. "Anyway, I don't want a gun that was messed with. So, it's got to be unmodified. Next, two extra magazines." I waited, knowing what was coming.

"Hmm, they're hard to find. Harder maybe than the gun itself. But I can get them. What else?"

"I might want to silence it, so I'll need a ½ by 20 to ½ by 28 adapter and a Dead Air Mask 22LR Suppressor. Throw in a couple of boxes of CCI Stinger, 22LR copper-plated 32-grain hollow points and we're good to go. Oh, might as well add a Sig Sauer P238 Nitron with a few boxes of Remington 88 grain HTP to go with it."

Mel just stared for a few moments. Then, "Jesus Christ, Choir Boy. Where did you find this one? I'm getting a hard-on just listening to her. And at my age, that's saying something."

"Mellllll..." Tony scolded.

"Apologies, my dear. It's just so rare to meet a beautiful woman who also knows so much about fine weaponry. Please forgive me."

"No problem, Mel. How much for the lot?"

"It's okay, Angelica, it's my present," interjected Tony. "So, Mel, what's the damage?"

"Normally, with everything, I'd charge five large, but for you, Tony, let's call it a deal at three."

Tony nodded. Then Mel turned back to me, rubbed his chin and smiled. "You know," he began, "Angelica, though not a rare name, is still not *that* common. The only Angelica I've ever heard of who might be so well versed in the finer things in deadly weapons was... Shit! You're Angelica Fortuna, aren't you? You're supposed to be dead. Wait until I—"

I leaped from my seat and slapped my hands down on the man's desk, hard and loud. I stared at him, and smiled. Yeah, my stare-smile. He had recoiled at my noisy attack and beads of sweat now appeared on his glistening scalp.

"Look, Mel. You seem like a nice guy, and Tony vouches for you, which says a lot. But let me explain a few things. Yes, I am Angelica Fortuna—*l'angelo della morte!* However, Vito Fortuna was *not* my true father. My real *padre* faked my death and then arranged for Don Fortuna's *unfortunate* demise. He and I went to a lot of trouble to convince the world I'm dead. There are some who, still loyal to their deceased Don, might be inclined to remedy that situation if they learned I am, in fact, alive. So you can see why I'd like to keep that fact a secret. My true father, if the word got out, and I were put in peril, would be very, *very* upset. Get my *draft?*" I know, sometimes I just can't help myself. Mel nodded. "And I don't think you'd want him more upset at you than he already is."

I let that sink in for a few seconds. Sweat accumulated on the man's brow as he silently went through a list of those he'd pissed-off over the decades. Then, "His name is Sammy Vivino. You've met, I understand."

I saw Mel's Adam's Apple move as he swallowed. "Lover Boy!" he said. Though it was voiced just above a whisper, it was done so with force—and fear. I nodded, handed him a tissue from the box on his desk, and then sat. "Sorry if I came across as too aggressive, Mel. My apologies."

The man used the tissue to wipe his bald pate. Then he smiled.

"Choir Boy, I *really* like this one. She's got fire!" He put his thumb and forefinger together and moved them across his lips. "Mummy's the word, my dear. One thing you'll learn about me is I'm a paradox of virtue. So, no worries. In fact, forget your money Tony, this is on me—a gift for Lover Boy's *bellissima figlia*. I'll have it all in three days." Tony would pick it up and it would remain at his home for safekeeping.

"Thank you, Mel. I'll be sure to tell *Papà* of your kindness."

We all rose; I shook his hand, as did Tony. "You sure I can't interest you in my son, Angelica? I'll throw in any car on the lot."

I made like I was considering the offer. "Hmm, does that include a loaded LC 500 convertible I hear is coming out this summer?" It would probably go for at least $120,000 before tax.

Mel grinned. "For that, my dear, I would need a guarantee you'd keep trying for at least two grandsons."

I shook my head. "Sorry, Mel. No can do."

He nodded. "Yeah, I figured. Well, as they say, 'nothing dentured, nothing gained,' right?"

I smiled at the man and patted his cheek. "Mel, you've said a mouthpiece."

Chapter 14

Sunday, January 5
Somewhere over the Atlantic
3 PM

The remaining two and a half days spent in Florida were filled with joy, sex, relaxation—and sex.

After the meeting with Mel, Tony and I returned home to find Linda all smiles. There were about a half-dozen shopping bags strewn across the living room with names like Macys, Foot Locker and Kaye Jewelers plastered across them. "Could be worse," the soon-to-be spouse explained after a long sigh. "The mall's got the likes of Nordstrom, Stuart Weitzman, and Tiffany, after all." He did, however, grin when he saw the Victoria's Secret bag.

"Don't get too excited about that one," Linda said, pointing to the same. "They're mostly presents for Angelica." Oh, my time to smile. Tony faux- frowned. "But there *are* one or two items for me that should make *you* happy, *mi amore.*" She gave the man a quick peck on the cheek and went into the kitchen. When she was out of earshot, Tony looked at me, frowned for real and said, "Good bet *those* items won't be the receipts."

Tony was the chairman of the condo's grievance committee and had to leave for an emergency meeting. One resident had recently pulled his licensed, concealed Smith and Wesson .45 on a gym

112

member who hadn't wiped down the handlebars of the elliptical after completing his routine. The committee had to decide what to do with the gunman. The choices were, Tony quipped, "Fine him, ban him, or give him a fucking medal."

Florida.

That night I tried on my gifts for Joe, making a costume change between our sessions. "Linda always had excellent taste in underwear," he said, pulling the evening's second pair of panties off my body. I reached behind, grabbed his ass, and guided him into me.

"In men, too," I added.

Saturday was Tony and Linda's wedding. Just beautiful. The vows were taken in the couple's backyard as the sun set, lending a golden-magenta hue to the sky. Luckily, and unusually for South Florida, not one drop of rain fell to dampen our spirits. Even the cold-snap concluded and the temperature rose to seventy-two by sunset.

I know it's cliché to say the bride was radiant, but fuck it, she was. Felicity was a lovely flower girl, Jane and Anna such beautiful bridesmaids and, of course, Joe, the handsome best man. In a very touching gesture, Linda had asked Morris to give her away, and I could see tears in the old man's eyes as he kissed the bride, passing her off to the groom. Joe did the usual *shtick* (see, I'm learning a little Yiddish, too), making it seem like he forgot the wedding rings, and I performed perfectly, keeping the gown's train from getting in the way. Not as easy as it seems. Thankfully, the hired judge kept it short and sweet.

The newlyweds had invited three other neighborhood couples they were friendly with, and the post-wedding festivities proceeded flawlessly. The food was exquisite, thanks to Anna's caterer, and we danced and drank until midnight, after which Joe and I made glorious love again. Just once though—it had been a long day.

Sunday was spent mostly at the pool, then we said our tearful goodbyes. We entered the stretch limo Anna and Jane had rented and proceeded to the airport; our Gulfstream G280 awaited.

While on board, we all caught up on the news of the world we'd blissfully ignored during our Florida stay. Philadelphia police had concluded Don Vito Fortuna's death was natural, probably hastened by sexual activity the night before. Some of his rivals, especially in the Maltucci Family (due to the license plate on the Lexus) were questioned but nothing came of it. Who the *mystery woman* was, was anyone's guess. Leo and the rest were quite uncooperative with the investigation. All the Families wanted was for the case to be closed, *immediatamente*, and the attention to Philadelphia gone; so, it was closed.

There was also some mysterious virus that seemed to have cropped up in China, but little was known about it, yet. Some big-shot doctor named Fauci said there was no cause for concern here in the US, though.

Joe and I had decided to live together at his home for the time being. The plan was each morning to drive my new car—picking it up tonight!—to *Papà's* and spend time with him. Then I'd take care of any errands until just after 3 PM when I'd begin my training sessions with Felicity and Maverick. I figured a week would be sufficient for the basic commands. It was just a matter of teaching the dog obedience to another. Whether I would add *"Fass"* to the repertoire was another matter. I'd have to discuss that with the parents.

So we sailed northward. Yeah, I know *flew* is the correct verb. But in the super-quiet, luxuriously furnished cabin, lunching on gourmet food and drinking Pappy Van Winkle twenty-three-year-old bourbon—at least $5000 a bottle!—I imagined us all on a 20th-century luxury steamship, cruising the Atlantic. The only thing better than having wonderful friends is having *rich*, wonderful friends.

Joe and I held hands, as did Anna and Jane. Sammy napped in one of the living areas, and Felicity played with Maverick on the cabin floor. We all looked forward to resuming our lives.

Sure, there were concerns. For the Franklins, it was Felicity's therapy. For *Papà*, how to advance his relationship with Helen. And for me, well, the foremost was *simply* what I was going to do with the rest of my life. No biggie, right?

But none of us saw much in the way of storm-clouds on the near horizon. We relaxed, blissfully content, cruising through the crystal-clear sky toward home. Not a hint of turbulence.

But tempests indeed were forming on various fronts. Now they were nothing more than mild squalls. Mere blips on the radar.

But soon the skies would darken, and hurricane-force winds would come for us... and for the world.

Floral Park
9 PM

Papà and I entered his apartment as Joe waited downstairs in my new car. As I was told Frankie had done under similar circumstances, my eyes misted upon first seeing the vehicle in the Franklin's driveway. Driving it from Lake Success to Floral Park along mere pavement, I felt as thrilled as those expert pilots surely had, powering their sleek Gulfstream through the heavens.

Now it was time to greet my—as fave film assassin, Sweeney Todd, called his razors—*old friends*. Sweeney had reunited with his

115

pals after fifteen years of unjust imprisonment. I only had to wait six months, but the relatively brief separation was sorely felt.

Before leaving for Henderson, *Papà* had laid everything neatly on his bed. I'll be a good girl and not disclose to Linda that Tony had correctly predicted my first act upon arrival.

I know I'd forsworn the assassin's life, but seeing again the tools of my past trade brought tears to my eyes for the second time this night. As already alluded to, I had felt naked, *incomplete* these six months. So many years spent with *my friends* could not be simply discounted or go without lament. I could never feel whole again without them—if not carried, then at least nearby—to touch. To clean. To sharpen.

First, I took the suppressed Beretta in my hands and caressed her. I'm sorry, I can't think of another word to describe the actions toward my primary weapon. I racked the slide, feeding a .22 mm round into the chamber. *Papà* had obviously cleaned and oiled her—the slide pull and release were buttery-smooth. I flicked on the safety and placed it in my overnight bag that lay open on the bed, left behind when I entered WITSEC. Next came the Sig Sauer. Small and light, it was my backup gun and fit perfectly in the custom-made, combination knife-sheath/ankle-holster that tied to my leg. The leather accessory was a gift from *Il Pugnale*, The Blade. He was my master instructor in all bladed weapons and had christened me *la padrona della lama*—Mistress of the Blade—a testament to my skill. As for the Sig, I similarly tested her workings and found them as perfect as the Beretta's; in the bag she went to join her sister.

Finally came Needle, my newly christened dagger. Clearly, *Papà* had sharpened the edges and oiled both surfaces to prevent surface oxidation and corrosion. I lifted her and passed one side against my left palm, then repeated the action with the other side. Smooth as silk.

All my old friends had, at one time or another, helped save not only my life but those dear to me. Being separated from them had left me sick at heart.

Until I figured out a way to legally carry my firearms in New York, at least Needle could always be with me. I lifted the sheath/holster and tied it to my lower leg, the soft leather scabbard at the calf, hidden from straight-on view. The blade was then slipped into its home, with just the slightest hint of friction.

Then, in a moment of pure, unbridled joy at this grand reunion, with the skill of the expert assassin, I extracted, blink-of-the-eye-fast, Needle from her sheath. Triumphantly raising her into the air at full arm's length, the movie-buff in me silently, but dramatically quoted Mr. Todd as he too had exulted in reunion with *his* old friends—

At last! My arm is complete again!

Chapter 15

Monday, January 6
Mineola, NY
7:30 AM

Dr. Joseph Peck entered his office and found the office manager, Helen, already at her desk, a pile of mail to the side. Whenever Peck was in town, she'd place the daily delivery on his desk. But when away for a while, as he had been, Helen loved to collect each day's mail and messages, place them in an ever-towering pile and finally put the large, cumulative stack personally into his hands. A "welcome back" present, so to speak; a little friendly reminder to the doctor that *getting away from it all*—and leaving her to hold down the fort alone—had its consequences.

Today's stack was unusually bulky, and he grimaced as Helen plopped it upon his outstretched hands. "Have fun," she said before going back to her computer. It would take Peck about an hour to go through it all. Any messages needing personal follow-up phone calls would be done during lunch hour and those he felt she could handle would be gleefully returned to Helen to deal with in her own inimitable style.

As for the holiday, Helen didn't ask for details. All she knew was Peck and Sammy had traveled to Florida to attend Tony and Linda's wedding and to welcome back Angelica after a six-month absence.

She had left to, as Sammy put it, "find herself." He'd been very vague about his relationship with the young woman. Helen had met her just that once six months ago, when she appeared at the office with Sammy, *sans* appointment. Normally, getting to see the doctor under those circumstances would have been a high hurdle to clear under the office manager's careful watch. But the man had charmed the woman almost immediately; Angelica was admitted and, it appeared, charmed Helen's employer as well. Since then, as they spent more and more time together, Helen sensed Sammy's reticence in talking about his daughter—so she didn't push. There was already too much involved in moving their relationship further, especially given the very unkosher elephant in the room—the religious differences.

She really liked the guy. Loved? Maybe. Hard to say. She found, as the years went by, defining love became harder, not easier, as one might expect with the wisdom of aging. But Helen did have strong feelings for the enigmatic Sammy Vivino, despite his keeping much of his past life secret from her. One mystery was the meaning of his unacknowledged nick-name—Lover Boy—blurted out by the Franklins during their desperate visit in search of help six months earlier.

Better to not ask than be lied to, she often thought, though never quite believed. He had promised one day all would be explained, and she had agreed to let that suffice for now. Because, when brutally honest with herself, Helen was scared. Scared the truth would be too much to accept and, along with that elephant, constitute a deal breaker—and their relationship would be at an end.

Joe dropped the stack on his desk and perused the day's schedule, already printed and laying there for his review. The first day back Helen always kept the day light, and he figured it would be done by 3 PM, plenty of time to get to the mall and find a present for his lover's birthday celebration in two days. *Nothing like waiting for the last minute*, he lamented. Helen would be invited, too, and

Sammy had told his friend between now and then he was going to tell the woman everything—about him and Angelica, even how the good doctor and the assassin had met. Joe was looking forward to *that* almost as much as he was sure Sammy was to opening up about his past—NOT. It would be interesting to see if Helen wound up attending the party after the revelations; or showed up to work for an employer who had been involved in the murder of two men.

Joe regretted his involvement with Franklin's death. But he'd never apologize for aiding in murdering that pedophilic monster, Vito Fortuna. Especially since it meant the return of his lover as a bonus.

It's going to be interesting, he thought.

Joe read down the list. Among the follow-up patients whose names he recognized, none struck a chord of dread. *Thank God.* Nothing worse than coming back from vacation and being greeted with a known *Patient from Hell*. The doctor was also happy to see Melinda-Ann Queen scheduled as first of the day. She was always a lot of fun—full of life, quick-witted and never one to shy away from a dirty joke or two. He wished all his patients were as enjoyable to treat. Today was a pre-op visit, so it shouldn't be long.

By 8:55, Joe had finished with the mail, read the morning headlines on the computer, and logged into the electronic medical record (EMR) system the hospital had forced upon him. It was called EPIC and was the single most used network in the country. Half of all US hospitals used it and north of 250 million patients were in its database. All that personal health information under one massive company's roof. What could possibly go wrong? The founder and CEO had become a multi-billionaire from the ubiquitous software—all without ever having gone to medical school or touching a sick patient. *What a country*, Joe marveled.

Anyway, EPIC the EMR was, as far as he was concerned, EPIC the epic nightmare. It added at least two to three hours of work a day to enter visit-data and tick off every required checkbox the program maddeningly required, even when it made little sense.

120

And, if there was a power outage?... Chaos!

Helen entered. "MAQ's here, and in rare form. She's so excited I think she'd pay you a thousand cash if you could just lie her down and take the damn cataract out in the chair and be done with it."

Joe chuckled. "Don't I wish it were that easy. Here's some busy work for you," he added as he passed some notes on matters Helen could handle from the earlier pile. "Send *La Reine* in."

Helen gave her best Gomez Addams imitation as she placed a hand on each of her cheeks: "Oh, *José*, I love it when you speak French!" Then she left; within moments, the patient appeared at the doorway.

"Melinda-Ann!" He approached and gave the woman a quick peck on each cheek. "Ready to rock and roll?" He pointed her to the exam chair and sat again at his desk.

"I was born ready, Doc. These cataracts are getting to be a real pain in my ass. I don't trust myself to drive anymore, so I Uber everywhere. Can hardly even read a book, either on paper or Kindle. Forget about newspapers. Writing emails has become embarrassing since I miss half of those already hard to see auto-correct warnings, and then get sarcastic replies from my so-called friends pointing out my spelling and grammar mistakes. Bunch of jackals. Anyway, once this operation is done, at least one eye will see crystal clear, and I can get back to the full pleasure of reading, writing and TV watching. Right now, Judge Judy looks like Judge Dredd. Then next month we do the other eye, right?"

"Yes, correct, but..." The doctor just noticed the stye on the woman's left upper lid, the one above the eye to be operated on in just two days. *Shit*, he thought. "MAQ, how long have you had that stye?"

"I was afraid you'd ask. About three days. Don't fucking tell me it's going to be a problem, Doc."

"The thing is, Melinda,"—Peck was one of the very few the woman let get away with truncating her full name—"you can't have an active infection so close to the operating area. We *should* be able to deal with it... though I'll still have to make a final decision Wednesday, at day-op."

Melinda-Ann was crestfallen. "What can I do?"

Joe went to the computer and pulled up the electronic prescription section. He clicked about seven places with the mouse and opened three separate screens, a process that took about sixty seconds— about fifty more than scribbling the Rx on a prescription pad would have in the "old days." "I'm going to e-prescribe an antibiotic. Your pharmacy is the one at the Towers, right?" Joe knew the woman not only lived at QueensGate but had been a member of Sammy's *Harem*. This was only the second time in the last six months she'd been to the office and before, as now, he'd prayed Helen wouldn't mention to Melinda she was dating a man in her building. That might prove very awkward. So far, so good.

The patient answered in the affirmative and with a final click, the Rx sped through cyberspace to await the woman when she returned home.

The doctor instructed the patient on the pill-taking regimen, ending with, "... one last one Wednesday morning before you head out to the day-op center. By the way, you've got to be there by 7 AM."

"I know. I'll set the alarm clock next to my bed for five right after dinner tomorrow. Just have to flip the switch before retiring. Anything else to do about the fucking stye?"

"Yes, and even more important. This stye is like a pimple and needs to pop. So get yourself a couple of small potatoes. Have any at home?"

Melinda-Anne laughed. "No, afraid not. I haven't eaten French fries, home fries or potatoes of any kind in years. I'm on the Atkins, low-carb diet. Potatoes are poison for that. How do you think I keep this beautiful figure?"

Joe had to admit, MAQ was in great shape for her age. "So that's the secret, huh? I was thinking you had some portrait hidden under your bed that grew wrinkly and fat as the years went by."

MAQ laughed again. "No Dorian, er, *Doreen* Gray here. Just good eating, Botox and exercise, including a good fuck now and then. I can get potatoes downstairs, but what do I do with them?"

Joe was still digesting those last remarks and appreciated how well she had fit into Sammy's *Harem*. "Er... all right, what I want you to do is this: take a potato and bake it, as if you *were* going to eat it, Dr. Atkins forbid! About an hour in a regular oven, maybe ten minutes in the microwave."

"I don't like microwaves. Don't trust 'em. Radiation and all that. Anyway, what then?"

"Once it's done, wrap it in a wet washcloth and hold it against the stye for a half-hour—we need concentrated heat on that bad-boy. Do this every two hours today and tomorrow. Hopefully, the pimple will pop, and some puss will come out. Don't stop, though. Keep at it until Tuesday bedtime. With the antibiotic taking care of the acute infection, and the heat popping the stye, we should be good to go. But I'll still have to decide on Wednesday. So be a good girl and spend all your leisure time with a potato on your lid—not a man in your bed. Unless, of course, you can manage both simultaneously. You ambidextrous?"

MAQ got a good laugh out of that. "Well, I do have *some* fucking to do this afternoon, but that's of the metaphorical kind, not physical. Got a board meeting to go to. By the time I'm done with them, they won't be able to sit for a week with what I'll be shoving up their asses. Anyway, that's all inside-baseball. Forget I mentioned it. The meeting shouldn't last more than an hour or so; it shouldn't interfere with the regimen."

Knowing Melinda-Ann for over ten years, Peck felt sorry for the members of the board if she was indeed after their behinds. But she was right; it wasn't his concern or interest. He was sure the waiting room was already filling as the two of them bantered about.

"Okay, MAQ. Let's go over the boring stuff, do the consent forms, and you can be on your way."

"You got it, Doc. Where do I sign?"

The rest of the day was uneventful except, as it always seemed to occur, for the last patient, a seventeen-year-old girl who wanted a prescription for colored contact lenses. She had dark brown eyes and wanted baby-blue lenses. *Stupid kid*, he lamented. To begin with, light blue over dark brown never looked good. Second, it was unnecessary. The mother, however, was all for it, even after being told about the small but definite risks. She said her daughter needed a boost for her Instagram career. They already had scheduled breast implants—*she's only seventeen!*—and Mom, whose own hair had obviously been dyed bright blonde, was hoping a color change to her daughter's eyes would be the final step to turn the child into an 'Instagram Influencer,' *whatever the hell that means. I'll have to ask Angelica. Shit, nothing like reminding my girlfriend she's dating a dinosaur.*

The mother brought out her iPhone and showed Peck the daughter's latest Instagram video. The teen wore a skimpy bikini and "danced" with jerky movements of the hands and hips, lip-synching—it seems Milli Vanilli were thirty years ahead of their time—to some vile rap song, turning and twisting her body around to emphasize her admittedly cute ass as often as possible. Then, mid-song, the mother—*the kind of woman who looks good, from a distance*, Peck inwardly quipped—entered, wearing similar swimwear. She tried, unsuccessfully, to mimic her daughter's moves, which, though banal, were at least performed gracefully. It was essentially very soft-core porn, set to songs which the performers couldn't even sing for themselves. *Pathetic.* The mother clicked the circular icon with the girl's picture and the following screen showed she had 775K followers! "We should hit a million by next month, according to our agent," the mother added. *We? Agent? For this shit?*

Well, a million followers or not, the doctor informed the girl that with her perfect acuity *without* glasses, it would be against best

124

medical practice to prescribe a foreign body to be placed unnecessarily on her corneas. Teenagers' general carelessness and poor hygiene were recipes for disaster—serious, eye-threatening infections which he'd seen more times than he cared to remember. He knew of two or three teens who, ignoring his advice, lost an eye as a result.

She didn't need glasses, so she certainly didn't need contacts. Period. End of story.

He tried to use humor: "You know what you get when you cross a brown eye with a blue contact lens, right?" No answer. "A *pink* eye." Crickets.

Well, I thought it was funny, the doctor dejectedly believed.

The budding influencer and her mom were not amused, and the latter vowed to seek out a more, Joe would say, *ethically challenged* physician. "Fucking eye doctors are a dime a dozen, *Dr. Seinfeld.*"

So are shitty mothers with no sense of humor, Peck silently added. *Anyway, best news I've had all day. Don't let the door hit your Instagrammed asses on the way out.*

And on that way out, the mother added, "My kid's going to be able to buy and sell you in a few years, you quack. And by then, so will I. Go fuck yourself!"

Nice role model.

"Yeah," the daughter repeated, "I'm going to be famous. Go fuck yourself!"

A chip off the old, dyed block.

On the one hand, Peck continued to muse, *there are great parents like Anna and Jane. Then you have this Mama Rose looking to glom off her soon-to-be artificially enhanced blue-eyed/big-titted daughter. 'Instagram Influencer.' Whatever happened to wanting your kid to be a doctor, lawyer, or a teacher?*

The learned physician inwardly sighed. *We're doomed.*

Helen had walked toward the office door on first hearing the ruckus and, as mother and daughter stomped by, adopted the *Apu* (from *The Simpsons*) voice she enjoyed using at such times and exclaimed, "Thank you. Come again!" Then she turned to Peck.

"Congratulations. Back less than a day and already on another shit-list. I think that's a record. I'll contact Guinness." Then she smiled, raised her palm, which the doctor high-fived.

"By the way," she added, "just got off the phone with Sammy. I'm invited to the Franklin's for Angelica's party! And it's so sweet of the ladies, too—they're using *Cho-Sen Village* to cater it!" Cho-Sen was a strictly kosher restaurant/caterer in Great Neck. "They're even using paper plates and plastic silverware, so I won't be uncomfortable eating off their dishes." She paused, seemingly in thought. Then, softly, "I'm sorta looking at this all as maybe they see me becoming more and more a feature in Sammy's future. What do you think? Am I right?"

It's amazing the many ways the human voice, through its inflections, can make three words take on so many meanings. That last trio of Helen's were said with a combination of optimism, joy—and dread. All were mixed together yet, to Joe, were easily dissected into their component parts. Before he could answer, Helen added, "Also, Sammy wants to come over to my place a few hours before the party. Says he has a lot to talk about. That I shouldn't be left in the dark any longer." She paused, and for the first time in Peck's over thirty years with his office manager, he saw fear on her face.

Seeing such a look had been unimaginable to him. But Helen's behavior this past half-year had been very unexpected—she had become a different person after meeting Sammy. She was still the same *"Don't take yourself so seriously, Doctor Peck,"* wisecracking, take-no-shit from anybody—especially rude patients—office manager he'd come to know and love. But now showing a soft side which, he'd always suspected, lurked just below the gruff surface. Yet this was the first time she had ever shown true vulnerability.

"I know you know what Sammy's going to say, or most of it, so don't deny it," she continued. "Should I be worried?" Her voice pleaded for a "no," in response, but Joe had to be truthful. She deserved no less.

"The thing is, Helen, I honestly can't say. There's a lot you don't know. All I can advise is... is to trust your heart."

Helen laughed. "What are you, Joe, a fuckin' Hallmark card all of a sudden?"

Actually, I read it in a fortune cookie, thought Peck, smiling. And then his office-manager grew somber. "But you're correct, *doctor*, of course. I've gone through a dozen scenarios and responses in my head, but when the moment comes... who the hell knows? Life is so damn complicated."

Truer words were never spoken.

Chapter 16

Roosevelt Field Mall
Garden City, NY
4 PM

Joe bent at the waist, staring at the fifth display case in the last thirty minutes. He felt like a *landlubber* shipwrecked in the ocean. Drowning. For he had come to a momentous, frightening and, especially for one so proud of his high IQ, highly illogical decision while driving from his office to the gargantuan indoor mall.

He was going to ask Angelica to marry him!

Quite a leap from only an hour before, when his major concern was just what to get for the woman's birthday.

You're batshit crazy, you know that, Pecker? he imagined Tony admonishing.

Well, haven't I known the girl for over six months? his inner voice answered.

Yeah, right, came the expected, sarcastic counter.

When he examined it logically, Joe understood he only had known the beautiful ex-assassin—*Jesus, how many soon-to-be fiancés had ever said those words in a sentence?*—for just a little over two weeks. And those two were separated by three-thousand miles and six months.

Well, since when did love and logic go together?

This wasn't his first rodeo, after all, and he hadn't felt like this for any woman since he had first met Linda almost forty years ago. Logic dictated they should get to know each other a lot better before tying the knot. Joe agreed, and he was going to recommend at least a six-month engagement; that is, of course, if she said "yes." *Shit, do I really think she'll say "yes?"*

Yes. Sometimes you just know, he tentatively answered himself. It was time to make a commitment. *After all, I'm not getting any younger, that's for damn sure,* he painfully understood. And, as if to underline the point, his back started to ache from all the bending done over the last half-hour.

Joe was sure Angelica Foster was the one for him, just as sure as he knew "diddly squat" about diamonds. So here he was at *Zales— The Diamond Store,* in the mall, adrift in an ocean of jewelry. The salesman had tried to help, but it was no use. Joe wanted to make sure whatever diamond he chose was worth what he was willing to pay, which was a lot. So, he gave up and took out his phone to, as they say on *Who Wants to be a Millionaire?* "phone a friend."

———————————

"Hey, Joe, what's up?" Anna had just finished helping Felicity with her French homework and was relaxing in the living room, reading *Twelfth Night,* yet again.

"Hi, Anna. Look, I've got a big request. And it must be a secret between us. Well, between us and Jane, I guess, since I'm sure you'll blab it to her the second we're off the phone."

"Well, if I weren't before, I'm certainly going to now. Give!"

Joe took a deep breath. "I'm going to ask Angelica to marry me."

Silence. Anna wasn't totally surprised. Nothing surprised the woman anymore. After all, Anna and Jane began their relationship as adversaries, then became lovers in less time than Joe and Angelica had known each other, so no, this wasn't a total surprise. In love, anything was possible, at any speed.

129

Anna smiled as she recalled, from *As You Like It,* how she and Jane felt about their own breakneck romance—

Who ever loved that not loved at first sight?

"Oh Joe, that's marvelous! And are you kidding me? Of course I'm calling Jane, *and* Linda, as soon as we get off the phone."

Joe chuckled. "Okay, but what I called for is this. I know nothing about diamonds and I'm here at Zales and feel totally inadequate about what to choose and how to make sure I don't get screwed."

"Well, Zales is a very reputable store, so you don't have to worry about that, but, as you recall, Jane and I have lots of loose stones sitting in the vault at the bank, and, as I think about it, some even still here in our safe, so..."

"Before you go any further, Anna, while we *are* on the same wavelength, I absolutely insist I pay you a fair price for a stone. It just wouldn't feel right otherwise. I called you because I'm clueless. I must have missed the lesson on engagement rings in med-school. Need help with a setting too. It's fucking embarrassing how totally ignorant I am of all this."

Anna was enjoying herself. "Well, my oblivious friend, you've come to the right place. Happy to help you out. I'll pick one of our stones—they're all basically the same, two carets, perfect, gorgeous—and meet you in half an hour at Jack The Jeweler, in Great Neck. I'll text you the address. Pretty sure I know some of Angelica's tastes, so I'll pick the setting. Jack will mount it and *voilà,* you'll have it by tomorrow. If for whatever reason Angelica's not happy with the setting, or we have the wrong size, he'll replace it, no questions asked. I've basically paid for his kids' education, five-times over these last few years.

"But take it from me, Angelica will be ecstatic. I'll also ask Jack to give us an honest, wholesale appraisal of the diamond, okay? You can pay me back over as long as you wish."

Anna could hear Joe's sigh of relief. "Thanks, Anna, you're the best." Then a slight pause. "You think Angelica will say *yes?*"

Anna was stunned. For as long as she'd known Joe, and true, it wasn't *that* long, she had never heard doubt in his voice about anything. He was always so sure of himself. But she had just heard a tremble as his words spilled out. She found it touching, poignant, and, she was almost 100% sure, unnecessary. "Come on, Joe. You've got to be an optimist."

The doctor laughed. "Tried that once. Didn't take."

Anna chuckled. "Well, if she doesn't agree, she'll need to go back into WITSEC—to escape Linda's, Jane's, and *my* wrath!"

Joe laughed. "From your mouth to God's ear. Text me the address and I'll see you in thirty."

The call ended, Anna texted the jeweler's address to Joe, and within a millisecond, dialed Jane. As she waited for her wife to answer, Anna reflected on how far Joe had come since she first seduced him into helping to plan her bastard—admittedly, super-rich bastard—husband's death. Not only had he grown a conscience about the deed, as had she, but had forsworn his wayward, satyr-like ways with the opposite sex and had undertaken a journey to find the right woman to settle down with. She looked at the text on her lap and smiled at the coincidence. Quickly flipping through the pages, she found it.

Shakespeare always knows best, she thought as she read the line from Act II, Scene III—

Journeys end in lovers' meeting.

Floral Park
4 PM

Melinda-Ann Queen quietly signaled the rest of the board-room's occupants to remain behind, allowing Tony and Carla to leave; the official meeting was over.

131

"*Celine, mon amie*," MAQ began, "we're going to go into executive session now, so you can go." Notes were never taken in executive session.

"You're new here, Melinda-Ann," said Crowe, the lawyer. You can't go into session once the official meeting is over; and certainly not without the entire board."

MAQ frowned. *Probably telling the truth*, she thought. *But he's a lawyer, so who the fuck knows?*

"Oh, okay. So, this will be an *informal* meeting; but I don't think you'll want notes taken, Abe. Believe me."

Mrs. Crowe looked at Mr. Crowe, who nodded. "Put the pen down, Celine; just sit and be quiet."

The wife complied.

Board President *Peter Prick*, co-op attorney *Asshole-Abe Crowe*, Building Manager Bill, *B.B.* Brown, Jack and Jill Ginsburg (not yet worthy of nicknames), Tina, *Dragon Lady* Thomas and *The Queen of QueensGate* took their seats around the ornate, rectangular mahogany table. MAQ noticed the large, gold cross that dangled between Thomas's recently enhanced breasts as she bent forward to sit. *Fucking hypocrite*, she disdainfully thought. *I wonder what Jesus would say about all that money you've been skimming?*

"Okay, Melinda-Ann," said Plick, glancing at his watch. "I know Jack has to get going soon for synagogue to say *Kaddish* for his father"—the yearly Jewish prayer for the dead. "So, tell us what *you* have to say."

And did she ever.

---

5 PM

By the time Melinda-Ann had finished her presentation, not only could one have heard the proverbial pin drop, but worrying about some prayer for his dead father suddenly took a back seat to Jack Ginsburg's concern for the living.

First, MAQ had repeated the earlier points concerning Plick's *gifts* to new board members and his girlfriend's rent payment avoidance. There was also the 2005 renegotiated co-op indemnity policy. Plick, an insurance agent by trade, took it upon himself to bargain, awarding the policy to a new company—at a personal finder's fee of $20,000; a fee which rightly belonged to the co-op. No one on the board at the time felt it was worth questioning. Finally, Melinda-Ann noted all contracts approved by Plick tended to be at full, bust-out retail. The man was many things, but stupid was not one of them. There had to be kick-backs. How the money was divided was for an IRS auditor to discover.

The Queen went on about Tina Thomas's barter agreements with the plastic surgeon and at least seven others over the decades. These included the owner of a Porsche dealership—three guesses as to what kind of car Thomas drove—and the manager of a chic, ungodly expensive catering hall in Muttontown where, coincidentally, Thomas's daughter was married soon after. All those buyers received excellent, below-market-value deals on their spacious apartments.

With *B.B.*, it was hard for Melinda-Ann to know where to begin. First, she had found a note in the minutes where it was decided, over a decade ago, to give the B.M. the ability to write a check to any person or business, even to the ubiquitous Mr. *Cash,* in any amount less than $7,500—without board approval! These checks were, of course, cashed, returned, and wound up sitting in many a dusty shoebox among the late Jack Wellman's official possessions. Wellman, and now MAQ, were given a small office in the bowels of QGT, a place that would make the famed Collyer Brothers' home seem tidy by comparison. The board never thought in a million years the fastidiously neat new chairwoman of the finance committee would dig out, let alone examine, the old records (laden

133

in dust an inch thick), and moldy, canceled checks. They thought wrong.

Queen had discovered a good many of those checks were cashed by members of the board, some now retired or deceased. In fact, *all* members in the room had received more than a few each year of their board *service*, none showing up in any balance sheet. All were simply ascribed to *miscellaneous spending* by the far-from-fastidiously neat Jack Wellman. Juggling Jack's name appeared on many of those checks as well. "How many of these checks were declared as income on your tax returns?" she asked. No answers were forthcoming.

This was exactly where the woman's arguments and threats were going. Bribery, graft, or outright theft among consenting crooks would be hard to prove. But tax evasion, that's where the action was. Al Capone killed hundreds in his day, either directly or by his orders. But it was tax evasion that finally got him shipped off to Alcatraz.

Everything MAQ had discovered could be cogently presented, say in a week-long series in The New York Post. Her son, Jason, toiled there, mostly consigned to writing pithy headlines for which the tabloid was famous. The man yearned for recognition from his peers. Well, if he were ever to write up all the information his mother had learned, recognition would come—possibly from the Pulitzer Committee for himself, and definitely from the IRS for the board-room occupants. It would be sweet for Jason—and very bitter for the others.

But Melinda-Ann wasn't done with *B.B.* yet.

Another profitable, little-known rule at QGT was the "alteration fee" of $500, paid by any shareholder who dared use an outside contractor for work on their apartment. No reason was ever given for this payment. It was just the way it was. *But*, instead of writing a draft to QueensGate Towers, this fee was to be included in the check written to the *contractor*, who then reimbursed Bill Brown, supposedly to be deposited into the co-op's account. MAQ could

134

find no evidence of such deposits ever being made over the twenty years she'd examined.

The over-priced, no-bid landscaper Brown had chosen for the entire grounds was Plick's cousin, who, of course, landscaped Plick's, B.B.'s, and the Ginsburg's summer homes in the Hamptons—probably gratis.

Gold Shield Security, picked by the B.M. to oversee security at the Towers, was run by an ex-cop, John Crane, who, when *B.B.* was a sergeant in the NYPD, was a rookie cop under his command. Also, a no-bid award.

An ex-security employee, who used to be *friendly* with MAQ, once related how one day, witnessing Crane approach Brown's office, the man slipped and dropped a non-sealed envelope. Scores of twenty-dollar bills fell out onto the floor, the money almost certainly coming from the $20 parking fee overnight visitors had to pay, in cash, to Security for a temporary parking sticker. Melinda-Ann could find no evidence of this cash in the financial records of the corporation. None.

B.B. was known to be colorblind. *I'm sure green is the one color he has no trouble appreciating,* MAQ thought.

Next, *The Queen* turned to Abe Crowe, Esquire. Abe was the brains behind all the arcane rules and regulations under which the cooperation governed, like the "alteration fee." His word was, literally, law at the Towers. So, for example, when QueensGate decided to allow dogs in the building, it was he who decided each dog had to pass *inspection,* at a *cash* fee of $250 to the man himself! He had to make sure the dog was a "QueensGate type of dog," whatever the hell that meant.

Additionally, Crowe often "encouraged," as shown in the written minutes, the board to reject an apartment sale to a younger person or couple. The older you were, after all, the closer your demise, which meant the sooner the apartment would be resold. With each resale came a Flip-Tax and renovations, the latter with

135

either *Park Avenue Remodeling* getting the work or the $500 "remodeling fee" charged. A win-win.

So, round and round, the senior-citizen carousel spun, its floorboards creaking in sync with the arthritic joints of its riders. And the average age of a QGT resident inched inexorably upward. Want a guaranteed approval by the board? Just show up for the interview in a wheelchair with two aides and a defibrillator.

Melinda-Ann continued, listing the many small and not so small ways Crowe bent rules and ethics for personal profit. But the real bombshell was saved for last.

QueensGate Towers, among the tallest structures on Long Island, also stood on one of its highest patches of real estate. Ergo, the roofs were the third, fourth and fifth uppermost outside of Manhattan, and the only ones within a hundred miles with direct line of sight to areas as far south as Atlantic City, after which the Earth's curvature finally intervened. It was a perfect spot to place high energy antennas and repeater towers. This allowed every small local newspaper, radio, and television station, along with their ubiquitous mobile news vans, to send signals directly to QGT with their own small transmitters. These signals were then bounced by the large, powerful microwave roof antennas to millions of homes and scores of similarly highly placed aerials many miles away, to be bounced again, etc. The roofs were also prime locations for the mobile-phone operators to place cell towers.

Name a large place of business—COSCO, BJs, Home Depot, Macys, FedEx, UPS, every Long Island shopping mall—and you'd find a communication antenna with their name on it atop a QGT roof. Hundreds upon hundreds of companies, many sharing antennas for savings. Then there were the government agencies who required multiple advanced communications and listening posts: NYPD, NYFD, FBI, CIA, DEA, NTSB, FEMA, NSA, and dozens of other abbreviated entities most people never heard of.

So, the three roofs were a potential gold mine for QueensGate. Yet, in November 2001, Apex Satellite Communications, the organization to which the corporation had sold the roof leasing rights twenty years earlier, renegotiated a new contract with Abe Crowe. This should have been a bonanza for QGT due to the unfortunate tragedy of 9/11 and the fall of scores of competing antennas atop the Twin Towers. Yet, *Asshole-Abe* gave Apex a sweetheart deal. The new *fifty-year* contract imposed a rental fee of a mere $200,000 a month, with a 5% increase each year for the first ten years. And no industry-standard, profit-sharing agreement!

Luckily for Melinda-Ann, Apex was a publicly traded company. According to their most recent year-end report, the income brought in by leasing out the three towers was an astonishing $30 million! One-hundred-and-five antennas in total sat like sci-fi, giant porcupine quills atop the Towers. And it only cost Apex $2.4 million—officially.

When MAQ first saw this discrepancy, she was astonished—and committed to finding why such a deal was entered into by someone who, despite being an asshole, was a financially very shrewd and savvy asshole. She assumed, given everything else she'd discovered, there had to be kickbacks, payments to those on the board at the time of the contract signing, plus *B.B.*, Crowe and Thomas.

The Queen had done accounting work for American airlines in the past and still had contacts, one of whom was willing to look back at reservation data. He found decades worth of first-class travel booked for Bill Brown and his wife, Tina Thomas and whoever was her *plus-one* at the time, and the Crowes. Each year since 2002, the above-mentioned flew via American to Europe, Asia, South America, almost everywhere on Earth with luxury hotel availability. MAQ was sure if she had contacts at other airlines, she'd discover Plick and Emi had traveled similarly. And the *one* location all of them had *first* traveled to was, of all places, Singapore. It turns out that the sovereign island city-state in Southeast Asia was one of the most popular destinations on Earth for hiding money from Uncle Sam.

The process was simple. First, you opened an account with one of the many island banks, each committed to a depositor's anonymity as zealously as any Swiss institution. This had to be done in person, thus those initial flights. Second, one obtained an American Express Black Card. Now, all simple or exorbitant personal purchases could be made with the card, linked and drawn from the Singapore bank. Seems that, in an IRS audit, if you didn't take credit card purchases as itemized deductions on your tax return, these receipts are never examined. Bank accounts—that is, American bank accounts—yes. Credit cards, no. Perfect.

Just how much Apex had agreed to send the lawyer and his co-op associates via Singapore MAQ didn't know, though she assumed it had to be at least a half-million a year per person. How else to afford the lavish travel, cars, watches, jewelry and vacation-homes each enjoyed? For Apex, it was an excellent investment.

Melinda-Ann was unsure of the power of the IRS to investigate offshore accounts, but the threat of the agency's involvement was enough to make even the most steadfast crook piss in his or her pants. Thus, the pin-drop lack of noise and many an open mouth Melinda-Ann faced at the end of her discourse.

"Now, you must wonder what I want in exchange for keeping this information in a Word file on my desktop and not light-speeding it to my son at the New York Post. Well, I'm a simple woman who is not looking, at this stage of my life, for wealth beyond my means to spend it. My finances, due to that prick Madoff, have been hit hard, as you know from the newspapers. I'm not too proud to admit I can use some external sources of income. The thought of having to sell my apartment for a smaller one is... is inconceivable. The false stares of pity...

"So, I need money. But unlike you fools, I don't intend on hiding it from the IRS. So what I want from you is this—$50,000 a month. All above-board and transparent. That's all. I don't care how you do it, whether it be checks from Bill, cash disbursements from all your under-the-table money, or transfers from your Singapore accounts. I don't give a fuck. You can justify it by calling me a 'consultant' or whatever bullshit title. Just get it done, month in, month out. You do that and the file remains on my computer, never to appear on the pages or website of The Post. Simple as that. Else... I can see the headline now." MAQ stood and outstretched her right arm. Then, mimicking reading with her index finger, she pronounced, *"SatelliteGate at QueensGate! Corruption reaches TOWERing Heights."*

Melinda-Ann snickered. "You have forty-eight hours. Send someone to my apartment no later than Wednesday night with your decision." And with that, the woman turned, opened the door, and left. There would be no Q&A session granted by *Her Majesty.*

For a few moments, silence. Then, Abe Crowe barked, "Celine... close the fuckin' door!" The secretary rose, shut the door—and all hell broke loose.

For thirty minutes, they screamed at each other. The two most vociferous, at least at the start, were Jack and Jill, of all people. They were royally pissed off that their cut over the years had been so small! Showing, up to now, unseen dynamism, they wanted more, especially a piece of the Apex agreement and would not cooperate with the others until that issue was resolved. Once it was agreed the two Ginsburgs would get an equal share of the antenna deal, the shouting and recriminations continued, echoing so loudly in the compact, paneled room that after a while *B.B.* removed his still licensed, .32 caliber Police Special revolver from its holster and placed it loudly upon the table. "Enough! All of you shut your fuckin' mouths!" he screamed. He then realized he had essentially included his patron, Tina Thomas, as an object of the outburst. He'd make sure to obsequiously apologize to *The Dragon Lady* later.

Plick took advantage of the sudden quiet and, as President of the Board, made his standard, executive decision: he punted. He wanted time to think—and plan. "We obviously can't come to a consensus tonight. Too many hot heads. It's too soon to rationally discuss all this. So, we will adjourn and meet again... day after tomorrow, Wednesday, 9 AM to come to a conclusion on which we ALL must agree. Plenty of time to think it through—rationally. Okay?"

Each in the room nodded and began to leave. "Remember," Crowe added, "nothing that has been discussed here leaves this room. The consequences would be disastrous. To us, and especially to whoever opens his—or her—big, fuckin' mouth!"

"Amen to that," added Plick. "You've all been warned!"

No further discussion was necessary.

As they all solemnly exited, it was clear there were two factions forming. One, the *appeasers*, wanted to give MAQ what she desired. After all, they believed, what was a little more than half-a-million dollars per year in the grand scheme of things? Just give it to her and be done with it. The other faction, the *hard-liners*, disagreed. They thought it was all a big bluff and, even not, if they stood together, got top-notch representation, they could prevail. After all, what was to stop Melinda-Ann from coming back at them next year, or the year after for more. Each, in their own greed, understood *that* was exactly what *they* would do given the same situation.

But there was one, a fiend, who, while outwardly agreeing with the *appeasers*, inwardly seethed with rage.

Who does that Jezebel think she is? Nobody, especially the Queen of Whores, fucks with me! She can suck my dick—the shrew's had plenty of practice, I'm sure. She's no better than that bitch Harriet Gold or those goody-two-shoes Ted Finberg and Jerry Chen. Well, I dealt with them, then—and I will deal with this cunt. Now.

And to this fiend, "dealing with" meant one and only one thing—

The Queen must die.

Chapter 17

Lake Success
6 PM

My first training session with Felicity and Maverick went extremely well, and I guessed within one or two more sittings my pet would respond to the child as obediently to me. I had to decide whether to teach Felicity the attack gesture and command. For this, I would need parental approval.

Anna had just pulled up into the driveway and we greeted her as we entered from the back sliding doors. I took a quick call from Joe, who said he'd been delayed at work and would meet me at home. I saw Anna whisper into Jane's ear, leading to both giggling and then they, after being informed of my discussion with Joe, suggested I stay for dinner. Since I wanted to discuss Felicity's training, I agreed.

We quickly ate, after which Felicity went upstairs to visit *Grandpa*, Jane's father, who lived in one of the bedrooms, 24/7 nurses at his bedside. His Alzheimer's Disease had recently deteriorated, despite experimental treatments which, until now, had proven effective. The child took the dog with her since Maverick's presence seemed to brighten the old man's spirits.

We three adults sat in the living room and sipped an after-dinner brandy. I then broached the subject of extending Maverick's usefulness in Felicity's therapy to that of a personal defense weapon. My opinion was it was a good idea, but we all knew where I was coming from, me being an ex-professional assassin and all. With Felicity and Marta's kidnapping still fresh in everyone's memory, I argued having the dog around could only be a plus, especially if she and Marta were home alone. The three of us had already decided, again as an aid in the child's therapy, to allow Maverick to have extended stays at the Franklin household over weekends and school holidays. So my dog would often be the child's and nanny's sole companion with Jane at work and Anna out and about with her many charities, foundations and daily two-hour stints teaching Pilates in town. The latter was an activity she enjoyed greatly, and it kept her in tip-top shape.

The women looked at each other, and then Jane spoke for them both. I found it uncanny how a quick look between the two was all they needed to understand and then agree on a course of action. I hoped such a deep understanding of a lover's thoughts would come to Joe and me as time went on. We were still a bit unsure of what the other was thinking. But one thing we both knew was we loved each other. That was all that mattered.

"We tend to agree with you, Angelica, and we'd feel better and more relaxed away from the house knowing Maverick was often around. And if we ever get Felicity her own dog, she'd already be used to training and taking care of it, both as an obedient pet and protector. But we want to run it by the psychiatrist first. We have an appointment on Saturday. We'll need your word that you would impress upon Felicity the absolute importance of never using her 'weapon' unless absolutely necessary. She looks up... shit, she *worships* you, you know."

I blushed at the compliment and perfectly understood their concern. I was about to say so, but Jane's phone rang, interrupting the conversation. She looked at the display. "Port Jefferson? Must be spam." She was about to cancel the call, then remembered. "Hmm, could it be?" She decided to answer.

142

"Hello?" A brief pause, then, "Yes, Marlene, of course I remember. So nice to hear from you again. How's Khaleesi?... Terrific... Really?... Sure, I guess... Okay. How about Wednesday? We're having a little party for a friend of ours and you and Khaleesi can join in for some Carvel cake and we can discuss... Oh, well, the three of us can adjourn to a private area if you wish... Okay, say about seven?... Fine. Oh, by the way, someone you know will also be here. Dr. Joseph Peck. He's Khaleesi's eye doctor, right?... Also, she can play with my eleven-year-old daughter, Felicity. Khaleesi's what, nine?... Oh, almost... Anyway, great, see you Wednesday at 7 PM." Jane gave the woman the address. "Bye." The call ended.

Jane had a concerned look on her face, and Anna noticed it immediately. "Everything all right, honey?"

"I guess," the detective softly answered. "That was Marlene Fell. I told you all about her." Anna nodded. Turning to me, Jane added, "I'm sure Sammy spoke to you about her fucking husband and how we, er, handled that situation."

I also nodded. No need to go over the details. "She wants to meet with me. With you, too," she added, nodding to her wife. "Says it's important; she didn't want to go into details on the phone."

"But?" asked Anna, hearing the suspicion in her wife's voice.

"Her voice. First, I would describe it as one of despair. I know that's very subjective, but she sounded like when she first asked for my aid with her husband. Desperate. Second, the very sound of it. Raspy, as you'd expect from a chain smoker. Very different from what I remember." She paused.

"Anyway, I guess we'll know Wednesday. We should warn Felicity in advance. She's not known for her tact and thinks anyone younger than her is not worthy of her attention." The two mothers giggled. "Another thing we have to work on with her, Anna, right?"

The older woman nodded in agreement.

We then continued with our brandy, each silently pondering what Marlene Fell had to discuss, not realizing the impact it would soon have on all our lives.

Chapter 18

Tuesday, January 7
Floral Park
7 PM

The display blinked 5 AM, on-off-on, until Melinda-Ann, having now dealt with tomorrow's alarm, moved the three-position switch from "SET" to "OFF." Tonight, before retiring, she would slide it to "ON." She could do it now, but the woman was a creature of habit. Whenever preparing a personal wake-up call, she would set it after dinner to be activated upon retiring, after once again seeing the alarm-time was correct. A final check.

Dinner completed, it was again time for the potato. Doctor Peck's remedies, the antibiotics and the high-carb vegetable, had so far worked very well. The stye had popped yesterday, after the third application of heat. The redness was gone, too. But MAQ was not taking any chances, so continued with the doctor's instructions.

The potato awaited in the kitchen. Already pierced, she placed it on a metal pan, lowered the door of her state-of-the-art electric oven, and slid the pan onto the upper rack. She closed the door and set the digital timer for sixty minutes. When the time expired, the oven would automatically shut off and announce the completion of its task with three high-pitched *beeps,* along with a "COMPLETE"

145

message flashed across a small display window, remaining until the door was reopened.

As Melinda-Ann hit the start button, she was almost immediately greeted with the ringing of her doorbell. Given the concierge hadn't called up, whoever it was, she deduced, must live in the building. She walked to her front door and opened it.

MAQ smiled as she saw the visitor.

"I didn't think *you'd* be the one chosen for the task," *The Queen* said. "And a day early, too. No matter. Come on in."

"Now, now, Melinda-Ann. Look, I bring good cheer, figuratively, and," an already opened and re-corked bottle of *Cabernet* was presented, "literally." The two made their way to the living room.

"I see you've had a bit of a head start," MAQ said. "No problem, I can catch up fast."

"Yes, but before we get into the details, let's have a little congratulatory drink. After all, you're about to become a much wealthier woman."

"Just what I want to hear." The host went into the kitchen, retrieved two wine glasses and returned, placing them upon the coffee table that now separated the two individuals as the fiend sat on one love seat and Melinda-Ann on another, facing her guest. The former poured two full glasses of wine. Each lifted their respective glass, then clinked them together.

The Queen hadn't noticed the guest's other hand resting in a jacket pocket. In it lay an ancient, low-tech toy known as a *joy buzzer*, a small device which, when pressed, made a buzzing sound. Its purpose was as a gag, but it also recreated the sound of a muted iPhone extremely well. As glass was raised to mouth, the buzzer was pressed. The noise wasn't loud but was clearly audible to both. Without drinking, the guest lowered the wineglass. "Shit, what's this?" Alongside the buzzer in the pocket was a phone, now removed.

"Hello?" A two-second pause. Then, "Sorry, MAQ, I have to take this little call." Walking slowly toward the kitchen and continuing the imaginary conversation, the visitor surreptitiously watched as Queen quickly downed the full glass of wine, refilled and began to drink again. Melinda-Ann was known to enjoy her *vino* and despite the fifty, ten milligram pills of Valium dissolved in the bottle, that love of wine, combined with the euphoria of her "victory," helped mask the somewhat bitter taste the medication lent to the liquid.

The visitor knew the effects of even one ten-milligram tab, having used them to relax for a few claustrophobic MRI exams. Such a pill would induce a pleasant drowsiness within ten minutes. Fifty, dissolved in wine, no less, should kick in about...

Melinda-Ann closed her eyes and lay back, resting her head on the back of the couch. Not asleep, but extremely relaxed.

... now. The visitor smiled and removed a pair of surgeon's gloves from a jacket pocket. That virus going around in China was getting lots of press and constant handwashing and glove-wearing were the recommendations. The guest was anything if not fixed upon staying healthy and alive, so had many pairs available. Proceeding to the first bedroom of the apartment, known by all visitors to MAQ's home as her office, the Apple MacBook was located. It was on a corner desk, connected to a printer and external hard drive. Its top was closed, and, upon opening it, a password was immediately demanded. Queen was a bit of a technophile and had proudly shown off her new computer's Touch ID feature to all members of the board at her last party, right after the election. The visitor unhooked the computer from its attachments and brought it into the living room where Melinda-Ann's index finger was placed on the Touch ID key. The desktop sprung to life. *"Et voilà."*

The laptop was returned to the office, the printer reconnected, and a thumb-drive produced from the guest's pocket. It was inserted into a USB port and after two seconds, the drive's icon appeared on the desktop. While waiting, the visitor scanned the

147

screen and soon found a file named *QGTScandals.docx*. "Bingo!" The file was copied to the drive icon and then the original was dragged to the *Trash*. Finally, and most importantly, the Trash was emptied. The file's retrieval now was almost impossible unless one was equipped with much skill and the right equipment. Given how quickly the police would dismiss this case—the visitor was certain—it was doubtful such efforts would be undertaken.

Once completed, a file named *Suicide.docx* on the thumb-drive was dragged to the printer icon in the dock, almost immediately bringing the machine to life. Within thirty seconds, Melinda-Ann's *suicide note* sat in the printer's out-tray. And there it would sit until discovered. The file was moved to the desktop.

The computer was powered down, the thumb drive removed and the small external drive, almost certainly containing a backup of the incriminating Word document, was placed in the visitor's pocket.

Melinda-Ann snored peacefully. "Come on *ma cherie*, time to get up," the guest jokingly said, shaking the sleeping woman. MAQ stirred and slurred a response that was not decipherable. Then, after a few extra, vigorous shakes, she said, "I'm not... feeling well. Sooo ti... ired."

Yes, quite the wooden mouth. "Maybe a little air will do you good. Let me help you to the balcony."

The guest's arms were placed under MAQ's armpits, and the woman was helped to her feet. It took five full minutes, but both finally arrived at the large balcony. The door was unlocked and slid open. Melinda-Ann was placed, slumped over the side railing, moaning. She was tall, raising her center of gravity to just above the low barrier. The visitor looked right, to the adjacent balcony and apartment. The room was dark, the terrace empty. Thirty stories below lay the courtyard, a central area of concrete, wood and grass that closed at sunset. It would not reopen until dawn.

The fiend quickly bent down, grabbed the prey's legs, just above the ankles, and in one swift, athletic move lifted and, using the railing as a fulcrum, flipped the woman over. It took less than five seconds for Melinda-Ann to fall, hitting the concrete at about 100 mph. Even thirty stories above, the sound of every bone, including her skull, shattering on impact caused the killer to recoil in revulsion. Quickly recovering, the murderer exited the balcony and kept the sliding door opened and unlocked. *After all, how can it be closed and locked if the only occupant jumped? And why would she close it once outside, anyway?*

Knowing the high winds on the 30th floor would wreak havoc with one's hair, the killer approached the bathroom, not wanting to look disheveled on return to the Security Office, where in a back room were spare keys to all residences in case of emergency. There were also important co-op papers all building VIPs could examine. Surreptitiously lifting the set to 30Z had thus been a simple matter for such a regular visitor and important person.

In the bathroom, the fiend used a comb and within seconds appeared to have spent the evening at home, quietly relaxing. Looking into the mirror, the guest smiled and pronounced, *"The Queen* is dead! Long live the—"

"HELP!"

What the fuck? Impossible. For a second, the killer, in horror, thought Melinda-Ann had survived and was now calling for aid. But the realization soon set in that the sounds from below, echoed through the courtyard and carried up by the wind, were not from *The Queen,* but were the words of a younger person. A teen.

Fucking kids! There were few residents of QueensGate under the age of twenty, but the ones who did live there with their parents were bored to tears and would often sneak into the courtyard at night. Though locked at this time, the fences were low enough for the athletically inclined to scale. Many of the teenagers would gather to drink, smoke and make out. Obviously, some had picked this chilly January night to do so.

Damn! The murderer had wanted to make one last pass through the apartment, just in case, but there was no time. Security would

149

be notified quickly. The guest went to the kitchen, wet a paper towel, and returned to the living room.

Preparing for tonight, and while pouring, the visitor had held the wine bottle only between the front and rear labels. Now it was time to lightly wash and wipe dry those labels, so no fingerprints but Melinda-Ann Queen's remained. The towel and the killer's wine glass were also placed into a pant pocket after dumping the liquid into the toilet and flushing. MAQ's glass remained, the Valium residue to be explained in the suicide note.

Apartment 30Z was at the end of a long hallway and next to the stairwell. A quick look through the peephole at the apartment across the hall showed no one present.

What's that smell? A very faint odor, an earthy, nutty aroma was detected. *Maybe it's MAQ's perfume? Can't worry about it now.* With that last notion, the assassin left and quickly locked the door. Moving to the adjacent staircase, the murderer walked down two flights and then took the elevator to the Mall level and Security. The hubbub occurring there made it even easier to enter without suspicion and return the keys.

––––––––––––––

Minutes passed. Now and then, if one were present in apartment 30Z, if the winds were swirling in the right direction, voices from below would echo through the open balcony door. Words like, "Call 911," and "We've got a jumper." After a while, there was silence as whoever remained at the scene stood quietly, waiting for police and paramedics. In an hour or so, the detectives and representatives of the Medical Examiner would arrive. They would soon figure out the possible apartments the jumper could have leaped from, and after a careful process of elimination, arrive at 30Z. They'd examine the balcony, find the suicide note, and do a cursory examination of the area. Within twenty-four hours, next-of-kin would be notified, and the M.E.'s office would determine

Melinda-Ann Queen died of massive trauma. The police would quickly declare it a suicide. Case closed.

But until 30Z was entered, the apartment remained eerily silent. It was an unusual state for the premises. For when Melinda-Ann was present, there was always noise—sounds of passion from the bedroom, she on the telephone, texting, watching TV, conversing with guests, even merely turning the pages as she read real, ink-on-paper books—though recently her cataracts had significantly curtailed that activity.

Yes, unfortunately, *The Queen of QueensGate* would not be showing up for her surgery with Dr. Joseph Peck tomorrow. She would be missed.

The silence in the apartment lingered.

Then, exactly one hour after the visitor had first appeared at 30Z's threshold, the quiet was broken by three high-pitched sounds.

Trivial noises, to be sure. Inconsequential——one would think.

Beep... beep... beep.

PART II–Scripture, Sisters, and Suspicion

"Thy people shall be my people,
And thy God, my God."

~The Book of Ruth, 1:16

"I could never love anyone as I love my sisters."

~Louisa May Alcott, 'Little Women'

"It's every man's business to see justice done."

~Sir Arthur Conan Doyle, 'The Memoirs of Sherlock Holmes'

Chapter 19

Wednesday, January 8
Ambulatory Surgery Center, Garden City
7:30 AM

"Any luck, Joan?" Joe asked the OR secretary.

"No, Doctor Peck. We've tried to contact Ms. Queen three times and called her emergency contact, the son. It just goes to voicemail. Should we start moving everyone up? Your second case, Mr. Jackson, he's here and almost ready to go."

Strange, thought Joe. *Very strange.* "I don't understand it. She was so looking forward to the surgery. I envisioned her showing up two hours ahead of time, in fact." *Maybe the stye worsened. Maybe she thought I'd just cancel when I saw it. No. She would have called, at least. Something's wrong.*

"Okay, Joan. Start calling. We've got five more to get through and we can always add Queen on if she shows."

And I've got an engagement ring to wrap.

That last thought made the surgeon shiver with apprehension. He could cut into five eyeballs over the next four hours and not raise a sweat; but the thought of Angelica saying "no" was enough to make his hands shake.

Stop being crazy. You've got a job to do, so fuck everything else and get with the program!

Joe sighed, shook his head, and, still stunned Melinda was a *no-show*, turned to greet Mr. Jackson. The man was now Peck's priority—his one and only concern. No shaky hands allowed.

Worrying about Angelica or *The Queen* would have to wait.

West Hempstead, New York
3:30 PM

Sammy Vivino completed his confession. Helen had asked Joe for the afternoon off and, since patients were never scheduled after a full morning of surgery, he had agreed. The answering machine could deal with any messages; she'd remotely check throughout the day.

Helen had listened for close to ninety minutes without commenting. Sammy had started at the beginning. He told of his beloved mother, abusive father, and how at age twelve, to save her from being beaten to death, he'd killed the man with his own gun. Then he spoke of the kindness of Mafia soldier, Vincent Esposito (Ace's father), who came to his and his mother's aid that night. Sammy continued with how Esposito took young Sammy under his wing, training him in the fine art of assassination. The soldier ultimately ascended to Don and young Sammy quickly became the family's number-one hitman, a legend among his peers.

Sammy tried to explain how, given these events, he never really had a chance—no alternatives, no other paths to follow. It was all he knew; the *Family* was *his* family. The man had done a good deal of homework the previous two days, using Google (with Angelica's help) to gather stories from the Old Testament, what the Jewish people call the *Torah*, to help him, he hoped, soften the blows of his revelations.

154

"You should know, Helen," he said at one point, "every person,"—*well, almost every* he silently, ruefully admitted—"who I was called on to kill was himself either a killer, wife-beater, or child molester. Some were all three. They had reaped what they had sown, as far as I was concerned. They were all seen as *enemies* of my Don and the Family. Just as in the *Torah*,"—Helen was shocked he knew the term—"the Canaanites were seen as *enemies* to the Israelites. And did not Moses send *his* soldiers to murder them all at God's command? And didn't Moses himself kill an Egyptian he saw oppressing a Jewish slave? Yet he's considered having come as close to God as any man according to the *Torah*, no?" Sammy didn't wait for a rebuttal, one he was positive Helen could come up with.

Next came the nickname, Lover Boy. There was no need to cite numbers; Sammy made it clear he had slept with many women, stressing that because of his mother's influence, he'd treated them all respectfully and tenderly. Sammy spoke of his now disbanded *Harem* (Helen's eyes widened when told he'd quit them for *her*) and of the two loves of his life, Chiara, gunned down during an attack on him just days before the two were to be wed, and Maria, Angelica's mother. Maria was the perfect segue to Angelica's story, culminating with Felicity's rescue, his daughter's battle with *Il Boa* and her subsequent entry into WITSEC.

Before he spoke of Angelica's return, he described how he'd met Helen's employer, Joseph Peck. Here was another chance to lessen the blow as the woman discovered the boss she thought she knew so well had not only had sex with another man's wife (that *I can believe*, Helen thought), but plotted to kill the husband and gain the wife and her money. That, was an entirely different matter.

"Does this story sound somewhat familiar?" he asked. Helen didn't answer, but knew where Sammy was going. "Was not David, second king of Israel, a 'man after God's own heart?' as the *Torah* says? And did he not commit adultery with Bathsheba and plot successfully for her husband to be killed in battle, so as to have the wife as his own? And yet we, Jew and Christian alike, to this day sing David's psalms, especially the 23rd, 'The Lord is my shepherd...' So please, do not think harshly of Joe. He proved, as David, to be a man with all of Man's weaknesses. I can tell you he has suffered tremendous guilt since, and fully regrets his deeds. Remember, he played an important role in Felicity's rescue and helped bring down a murdering monster and child molester, a man who—if *anyone*— deserved to die a horrible death." At that point, Sammy told Helen of the death of Don Fortuna. If he and the woman were to continue their relationship, she had to know all—about him and his friends.

Now he was done. The entire confession had been spoken in hushed, calming tones. If not for the subject matter, Sammy might well have been telling a child her bedtime stories. Helen had listened intently. There were times during the recitation she considered asking the man to leave, to get out of her house. But each time would come an explanation, either a story from the *Torah* or Sammy's own justification. And each time the woman's heart, unlike Pharoah's of Exodus, would soften, and she'd continue to listen. She could hear in his voice that Sammy was filled with regret, and he'd emphasized how over these past few years he'd come to fully realize how his actions had caused his soul to, most likely, be lost. He also stressed how Angelica felt similarly. But he hoped the good he'd achieved in helping save the child Felicity, battling for his daughter's life and contributing to ridding the world of Don Vito Fortuna could be a new beginning—a new road back into grace with God... "and with you, Helen."

Then Sammy took the woman's hand and told her he loved her. It was then Helen realized the true reason she had not asked Sammy to leave was because she felt the same—and she had sensed it for some time.

But where could this go? she thought. *Where? How?*

And, as if to answer, Sammy continued. "Which is why I've decided to convert." He paused. Helen just stared, stunned. Her hand, already grasped in Sammy's, clenched tighter. "I met with an orthodox rabbi on Monday. He tried to convince me against my chosen path." The man laughed. "He reminded me of all the beautiful Italian girls available to marry and all those delicious seafood and meat/parmigiana dishes I'd be sacrificing. And the possible conflicts with family members. I told him all my family were gone except for Angelica, and she has encouraged me to follow this path." Helen was happily surprised the girl had given Sammy her blessing. *We must get to know each other better*, she thought. "But in the end, I guess, I passed, for he sent me to a *Beth Din*"—a biblical court, composed of three rabbis who specialized in conversion. "They too tried to persuade me to give up my goal. Very persistent. I guess this is some sort of test of one's resolve. They stressed how difficult the road ahead would be. The sacrifices. The studies. But again, I stood fast.

"Thankfully, they never asked about my past. They were just interested in my future. I appreciated that. No prejudices going into the training, which they said usually takes two years to complete. I reminded them I wasn't getting any younger, at which point the oldest of the three, ninety-five, agreed to spend as much time as I could give him to speed things up." Sammy chuckled. "He said *he* wasn't getting any younger either, and if this were to be his ultimate achievement, leading me to God, who he called *HaShem*, it would be a fine, last act indeed.

"So, they have agreed to begin the process. For me to become one with you, spiritually as well as physically. So, when the time comes, when I have passed all the tests... if you will have me... we can be married."

Helen was in shock. *The Beth Din has agreed!?* she marveled; and tears came. She knew a decision had to be made. Yes, Sammy had confessed to terrible sins. Yet, she understood how, brought up in the underworld culture as he'd been, it would have been a miracle had he not succumbed to that way of life. It was inevitable. *But he seems to be truly repentant, ready to turn the page, abandon that life, his Harem—for me! The Beth Din believes in him. Shouldn't I?*

"I have to know one thing, Sammy," Helen began. "I have to know there will be no more killing. You can no longer be involved in such things. Can you promise me that?"

Sammy Vivino—the legendary assassin, Lover Boy—took both the woman's hands in his. "You know how some people are accident prone? For me... well, your God... our God... *HaShem*... has seemed prone to putting me into situations where my skills were required—to save *my* life and those of others. Where there was no alternative." He paused, then, "What I can promise you is this: I will never take up the gun, the knife, any lethal means for personal gain, or vengeance. But, if *you* or any of those I love face a situation where I *must* use my skills to avoid losing that which is most dear to me, then I will do whatever is necessary. In that event, I cannot promise blood will not be spilled." And then he waited.

Helen had expected *some* revelations when the two had met, prior to Angelica's party; but what she wound up facing was overwhelming. What she knew was this man holding her hands loved her. And she loved him. She had once let her strict upbringing and beliefs lead to a painful result, her son's estrangement. That conflict, now after a decade, had finally, and happily, been resolved. She vowed to not make the same mistake twice.

Sammy was making an extreme sacrifice, she knew. And he was doing this *for her*. It was time to do the same—for him. She took his hands and kissed them.

"I can live with that," she said, smiling. Then, "They *did* tell you..." she paused, looked down, then up, "... about the? ..." she made a snipping gesture between her thumb and index finger.

"You mean circumcision?" Helen nodded.

"Yes, though it was unnecessary. Joe had already, much too cheerfully I might add, informed me of that fact. I guess *I* can live with that, too."

There was a twinkle in Helen's eye as she added, "You probably mean you can live *without* that, no?"

It took Sammy a second or two, but then the man heartily laughed—

And they embraced.

Chapter 20

Lake Success
6:00 PM

We retired to the living room after dinner. It was time for presents! I hadn't had a birthday party with so many guests in my entire life; I felt giddy as a five-year-old.

Before dining, I spoke with Helen and found her very entertaining. I liked her acerbic wit and saw how she loved my *padre*. She asked if I was really okay with his decision to convert, and I told her the truth: my only interests were whatever made him happy. Right now, she seemed at the top of that list; so, it was fine with me. We hugged and agreed to spend more time together, alone and as couples, though she noted it was going to be weird double dating with her employer. I told her not to think of Joe as her boss, but "should things progress as expected, think of Joe as... as your future son-in-law!" She faux—I think—gasped in horror and then we both broke out laughing as she added, "Great. I can double as both office manager *and* mother-in-law from Hell!"

Yeah, I really liked Helen.

Linda, Tony, and Morris joined us via Apple Facetime and were the first to present their gifts. From Linda, more clothes—barely there bikinis plus a one-piece that promised "to show more of your ass-cheeks than should be legal," she admonished. Also, a few sunsuits and other Florida-appropriate casual wear. The clothes would wait for my next visit. Then Tony informed me Mel had come through with my "order," and then produced his gift: a deluxe, Sunfiner multi-function tactical bag to carry all my equipment. He also had purchased life-time admission to a local gun range as part of the deal. I could see Linda wasn't thrilled, but she accepted the fact that parts of Tony's and my pasts could not be wished away, so, if they made her man and her friend happy, she'd live with it. Then Morris showed me three bottles of Knob Creek Single Barrell Reserve (120 proof!)—one of my favorite bourbons; very hard to come by. As much as they tempted him, Morris promised not to touch a single bottle till I was there to open one and share it with him. I do love that old man.

Felicity and Marta were next. They had chipped in and bought the most precious personalized collar and name/rabies tags for Maverick plus an adorable fleece jacket—with a hood! How cute is that?—for the cold New York winters. Jane and Anna produced two front-row-center seats to the Broadway revival of *Plaza Suite* for opening night, April 13. It also included a backstage pass with the stars. They obviously had remembered a comment on our trip back from Florida that watching *Sex and the City*, starring Sarah Jessica Parker (who would also headline the upcoming play) was one of my favorite viewing activities, along with *Game of Thrones*.

Penultimately came *Papà*. He had realized carrying a firearm in New York was not in the cards right now. Therefore, my combination sheath/gun holster was rendered half superfluous. So, he took the beautifully fashioned piece to a master leather craftsman he'd used over his career, who created an exact copy of the sheath alone, plus ties, thus allowing a sleeker carry for Needle on my calf and making for a faster pull.

Then it was Joe's turn. He lifted a three-foot square box, a red bow tied to the top, and placed it at my feet. I was sitting on the couch, surrounded by Jane and Anna, and they rose, allowing Joe and me to sit alone. Either could have just slid over, yet they left me and my man unaccompanied. *Hmm.*

I lifted the box and was immediately struck by how light it was. Whatever it contained weighed next to nothing. *Strange. Oh well, just*

161

open the damn thing and find out what gives. I tore at the wrapping paper and lifted the cover to find—another box; but I immediately realized it was not just any box. Though it was wrapped, the size and shape were unmistakable. It was a jewelry box. I looked at Joe, then the others. All were staring at me as if I were expected to spontaneously combust—and it gave me the chills. I slowly unwrapped the small gift and opened it.

Oh my.

Joe removed a gorgeous, large, round diamond ring surrounded by small stones encircling the entire band. I was told later those were called Pavé diamonds and the band itself was platinum. He placed it on the ring finger of my left hand, which now was trembling. Then he looked at me and smiled.

"Angelica. Will you marry me? And before you answer, I know we've not known each other long, so nothing says we can't wait six months, a year or whatever you want until we marry. Of course, if you want sooner that's okay, too, but I thought six months was a good time and—"

"Will you just shut the fuck up?!" I cried. The room went as silent as the grave, except for a giggling Felicity responding to my language. *Hmm, I may have given them all the wrong impression.* So I smiled, gave a soft punch to the shoulder and said, "Of course I'll marry you, you big jerk!" Then I softened. "Of course." I threw my arms around him and held on for dear life. The room erupted in applause, joined by the Florida group. My eyes were filled with tears and as I went to wipe them away, Joe put his hands on my cheeks and kissed me deeply. Then, coming up for air, I heard Morris exclaim—

"B-T-W, happy birthday!"

6:55 PM

162

Jane had produced a bottle of champagne while Joe and I were in mid-kiss and the group toasted the newly engaged couple, along with Tony, Linda and Morris, who drank their own bubbly, fifteen-hundred miles away. Even Felicity was allowed to join in with half a glass. She really got a kick out of the bubbles. Then we all relaxed. The Florida contingent said their goodbyes, and, to prepare for Marlene and Khaleesi's visit, Marta cleared the glasses. The women had told us about the visitors during dinner and we were all very curious about what Marlene had to say. Anna again reminded Felicity about Khaleesi. "Mama and I know your opinion of kids younger than you. Frankly, of most kids. Please—be—nice, okay? She's probably very anxious about being around so many strangers."

Felicity was petting Maverick and stopped, placed her hand over her heart, and said, "When am I not nice? Don't answer that! Okay, I swear, cross my heart and hope to die, I will be nice to the little pipsqueak." Both her parents scowled and were about to speak when the doorbell rang. Marta started to rise, but Jane said, "Don't bother, Marta. We'll get it." At which point she and Anna walked toward the front door. The rest of us waited. We heard the door open, some pleasantries exchanged, and then the two visitors were led into the den.

"Okay, everyone," said Jane. "This is my friend Marlene Fell and her daughter Khaleesi."

Marlene nodded. "Glad to meet you all. Khal?"

The bespectacled child grabbed her mother's arm, obviously intimidated, but said, "Hi."

Joe rose and went over to the pair, and as soon as the girl saw him, she smiled. "Mommy, it's Dr. Peck!"

"Hello, Marlene." They shook hands. Then, "And hello to you, Khaleesi. How's it going with the patching?"

"Great. It's really easy now that I'm down to just one hour a day. I do it after school while doing my homework."

Joe smiled. He had told me Khaleesi had been quite the success story. When she first appeared with Marlene and that brute Monty, the father refused to even consider putting his child in glasses, let alone patch her good eye to help the poor-seeing one, almost legally blind. But once he was dealt with, thanks to *Papà* and Jane, she had improved dramatically (20/20!) under Joe's care and soon patching would no longer be necessary. She was a cute child with short, black hair and wire-rimmed glasses that complemented her face.

Jane then introduced Sammy. "This is my friend Sammy Vivino. He was, er, quite helpful to me with solving your... problem a while back..." Jane trailed off and Marlene looked at Sammy and understood. "Thank you, Mr. Vivino. I can't tell you how grateful I am for your help. You and Jane saved both our lives. I've always thought of Jane as our *guardian angel*. Now I can include you, as well."

Sammy smiled. "It was a pleasure, my dear." Then, realizing he'd told Helen the tale, he looked at the woman, fearing her response to the pride in his voice. But Helen had been touched by the story, so sympathetic to the abused family that now, seeing them and hearing Marlene, she nodded at Sammy, as if to say his words were appropriate. Lover Boy smiled. Relieved.

Next came Marta, Helen (who they knew), and then I was introduced. When Marlene was told of the recent engagement, she beamed. "Khal, this nice woman and Dr. Peck are going to be married! I'm so happy for you, and *you*, Doctor. So happy." Joe and I thanked her.

"Felicity?" Anna motioned for her daughter to join them. She and Maverick together walked over to the Fells. The girl first shook hands with Marlene and then looked at Khaleesi. She handed her a doggie treat. "This is Maverick," she explained. "If you give him the treat, he'll be your B-F-F." To Felicity, this was a test. First, she wanted to see if the *pipsqueak* was comfortable with dogs. If not, that would end things right there. Second, she had learned the dog's initial reaction to a stranger was important. Even with a treat, if

Maverick didn't *approve* of the presenter, he would not accept it. He'd look for guidance from either Felicity or me.

Khaleesi smiled, petted his head, bent down and presented the treat. First test passed. The dog quickly lapped up the offering and then started licking the girl's hand. Felicity was pleasantly surprised. "Well," she began, smiling. "Maverick seems to like you. That's good enough for me." And she took the younger girl's hand and shook it. "Nice to meet you, Khaleesi."

"Me too, you," the guest replied.

Jane and Anna looked at each other, and an unspoken sigh of relief was shared. "Why don't you take Khaleesi and Maverick upstairs while Marlene and we talk, sweetie?" said Anna.

Felicity faux frowned. "Hmm, the adults want to get rid of us. You still play with Barbies?"

The girl briskly nodded.

"Well, I think I know where I put them. We can start there, then see what else we can do. Maybe watch some videos, okay?"

"Sure. Can I, Mommy?"

"That's fine, dear. Have fun with Felicity. I'll see you in a while."

And with that, the two children and the dog left, bounding up the stairs.

"Would you prefer to talk to Jane and me privately, Marlene?" Anna asked.

"I thought I would, but seeing as everyone here is a friend, I figure it might be better to explain to you all. It's always good to have the opinions of good friends, don't you think?"

"Yes," Jane answered. "We do. Please sit." She pointed to the couch. Marlene sat, as did Jane and Anna, on each side of her.

The visitor lowered her head. A few uncomfortable seconds passed and then she looked up. Tears had formed under both eyes.

"Well... the thing is..." she began. "I'm dying."

Thirty minutes later

"My Mommy's dying."

The girls had spent a few minutes dressing up some old Barbie dolls Felicity found under her bed in plastic containers but Khaleesi, noticing today's NY Times crossword puzzle, partially completed, laying on her host's bed, suggested they try to finish it, together. Felicity was surprised and, in amazement, found the younger girl's vocabulary very advanced for a nine-year-old—and she was good at the tricky clues, too. The two of them finished the puzzle and then, noticing *The Complete Works of William Shakespeare* on Felicity's bookshelf (Jane and Anna had started their daughter early), Khaleesi commented how she had just started to read the plays, especially the comedies. She admitted to problems with the old English and relied on the Folger editions to explain many of the words and phrases.

Felicity must have realized her mouth was agape, because she forcibly closed it. Then she recommended playing the "complete the quote" game she had often heard her parents engage in. They played about ten minutes and though the older girl won handily in the end, the younger child was competitive early on. Felicity was impressed. *She's really smart.*

The last ten minutes or so were spent reading the Manga comics found among Felicity's books and then taking turns drawing with colored pencils on paper some of each girl's favorite characters. Felicity was having an unexpectedly good time with the younger child when, out of the blue, came the statement about her mother.

"Oh. That's terrible," was all Felicity could think to say at first. *That was profound, you idiot,* she berated herself. She was too busy imagining how she would feel if one of her parents died. A hollow sensation developed in her stomach. Then she thought to ask a question that, to now, she'd not considered. "What about your dad?"

Khaleesi was still looking down at her drawing paper. "He's dead, almost two years now."

That discomfort in Felicity's stomach grew stronger. Now she envisioned both her parents gone—being an orphan. It was too frightening to contemplate, so instead, she quickly said, "Oh, I'm sorry."

Khaleesi swiftly raised her head. "Don't be!" she sharply said to Felicity's astonishment. "He was always mean to me. And a bad man—used to hit Mommy all the time. And... and..." Now tears came to the child's eyes. "... he was starting to touch me... you know, not nice type touching... in my private areas. Started about a week before he drowned." She paused. Then, "*That,* was the happiest day of my life!" And then the tears increased in volume.

Felicity was shocked and deeply distraught. Khaleesi's words had hit home, tearing at her own, still-open wounds, things she had not discussed with anyone—not with her parents, not with her psychiatrist. No one. And though she subconsciously knew better, Felicity believed those things that had occurred were unique to her—and somehow her fault. But now, with the younger girl tearfully confessing, the older, much to her amazement, had found another who had experienced what she had faced—and Felicity felt compelled to comfort Khaleesi; tell her that *she* was not alone.

The older girl was shocked at how she felt. This was *empathy,* the child recognized; the ability to share another's feelings that her parents had often encouraged her to cultivate—unsuccessfully, until now. *She opened to me, as I should have with Mommy and Mama,* she thought. *Maybe...*

"Khal?" Felicity began, using the nickname she'd heard the girl's mother use.

"Yes?" the younger girl sniffed, wiping her eyes.

"I'm going to tell you something—a secret I've told no one. Neither my parents nor my psychiatrist."

The young girl's eyes widened. "You see a psychiatrist?"

Felicity nodded. "Yes. Primarily, I think, because of what I'm about to tell you. My parents suspect, which is why they sent me to the doctor in the first place. There's another reason, something they swore me to secrecy about, though maybe we can talk about it in the future. But *this* thing, what I tell you now, is our secret. Between *us*. Okay?"

The girl nodded.

"My father, he, too, touched me inappropriately. You know that word, right?" Khaleesi nodded. "Yeah, I was sure you would. Worse... he made me... he made me touch him, too. There were nights I lay in bed, waiting for him to come—and thought of ways of killing myself." Khaleesi gasped and her hand went to her mouth. "Mommy didn't know. He always came after she had gone to bed. Once or twice, I tried to gather the courage to tell her, but, well... you're not going to believe this, but I was a real brat back then." She chuckled. "Yeah, I was quite the bitch. Some of it, maybe most of it, I'm sure, was a reaction to what was going on—I've read some stuff about that on-line. But I figured Mommy would believe I was just making it up and, frankly, I don't think she liked me much back then. I was a shit-load to handle, I can tell you."

Khaleesi giggled at the mild curse, but then took Felicity's hand and squeezed gently. The older girl continued. "Then, one day, he was dead. Gone. Like you said, that was the happiest day of my life... Until now, I've not told a soul. I've been thinking of opening up to the psychiatrist. He seems nice and I know that's what my moms would like, and I want them to be happy. I love 'em both to death and I know they love me... Anyway, you are the only one who knows, Khal. The only one." She squeezed the younger girl's hand.

"So, you see, we have something in common, right?"

Khaleesi nodded, smiled and added, "Yeah, lucky us, huh?" They both laughed—it was preferable to crying. Felicity was again surprised by the child's maturity.

"Now we both know each other's darkest secrets. Like sisters, right? All you read is about how sisters share stuff like that. But I

168

have a question now. Why did your mom and you *really* come tonight? My moms didn't know when I asked."

Khaleesi's grip on the older girl's hand tightened even further. "Mommy told me before we left today. Everything, though I'd figured out the dying part already from phone conversations I'd, er, listened in on. She's going to ask your parents to take me in, once... once she's gone." She sniffled, holding back any more tears.

"You mean adopt you?"

"Yeah."

"Is that what you'd like?"

Khaleesi nodded. "If Mommy dies, then sure. Your parents seem real nice. Are they? Is it strange having two mommies?"

"They're the best! Sure, you'll have to train them a bit, like Maverick here." The dog, laying on the floor at the foot of the bed, raised his head upon hearing his name. "But yeah, *real* nice. The two-mommy thing is no biggie. Sure, now and then there's some jerk in school who teases me about it, but *fuck 'em!* Better to have two mommies than a mommy with a daddy like ours were, right?"

Khaleesi grinned and then nodded as Felicity continued. "I couldn't imagine... I couldn't imagine losing them... Hey! If they adopted you, that would make us sisters. Real sisters! Would you like that?"

The younger girl vigorously nodded, then tentatively asked, "What... What about you, Felicity? Would you like to be my sister?"

Felicity took her hands and placed them on Khaleesi's shoulders. "Khal, like I said. We've already told each other stuff only sisters could tell one another. No matter what's decided downstairs, as far as I'm concerned, we two already *are* sisters." And then they hugged, at which point Maverick bounded onto the bed and they both surrounded him with their arms and hugged as three.

"Wait!" Felicity interjected. "Those *adults* are downstairs discussing your, *our* future! Don't you think we should have a say in that?"

Khaleesi nodded furiously.

"I say we go down and say our piece. Right?"
"Right!"
The three leaped off the bed and headed for the staircase.

Chapter 21

Marlene had come to the end of her story thirty seconds ago. We all just sat still, the room deathly silent except for some soft sobbing from Helen. The rest of us were non-vocal, but, as the saying goes, there wasn't a dry eye in the house. Finally, Anna, taking the woman's hand in hers, spoke.

"First, Marlene, I want to allay your fears about one thing straight away. You don't have to worry how Khaleesi will get to school, get her meals, or how you'll deal with doctor's appointments while simultaneously taking care of her. I was a nurse and have lots of old friends who do private nursing. I'm positive I'll be able to have a few of them agree on a schedule to be at your home, 24/7. They'll make sure Khaleesi gets up for school, is fed, etc. Someone will be there to help even when you're feeling well. I can probably get them started next week. And on those days when you're not feeling up to it, or you must be at a doctor's appointment, again, one will be available to take care of you or drive you wherever and another to make sure your daughter is cared for. If you need to stay overnight at the hospital, well, one of them can remain with Khaleesi or she's always welcome to stay with us. One of my friends, or even I, can drive her to school in the morning and pick her up. So, don't let any of that burden your thoughts. You need all your strength and resolve to fight this thing. Jane and I will cover the expense."

Marlene managed a smile. "Thank you, Anna, Jane. That's so kind." Then she waited. The Franklins looked at each other. Then Jane took over.

"As far as what happens... after. That's... that's something else. Anna and I *have* been discussing adding another child to the family. A baby through artificial insemination. We've even started looking at sperm donors. Felicity has expressed the desire to be a big sister, though she's not thrilled with the thought of a newborn. 'Too much work,' she says," and Jane managed a quick, nervous giggle. "Anna and I hadn't really considered an *older* child. I guess... I guess nothing stops us from doing both but... but, well, we'd have to all discuss it, together. As a family. We'd need to know Felicity's feelings on the matter and—"

"Well, we can discuss it now!"

Felicity and Khaleesi appeared at the doorway. "Jesus, child!" exclaimed Anna. 'You've got to stop creeping up on people like that."

"I'm sorry, Mommy, but Khal and I were talking, and we figured, since what you're discussing affected us both, we should have at least *some* say in it."

The three parents looked at each other and nodded as one. "Okay," Jane began, "let's hear what you've got to say, then."

Felicity looked at Khaleesi. "You go first."

The two children took a few steps into the room. "Mrs. and, er, Mrs. Franklin..." Khaleesi started.

"Anna and Jane are fine for the moment, dear," said Anna.

"Okay. Anna and Jane? Obviously, I don't want my mommy to go away. But... but I don't want to go live with strangers, and if I *had* to come live with another family... and Felicity and I discussed this... well, I would be very happy to live with you." She paused. Up to now, the cadence of her speech had been normal. Now, it sped up dramatically. "And I wouldn't be any trouble, really, I swear. I would be a good daughter." Tears were forming and Helen had again begun to sob. Khaleesi rubbed her eyes and added, "Really, I'd be a good girl. I promise...anyway... that's all I wanted to say. Oh, and I also like Shakespeare, too." Jane and Anna chuckled, though it was a difficult task for the sounds to not come surrounded by sobs.

The girl began to step back, but Felicity took her hand, keeping her alongside. "Look, I know you guys have been thinking about having a baby. But really, all they do is cry and poop their pants all the time." She turned to Khaleesi, smiled and added, "*You* don't still do that, do you?"

The younger girl laughed and gave the older a soft punch in the shoulder.

Hey, that's my *signature move.*

"No, not since last week, at least." Felicity's smile widened. She, as I, appreciated a good sense of humor.

"Well, now that we've cleared that up, Khal and I had a long talk upstairs. And we shared some secrets... some terrible secrets I've not even shared with you guys." She looked down, then up. Her voice became almost too subdued to hear. "And I'm sorry about that, Mommy. Mama. But I've been afraid to talk to you about it. Afraid what you'd think—of me."

I could see a look of sadness now creep over both parents' faces. From conversations with Joe and *Papà*, I had a pretty good idea what Felicity was referring to. The two women definitely believed they did—and the look of despair on each of them tugged at my heart. "This Saturday," the child continued, "I'm going to discuss this with Dr. Thorpe; and then maybe we can have a long talk about it?"

Both parents, still stunned, could only nod. They realized the almost nine-year-old child who pleadingly stood before them, essentially a stranger, had somehow gotten their daughter to speak of things they had not, with all their love, been able to extract, either on their own or with help from the psychiatrist.

173

"These things we talked about, these are the type of secrets only sisters usually share. So I want you to know," she put her arm around Khaleesi's shoulder, "that no matter *what* you decide, Khal and I consider ourselves sisters—now and forever!"

At those words, Jane and Anna both looked my way. I knew why. Those were, after all, my exact words to them when we first reunited in Florida. I smiled and nodded. Then the two of them took a long look at each other. I could see their Vulcan mind meld, or whatever the hell you want to call it, revved up to full strength. Eleven on a scale of one-to-ten. Time seemed to stand still as I saw tiny, micro-expressions flutter across each face, accompanied by almost imperceptible movements of their heads. Maybe I exaggerate, but I don't think so. It was uncanny. Then, they both smiled together, and each took one of Marlene's hands and rose, the doomed woman rising with them. Maverick, who had been lying at my feet, also stood.

"Well," began Anna as the three mothers reached their children, "I'll call my lawyer tomorrow and we'll start the paperwork. Okay?" The children looked at each other and grinned widely. Then they rushed forward, forming a group hug. Five individuals, yet more.

"Khaleesi... Marlene," Jane added, the words catching in her throat—

"Welcome to the family."

10:00 PM

Tomorrow was a school day, so, after the Carvel birthday cake was voraciously consumed, Felicity went to bed and Marlene and Khaleesi departed for Port Jefferson. The rest of us sat in the living room, finally able to relax among friends. Marta had made coffee and retired so now Jane, Anna, Joe, Helen, my *padre* and I absorbed the caffeine, not that we really needed any more stimulation, and

174

engaged in unwinding from the whirlwind of events that had made the night so memorable.

Helen was the first to speak. "Ladies," she began, addressing the Franklins as they rested on their *objet d'art* couch, "you're doing a wonderful thing here. Wonderful. Sammy has told me about what happened to your husband, Anna." She turned to Joe and gave him a look he recognized well after thirty-one years of similar, Medusa-like stares from his office manager. She then turned back. "And the rescue of Felicity and Marta, the snake-guy and that monster in Philadelphia. My whole life I've always seen things in black and white, right and wrong, good versus evil. But I have to admit the shades of gray I've encountered since meeting *this* guy," she looked at Sammy and took his hand, "have been a revelation. Now tonight, what you're doing for Marlene and her child goes beyond kind and generous, so totally at odds with actions in the past that looking at them from the outside, without the context, would seem so much the opposite. I'm feeling quite overwhelmed with the contradictions." She took a sip of her coffee and continued. "Anyway, I just wanted to say anything I can do to help you with Marlene and Khaleesi, you just have to say the word." I saw my *padre* smile, and he reached over and gave Helen a kiss on the lips. Remarkably, despite the onlookers, the very religious woman did not pull away.

"Thank you, Helen. We will certainly take you up on your offer. But let's not forget what started the ball rolling tonight—Angelica and Joe's engagement!" I smiled and looked down at my ring, sparkling brightly on my finger. A little tight, but easily fixable. "Whenever you decide to tie the knot, I hope you will do it here, in the backyard. We have more than enough room and, as you'll recall, Joe, from Felicity's birthday party, we have experience with setting up a tent to handle any difficult weather."

"That's very sweet, Anna, Jane. I would like that. Definitely," I answered. "Joe?"

175

"Of course. It's a perfect setting. Oh, and speaking of settings... Angie, I've been thinking for a while of downsizing. The house and all the problems that go with it are getting just too much. I know you'd like to be close to your father, so I thought maybe we'd look for a unit at the Towers. What do you think?"

Now *that* was unexpected, and I was almost as surprised at the suggestion as I was with the engagement ring. After all, "I thought you didn't even like visiting there. You said all those residents in walkers and wheelchairs depressed you."

"True," he answered. "But as long as I'm not yet one of them, it's okay with me. I know you'd like to be close to Sammy, so..."

We were sitting right next to one another, so I leaned over and kissed him passionately. I knew this decision wasn't easy. It was a sacrifice, no matter what he said. But he was willing to do it—for *me*.

Finally, released from the lip-lock, he smiled and looked at his watch. "I'm sorry but I've got, we've got," he turned to Helen, "an early day tomorrow, with all the post-ops. So, I think we should go, no? Angie?"

I nodded and Helen said, while rising, "Just wait a sec. Let me check in with the machine and see if there are any messages we need to know about before morning. Be right back." She walked into the kitchen and dialed the office number from which, with a series of phone-button presses, she could play any messages recorded since last checked, right before dinner.

We all sat, finished our coffee, and mostly just snuggled—me with Joe and Anna with Jane. I grabbed *Papà's* hand so he wouldn't feel left out. In about three minutes, I heard Helen re-enter. Our two hosts were first to see her, given they were facing in the direction from which she entered, and when the rest of us saw *their* expressions, we turned to see for ourselves.

Helen's face was pale, a look of puzzled disbelief painted across it. It reminded me, in a way, of the agonized face in Munch's *The*

176

Scream, except her hands were at her side, the right holding a piece of scrap paper on which she had hastily written.

Sammy quickly rose and went to her. "What's wrong, my dear?"

The woman took his hand. "There was a message from Melinda-Ann Queen's son. He apologized for not getting back to us sooner. He said... he said Melinda was dead. She committed suicide last night."

Silence. At least ten seconds' worth. Then, Joe was first to react. "No, no, no. I can't believe that. She was *so* excited to have the operation. I just saw her two days ago! She was bursting out of her skin, wanting to get it over with so she could get on with her life. This doesn't make any sense." Joe had mentioned to me earlier he enjoyed having the woman as a patient more than any other. He was devastated.

"I have to agree," was all Helen could add. She was still in shock.

"You're right, Joe," Sammy added emphatically. "I knew Melinda-Ann very well. I have never met someone so full of life and who enjoyed living it to the fullest." He turned to Helen. "She was one of the first members of my *Harem, mi amore.* I'm sorry to bring it up again, but it's important to know. She was *not* one who would take her own life. It's unthinkable."

"I assume," I began, "the police will investigate, right Jane?" She nodded. "If there's anything fishy about it, I'm sure they'll find out," I finished. But I could see the two men were not convinced. Frankly, neither was I.

"Anyway, it seems Melinda wanted a graveside service, just close family," said Helen. "But the son will be sitting *shiva* tomorrow. He's not religious and is just doing one night. He gave me his address," she noted, raising the scrap of paper. "It's in Huntington. You and I should go, Joe."

"Yes, of course," my man answered.

I looked at him and said, "I'll go with you. We're an official couple now, after all. You know, I'm certainly no expert on this stuff, but I was a psych major, and we had quite a few lectures here and there on suicide. As I'm sure you did too, in medical school, Joe. What I learned was frequently there are no outward signs preceding such an event. Relatives and friends will often say they had no idea the person was considering suicide. It comes as a great shock. You really don't know what was going on in her life that might have driven her to this. Maybe the son can shed light on that. But now, I have an embarrassing question to ask—what's this *shiva* thing?"

Joe smiled. "It's like a wake. For a week or so, after a death, the immediate family sits in their homes and receives guests. Relatives and friends come to pay their respects, provide food, and tell stories of the departed. It's meant to soothe the grief of the immediate family members, having company during this early time of mourning. Usually, the immediate family will sit on small boxes. I forget the significance. Helen?"

"Actually, you're supposed to sit close to the ground," the woman began, "so short boxes have become traditional. It's a symbol, showing the humbleness, sorrow, and pain of the griever being brought 'low' by the death of the loved one. It's supposed to be for a week, but, depending upon how religious the family is, it can be one or a just a few days. Anyway, we should be done at the office by five tomorrow, and he's sitting from seven to ten, so Sammy, why don't you and Angelica meet Joe and me at the office. I'll bring some cold cuts; we can have a quick bite, and then head off for Huntington. Okay?"

We all nodded in agreement and slowly headed for the door. My attempt at an explanation seemed to be a dud, for I could hear *Papà* mumbling and could make out words like "impossible" and "full of life" and Joe too just shook his head, repeating "no way," over and over.

"I'm sure the NYPD will figure out if there's anything untoward going on here," Jane said as we parted. I respected Jane greatly, as a woman, mother, and detective. But as alluded to earlier, I had my doubts concerning her belief in a thorough investigation. I guess I'd dealt with too many members of the Philadelphia police department, many on Don Fortuna's payroll, to whom getting to the truth was often way down on their list of priorities. Exhibit A— the quick, official determination regarding the Don's demise.

I hoped the local detectives in the NYPD who'd be investigating this death would be methodical, for *Papà* and Joe's sake. But, my *Spidey-Sense,* the ever-present Fortuna pessimism was again taking hold. Joe and *Papà* seemed ready to mount a crusade to get at what they believed was the authentic truth—something—anything, other than suicide. Yes, for the two most important men in my life, their most fervent wish, it seemed, was for this truth to emerge.

As we walked to the car, I suddenly shivered, feeling very cold. I interlocked my arm with my man's and squeezed tightly. And I was reminded of that ancient proverb, probably from Confucius, or Aesop—

Be careful what you wish for...

Chapter 22

Thursday, January 9
Huntington, NY
7:10 PM

The door to Aaron Queen's home had been left ajar to accommodate guests, so Joe, Helen, *Papà* and I entered. We found the son in the living room, sitting on one of those small wooden boxes. When he saw us enter, the man rose. There were currently only two other couples present.

Queen seemed to be in his mid-forties. He was slightly balding, and, it appeared, had inherited his mother's bubbly personality. He greeted us, not knowing who we were, with a verve belying the occasion. I assumed this was his way of coping. On the other end of the spectrum, I, on my *Mamma's* passing, had not been in the mood for *any* companionship, and my funereal mood lasted weeks.

Joe made the introductions.

"Mr. Queen, I'm Dr. Peck. This is my fiancé Angelica, my office manager Helen and our and your mother's friend, Sammy Vivino. We're so sorry for your loss." And though Joe certainly was sorry, more so than the son probably appreciated, I still found the words, rote spoken by almost every mourner in the history of civilization, banally routine. Yeah, I'm just a joy to be around on all occasions, right? Hope Joe knows what he's getting into with all my moods and often contrary opinions. But I put on my game face, or at least what I assumed was a proper mien for a respectful mourner, and the son thanked us all for coming.

"Yes, Doctor Peck. I'm sorry I didn't get back to you and," he turned to Helen, "answer your voicemails until late last night. It was obviously all a shock, and then came the added tasks of dealing with the police, the medical examiner, identifying mom's body... and then, the funeral arrangements."

"Please, Mr. Queen. There's no need to apologize." Joe quickly said. "You had a lot thrown at you all at once. We're grateful you got back early enough so we could come and pay our respects. Except for Angelica, we all knew and loved your mother. I've told them and I'll tell you—she was my favorite patient, and I was really looking forward to helping her regain her sight. Thought she was, too, which is why I find this all so inexplicable."

The son nodded. "You and me, both, Doctor." Then he turned to *Papà*. "So, you're Sammy. My mother spoke of you often. You'll be happy to know you were often a great comfort to her,"—*that's a way of putting it,* I thought—"and she always spoke highly of your friendship, especially during those first dark months of the whole Madoff business. As I learned from her suicide note, that son-of-a-bitch is partially responsible for her death. He should burn in Hell!"

Sammy nodded. "Thank you for saying so, Mr. Queen. I was very fond of your mother. I just can't believe she would have taken her life. You say she explained it in a note?"

I was surprised. Though certainly not an expert on police procedure, I would have thought the note would remain in evidence until the investigation was... *oh shit.*

Joe was way ahead of me. "Are you saying the police are done with their investigation? It's just only forty-eight hours or so."

"Didn't even take *that* long," the man ruefully explained. "Before they even called me, they had examined the apartment and found the note. I was called early Wednesday morning, about five, and went to identify her. By the afternoon, they had already made their determination and allowed me to enter the apartment. Not wanting to spend a lot of time there, I just gathered mom's valuables—I didn't want to take chances of anyone, knowing it would be empty, breaking in to steal things. Also took her laptop, since she did her banking on it, and there were personal account numbers and passwords I didn't want to fall into anyone's hands. Then I left and have no intention of going back until it's sold. Afraid there'll be some rotten food to discard by then.

"Afterward, I arranged with the cemetery for the graveside service and finally checked my voicemails. Which is when I was reminded of the surgery." He stopped for a moment, probably not knowing what to say. Some other guests entered, and he nodded their way.

Joe entered detective mode. "You say, Mr. Queen, you feel the Madoff scandal had something to do with this. Why?"

The man went into his jacket pocket and withdrew a printed sheet of paper. "This is a copy of mom's note. The original has to stay with the police. I've got to say hello to my aunt and uncle over there, but here," he passed the paper to Joe, "you can read it for yourself. I'll be back shortly." And with that, he left to greet the new arrivals.

The four of us took chairs and moved them so we could surround Joe and read along with him as he positioned the letter on his lap. It was obviously computer printed (unless the woman had a typewriter, which was doubtful) and about half a page, double-spaced. It read:

January 7, 2020

To my friends and family:

Please forgive me, but I cannot continue on. I've tried, God knows I've tried, but the shame and the constant reminders of my poor financial state have become too much to handle. I just barely make my maintenance payments each month and have had to forgo the simple but expensive pleasures in life that have always brought me joy. That bastard Madoff has stolen everything from me-my money and my self-esteem, to name two. When the newspapers listed my name among those he had swindled, that began my downward spiral. Yes, though many would come to me in the Mall and commiserate, I knew, behind my back, they were laughing at me. 'The Queen of QueensGate,' brought low and swindled, despite her acumen, taken in by that vile bastard. I'm sure they noticed, over the years, how my apparel, reduced time away on vacation and even what I ordered at the restaurant, all pointed to someone who could no longer afford to live the life she'd become accustomed to. I dealt with it for a long time, but the shame has become too great, especially since I now fear, maybe, having to move. The looks of pity that would come my way, being forced to move to smaller and cheaper quarters, would be unbearable. The shame of having to give up my cherished apartment is not something I can live with. No, it's much too much.

So, I've decided to leave this life and I might as well do it in spectacular fashion, fitting for a queen. I've needed extra courage, though, so I've added a good many Valium pills to my wine bottle and I can already feel them taking effect. It won't be long now. So, I'd better make my way to the balcony. I'm sorry I've let you all down, but you'll be happier not having to provide the fake smiles and sympathies. I am going to a better place.

Melinda-Ann

Papa was first to speak. "I never knew she felt that way. With me, she even joked about that *figlio di puttana,* Madoff. I noticed she hadn't traveled as much these last years, and maybe re-wore the same clothing now and then, but put it off to age, forgetfulness. Nothing more. Until I made my decision to say *arrivederci* to my *Harem,* I noticed no such depression." He paused. Then, in a much softer tone added, "She fooled me into thinking she had managed to put it all behind her." And then he stopped speaking, and put his face in his hands, his elbows on his thighs. Helen put her arm around him.

183

I looked at Joe, who was still staring at the letter. "Are you convinced, Joe?" I asked, hoping to put this sad chapter to bed.

"I guess," he said. "Still hard to believe, and there's something about this letter that just isn't right. She didn't even mention her son. There's more, but I can't quite put my finger on it."

I was fearing the woman's death was becoming somewhat of an obsession with my man and took his hand. "*Mi amore,*" I began. "The woman was very depressed. From what you've told me, she was a very proud person, enjoying life to the fullest. Then this bastard comes along and not only steals her money, but, in a way, steals her self-respect and esteem among her neighbors and peers. You and I might shrug these things off. But obviously, she couldn't. Why did she wait until the night before surgery? Who knows? But it certainly seems her mental state was poor. Now, we see the result."

Joe nodded and looked at me. "I guess you're right, Angie. It's just," he looked again at the note, "It's just..." Joe reached into his pocket and removed his phone. Before I could say what he was about to do seemed inappropriate at this wake, er *shiva*, he quickly snapped a photo of the letter and replaced the phone.

"Just want to get a look at it again tomorrow. When my mind is fresh, that's all. Don't worry, I'm not becoming obsessed. We can..."

Mr. Queen had left his latest visitors and rejoined our group. Joe returned the note and the son nodded. "So you can see," he began, "it seems she was very depressed. It's funny, because just lately she had asked my help in a little "research project," as she called it. Using my newspaper's resources to investigate some suspected shady doings at QueensGate. She even said there might be a big story in it for me. But Tuesday morning, when I called to confirm her surgery schedule—I was going to pick her up after the operation—she mentioned she was incorrect, and there didn't seem to be any funny business going on, after all. Who knows, that, in and of itself, might have been enough of a disappointment to be

184

the last straw." He sighed. "And she really enjoyed living at the Towers so, I guess, the thought of possibly losing her apartment was also just too much."

"Yeah," Sammy added. "She loved the Towers. Joe and Angelica, in fact, are considering moving there soon."

Queen's brows raised. "Really? Well, if you don't mind waiting a month—I figure that's how long it will take to deal with all her affairs—I'm going to put the apartment on the market. Not looking to make a killing, just a fair price. If you want, I'll give Samantha Tate, the agent, your name and number and tell her to call you right away when I do. I'll let you have the first crack at it. I think it would make Mom happy to know her place didn't go to strangers. That it did, in fact, go to someone she was quite fond of."

I looked at Joe, smiled, and nodded. He did the same.

"Yes, Mr. Queen. Let me write down my info. I think we would indeed be interested. A month is fine. There's no great hurry." Joe took one of his business cards and wrote his cell number on the back. He handed it to the son, they shook hands, and the man excused himself to greet others.

We stayed in the house for another thirty minutes or so, then said our goodbyes and left. It was a sad night, but I hoped, at least, with the note and the promise of an apartment, Joe could move on. And he seemed to have done so. We returned home, watched some TV and made slow, tender love. Hopefully, our lives would now continue forward, and suspicious thoughts of Melinda Anne Queen's death would fade from Joe's and *Papà's* imagination.

And, it seemed, they did. That photo Joe took of the note was forgotten and we talked no further about the woman except once or twice over the next month as we awaited the realtor's call. Each time she *was* mentioned, it was only in the context of buying her apartment, not regarding the circumstances of her death. I was happy. After all, I was engaged to the love of my life, and was surrounded by good friends. There was also the hope of moving into a home of my own, close to my father. I even started thinking about what to do with the rest of my life.

I enjoyed planning for the future.

I didn't think of it then, but in retrospect, I'm reminded of one of Morris's favorite quotes. It's an old Yiddish adage. You might have heard Joe mention it before—

Man plans... and God laughs.

Chapter 23

Monday, February 10—One Month Later
Floral Park
9:10 AM

Joe and I entered apartment 30Z. He was called by the agent, Samantha Tate, the previous Friday and notified Melinda-Ann's apartment was now up for sale. She was instructed to give him and his fiancé—I love saying that word!—the first look. We agreed to meet this morning.

It had been a little over four weeks since her death, but much had occurred in the lives of the individuals who were parts of Joe's and my world—and the world at large.

The World Health Organization had declared on January 12 that this new virus, COVID-19, was now a global health emergency. It was only a matter of time until the US would be affected, and plans were already being discussed to shut down the country to slow the inevitable spread. For Joe and me, the most troubling rumor was gatherings of more than a few people might be banned within a month or two, thus making a wedding reception problematic. There were also rumors of airplane travel bans and restrictions on car, train and bus transportation between states. That would make Tony, Linda and Morris unable to attend any celebration for the foreseeable future. And there it was, that word—*foreseeable*. For if history tells us anything, once Draconian measures are initiated, it's anyone's guess as to when they'd be lifted. Our government was talking about simply shutting the country down for a week or two, just to *flatten the curve*—yeah, right.

Anyway, because of all this, and the fact both Joe and I were convinced the other was "the one," we decided not to wait any longer—and marry on Sunday, March 1.

Once the date was set, Anna went into overdrive. She and I decided upon a wedding dress very similar to the one Linda had worn. Anna arranged fittings with a seamstress in Roslyn (for me and all concerned parties), as well as at her Palm Beach contact for Linda. No one doubted the dresses, caterer, photographer, and string quartet would be ready in time. When you're as rich as the Franklins, not only does money talk—it shouts. And when finances are not a concern, it's amazing the speed at which tasks can be accomplished—unless, of course, you're dealing with government contractors. There, the opposite is usually the rule.

I had spoken to Julie occasionally since I returned and was always cheered to hear her voice. Unfortunately, there was a new owner of the 7-Eleven—and he was a prick. An understaffed prick. He refused to let my friend take a few extra days off to travel to New York for my wedding and, since she needed the job, antagonizing the new boss was not an option. Julie was also using all her free time to search other towns for places to live and work, since her incarcerated ex-boyfriend's possible release date was now only four months away. I was happy to hear that, at least, she had decided to escape from both Henderson and him. But I was sad she'd not be here to join and take part in (she would have been maid of honor) the celebration. But I understood. I'd e-mail her lots of photos and Joe and I were discussing traveling out west for the honeymoon, COVID permitting. Any such trip would include a stop to visit my friend.

Marlene Fell had begun her treatments, but her health was deteriorating faster than expected. She had to be admitted to the hospital on two occasions. One admission was for infection. The other was for a procedure to insert a tube into her stomach for feedings—the pain of swallowing had gotten too severe, and she was losing weight rapidly. Just thinking about the poor woman's life made me cry, but I could tell Anna and Jane's decision had, at least, brought her some peace. She knew her little girl would be taken good care of and I, too, vowed to be as much a friend to Khaleesi as possible. More than just a friend, in fact.

All three women, Marlene, Anna, and Jane agreed the young child should spend the weekends and off-days from school at the Franklin's home. It would make the final transition easier. Both girls insisted they sleep in Felicity's room and a bed was moved in. Jane and Anna were amazed their daughter, so territorial, so demanding of the privacy of her bedroom, had not only allowed it but was the one who suggested the two girls share the older one's living quarters. Touchingly, more often than not, when the women entered the room in the morning to wake them, they'd find Khaleesi curled up next to Felicity in the latter's bed, despite having first retired separately to opposite sides of the room.

On the Saturday after the girls had first met, Felicity, as promised, spoke to her psychiatrist about Jonathan Franklin's abuse. That night, she and her mothers sat in the living room, crying, hugging, and kissing as the child emptied her soul, heartbreakingly describing what she had endured at the hands of her father.

While many more months of therapy, both individually and as a family group, would be necessary, Felicity and her parents were now well on the road to healing. As far as the kidnapping, the doctor believed the girl had rebounded well, and it was not seen as a reason for concern. He gave his blessing to Maverick's additional training and felt when Khaleesi was finally fully integrated into the Franklin household, she too would benefit from therapy of her own. Actually, given the brief interval of actual abuse, much of her therapy, the doctor believed, would be grief counseling once Marlene had succumbed. The women agreed.

Another unfortunate turn of events concerned Marta. Her father, living in Colombia, had recently been diagnosed with cancer and given his own six-month death sentence. He refused to leave his home, so the woman felt she needed to be there for him and, via Franklin's private jet, had flown down February 1. Anna and Jane understood and noted Marta's job, of course, would be waiting for her when she returned. Any monies needed for funeral related or any other expenses, she'd just have to ask of the ladies, and it would be hers. In the interim, Anna had taken over the extra household duties. They had thought of temporary help, but their sense of trust in strangers, despite references, had diminished greatly since the kidnapping.

I had spent the Monday after my birthday with Felicity and Maverick, training the dog to accept the girl's attack command. Anna had purchased male and female mannequins, just as I'd done in Henderson. I was surprised with how little time it took. On the first try, after Felicity pointed and gave the command, Maverick looked at me for confirmation. Once given, he performed as expected. After that, all the child's orders were treated as coming from me. Their bond was complete.

Felicity was very proud of her accomplishments, and I was so happy to have been helpful in building the girl's self-confidence. These achievements had imbued in her a sense of self-worth and responsibility severely lacking, all traced back, no doubt, to her father's abuse. Yes, I was proud of her. But even so, we needed to have "the talk."

We were eating mint-chip ice-cream, a wide grin spreading across her face.

"Okay," I began. "I want to congratulate you. You've done a great job and showed much determination in getting Maverick to respond to you. I'm proud of you. But,"—*best to learn early, sweetie, there's always a 'but'*—"I want you to wipe that silly grin off your face!"

The girl was taken aback and quickly complied. I felt like a heel. "You now have great power at your command. A deadly weapon, as lethal as any gun. Yet as Spider Man says, 'With great power—'"

"'Comes great responsibility,' yeah, I know."

190

"Well, don't let the fact that those words come from a comic book hero make you think they're a joke. They're not! Maverick is a pet, first and foremost. But just like an empty gun, which can become lethal when loaded and fired, so can he. And just like that gun, the one who uses the weapon will be called upon to explain. If the explanation is not satisfactory, that person is in *big* trouble. You may think because you're a kid, there's little that can be done to you. Don't count on it! And there's a *lot* that could, and *will* be done against your parents and Maverick, if you ever use him inappropriately. The only time, the *only* time that command should be used is if you or anyone with you is in mortal danger. It can't be because you're pissed at someone, or they say something mean to you or your parents or Khaleesi. You want to punch them out, fine by me. I'll even teach you how to kick ass with the best of them. But Maverick stays out of it. Because, once you unleash him, not only can he be taken away from us... he'll be destroyed. Killed! That's the law. There's nothing me or *Officer* Jane can do about it. You understand?"

Felicity obviously had not considered this because her eyes widened and, for a rare moment, she was speechless. Finally, she nodded.

Not good enough.

"I have to *hear* it from you!" I added harshly. "You *must* tell me you understand. I would never forgive myself if you or your parents got in trouble. And, I *can't–lose–my–dog!*"

Now tears started flowing from the child. She had never heard me talk to her this way. So sternly. I was feeling terribly guilty. After all, this had already been a very emotional week, starting with Felicity and her parents' conversations. Maverick had become more than a pet to her. He was a loving companion, almost as much as her parents, Khaleesi and me. But I would be remiss if I hadn't reminded her of her responsibilities.

"I promise, Angelica," she began, through sobs. "I don't want anything to happen to Maverick." The dog, laying on the couch, now hearing the child cry, rose and approached, whining. Felicity patted his head and kissed him on his snout. "Don't worry, boy." She looked at me. "Don't worry, Angelica. I would never do anything to hurt your dog." I believed her. I took the girl in my arms, and she continued to sob.

"I believe you, honey. I believe you. Remember, this is between us. Maybe we'll consider adding Khaleesi when she's older. As smart as she is, she's still too young to take on this responsibility. Okay?"

The child, her head still pressed against my breast, nodded once again. Then, after a few moments, we separated and returned to our seats.

Finally, to top off this month-long summary, a few nights ago Khaleesi was sleeping over for a weekend and she, Felicity, Maverick and I were all sitting on the older girl's bed, shooting the breeze. Not knowing I already knew much about them, they each began to relate the facts concerning their fathers. Then, once done, the younger girl said, "So now you know *our* deepest secrets, Angelica. But Felicity and I have been talking and, you know, we don't really know much about *you*. You sort of just appeared seven months ago, out of nowhere, to save Felicity's life." Yes, the older girl had asked and received her parents' (and my) permission to tell the younger about what had occurred. Khal was happy to be sworn to secrecy to never relate the tale to anyone. "Where did you grow up? Where is your mother?" They knew *Uncle Sammy*, as they now both called him, was my father.

They continued asking questions, so I decided to open up, somewhat, with an abridged story of my life. I didn't go into any specific details about my work, but they understood what it meant to be a paid killer—and I made it clear what a terrible stain that had placed upon my soul. I spoke of Don Fortuna and how he forced the assassin's life upon me, *Mamma*, and how *Papà* was discovered. Nothing was mentioned regarding my dad's involvement in the deaths of both girls' fathers. Felicity had had a front-row seat to the duel with *Il Fucile* so no need to repeat *that* harrowing adventure. I ended with *Il Boa*, WITSEC, Henderson and Julie.

When I was done, I could see the open-jawed amazement on their faces. "What I've just told you, if repeated to strangers, even in part, could lead to serious consequences for me. There are some who, if they discovered I was alive, would hunt me down and try to kill me. By telling you these confidences, I have entrusted you with my life. Do you understand?" Both girls nodded as one. Felicity then added, "Don't worry, Angelica. I would die before giving up your secrets."

"Me too!" added Khaleesi. And I believed them.

"Well, hopefully it won't come to that." I then gently stroked each child at their neck. "Now we have all shared our secrets, as only sisters do. So I guess that makes us *all* sisters, right?" The two nodded vigorously. I brought our heads together, kissed them both on the foreheads, and we, sensing each other's thoughts, whispered as one—

"Sisters."

Chapter 24

The first aspect of the apartment Angelica noticed was the view of Manhattan from the living room window. Almost exactly like her father's. However, her exhilaration was tempered somewhat when she realized the window opened to the balcony from where Melinda-Ann had jumped. Also, sadly noted, were the many plants, now wilted from neglect.

Joe was familiar with the setups of most apartments due to his father having lived at The Towers for many years, as had his relatively new friend Sammy. So as Samantha guided Angelica about, showing the bathrooms and bedrooms, Joe wandered off to the kitchen. One thing had been made clear to him during the little time they had lived together; if he and Angelica intended to not starve to death, the couple would either be ordering out a lot or Joe would do most of the cooking. Despite being the Italian daughter of an Italian mother, Angelica's many talents did not extend to culinary excellence. With tutors such as *Il Pugnale* and others, *Una Grande Cuoca* wasn't, unfortunately, among them. But it turns out, Joe loved to cook! *How lucky can a girl get?* she had thought when first learning that delicious fact. He considered himself a bit of a gourmet and the two decided Angelica would set things up and clean things away—and Joe would take care of everything in between.

So it wasn't a surprise the man found his way to the kitchen. He pleasantly noted the first-rate, Sub-Zero side-by-side refrigerator-freezer combo. He opened the doors to find it well stocked, though mold had already formed on the cheeses and the vegetables had rotted.

Joe then noticed a standard, built in, original-equipment microwave. He didn't expect more here, remembering Melinda-Anne's fear of invisible radiation. There were plenty of shelves and cabinets and what appeared to be a very modern electric stove. *Nice kitchen*, he thought and then, hearing Angelica and the agent approach, he started walking to meet them at the front door—

And froze.

Looking back at this moment, Joe realized surgeons and detectives have one aspect of their professions in common— they're both trained to carefully observe. For cops—objects seemingly out of place, how victims fell, the splatter pattern of blood, etc. For the eye surgeon—the newly seen iris freckle that might be cancerous, the slightly drooping eyelid indicative of a brain tumor, or a slight tilt of the head pointing to an eye muscle problem. Little things that would go unnoticed by the layman. So, it was not surprising when, in passing, he noted the blinking COMPLETE on the oven's display. It was out of place here, now. The apartment and all it contained, up until a few moments ago, had been dead for a month. Even the food and the plants had rotted away.

Yet, the oven had been alive! Waiting... pleading to be opened— its flashing COMPLETE seeming, to Joe, as desperate as a semaphore blinking an SOS from a stricken vessel at sea.

And in a millisecond, the hairs on his neck stood erect as the man contemplated just what that pleading prompt implied.

———————————

The apartment was a dream. Not as spacious as *Papà's* penthouse, but not far off, either. The view was the same: magnificent. The bathrooms were bathrooms and the bedrooms, bedrooms. I know, I won't be getting a job writing real estate copy any time soon. What I mean to say is those rooms were standard fare—more than sufficient. As a whole, the apartment was perfect and, since Joe had already told me if I liked it, he'd put in a bid, I was looking forward to telling him my approval.

And then I saw him.

Staring at the oven.

The look on his face was a cross between an inquisitive child and a terrified adult. I found it very disconcerting.

"What is it, *amore?*" I tentatively asked.

Joe continued to stare. I was about to ask again, but he bent from his knees and lowered the oven door.

The cold look that had been on his face turned to ice. He quickly stood and brushed past me. "Where's the master bedroom?" he asked Tate. She pointed the way and he hurried in that direction.

I was about to follow, but the open oven door beckoned me. I bent down and looked in, saw the object and withdrew it.

A potato? Are you fucking kidding me? That's what's got him so rattled?

I quickly left the kitchen to join Joe in the master bedroom. I saw him examining a fancy, digital radio/alarm-clock on the end table next to the queen (of course), sized bed. "Finally," he said, finding the switch to set the alarm. He moved it from OFF to SET and 5:00 AM blinked on and off on the display. After a few seconds, watching the LED dance between brightly lit and dark, he turned the switch back to OFF and sat on the edge of the bed, legs on the floor. I joined him.

"Joe, you're frightening me. What's wrong?" My love turned to me and was about to speak, when a thought suddenly rose from his subconscious, buried deep for a month. "Shit, of course!" Joe pulled his phone from his jacket pocket, and with a few strokes, was in the photo library, finding the picture he'd taken of Melinda-Ann's suicide note. He read it once more, then handed it to me, a look of determination on his face like I hadn't seen before.

"Take a look at that. Read it and tell me what you find wrong there."

I took the phone and read through the short note. Now I was really getting alarmed because I felt he might be losing it, seeing things that weren't there. But I had to answer truthfully.

"I'm sorry, Joe, but I see nothing wrong." I waited. And of all the possible replies I anticipated, the one I received was totally unexpected.

"Yes, exactly! There's *nothing* wrong with the letter. It's perfect!"

Now I was really confused, and it showed. Joe took my hands, but then noticed the agent at the door with her own perplexed look.

"Samantha, we'll take it. You can go back to your office and get in touch with Mr. Queen. No haggling. We'll give him what he wants."

The real estate agent forgot everything that had preceded this announcement and beamed. "Okay, I'll go right now. Just close the door on your way out. It'll lock behind you." And she quickly left, visions of a six percent commission dancing in her head like Christmas sugar plums.

Joe waited until he heard the door close. Then, "Look, Angelica. As I've said, Melinda was really looking forward to the surgery. She bitterly complained she couldn't see the TV—*or her computer screen.* She was being teased by friends for all the spelling and grammar mistakes she was making in emails because she probably couldn't see the keyboard well and certainly couldn't make out the dim, thin underlining of the spell and grammar checkers. Yet here she was, distraught—about to commit suicide, for fuck's sake!—her stomach full of Valium, writing this *suicide* note—AND DOESN'T MAKE ONE—FUCKING—ERROR! As you said, it's perfect. I doubt either of us could write such a note, under the same duress, drugged up, knowing we were minutes from our deaths, and not make a whole shitload of spelling and grammar mistakes. Yet, she didn't. NOT—ONE."

I was seeing Joe's point. "And the stove?" I asked.

"Yes! Again, she's contemplating suicide, right? Yet, the night she kills herself, she's *still* following my pre-op instructions? *Still*

197

treating a stye which, if not dealt with, would mean postponing the surgery? Think about it. You're about to jump off a fucking balcony, for God's sake! Why care?"

It was clear Joe meant this as a rhetorical question because he immediately replied, "Because she *did* care. She *didn't* want the surgery to be postponed! She was to put a baked potato on the stye multiple times a day, and obviously, Melinda *was*, right up to the moment she," he made finger quotes, "*jumped*."

"But how do you know she didn't just put the potato in to eat?" I asked, playing devil's advocate but getting more and more convinced of Joe's suspicion.

"Because she hadn't eaten a potato in years! She was on the Atkins Diet. Potatoes are full of carbs and, as far as Atkins is concerned, strictly *verboten*. She told me herself, just the Monday before the surgery was to be."

"And the alarm clock?" I asked, though already pretty sure of its significance.

"Again, it's the night before the surgery. She told me she was going to set her alarm after dinner and switch it on upon retiring, checking again the wake-up time. So, just an hour or two before she decides to *end it all*, she goes and sets the alarm to wake her for surgery?! It's crazy. There's only one answer."

Silence. We both looked at each other, and, not unlike the Franklins, could sense what the other was thinking. The potato, the clock, the suicide note. Each, by itself, might be argued away. But together? No. In totality, there could be only one explanation.

And knowing my Joe and my *padre*, I realized their search for the truth wouldn't end until they'd found the one responsible for the following, now seemingly incontrovertible fact—

Melinda-Ann Queen, *The Queen of QueensGate*, had been murdered.

PAR III–Quests, Questions, and QueenSlayer

"To begin is the most important part of any quest,
and by far the most courageous."

~Plato

"I am just a child who has never grown up.
I still keep asking these 'how' and 'why' questions.
Occasionally I find an answer."

~Stephen Hawking

"Violence does, in truth, recoil upon the violent, and the schemer
falls into the pit which he digs for another."

~Sir Arthur Conan Doyle, 'The Adventure of the Speckled Band'

Chapter 25

Lake Success
8:45 PM

"Well, Joe, if you ever decide to quit medicine, you'd make a good cop."

Detective Jane Rieger-Franklin had just finished listening to my fiancé explain his theory regarding the murder of Melinda-Ann Queen. Yes, as far as I was concerned, this was a case of murder, so we might as well refer to it as such. Given my love of *Game of Thrones*, I also decided to refer to whomever had killed the woman as *The QueenSlayer*, an homage to the show's Jaime Lannister, whose *nom de guerre* was *KingSlayer*. So far, however, I had managed to keep that pop-culture characterization to myself. No need to be looked upon as too geeky to play with the adults.

Joe had called all interested parties after we'd left QueensGate and had arranged for this meeting of the minds. It would have been earlier, but *Papà* had a two-hour lesson with the aged rabbi of the *Beth Din* already scheduled for six.

Just saying those words makes me feel as if I've entered an alternate universe.

We sat in the Franklin's living room—me, Joe, *Papà*, Helen, Jane, Anna and, yes, Felicity. She normally would have been told to go to bed, but by now we knew she'd just saunter on down and stealthily listen in, anyway; might as well let her stay. Ever since the Franklin family had discussed the girl's ordeal among themselves and began working on the healing process—at home and with the psychiatrist—they had become closer. Much closer. The women now treated the child as worthy of an adult's respect—not to be dismissed because of age. It was wonderful to watch. Anyway, they, and we, all knew she had a keen mind and, as has been said before, "out of the mouths of babes..."

Joe started by recounting what had occurred at the *shiva*. Then he related the events of this morning. It took about thirty minutes.

"So, you convinced?" He was looking directly at Jane as he finished his presentation.

The detective smiled. "From a personal standpoint, absolutely. But from a legal one, we're going to need, you know, *actual* evidence. And suspects. Right now, we have neither."

One person who didn't need convincing was my *padre,* who now rose, unable to contain his fury.

"There is *no* way we're going to let whoever did this get away with it! This woman did not deserve to die, and we must begin, I think in the olden days it was called, a 'quest.' Like that Don Quixote guy." We were all amazed the high-school dropout knew of the fictional character, but he later told me he'd seen, and enjoyed *Man of La Mancha* on Netflix. "Yes, we have to go on a quest for truth—and vengeance!" He quickly glanced at Helen. "I don't mean vengeance as in an *eye-for-an-eye,* my dear. I mean to find the *bastardo* and bring him to justice." He turned back to the detective. "Jane, you have to go to the police and tell them what we've got." He sat, rejoining Helen. I'm sure he was trying to reiterate for the woman his move away from "The Dark Side." Yes, those words of explanation he had added were, I'm sure, mostly to placate her. I was positive if, during his *quest,* the murderer wound up dead, *Papà* would not be disappointed. And, I must say, neither would I. I had seen too many murderers slip through the fingers of the justice system during my time working for Don Fortuna. Just look at me— Angelica Foster, née Fortuna.

201

Helen took his hand and added, "Well, Sammy, that's what we all want. But The New York police have already decided it was suicide. Unless I'm mistaken, Jane, it's going to take more than just theories to get them to re-open the case. I watch lots of *Law and Order* TV shows."

God save us from amateur sleuths, Jane thought. But in this case, the woman was correct, and the detective nodded. "You're more right than you know, Helen. I have absolutely no jurisdiction there. I can go to the investigating detectives and present our findings,"—she purposely didn't say "evidence,"—"but I can tell you there's little a detective appreciates less than another cop putting her nose into his business; especially in a case he's already closed. I know *I'd* be annoyed. The truth is, unless we can come up with something a bit more concrete, going to the NYPD is a waste of time. Let's not forget, I *do* have a day job. My superiors will not take kindly to my spending office time on a case in a different jurisdiction. Whatever I do will have to be mostly after hours."

"Well," Felicity chirped in, "then let's go *find* something!"

Now it was Anna's time to smile. "Okay, Nancy Drew, just how do you suggest we do that?"

The child grinned. "Glad you asked, Watson." Anna scowled. "I mean, Mommy Watson. Anyway, Joe, you said the son mentioned Melinda-Ann—and from now on I'm just going to say Melinda, okay? Name's much too long—told him she was looking into fishy things going on at that old-age-home you're about to move into." Now it was Joe's turn to scowl. "Unfortunately, it seems she didn't really clue him in with any details. But doesn't it strike anyone as suspicious that while doing the investigation, she winds up murdered?"

I decided it was time for me to chime in. I was feeling left out. "Yes, Felicity, but Melinda told her son she was wrong, there was nothing to her suspicions." But as soon as the words were out of my mouth, I knew what the response would correctly be.

"Well, there you go! She's investigating something suspicious, someone gets to her, puts on the pressure, maybe threatens her and so she suddenly says, 'never mind.' Then BANG, she's taken out." *Taken out? Like Helen, the kid's been watching too many crime shows.* "Now, I don't know yet how to connect the dots. I'm not a *detective* after all," she nodded toward Jane, "but if you ask me, we find out more about what Melinda was investigating and we're closer to the killer. No?"

Silence. We all just stared at each other, and at Felicity. Joe finally broke the quiet.

"You know, kid. I can't believe I used to fear your visits to my office. I won't repeat how I used to refer to you."

The child smiled. "I can imagine, especially since my first and last initial begins with an F."

My God, this girl has quite the insight. Joe had told me how he dreaded the girl's visits. He called her 'Felicity... Fucking... Franklin.' Amazing how much she, he and everyone else had changed in so short a time. My lover was about to show just *how* much.

First, he laughed. "Yeah, well... I apologize. You are really something else." And then Joe approached the girl, reached out... and they hugged. I think it was the very first time they had done so, and the mothers were visibly touched. As was the child. They separated, and Joe kissed her on the forehead.

My father, though enjoying the scene, was getting inpatient. "So, young Sherlock, any idea where we go next?" It indicated *Papà's* thirst for vengeance that he considered asking a mere child for her opinion, her intelligence notwithstanding. I'm sure his thoughts on the matter were influenced by the fact he himself had killed his first man, his own abusive father, at the tender age of twelve. So, he was willing to listen to her, to anyone, in order to succeed with his quest.

Felicity's smile slowly disappeared. It was clear she was stumped. "I'm going to go call Khaleesi, see what she thinks!" She jumped up and rushed out of the room, up the stairs, before anyone could say anything to dissuade her. *Papà* looked exasperated.

203

"*Mio Dio!*" he cried. Then, turning to Jane. "And you, detective? Any ideas?" The woman frowned and shook her head. "Well," my father continued, "neither do I. We need to think... hard. Felicity has come up with a good idea, the only idea, at least for the moment—unless, of course, *Khaleesi* solves the case!" We all got a slightly embarrassed chuckle out of that one. "So," he continued, "where do we go from here?"

Joe hadn't weighed in yet since his embrace of the child. He'd been thinking. And remembering. Now it was his turn.

"Sammy, it's going to take some luck... but I think I've figured out where we can start looking."

Chapter 26

"Thank you for seeing us, Mr. Queen."

Joe, *Papà* and I sat in the man's living room. Queen often worked from home, so meeting him mid-afternoon was not a problem. Joe had moved his afternoon patients to the morning, so he was beat; but, having worked over one-hundred-hour weeks during his internship, he, as most doctors trained "in the days of the giants," as he called them, was used to work-exhaustion. And just like back then, when he shrugged away the fatigue for an emergency, he now ignored his tiredness for the *quest*.

"No problem, Doctor. In fact, now that you've told me your suspicions, I want to do anything I can to help you and the detective friend of yours you mentioned on the phone. If you all believe Mom was murdered, I want to find out *who* and *why*. So, what can I do?"

"Well," began Joe, "you mentioned Melinda had asked you for some information about QueensGate, and she might have a juicy story for you to write about. Can you elaborate?"

The man sighed. "Unfortunately, I don't have much. She wanted me to investigate the ownership of the contractor that has a business in the building's basement. Madison Avenue, or Park Avenue Remodeling... something like that. It turned out it's owned by another business that's finally owned by a third in Boston whose CEO is the cousin of the Building Manager at QGT. Having dug a little deeper, I found whenever work was done, about 20% extra was tacked on to the price and disappeared into the morass that is

205

the company books of all concerned. Graft, yes, but nothing spectacular in and of itself. I'm sure this sort of thing goes on at all such large co-ops and condos. Business as usual, I would think."

"That's all?" *Papà* asked in a dejected tone.

"Yeah, I'm afraid so. She did mention to me that this was just the 'tip of the iceberg.' She was preparing a *blockbuster* report but warned me there still were many a *T* to cross and *I* to dot, and it was possible the house of cards might come crashing down. I hoped for the best. Then, as I mentioned at the *shiva*, she informed me that the house had indeed tumbled and there was no Pulitzer Prize on my horizon. It's strange, but in a way, Mom actually sounded happy, it seemed, to find her initial suspicions proved wrong. I guess, given how much she loved QueensGate, she preferred there be as little as possible to mar its reputation. Though, why she would investigate in the first place, instead of letting sleeping dogs lie, is beyond me. Doesn't make sense."

I could see Joe thinking, his eyes darting about as if he were visualizing characters moving to-and-fro on a stage. Then, finally, "No, it doesn't. But, as you said, she told you she was preparing a report. I would expect she'd write it down, probably type it into her computer. Maybe there's a file on her laptop that might give us some information." Joe now seemed to hold his breath. I certainly was holding mine. There were two possible responses from Queen. One, the most disastrous, would be he had wiped and discarded the laptop—thrown it into some dumpster somewhere, now crushed and useless. The other would be it was still in his possession. That was where our hopes lived.

Thankfully, he answered, "Sure, give me a second and I'll get it. I haven't gone through all her files yet. I've been concentrating on the Excel ones in which she had all her investment and banking information. There are many accounts. Though, because of that Madoff bastard, not much is left in any of them. I could see why a major depression might have set in." He rose and walked out to retrieve the computer. The three of us were silent, each in his/her

206

own way, praying the laptop would prove useful. At least it was now clear that the man had access—whatever password his mother might have used was known to him.

Mr. Queen returned within a minute and placed the laptop on the coffee table around which we sat. "My mother used her fingerprint as her log-in preference, but had a password as a backup, just in case, like now, she needed me to get into the computer and she wasn't around, say, sick in the hospital. The password is *exclamation point, Aaron*—that's my name, capital A—*exclamation point.*" For a moment, the man seemed to choke up, noting his mother had included his name in her secret password. Such a small thing, yet so telling it could bring on such emotion. He composed himself and typed in the characters. The screen came to life, and I asked the man if I could have a look. Of the three who sat before him, I was the most computer savvy, Joe second, and *Papà,* well to call him a *dinosaur* when it came to computers would be an insult to T-Rex and his pals. Once, mentioning Facebook, *Papà* thought I had meant a police mug-shot album.

The laptop turned out to be a MacBook, which was a plus since it was with them I had the most experience. However, I could navigate a Windows machine if necessary. I checked the Finder and searched for all files with a .doc, .docx, .pdf or .txt extension, though, seeing Word in the Dock at the bottom of the page, it made the most sense to assume she'd used that ubiquitous program for her work. There were seven .docx files—none of the other types. I opened each one and found nothing but letters to various people and businesses. Then, I thought maybe she had hidden the file. I knew it could be done by a command entered in a Terminal window, but I doubted she would know how. Still, I needed to look.

I had forgotten how to unhide such files, so I had to Google the answer. Then, able to search all files, including hidden ones, I found no added Word, PDF or text files. Everyone's disappointment was palpable. "Hold on. Let's look at the Trash." I clicked on the Trash Can and it opened.

Empty. Nothing. *Nada.*

Papà let out a Sicilian curse I was unfamiliar with. Joe added a simple "Shit," to the discussion, but I, though disappointed, was intrigued.

"Let me explain something to you guys. The fact the Trash is totally empty tells me something. Whenever you delete a file, it goes into the Trash and sits there, easily recovered if desired. Normally, if I picked any computer at random and looked in the Trash, it would be chocked full of hundreds, maybe thousands of files. To totally empty the Trash requires the user to perform a discreet action. Actually, a series of clicks and affirmations you really want to get rid of all those deleted files, since once done, it cannot be undone. Or, and this is key, cannot be undone without the proper software. Anyway, the point I'm making is, Melinda, *or someone,* deleted all the trash in the Trash Can—something rarely done by most computer users. That means there was some file, now deleted, that *someone* felt needed extra obliteration. Someone who didn't know that, under the right circumstances, the file could be recovered."

I now had their attention. "Just what are these circumstances, Angie?" Joe asked. There was a hint of hope in his voice.

"One, you need someone who knows what they're doing and who has the right software. Two, from the time the file was deleted, we must hope no other file was written over the disc-space the deleted file occupied on the hard drive. Have you created any files on the computer since it's been in your hands, Mr. Queen?"

The man shook his head. "No, all I've done is look at those Excel files I mentioned. I haven't typed in a word except for the password."

Thank God, I thought. "Well then, we have a chance. The scenario I see is this. Somehow, the murderer got access to your mom's laptop and deleted some file or files she had created for her investigation. The killer probably didn't take the MacBook knowing it would be missed, especially by you, Mr. Queen. Also, since the bulky printer couldn't be easily removed, seeing it, minus a connected computer, would be very suspicious.

Anyway, after deletion, those files, along with all the others, were wiped from the Trash—permanently emptied. Now, if this person had the savvy, or the time, to overwrite the sections of the hard drive where these deleted files were stored, we're screwed. *But*, if not, and we can find someone incredibly skilled to look for these emptied, deleted files, we might be in business."

I looked at Joe, and there was a big smile on his face. He reached over and gave me a big kiss. Obviously, my man thought I had provided useful information. I also guessed he knew of such a skilled person. Then, "Mr. Queen, is it okay with you if I borrow the laptop for a few hours?"

The man hesitated. There were sensitive financial files on the disc drive, after all. But, if his mother were indeed murdered, he said, then he wanted "the bastard" brought to justice. So, he agreed, especially after his mother's trusted eye doctor told him to whom he would deliver the computer.

Joe picked up his phone and dialed. "Hi, Jane. It's Joe. Listen, you free at the moment?... Good. I'm coming over with Angie and Sammy and bringing Melinda's laptop. Are the *geeks* busy?... Okay, sorry. Forgot. Are the *boys* busy?" There was a pause as Jane must have gone down the hall to look and walk back.

About thirty seconds later, I heard a muffled sound from Joe's phone. He smiled.

"Perfect! Be there in forty—thirty if Angelica drives."

After Joe disconnected, I looked at him and smiled; no, smirked would be a better word. "You realize, of course, not only am I *going* to drive, but I'll be aiming for *twenty* minutes now, right?" I glanced at my watch.

Joe smiled right back. "I know, Angie. I know."

Chapter 27

Nassau County Police Headquarters
Mineola
3:58 PM

The Intel Group, known by many as the *Geek-Squad*, were three men—Tony, Thomas and Harold. Jane had also used the affectionate, but still somewhat derogatory phrase to describe them until seven months ago. But, after they had all risked their jobs to help save Felicity and Marta, they, as all the others involved in the operation, now occupied a warm spot in Anna's and Jane's hearts. So, as with Frankie, the use of disparaging names was discarded.

The ladies had rewarded each man with his own two-caret diamond, to be used as deemed fit. Tony, recently married, had used his for his bride's engagement ring. The others, as per Anna's suggestion, had placed theirs in safety deposit boxes to be presented when the time was right. For Thomas, that would be very soon— he was days away from popping the question to his girlfriend, a nurse he'd met at Felicity's tenth birthday party. Only Harold, the youngest, was still unattached, and the Franklins were always on the lookout for someone suitable for him.

We met Jane at her desk after the downstairs sergeant, alerted beforehand, let us pass. I had left Needle in the car, not knowing if we'd have to subject ourselves to a metal detector. Good move.

We walked the short distance to the office of *The Intel Group*. The door was open, and we entered.

The three men were, unusually, not peering at their computer monitors. Instead, they were just sitting and talking.

We listened for a few seconds and then Jane began with what seemed a very practiced, "Ahem!" Then, "Hi guys."

The three turned to the woman and Tony, the senior analyst, spoke for them all. "Oh hi, Jane. What's up?"

Jane closed the door. I saw a slight frown appear on Tony's face. The detective's move was probably never considered a particularly encouraging sign. "First guys, I'd like to introduce Angelica," she began, pointing at me. "You remember our little adventure seven months ago? Well, this is *the* Angelica, the one who took out the kidnapper with the shotgun. She's been away but has now rejoined us and I thought you should all meet."

I smiled and didn't wait for any of the group to approach me. I moved quickly to Tony. "Without you guys, we'd never have located those bastards and, for sure, Felicity and Marta would have been killed. Probably along with Jane and Anna if they had tried a ransom swap. Jane, and all involved in the rescue, have become family to me. I want to say to you," and then I looked at the others, "and to every one of you—I consider you all family as well." And then I kissed the newly married Tony on the mouth—wonder if he'll relate *that* detail to his new wife?—and did the same with the others. The still single and unattached Harold lingered a bit and Jane noticed. "Down, Harold. She's engaged." The man released me from the pucker and gave an embarrassed smile. "Sorry," he said. I grinned. "No problem, Harold."

"This," Jane continued, pointing to Joe, "is Angelica's fiancé, Joe, an ophthalmologist here in Mineola who also aided in the rescue."

Joe gave a quick, two-fingered salute and added, "You guys ever have an eye problem, just call me. Anytime."

211

"And finally, this," pointing to *Papà*, "is Angelica's father, Sammy, whose presence at the shoot-out was key to its success, though I can't go into any details, I'm afraid."

My *padre* went over to each and shook their hands vigorously.

"I know this comes on short notice, but Angelica and Joe are to be married in our backyard March the first, so mark your calendars. You are all invited, of course, with significant others. Speaking of which, when are you going to grow a pair and ask Jackie to marry you, Thomas?"

The man grinned. "This weekend. I have a nice restaurant picked out, and then we go back to my place. I've got the ring with the diamond you and Anna gave us all set up."

"That's terrific. Good luck. Anyway," Jane began, lifting the MacBook, "I have a minor task for you guys which, I'm assuming, will be a piece of cake." She lowered the laptop onto Tony's desk. "Angelica tells me this laptop's Trash has been wiped. I know... well, I'm hoping there's a file there we need to see. Probably a Word file, deleted on or about January eight. We're also almost sure no one has written to the hard drive since. At least we're praying none has. Retrieving the file should be no problem, right?"

Tony smiled. "You've come to the right place. Even if there've been a few writes, we should be able to work around that. Harold, care to do the honors?"

The junior member picked up the computer and placed it on his work desk. He inserted a USB cable (one end already connected to his desktop), into the MacBook, went to his keyboard and typed furiously. "This shouldn't take long," said Tony, and, remarkably, it didn't. About sixty seconds, in fact. Amazing what having the right software in the hands of the right person can accomplish.

"There," Harold began. "You were right, Jane. All the files are totally intact, so no one seems to have written over any of them. I see one, deleted on the eighth, called *QGTScandals.docx* and—"

"Bingo!" I exclaimed. "That's got to be it. Can you print it out, Harold?" The man pressed a few buttons and one of the many laser printers in the room came to life. In a few seconds, we had our file—all eighteen pages.

"Beautiful, guys. Just great," I added. Harold disconnected the laptop and handed it back to Jane. She gave it to Joe, saying, "Why don't you return this and then you and Angelica go home and read through the pages? I've got to get back to work and these guys have to get back to... whatever."

We all said our farewells and left. Joe and I would make a quick stop to return the laptop to Mr. Queen and then, after depositing *Papà* back home—he had a 5 o'clock, two-hour meeting with the rabbi—head over to Joe's house. We all planned to meet up at the Franklins tomorrow at six for an early dinner, after which we'd go over our findings. Tonight wasn't good, since Jane and Anna had a late afternoon appointment with the lawyer in charge of Khaleesi's adoption. They didn't know how long it would last.

When Joe and I finally arrived home, I poured some coffee—no wine; we wanted to be able to think straight—and we began. I'd read a sheet, then pass it over as I started another. We repeated this until Joe had finished the last page. There were many spelling and grammatical mistakes, as Joe had expected in one with the woman's failing eyesight.

We looked at each other. Then we smiled, realizing we were both thinking the same thing, which we announced as one—

"Holy shit!"

Chapter 28

Friday, February 14
Lake Success
7 PM

Jane was being a bitch. Well, that's not fair—she was just playing devil's advocate. Still, her pessimism was making both my father and my lover unhappy, and that made me unhappy. Yet, I knew the detective was correct.

We had eaten a quick meal, again catered by Chosen Village for Helen and Sammy, and retired to the living room, our permanent command post, it seemed. Felicity was there too, as if anybody could keep her away. Joe and I went over all the evidence Melinda-Ann had gathered during her three-month inquiry. At first, it seemed like we had more than enough to get the NYPD to re-open the case. But Jane, as mentioned, had quickly rained on that parade.

"Look guys," she began, "what we have here is evidence of gross misconduct and graft among the board members of QueensGate. If we present this to the correct authorities, maybe an investigation will be instituted regarding that *misconduct and graft*. I'm sure the IRS would be interested. But... regarding the murder, and I do believe she was murdered, these pages don't prove a thing. Though I'm willing to talk to the lead detective in the case now, which I'm sure he'll be *just thrilled* about, I seriously doubt he'll do anything but tell me to take a hike."

"But," began Joe, "Melinda told me she was going to a board meeting and was going to *fuck them over*—you didn't hear that Felicity—and shove something up their asses—that too." The girl chuckled. "Well, it's clear that *this* information was what she was referring to."

Jane sighed. "Maybe yes, Joe. Probably. But we have no proof of one, whether she confronted them with her findings at the meeting, and two, if she did—I sincerely doubt minutes were taken—for what reason? Let's say, for argument's sake, she presented her evidence. What was her goal? If she just wanted them to pay for their crimes, why warn them in advance? Why not just have her son publish the info? The only reason I can think of, and I know she was a friend of yours, Sammy, and you really liked her, Joe, but the only reason would be for blackmail. She wanted in. Why? Well, we know from two sources she had money problems. First, she's on Madoff's public list of victims. Whoever wrote the fake note also knew this, which is why reference to it was included as a reason for her suicide. There's also the testimony of the son, confirming his mother's poor financial state. So, we know she needed money. Threatening to go to the authorities would be a perfect way to get them to either provide a nice payout or be allowed to share in their schemes." She paused. Then, "One, or more than one of them, however, decided upon an alternate solution, it seems."

Jane let that all seep in. Nobody said a word for a while until, out of the mouth of babes—

"So what if this lady was a crook?" the child asked. "She didn't deserve to die for it, right?"

We let that seep in, too. Then, Sammy rose, went over to Felicity and tenderly petted her head, like I do with Maverick. "You're right, Felicity. Of course, you are. I, and Joe, intend to get to the truth. But I must agree with your mother that as of now, we do not know enough to eliminate what seems a fairly large list of suspects. I think it's time to find out some more information. For example, I've heard of other similar suicides over the years at The Towers. Is there a pattern? Was Melinda-Ann not the first to threaten exposure? And we also know nothing about the board

215

members. Sure, I *know* them, casually, and have even spoken to many over the years. But I really know little about them. So, I think the first step, Jane, is for you and me to have a talk with the one person who can give us a wealth of the information, prior to any further, one-on-one investigative work."

"One-on-one, Sammy? Don't forget, I have no jurisdiction."

"True, my dear. But you have an ID and a badge. I doubt most would notice that both are from Nassau County. If they do, they have the right to remain silent, right? All I'm asking is for a few hours of your time, Jane. If, in the end, we get nowhere and the search for the killer seems hopeless, then at least Joe and I can say we tried to get justice for the poor woman. But, sometimes," he looked at Helen, "without taking justice into our own hands, we must admit defeat and move on. But we should at least try, don't you think, *detective*?"

Jane smiled. "Okay, Sammy. Just who is this person who can provide us with some answers?"

Now it was Lover Boy's time to smile. "Her name is Agatha Monroe, and before you ask, she was never a member of my *Harem*."

"What harem?" asked Felicity.

"Never mind," Anna quickly answered. "Continue Sammy."

"Yes, well Agatha is, as far as I know, the oldest living resident of QueensGate Towers; she's been living there from the very beginning, when it was a simple apartment complex. Haven't seen her in maybe two months, but I'd've heard if she had passed. About five years ago, her companion of over seventy years died and Agatha has become somewhat of a... what's the word...? recluse, I think. Yes. I see her rarely, now and then in the Mall—as I said, the last time was a couple of months ago. She was as elegantly dressed as always—and still as sharp in mind as ever. But mostly she stays in her apartment, ordering everything she needs, I assume, over the phone. I visit, now and then, to check up on her. But until her companion died, I would see them often, strolling around the grounds, eating in the restaurant. Though we were never close, I had many pleasant conversations with the women, both of whom were quite extraordinary. Refined. Cultured. She'll talk to us, I'm sure. I was the only QueensGate resident who attended the wake for Suzanne, her partner. Though, it should be just you and me, Jane. Over two people might be too much for her. I also believe she will find a bond between the two of you."

Companion. Partner. Sammy didn't need to spell it out for Jane or the other adults. But now, something else the man had said struck her as surprising.

"Wait a minute. You said, 'companion of over *seventy* years?' How old is this woman?"

Sammy thought for a moment, then, "I believe one-hundred five, give or take a year or two."

Everyone sat silently until Felicity's curiosity prompted her again to ask—

"What harem?"

217

Chapter 29

Webster defines *doyenne* as: *a female, senior member of a body or group who's considered being knowledgeable as a result of long experience.* The famed dictionary also defines *dowager,* in its modern usage, as: *a dignified, elderly woman.* Based upon the conversation Sammy and Jane had just completed in the man's apartment, the detective understood Agatha Monroe was an example of both. She had lived at QueensGate since day one and knew its history and more about the *dramatis personae* who had navigated the halls and grounds than any other living resident. Thus, the justification for the former title. Based on Sammy's description of the lady, Jane knew she would agree with the latter label as well.

Sammy had called the woman last night and told her he and a detective friend of his were looking into the death of Melinda-Anne Queen and asked if she'd be amenable to speak with them. Jane had Saturday off, so any hour convenient to Miss Monroe was fine. The woman, after hearing Sammy's request, was intrigued and immediately agreed. The man mentioned he and his friend would ask about previous suicides and information regarding the current board members. They set the time for 6 PM and now Sammy and Jane, the latter with notepad in hand, stood outside Agatha Monroe's doorway. The man knocked.

When the producers of *Downton Abbey* were casting for the role of Violet Crawley, if Maggie Smith hadn't been available, Agatha Monroe would have been perfectly cast, Jane thought. By the end of the visit, the detective was convinced the elderly lady could have

218

mastered the required British accent and shone as the Dowager Countess.

The oldest resident of QueensGate Towers greeted the two visitors at the door as if she were on her way to dine at the 21 Club in Manhattan, circa 1940. She was wearing a navy-blue, ankle-length dress with a pan collar, tiny heart-shaped buttons, and yoke and sleeves in a complimentary spot net. The only things missing for a night out on the town were long velvet gloves. The dress seemed to be made in a soft, crepe-like fabric and the shoes were wedged-heel, solid slip-ons with peep toes, also in navy. Topping it all off was a string of magnificent pearls. Jane was no expert—Anna would know for sure—but they appeared real. This was a woman of elegance, out of another century. And indeed, she'd spent most of her hundred-five years living in the previous one. Jane was wearing what she thought were nice jeans and a fancy satin blouse, but she felt woefully underdressed.

The handsome woman, who to Jane seemed no older than in her seventies, beckoned her guests in, needing only an ornate wooden cane to aid her in her ambulation. She had a full head of gray hair Jane assumed was a stylish wig, cut short and colored to match the age of the wearer, not unnaturally dyed to represent a shade decades younger. The woman led her guests to the living room, where the two visitors sat on high-back upholstered chairs while the host relaxed on a small sofa. Between them was a coffee table on which sat three crystal wine glasses. One was filled with a liquid Sammy recognized immediately.

"I seem to recall you had a love of anisette, Sammy, so I took the liberty of pouring you a glass." The man smiled and said, "You have an excellent memory, Agatha. Thank you."

"An excellent memory for someone of my age, you mean, no?" She smiled, signaling to her guests she was joking. Mostly.

"And may I say, Agatha, and I never joke about someone's looks—you look marvelous. Radiant. I take it you're in good health?"

"As best as a hundred-five-year-old can expect, I suppose. Many of my parts—hips, knees, eye lenses and such have been replaced with metal and plastic. But the internal organs, mostly, are still behaving themselves. But I'm being rude. What would you like to drink, detective?"

"It's Jane, Miss Monroe, and lately a friend of mine has introduced me to the joys of bourbon. If you have."

Monroe's smile broadened. "Ah, a woman after my own heart. I'll call you Jane if you call me Agatha. Will Jack Daniels suffice? I know there are some who sneer at the name, but if it was good enough for Ol' Blue Eyes—he was buried with a bottle, you know—it's good enough for me."

"Jack will be fine, Agatha. Thank you. I, too, am a big Sinatra fan."

The woman slowly rose, smoothing down her dress, and went into another room. She soon emerged with a whiskey bottle in her hand. Sammy stood. "Let me pour for you, Agatha," he said, and she handed him the bottle and retook her seat. Sammy poured her glass first, then Jane's, after which they all raised their glasses and clinked them together. "Down the hatch!" Monroe cried, and the three drank.

After having a few sips, Agatha looked at her fellow elderly resident. "Sammy, I want to thank you again for paying your respects at Suzanne's wake. I know it was five years ago, but to me it's like yesterday. *None* of the other residents here deigned to come, Jane. I have never forgotten." And a tear came to her eye, which she quickly wiped away with a silk, lace-trimmed handkerchief the detective just noticed on the sofa.

Sammy nodded. Agatha now turned her attention to the young woman. Looking her up and down, the detective felt she was undergoing a forensic evaluation and again felt miserably underdressed for the occasion. But, maybe suspecting her guest's discomfort, the dowager said, "That's a lovely blouse, my dear. Quite stunning on you."

Jane relaxed. "Thank you, Agatha. You dress, by the way... well, I could never carry it, as you do."

The aged woman smiled and continued. "I see by your finger you're married. What does your husband do?"

Jane answered without missing a beat or stressing any particular word. "My wife is a wealthy woman who sees it her job, her responsibility, to give to charities, hospitals and the like and spends much of her time on their boards, deciding how best to spend the money she provides. Given my job and sometimes long hours, she also has the primary responsibility of caring for our daughter. We are in the process of adopting another."

Miss Monroe had been lifting her glass for another sip of whiskey but stopped, waited a beat, then placed it down on the coffee-table. She just sat there, very still except for a slight tremor which Jane just noticed, and within a few moments, a tear again came to each eye—followed by a few others. Jane was flummoxed, unsure of what she might have said to elicit such a response—and it saddened her. She was about to speak when—

"I'm sorry, everyone," Miss Monroe said, wiping her eyes once more. "I was just overwhelmed for a moment. With joy for you, Jane."

"Please, forgive me, Agatha, but I don't understand."

Monroe waved her hand and smiled. "Nothing to forgive, my dear. I'm just a silly old woman who, upon hearing your words, became sorry for myself. Not that I don't have reason to be, but those moments should be in private, not among guests."

Jane thought she had an idea of the wounds her words might have opened and looked down. Her hostess, as with the blouse, intervened to unburden her guest.

"Let me explain, Jane. I moved into this apartment in 1980, when the buildings opened, with the one true love of my life. Suzanne. In our later sixties then, we'd known and loved each other since we were both twenty-five. I was a schoolteacher, first grade, and Suzanne a pediatrician. We were so in love but, back in those

221

early days, it was a love that could not be openly expressed. We first moved in together in our late twenties, but always in public kept a slight distance, never daring to hold hands or show any signs of affection beyond a simple kiss on the cheek. Our very livelihoods could be put in jeopardy if our relationship became public knowledge. But alone, privately, in our home, there was grand passion, often enhanced by the lack of it in public. We both loved children and so desperately wanted to adopt. But, as you can imagine, an unmarried, same-sex couple had zero chance of adopting back in the thirties and forties, and we had to remain childless. It was the one source of sorrow and regret in our otherwise happy lives together.

"By the time we came to QueensGate, in 1980, the country was changing, and we were more open with our affection toward one another. Still, despite the supposed high-class, liberal inhabitants of these buildings, we were looked upon by many as anomalies—exotic zoo animals—two lesbian spinsters. Outside of Sammy and a few others, no one chose to become friends, despite our attempts at outreach.

"So, you see Jane, I'm sorry if I made you feel uncomfortable. But just hearing you talk about your wife and child with such love in your eyes brought back a slew of memories—and believe me, most were joyful—of my Suzanne and our lives together. My tears were of happiness for you and your family. Finally able to speak openly and be accepted into society. Finally able to have children." She paused, then, "I can't tell you how happy I am for you, my dear." And then she stood, *sans* cane, as did Jane, and the two embraced, Jane sniffling due to tears of her own.

After a few moments, the women separated. Agatha Monroe sat again, straightened her dress, had another sip of her whiskey and began—

"So, I hear you have some questions for me. Shall we begin?"

Chapter 30

"First," Jane said, "we're interested in what you know about all previous suicides at The Towers."

"After I got off the phone with Sammy last night," Miss Monroe began, "I sat down and made a list." She reached over to an end-table adjacent to the sofa and retrieved a piece of personal stationery upon which was written, in script, the results of the woman's remembrances. She looked down and spoke.

"The first one I can recall was in 1992, two years after the buildings turned co-op. The man's name was Ted Finberg. He was on the first board of directors and since he was a retired CPA with a huge practice, it was thought the president at the time would elect him head of the finance committee. Even though Ted was already seventy years old, he was still sharp in mind if somewhat frail in body. Unfortunately, the president, for life it would seem, Plick, said Ted was too old for such an important position. Instead, Plick appointed Jack Wellman, a much younger man of no distinction. Not technically an alcoholic, Jack was known to get smashed at many country club functions. There were rumors Ted and Jack fought over elements of the budget at board meetings, but Jack was the head of the committee and what he decided was law. Ted did not leave a note and most everyone in the buildings didn't even know of his death, which is a repeating theme, as you'll see.

"Next came, in 1998, a real juicy story—murder/suicide. A man by the name of Harry James, not the trumpet player, obviously, but a cop. One hot summer's day, suffering from a migraine, he unexpectedly came home mid-afternoon from work and found his wife in bed with one of the porters." The woman smiled. "If she had wanted to sleep with the help, you'd think she'd have enough self-respect to have chosen, at least, from the superintendents. Anyway, Harry catches them *in flagrante delicto,* takes out his gun, shoots and kills them both, sits down to have a beer and then jumps off the balcony. Landed in the swimming pool. It was sheer luck the lightning warning had been sounded ten minutes earlier, and the pool cleared, or poor, cuckolded Harry would have certainly landed on someone—the pool was mobbed. The poor children there must have been scarred for life. Obviously, there was no note."

"Was this Harry a member of the board?" Jane asked, then realized she'd discount any answer. The crime and subsequent suicide were clearly acts of passion and irrelevant to her investigation.

"No," Agatha replied. She took another sip of her drink and continued.

"The next one I remember, a short time after the tragedy of 9/11, so that would be late 2001, was poor Harriet Gold. And before you ask, she was not a member of the board, either. Too boring for her, I would think. She was a bit of a wild one. Never short of paramours among the single men here, but it seemed, at the time of her death, she was having an affair with a married man. Someone either on the board or among the other powerbrokers in the building. We know this because she *did* leave a suicide note. Typewritten on an old Underwood she kept as a relic of the past. I don't think she had a computer. Elements of the note somehow made the rounds among the gossip mongers and from what Suzanne and I could gather from snippets we overheard, Harriet was extremely distraught over the man's calling off the affair. He supposedly made her feel as if it were all her fault they had engaged in *his* adultery. Called her a *Jezebel,* of all things. She didn't name him, however, which I always found strange. Anyway, one night she took a bottle of sleeping pills, washed them down with wine for courage, and jumped. What a tragedy. I actually liked the woman. She, at least, had life to her, unlike most of the other old crones."

Jane and Sammy were struck by the similarity between Harriet Gold's pre-jump routine and Melinda-Ann's. But the woman was not a board member, so, at least for the moment, did not fit into their hypothesis. *Probably just a coincidence*, each thought, though neither Jane nor Sammy was a big fan of coincidences.

"There was a bit of a lull," continued Agatha, "until about 2008 or nine, can't quite remember which. The man's name was Jerry Chan. He was a widower, board member and a big-time money manager at Morgan Stanley, or one of those firms. Should have been the finance chairman, but by then, Jack Wellman was fully ensconced and not going anywhere. So, Jerry had to settle for, I think, head of the Country Club Committee. But a bone of contention was he liked to sit in on the Finance Committee meetings. Drove Jack up the wall but there was nothing in the co-op's bylaws forbidding another board member from visiting and observing any committee he or she pleased. Anyway, turns out, about six months before he jumped, poor Jerry was diagnosed with pancreatic cancer. Lost a lot of weight and became very thin. But, despite undergoing chemo and radiation treatments, he never missed a meeting of either the board, his committee or Jack's. Anyway, he left a note, printed out on his computer—"

"Don't you find that strange, Agatha?" Jane interrupted. "To me, suicide is a very personal choice to make, one which, if you were going to leave a note, I'd think would be hand-written. Don't you agree?"

The woman thought for a moment and then replied. "Yes, Jane. I certainly think I would, but one never knows what's going through the mind of someone on the brink of ending his or her own life. With Harriet, I know she adored her typewriter—it was her mother's. Considered it an heirloom, so maybe that's why she did what she did. For Jerry, well, I once asked him for some advice on a financial matter and he hand-wrote a response. I had to track him down for interpretation; I could not make heads or tails of his penmanship. You'd think he was a doctor! Maybe he realized

225

printing out his last words would save the world from trying to guess his motive. Which was, by the way, his health. He wrote the pain from the disease and the chemo were just too much to bear any longer. So sad.

"Anyway, that's it, at least among the residents. There was one crazy guy who, I think three years ago, was able to get past the concierge and make his way to the roof. Took off his clothes—it was in the dead of winter!—and jumped. That one made the papers, though only for a day. Seems he had just been discharged from a psychiatric hospital. Schizophrenia. Probably heard voices telling him to jump or some such."

"Yes," Sammy interrupted. "I read about that one myself. Was the talk of the complex for quite a while. You're right, Agatha, it's the only one I can remember reading about."

"Why is that?" Jane now asked. "You'd think jumping from such prominent buildings would be news. Front page for tabloids like the News and the Post."

Monroe smiled. "Yes, you'd think. But it seems the local precinct has been headed for decades by just two or three different commanders. Turns out, they've all been friends with our ex-cop Building Manager, Brown—more on him later. The powers that be here don't like to publicize any scandals, crime, etc. that go on. Bad for business, property values and all that. So, when the police are called, they're warned by their commanding officer to just go about their business as quickly as possible, return to the precinct, write up or do the most cursory of investigations and never, ever leak a word to the press. He's very adamant about that and any violation would be met with swift... payback, I think is the modern term for it?" Both guests nodded. "I'd bet Brown, and the commanders had, and still have, a monetary deal going on between them, but it would be pure speculation on my part and not proper for a lady to engage in." And she winked.

Jane poured herself another *half* shot of bourbon—she had to drive home, after all—and said, "Well, Agatha. That was very helpful. It'll take a while to digest it all, but now, what can you tell us about the current board members and the other major VIPs?"

The elderly woman let out a sharp, "Hah!" She then poured a double into her glass and took a nice amount in one swallow. "Not a decent human being among the lot of them. I'm reminded of a quote from a Carole Lombard movie from the 30s—*Nothing Sacred*—that's always stuck with me: 'The hand of God reaching down into the mire couldn't elevate one of them to the depths of degradation.' Though, to be fair, the most recent two, Anthony something and Carla Weinberg, have only been on the board three and two years, respectively, so I really haven't gotten to deal with them at all. Since poor Suzanne died, I've lived much of my life here, among my memories... my God. I've become a lesbian Miss Havisham, though with a more varied wardrobe." The woman briefly snickered, but there was no genuine mirth to it. "So, it's possible they haven't been corrupted by the system yet. But the others? Where do you want me to begin, my dear?"

"How about," said Jane, "we start at the top, the president of the board, Plick?"

Monroe smirked. "Sure. After all, what's the expression, 'the fish rots from the head down,' right? Anyway, first a word of advice. If you ever interview the man, make sure to sit upwind. He has the worst taste in cologne and slathers it on to an extent that often makes one gag. I don't know how that liquor-store bitch he sees can stand it, if you'll pardon my French. Probably has to drink a good deal of her profits to tolerate that man in her bed so often. Anyway, you up on your Shakespeare, detective Jane?"

Both Sammy and Jane smiled. "A bit, yes," the younger woman playfully answered.

"Well," continued Agatha Monroe, "when considering Plick's aroma, I'm reminded of this ditty from the Bard: '*The rankest compound of villainous smell that ever-offended nostril.*'"

Jane's smile broadened. "*Merry Wives of Windsor,*" she commented.

The host was amazed. "Very good, my dear. Why am I not surprised you're as cultured as you are beautiful?" Janes blushed a bright red, but when Sammy recalled this reaction to their friends the next day, the detective playfully denied any such shade had appeared on her countenance.

"But to get back to business. Plick has been president of the board for forever. Thirty years. When he wants, he can be quite charming, and if your sense of smell is defective, you could have a decent conversation with the man and understand why many of the women in the building have wound up in his bed, if the rumors are to be believed. By the way, those same rumors are not kind regarding his bedroom skills." Agatha chuckled. "Anyway, I wouldn't trust a word he says. An insurance salesman by trade, so that tells you something there—always trying to convince people they need more coverage than they can afford. Silver tongued, when need be. But try to collect on the insurance? Well, you know what happens then. He's a ruthless bastard, from what I hear. Not one you want to cross. Though, since you two are investigating Melinda-Ann's death as a possible murder, I must say I can't see Plick having the guts to do it. He's a bully and like most bullies, if push ever came to shove, he'd get one of his goons to do the dirty work. Like B.B."

"Nice segue there, Agatha," said Jane. "What can you tell us about the Building Manager?"

The woman took another few sips. "Be careful with that one. Ex-cop. Still carries a gun, I'm told. Tall, thin and muscular, it would have been no effort at all for him to have flipped poor Melinda off her balcony. '*He doth bestride the narrow world like a Colossus.*' She looked at Jane, an unsaid question on her face. Jane answered, "*Julius Caesar.*" Monroe couldn't contain her glee. "Yes. Wonderful, Jane. Sammy, I'm so glad you've introduced your friend to me! Anyway, in B.B.'s case, it's the narrow hallways of the Mall where you'll often find the man bestriding—actually, more like strutting like a peacock. Very unpleasant to deal with—treats the shareholders, as a group, as if they were *his* employee, instead of the other way around. A coarse thug who feigns sophistication by peppering his conversations with French, though he was born and bred in the Bronx. He seems to think spreading whipped cream on shit makes it *mousse au chocolat*." Sammy and Jane looked at each other and grinned. "Unaccountable to no one save Plick and that witch, Thomas."

"There you go with your segues again, Agatha. A very flowing narrative. So, what about Tina Thomas?"

"The *Dragon Lady*? Are you aware of her position and the power she wields?"

"Yes," Jane replied. We know all about the votes she commands. And the conflicts. Melinda-Anne wrote an eighteen-page expose on the board members. I don't think we've mentioned that yet."

"No, but it's interesting. Anyway, the woman is a shark. Suzanne called her 'The Wicked Bitch of the East.' Divorced—*quelle surprise!* Totally conflicted in her job since it is, theoretically, to sell apartments, yet she, I've been told, constantly puts roadblocks in front of prospective buyers, mostly her unwillingness to budge an inch on the price. That alone puts a sour taste in their mouths. Everyone wants to negotiate, to think they've been able to knock the price down, even a little. But not Tina, so there are still many unsold sponsor apartments after all this time. Don't know why her employers let her get away with it. Lives in a very nice, high floor unit and does, I'm told, a lot of traveling. Unless she's independently wealthy, there's got to be some shenanigans going on. A tall woman, and when I was younger and Suzanne and I went to the gym, we'd always see Tina there working out, lifting weights."

"So, certainly capable of overpowering someone like Melinda?" Sammy asked.

"I would say so. Though, unless she could get the upper hand on MAQ, or took her by surprise, it would be a tough fight. *The Queen* is... was... tall and athletic herself."

229

The guests didn't mention the Valium. No need for Agatha to envision a helpless Melinda-Ann, powerless in the hands of her murderer. To Sammy, drugging a victim was indeed a woman's method; but the detective, prior to joining Homicide, had dealt with enough date-rapes secondary to spiked cocktails, and knew better.

"What about the co-op lawyer?" It was Sammy who asked, but Abe Crowe was next on the detective's list as well.

Agatha smirked. "*Asshole-Abe*. And his frog wife—been here forever. There was a time I heard they were headed for divorce but decided against it. About as useful as a teapot made of ice. Anyway, look up *shyster* in the dictionary and I'd bet Abe's picture will be prominently displayed. Every year, it seems, I get some notice in the mail about some new rule or regulation he imposed that not only seems unnecessary but almost always winds up putting money in the man's pocket. Just about everything you'd want to do as a shareholder needs his legal approval, often coming with a not insignificant fee. Suzanne and I had wanted a little dog forever. But, until about four years ago, it wasn't allowed. By then, Suzanne was gone. Then Abe decides dogs are allowed, but *he* must give them his okay. Charges $250 to make sure the dog in question is a *QueensGate type of dog*! What the *fuck* does that mean?"

Sammy and Jane were astonished, never expecting so colorful a word to escape the dowager's lips. The woman realized she'd shown emotion, and a vocabulary she'd never exhibited to anyone but her lover. "I'm sorry, Jane. Sammy. It just gets my blood boiling. All the years I, and especially my sweet Suzanne, wanted a puppy, and it was refused. Now, once she's gone, this SOB, *for a price*, allows it." And again, the woman had to use her handkerchief to blot away some tears.

The visitors waited for their host to compose herself. Then Sammy said, "I'm sorry, Agatha, if our questions have brought up some sad memories."

"Yes, Agatha," Jane added. "That was not our intent."

The old woman, now appearing closer to her true age, nodded, still wiping away the last of the tears. "Oh, no need to apologize. Sometimes it's best to be reminded that there are some cruel and vindictive people in this world." She smiled. "It helps me to appreciate the kind ones, such as you two, even more.

"One more thing with Abe," the woman began, getting back to business. "He likes to go on and on about things of zero relevance. Don't know if it's for obfuscation or he just loves to hear his own voice. He certainly speaks '*an infinite deal of nothing*,' that's for sure." She smiled directly at Jane, who returned it in kind with a nod, acknowledging the reference to *The Merchant of Venice*.

"As for the rest, Jack and Jill Ginsburg I've rarely spoken with. Have heard nothing bad about them but seeing as how they continue to get re-elected every three years, *The Dragon Lady* must approve of them—that says something right there. The last two, Tony and Carla, as I said, are non-entities. Never met them and don't know anyone who has or will admit they have."

The woman now downed the rest of her glass. "You need to look at the Board of Directors as similar to a Mafia Family. Plick is the Don—nothing gets done without his approval. He gives the orders. Crowe is the *Consigliere*, making sure any illegalities *appear* on the up-and-up while making sure he always gets his taste of the profits. B.B. is the enforcer. The man who makes sure things get done, no matter who gets hurt in the process. And Tina? The ruthless sister to the Don, like what Connie became in Godfather III. Always scheming—and potentially deadly."

Sammy looked at Jane and they both seemed to agree now would be a good time to let the woman rest. They and their friends would get together tomorrow and go over Jane's notes.

The *doyenne* of QueensGate walked her guests to the front door. "It was wonderful visiting again, Agatha," said Sammy. "I promise not to be a stranger." And with that, he kissed her, alternating on both cheeks.

"And it was a great pleasure to have met you, Agatha," added Jane. "You've been an immense help. If you don't mind, once this affair is complete, I'd like to come by again and introduce you to my wife and child. We may even have our second by then. I'm sure they would all love to meet you. *I* certainly would appreciate your company again."

The woman seemed to perk up at Jane's words and literally, as the cliché goes, clutched at her pearls. "Yes, Jane, *please* do. I've kept myself a hermit for too long. Let's face it, I haven't much time left on this Earth and would like to spend it in the company of lovely people such as Sammy, you and your family."

With those words, Agatha Monroe approached Jane for a farewell kiss. The detective began to turn her head to the side, but the woman took her hands and placed them gently, tenderly on the younger woman's cheeks. She brought her lips close, her lonely eyes pleading with Jane to allow this one, quick, intimacy—sorrowfully, long-ago abandoned with the loss of her lover. A delicate kiss on the lips.

And Jane, understanding the old woman's heart-breaking wish, did not pull away.

Chapter 31

Sunday, February 16
Lake Success
10 AM

We gathered in the living room after chowing down my favorite breakfast of bagels and lox from Bagel Boss in Roslyn. Present were me, Joe, *Papà*, Helen, Jane, Anna, Felicity (of course), and, since she was spending the weekend, Khaleesi. The youngest of our group had been brought up to speed by her newly anointed older sister. Anna had suggested they go to Felicity's room with Maverick to play.

The two children looked at her as if she'd grown another head.

Joe informed us he'd received an email from the co-op lawyer, Crowe, and a meeting was scheduled for *tomorrow* at his QGT office, regarding the dog. Nice of the prick to give us so much notice. Oh, and we were to bring $250—cash! I fumed and inwardly relapsed into my old Fortuna self, threatening the man with all sorts of painful torture if he dared deny Maverick's acceptability.

Jane and Sammy painstakingly recounted their conversation with Agatha Monroe and then Jane, in full detective mode, took the floor.

"Okay, then. If I may summarize. We can all agree Melinda-Ann was murdered. It appears it was due to the threat she posed to the members of the board and the two other VIPs, Crowe, the lawyer, and Brown, the Building Manager. Did the woman threaten them with exposure for the sake of justice? Doubtful—it just doesn't

233

make sense to warn them. No, despite Sammy and Joe's feelings for her, the scenario which makes the most sense is she threatened to use her information for blackmail. She needed money and here was a golden opportunity for either a large, lump-sum payment, or more likely, long-term income from inclusion into the schemes she'd uncovered. They probably had come to some sort of agreement, which is why Melinda-Ann told her son her investigations had come up empty.

"Then one or, unlikely, more than one of the participants in said agreement changed the terms and did away with the woman. This *QueenSlayer*, as Angelica has dubbed him or her,"—yes, I had caved and told everyone my nickname of the killer—"is the object of our quest. Assuming we're correct as to motive, this person will be found among those at the meeting Queen mentioned to Joe. That's eight people, way too many suspects for us to handle, especially when, as I've said many times, I cannot use most of my resources and time to investigate, given the lack of jurisdiction.

"I should tell you that yesterday afternoon, I called a friend of mine in the NYPD who tracked down the lead detective on the case for me. I spoke to him and discussed my concerns and theories and, as expected, he was none-too-pleased to have his investigation questioned. However, he was a nice guy and, off the record, admitted, given the lack of any physical evidence—the forensics team did their job appropriately—he was told in no uncertain terms to end the investigation. His commanding officer is, as was the one before him, it seems, quite friendly with the Building Manager, an ex-cop, and, unless there's clear evidence of murder, all such suicides over the years have been quickly labeled as such. In addition, this detective and all who work in his precinct know full well never to discuss any wrongdoing at The Towers with the press. Another favor their CO gives to Brown. We decided not to speculate on any recompenses.

"So, where are we? No physical evidence and too many suspects. First, my feeling is if we have any chance of sorting this out, the

234

suspect list has to be whittled down. The only way to do that is to take a leap and assume Melinda-Ann, in the long history of QGT, was not the first board member—and it would *take* a board member to obtain the needed information—to discover irregularities. Whoever killed her, making it look like a suicide, had done so before. I know it's a big, big leap, but without it we have nowhere else to look. So, according to Agatha Monroe, there have been two other so-called suicides of board members since the co-op was created—Ted Finberg and Jerry Chan, both, coincidentally, experts in finance. Finberg left no suicide note and Chan printed his out as did Melinda–Ann, which, I might add, still bothers me. So, assuming our killer was responsible for all the deaths, that leads us to four major suspects who have been at The Towers at, and since, Finberg's death—Plick, the president, Brown, the Building Manager, Thomas the builder's representative and Crowe, the lawyer. Four. Better, but we're pretty much grasping at straws here, guys.

"This is what I propose. Tomorrow, Joe and Angelica are to meet with Crowe about Maverick. Sammy, you should come too since he and all the rest of our suspects know you, even if casually. Also, and I've discussed this with Anna, Felicity will miss morning school and come too. NOT in any investigative role you understand"—she stared, laser-eyed at the child—"just to show this guy how tame and well-behaved Maverick is, even an eleven-year-old child can be around him. I'll take a personal day and come, too."

Jane's last statement surprised me and all the rest who were not made privy to it in advance. "We have no physical evidence and no proper way of investigating further. I see no other course of action now but to rattle some cages and see what happens. I will be there representing the police, quickly flashing my badge and hoping no one notices I'm not NYPD. Maybe someone with a guilty conscience will give a sign or do or say something incriminating. I know it's a long shot, but it's all we've got. Afterward, if nothing turns up, Sammy, Joe, we've got to move on. I'm sorry. I know you

235

were fond of Melinda-Ann, but this quest *must end*, one way or another, tomorrow. Okay?"

We all looked at both men. Helen took Sammy's hand, and I clutched at Joe's. Then each of them, in turn, nodded in agreement.

"Okay then," Anna chimed in. "On a much happier subject, let's talk wedding!"

Chapter 32

Joe and I sat with Maverick and my *padre* in his apartment, awaiting Jane and Felicity. We had just decided that although we'd answer any queries posed during the interview, the detective would do any asking, despite Joe's and *Papà's* desire to be Grand Inquisitor.

Once the team was fully formed, we made our way to the elevator, down to the Mall level. It was a short walk to Crowe's office. Almost there, we noticed a woman exiting. She was striking and way out-of-place for QGT. Slim, about six-foot one and in her mid-thirties with short, Scandinavian-blonde hair, the woman wore slacks and a golf shirt. The top two buttons were undone, revealing just enough cleavage to entice a stare from just about anyone past puberty. She walked by the group, nodded to Lover Boy, adding, "Hi, Sammy," and continued on her way. Joe turned to follow her for a moment until I tapped him on the shoulder, adding, "Eyes front, soldier. That's an order."

My man sheepishly grinned as he turned and asked, "Who the hell was *that*, Sammy?"

"*She*," the older man responded, "is the assistant golf pro. Came on about two years ago. I'm told the number of scheduled golf lessons has skyrocketed ever since." He gave a devilish smile. I shook my head and added, "Just remember Joe, if you intend to

237

take up golf once we move in, my *padre* is not the only member of the family who is an expert at making violent death seem accidental."

Felicity chuckled. "You two make such a cute couple." And then we all laughed and entered the office.

All laughter stopped as we spied the secretary at the desk. Agatha Monroe had used the word *frog* to describe Mrs. Celine Crowe, Jane had told us. But, upon seeing the woman in the flesh, *toad* seemed more appropriate. The woman was maybe five-foot-five and thick. She wore a short-sleeved, loose blouse which allowed her stocky arms room to maneuver. She had a round, plain face without makeup with hair done up in a style reminiscent of a 60s beehive. Completing the first-impression picture were various examples of fine jewelry, including an imperial jade, four-leaf clover necklace and a *Cartier* watch.

I saw Jane take a quick overview of the outer office. It was, I assumed, usual fare for a lawyer's lair, maybe except for the many framed, personal photographs of husband and wife who, it appeared, liked to travel. There were snapshots of the two in front of the Eiffel Tower and the Louvre. Also, one from somewhere in the Far East which I, having read Melinda-Ann's thesis, guessed to be Singapore. There was also a large wedding photo on the woman's desk with the date July 1, 2000, beautifully carved into its frame. *Hmm*, I thought. *Married twenty years. Not bad for a couple once considering divorce.* Jane also admired the frame and told the woman so.

Mrs. Crowe looked us over and seemed surprised—expecting two visitors, she faced five. However, her surprised expression was quickly replaced with fear as she rolled her chair as far away from us as she was able.

"Please make sure that dog is held firmly, little girl!" Felicity had Maverick on the leash and tried to be reassuring. "Don't worry, lady. Maverick is very gentle. Wouldn't hurt a fly, would you boy?" She then patted his head.

"Yeah, that's what my next-door neighbor told my mother when I was a little over six. Took a bite out of my leg—twenty-two stitches. I've been petrified of dogs ever since. They're my worst nightmare, so just please keep him away."

Felicity tightened her grip. Mrs. Crowe quickly lifted her phone, pressed a button and said, "The applicants and dog for the Queen apartment are here." Not waiting for a response, she pointed to a door and bade us enter and leave her in one piece. Which we did, though the child couldn't resist looking back and smiling. It was her Joker-like smile, and the woman recoiled.

Abraham Crowe, Esquire, sat at his desk, his suit-jacket cuffs pulled up just enough to show off his Rolex Submariner. He appeared to be about five-feet-nine, slightly graying, with a very unsightly growth on the tip of his nose. *You'd think with all his money he could afford to see a plastic surgeon about that*, I mused. He looked up and saw Sammy, rose with a wet, squishy sound, revealing a potbelly protruding over his belt. Yeah, every woman's dream was old Abe.

Unlike the outer office, I noticed only one photograph here, a portrait of a distinguished-looking man, in middle-age, prominently displayed on a side wall dedicated to just that one print. I saw Jane notice it, too. It was probably the attorney's father, himself a lawyer, we had learned.

"Hello, Sammy." Crowe reached out his hand and *Papà* shook it.

"Nice to see you, Abe. Let me introduce my daughter, Angelica Foster, her fiancé, Dr. Joseph Peck, my friend, Detective Jane Rieger-Franklin and her daughter, Felicity. And, the star of our show, Angelica's dog, Maverick." As my father made his introductions, he pointed to each of us when named. There were not enough seats for us all, so Felicity sat on the floor with Maverick and commenced petting. We had decided on that tactic beforehand.

"As you can see, Abe, my *daughter's* dog, is quite tame. Even an eleven-year-old has no fear of him. So, as a favor to me, I hope you give him your quick stamp of approval. I would be very disappointed if you felt differently." *Papà* let that hang. We had discussed the fact that the Building Manager, an ex-cop, knew, or at least must have heard rumors of Sammy Vivino's history. *Papà* had never been arrested, but his role in the Esposito Family was well known among the local cops in Brooklyn. Given many of the security detail at The Towers were ex-NYPD from some of those same precincts, we were sure word had trickled down to at least the B.M., if not the lawyer and others. So, it couldn't hurt to subtly imply Lover Boy would be *disappointed* if Crowe's decision did not go the way of the ex-assassin's daughter.

The lawyer seemed to have received the message. "Yes, Sammy, he does seem quite tame. If you're willing to vouch for his gentleness, that's a plus. Most of the dogs here are those small, carry-in-your-purse, yip-yip types. Can't stand the little shits, myself. I had a golden retriever growing up. Now, there's a *real* dog. I wanted to get one when I married and moved into a house with lots of property. But Celine is deathly afraid of all dogs, so there went that. Now," he turned to Jane, deftly changing subjects, "why, may I ask, are you here, Detective Rieger-Franklin?"

Jane smiled and began. "Well, Mr. Crowe, I planned to meet Sammy today, anyway. He and I were going to interview a few people, you included, about the death of Melinda-Ann Queen. Your setting up this appointment was just a happy coincidence."

The lawyer stared for a moment and, in lawyerly fashion, began to choose his words carefully. "I was under the impression, Detective, the NYPD had closed the case. In fact, I'm sure of it. Suicide is the official determination."

"Yes, that's true, Mr. Crowe. But Sammy and the woman were good friends, and he is not convinced of the official, local police conclusion. So, he asked me to investigate. As it turns out, I've come up with some evidence not presented at the inquiry." Jane let that sink in for a while. So far, she'd skillfully avoided mentioning her lack of jurisdiction, keeping Crowe thinking the detective represented the NYPD, possibly a more central investigative unit. It was only a matter of time, I knew, before he'd catch on.

"And what might this evidence be?"

"We discovered a file on the woman's computer a few days after the funeral. In it she describes many financial scandals perpetrated here at The Towers by members of the board, plus others, including you, counselor. We felt it was possible one of these individuals might have gotten wind of her investigation and decided to put an end to it—by putting an end to her. Would you mind telling me where you were the night Melinda-Ann Queen died?"

The man's face revealed nothing. He was probably a good poker player. And like all good, crooked players, he had an ace up his sleeve which he now, with flair, produced.

Crowe smiled broadly. "No, I don't mind at all, Detective. I was in Manhattan, at the Lotus Club, receiving an award from the Queens Bar Association—*Queens Co-op Lawyer of the Year!*" He beamed and, I thought, almost added, *"Touché!"*

Are you fuckin' kidding me? I continued to ponder. Who would have believed there was so *specific* an honor? *I'll have to ask Joe if the AMA gives two separate 'Ophthalmologist of the Year' awards—one for the right eye and another for the left.*

Jane was a good poker player herself and showed no disappointment. "Feel free to check with the club and the Bar. I was there until midnight. Many attendees can corroborate my story. There were many surveillance cameras, too."

Hmm, thought Jane, *not only does the Shyster of the Year have his ass covered, he seems to have the video to prove it, too. Convenient.*

Crowe now seemed to become more confident. "May I see your badge and credentials, Detective?"

Jane reached into her pocket and produced what was asked. The man looked at them, and for the first time, exhibited true annoyance. "What is this?" he began, throwing Jane's shield and ID on his table. "You're not NYPD. You're Nassau County. How dare you impersonate—"

241

"Now, now, counselor. Watch the insinuations. Before you get your knickers in a twist, neither I nor Sammy ever said I was NYPD. Just a detective. We can't be held responsible for your assumptions." The man's face reddened, but he remained in control. Jane, I think, decided, with his alibi rock solid, there was no need to continue and risk putting the approval of Maverick in jeopardy. She collected her credentials. "Look Mr. Crowe, and by the way, congratulations on your award, I'm just helping our mutual friend here, Sammy. He was distraught over the woman's death. You can understand, I'm sure. Neither he nor I really give a shit about what improprieties she may have unearthed. I'm from Homicide, not Grand Larceny. Frankly, even though *she* may have believed her info, *I* have no reason to. No real reason to investigate her allegations other than how they might relate to her death. You have an excellent alibi. Congratulations again. So, since I'm *sure* you're a stand-up guy and will approve of my friend's dog, I see no reason to ask further questions of *others* about any of Queen's disparaging accusations toward *you*. I know how rumors and innuendos get started and certainly wouldn't want to do anything to tarnish such a fine, award-winning reputation as yours. So, I think we're done here, right?"

Jane had done two things there. One, she had assured the lawyer he was no longer a murder suspect, and second, she'd said she'd not spread rumors concerning any financial indiscretion *if* he approved Maverick. A thinly veiled threat. Yet, it still was a win-win for the man, since he was almost certainly going to approve Maverick, anyway. Yet, as Jane would find out later, he was livid at being at the other end of a police interrogation and threat, like a common criminal, even if it were only for a few moments. I'm sure his fury would not have been as restrained had not Sammy, Lover Boy, Vivino been sitting across from him.

He'd deal with what he perceived as Detective Jane Rieger-Franklin's impertinence later.

"Agreed," the lawyer said. "The dog is approved, and I'll also see what I can do to expedite the sale of Queen's apartment to you two." He pointed to me and my fiancé and we grudgingly, but profusely, thanked him. *Gag me with a spoon!*

Joe placed $250 on the man's desk. We all rose, the adults shook hands, and we exited. On the way out, Mrs. Crowe again moved her chair as far from Maverick as possible. The child tarried behind the others. "Say goodbye to the nice lady, Maverick," she said, adding a quick hand movement which produced the expected, trained response. The dog barked loudly. Twice. Crowe shook. Felicity smiled, turned and left to join the others already in the hallway. Jane looked at her daughter sternly. "I heard *and saw* that."

"Well, she was mean. I didn't like her, and neither did Maverick. Anyway, it's good for her. She needs to get over irrational fears. Don't you, Dr. Thorpe and Mommy tell me that all the time, Mama?" Felicity was referring to a recurrent nightmare where Jane was killed in the line of duty. The child would wake, screaming in terror and it took both her parents usually a good thirty minutes to calm her. Jane and Anna kept telling her the fears regarding her mother's safety were irrational, not backed up with statistics. But Jane knew the child was smart enough to look up, on-line, the actual numbers and learn for herself the real odds of her dying in action. Just as she knew Felicity could look up *cynophobia*, the fear of dogs, and learn it was no more easily discarded as her own fears. The mother recommended her daughter do just that and then moved on.

"Okay. So, Angelica, as we discussed, you'll take Felicity and Maverick back to Anna. Joe goes to his office. Sammy and I will continue our interviews, right?"

"It's not fair," Felicity whiningly chimed in. "I've got to go back to school, yet Khaleesi gets to spend the whole day with Mommy."

Jane sighed. "I thought we'd discussed this. Khaleesi has the next two days off from school because of some chemistry lab spill they've got to clean up. So, she gets to stay a little longer. It will be

243

good for her to have Mommy to herself for some bonding time. The day when she'll be permanently joining us is, sadly, nearing. You understand this, right, honey?"

Felicity nodded. "Yeah," she said, morosely. "I know. I'm just being selfish, I guess."

Jane smiled and caressed the girl's cheek. "Anyway, I hear tomorrow, since it's a teacher's prep day at *your* school—whatever the hell that means—you two and Angelica are having a girl's day out at Roosevelt Field. So, since you're so understanding, I'll slip you another $20 for shopping."

Felicity turned to Angelica and smiled. "See, empathy—works every time." Then, before Jane could respond, the child hugged her. "Just kidding. Love you, Mama."

"Me too you, you little con artist. Now get going."

And so, we left.

———————————

The Building Manager's room was at the back of the Security office Jane and Sammy now entered. The QGT resident knew where he was going, and the detective followed. A guard at the front desk began to object, but Jane flashed her badge and that was that.

Brown was seated at his desk, reading the New York Times. He was a tall man, a good six feet, and even though it was cold outside, he wore a short-sleeved dress shirt which allowed the world to appreciate his muscular arms and, of course, the Rolex he too wore. *Boys and their expensive toys* silently quipped Jane. In his sixties, with a full head of dark hair, he was an imposing figure. He looked up upon hearing us enter his sanctum and, though his first facial expression started as a frown, it instantly turned upside down when he saw Lover Boy.

"Sammy, *mon ami*." The Bronx-born man pronounced it "moan" *ami* and Jane smiled, remembering Agatha Monroe's chocolate mousse quip.

244

"Hi, B.B. This is my friend, Detective Jane Rieger-Franklin."

Jane proffered her hand, and the man shook it, much too tightly than necessary, Jane thought; it was not an uncommon move, in the detective's experience. Men in positions of power, she felt, often enjoyed showing what they perceived as their superior standing on the evolutionary scale—that is, above all professional women who dared enter their workspace. She accepted the grasp and squeezed back, equally hard. *I'll match my balls with yours any day, B.B.*, she thought.

The B.M.'s theory on Darwinism might have been outdated, but his police training was not, and he quickly asked, "May I see your credentials, *Mademoiselle Detective?*"

No beating around the bush with this one, Jane mused as she showed the man her badge and ID. *And that's* Madame *Detective to you, fucker.*

The ex-cop examined the articles and handed them back. "So, what might possibly interest an NCPD detective in QueensGate Towers?" He pointed to two chairs into which Jane and Sammy now sat.

"My friend Sammy, here, was a good friend of the late Melinda-Ann Queen and feels the NYPD's investigation was a bit hurried and incomplete, especially given some new evidence. So he asked for my help."

The man sat for a moment, analyzing and then, "The NYPD has closed the case. Suicide. You wouldn't be withholding this additional evidence from them, would you, Detective?"

Very good, B.B. "No, not at all. I discussed it with the lead detective, a man by the name of Schiff. He did not feel it sufficed to reopen the case, so I find myself alone here, just trying to help my friend Sammy get some closure. Just want to dot the *I*s and cross the *T*s, as it were. I'm sure you would like to help him out as well, no?"

Nothing like playing the Lover Boy card again, Jane thought. Certainly, the B.M., like the attorney, would not want to find himself on the ex-hitman's bad side. "Of course, Detective. Just what is this new information?"

Jane described, as she did with Crowe, the deleted file with MAQ's allegations and again stressed she wasn't interested in investigating the claims themselves, just in speaking with all those the woman had mentioned—to see who might have taken matters into their own hands. "Are you willing to tell me your whereabouts on the night of the suicide, Mr. Brown?"

Jane purposely and respectfully asked permission and used the word "suicide" in order to give the man the impression she was just going through the motions to placate Sammy, and she believed in the NYPD's conclusion.

Brown took a little longer to answer this time. Jane noted some rapid eye movements and understood he was weighing multiple responses to her question. They could range from flat-out refusing to answer, all the way to full disclosure.

The eyes stopped darting, and he said, "Of course, I'm willing. But I need your word as a professional, and yours, Sammy, as a friend; what I say goes nowhere beyond these walls. *Oui*?"

The two visitors nodded. "I was with Tina Thomas. In her apartment, from around six PM to midnight. My wife thought I was just working late." He looked down, as if ashamed of his adultery, but Jane, always the cynic, didn't believe the man knew what the word meant. "Ashamed," that is—not "adultery."

"I assume that Ms. Thomas can corroborate?"

Brown looked up. "I'm positive she'll confirm what I've said."

I'm sure you are, Jane concurred, silently. *Just as I'm sure you'll be on the phone with her the minute our asses are out the door.* She sighed and then realized it was more audible than she would have liked. The man would take it as a sign of defeat and, Jane had to admit, if both B.B. and Thomas backed each other up, it was. She rose and Sammy, seeing her do so, followed the lead.

"Well, that would seem to settle that. Don't worry, Mr. Brown, your secret is safe with us. As I said, Queen's financial theories are of no interest to either of us."

Joe and Angelica are going to be living here, she thought. *No need to unnecessarily taint them with their association with me. I need to play nice.* Jane extended her hand and Brown shook it, maybe even a little stronger this time. *Prick,* Jane fumed. *You think you've won, don't you?*

Sammy also shook the B.M.'s hand, but Jane had one more question. "By the way, Mr. Brown. Do you have any idea where Mr. Plick might be found?" Sammy knew where Thomas's office was, but the board president, now retired from his day job, had no office. The detective fretted he might not be easily found on this one day she was available for interrogation. She needn't have worried.

Though B.B. and Plick were on the same side *vis-à-vis* their extracurricular, money-making schemes, most everyone at QGT knew each despised the other. Greed makes strange bedfellows, it could be said. The Building Manager looked at his watch and smiled. "It's 11:15 now. In forty-five minutes, you'll find him in the restaurant with Sucki, his girlfriend."

"I think the name is Emi," Sammy interjected.

B.B. chuckled. "Yeah, I guess you're right. They have lunch, noon every day—on the dot. You'll find them in the back. Peter will be having *The LBJ Special.*"

"Cute. I didn't realize the restaurant named sandwiches after past presidents," Jane innocently remarked.

Brown laughed. "You misunderstand, Detective. The *LBJ* stands not for dear old Lyndon Baines Johnson, but for *Lunch and Blow Job.* They eat and then return to the liquor store. The back room has a comfy couch, so I've been told. Nothing like being *eaten,* after eating, right?"

Jane couldn't help but smile at the juvenile pun. "Thanks for the tip, Mr. Brown." Turning, she and Sammy exited the office.

"That was," the man began, prefacing his favorite social-media expression, "*T-M-I*, no?" Jane laughed and borrowed Angelica's soft punch to the shoulder as her response.

As soon as Brown heard the two close the exterior office door, the temporary mirth from his jab at Plick faded. He picked up his cellphone and speed-dialed Thomas.

"Tina, *mon cher*. It's me. Listen, you're about to get some visitors. We need to get our stories straight."

Jane and Sammy rushed to Tina Thomas's office. They wanted to talk and be done with the woman in order to catch Plick between the L and the BJ phase of his lunch hour. The detective amused herself along the way, coming up with various variations on what the initials of a JFK special might represent.

The Management Office where Thomas held court was adjacent to the restaurant, tucked away in a corridor leading to the library. They entered and found two young male secretaries—*eye candy for the boss?* wondered Jane—stationed in front of Thomas's spacious enclosure. It had glass windows with blinds that could be shut, say if ever Tina and B.B. wanted to get kinky and go at it, mere steps from the staff.

Jane wasn't in the mood to mince words, so she just brandished her badge as she and Sammy made straight for *The Dragon Lady's* den. Since the blinds were open, the detective could get a good view of her next suspect—and marveled. Having Googled last night for some quick facts regarding the board members, she had learned Tina Thomas was sixty-two years old. Yet the woman, standing in profile, braless in a tight designer tee, had breasts that defied gravity and a perfectly tight round ass (easily shown by the spandex leggings which enclosed it). And, at least from a distance, a face free from the wrinkles one would expect in someone her age. Jane would have thought she was about to interview someone in her

248

thirties—tops. In reading Melina-Ann's report, the detective had learned of the *quid pro quo* with the plastic surgeon and thought, *That guy deserves a Nobel Prize in medicine. Maybe, if I'm nice, Tina will give me his name.* But then she realized, at this stage of her day, the last thing she was in the mood to do was play nice. She was also getting hungry.

Sammy and Jane walked through the open door, but before a word could be uttered, their quarry said, "Please come in, Detective. Sammy. I've been expecting you."

Quite the brazen bitch, thought Jane. *She's got no qualms in letting us know she's already spoken to her lover.*

The duo entered and was beckoned to sit on the two chairs opposite Thomas's, across from a large, rectangular white oak desk. The detective immediately looked to the woman's watch and noticed it wasn't a Rolex. The Dragon Lady, like Mrs. Crowe, had *settled* for a *Cartier*.

"I was surprised to learn of your impending visit. After all, the NYPD has already closed the case and decided MAQ's tragic death was a suicide."

Everyone seems to be reading from the same script today, Jane mused.

"Yes," Jane began, "but we've learned from a recovered file on her laptop that she believed you, the rest of the board plus Brown and Crowe, have been robbing the corporation for decades. So, we posit one of the above mentioned might have done away with the woman before she could alert the IRS or present her information to her son at The Post."

Thomas made a gesture with her right hand that, if the appendage could speak, would probably translate to, "Tish, Tosh."

"Melinda-Ann, and I hate to speak ill of the dead,"—*but you will, anyway*, thought Jane—"can go suck my dick. Always thought she was better than anyone else. CPA to the stars. *Sooo* smart. Yet, she still got taken in by that Jew-bastard, Madoff."

I looked at Sammy, not only a good friend to Melinda-Ann but also well into his conversion process, and could see he was primed to explode, his hands clenched tightly into pale fists. But he was on a quest, and, if necessary, would put his personal feelings aside—though Jane was glad he wasn't armed. At least, she hoped he wasn't.

"Anyway, B.B. assures me if I'm honest with you about our whereabouts on the night in question, you have no interest in passing on those scurrilous accusations. Correct?"

The detective hated to let this ship of thieves get away with their rape of the QGT shareholders, but unless she could bring the murderer to justice, for Angelica and Joe's sake, she would, yes, ignore the financial improprieties.

"Yes, Ms. Thomas, that is correct. But..." Unlike Brown, Thomas was not a cop and Jane felt she could exert more pressure on the woman than on the man, even if it meant stretching the legal truths. "... before we begin, let me warn you. If what you say to me is later proven false, then you're opening up yourself to a world of legal hurt."

Tina Thomas smiled. She might *look* like she was born not far removed from yesterday, but she'd been around the block and knew bullshit when she heard it.

"Oh come, now, Detective. One, you have not read me my rights, so, unless you intend to, everything I say from here on will be thrown out of court. Considering you have no standing in this case, frankly, I don't have to answer one damn question if I don't want to. But, given your promise to B.B., I'm happy to comply with answering the main query at hand: Bill and I were *fucking our brains out* during the time in question. Gives a good foot massage, too. So, *voila*—there it is, all I've got to say. Now, unless you want me to call security and, since you're neither a resident nor an officer of the law in New York City, have you removed for trespassing, I'll ask you to leave."

Jane, seething, stood, followed by Sammy. "Have a nice day," she said aloud, silently followed by, *BITCH! I wouldn't rub your feet if it were guaranteed a Genie would emerge from your toes and grant me three wishes.*

In the outer office, Jane turned to her friend. "You showed great restraint, Sammy. I'm proud of you."

The man sighed. "I guess being with Helen has been good for my soul." He paused, then, "As far as that *puttana's* soul, Satan will welcome it soon enough."

Jane wasn't sure if that last sentiment was a wish, prediction, or promise. She decided any one was okay with her, and they left.

Jane hadn't felt it was worth correcting Thomas about the trespassing remark: as an officer of the law in New York State, *I can go anywhere I damn well please*, she seethed. But they had gotten all they were going to get out of *The Dragon Lady*—which was "jack shit," as she told Sammy as they entered the restaurant.

Sammy said nothing. He knew Jane was correct and his hopes were fading fast for any revelations coming from this morning of investigation. He led Jane to the back. "There's Peck and Suck, er, I mean Emi," he said as he pointed to a table along the far wall. The two walked toward the last of their suspects. Jane was pissed-off and not in the mood to be cordial.

She noisily grabbed a nearby chair, and Sammy followed suit. Jane brought it to the head of the couple's table and immediately understood what Agatha Monroe had meant about sitting downwind. The smell was, if not unbearable, certainly unpleasant. She looked for the nearest blowing HVAC heating vent and maneuvered her seat between it and the man. Not a perfect solution, but the best she'd get. Both wore sweaters which covered their wrists, so the detective couldn't ascertain what obscenely expensive watch each sported. She came to the point quickly. "Mr. Plick?" She produced her badge. "I'm Detective Jane Rieger-

251

Franklin and I'm sure you know Sammy Vivino. I need to ask you some questions about the death of Melinda-Ann Queen."

It's not worth boring you with the details of the conversation. Jane went at the couple as quickly as possible so she could reach fresh air before gagging. *The NYPD has already made their determination* mantra was repeated by the man, who then claimed, unsurprisingly, to be at home with Emi at the time of death. The woman, low and behold, confirmed she and Plick were indeed home, drinking *sake* or some such bullshit. Another couple willing to lie for each other it seemed, though to be fair, Jane admitted to herself, she had no proof of being lied to by them or even by Brown and Thomas. She was letting her frustrations get the better of her and was getting hungrier by the minute, watching all the patrons eating their lunch. Emi, except for confirming Peck's presence at home with her that night, said nothing. Since she'd already been able to chronically accept his odor and, per Agatha Monroe, lack of bedroom skills, adding potential murderer to his resumé was not as worrisome, it seemed, as possibly losing her store's rent exemption.

Plick stood, though stooped a bit, and Emi followed. "I'm sorry, but I have an appointment at the radiologist—another MRI for my fucking back. So, if there's nothing else, we have to make a quick stop at Emi's store."

Yeah, Jane thought, *wouldn't want to miss your pre-MRI BJ, would you?* But the detective didn't think she could shake any more out of them than she already knew, so she rose and thanked him for his time, again stressing the financial doings were not her concern—*Joe and Angelica, you owe me, big-time.*

As the couple left, Emi turned and presented her middle finger. "*Kutabare!*" she spat, and continued on her way. Jane learned later that word was Japanese for "Fuck you!" As per usual, it was said without a smile.

Jane noticed an exit to the golf course and told Sammy to wait a moment and left. She inhaled and exhaled the fresh, cold air about eight times, then rejoined her friend.

"How about some lunch, my dear? On me."

"You're on, Lover Boy. I'm starved."

The two made their way to the front of the restaurant, but Sammy stopped suddenly and nodded toward a couple in one of the nearby booths.

"I know they're not really on your radar, Jane, but there's Jack and Jill Ginsburg. Want to talk to them?"

The detective was hungry and tired—not a good combination, she'd learned from experience. But she'd also knew many times assumptions she'd made in a case turned out to be wrong, and maybe the supposition the killer was involved in *all* the "suicides" was one of them. Maybe Finberg's and Chan's deaths were truly by their own hand, and only MAQ's was murder. The Ginsburg's had joined the board in 2009, after Chan's death, so they were not implicated in his death or any previous other's, at least as per her theory—which, she inwardly admitted, might be pure horseshit. It couldn't hurt to give them a shot. "Lunch can wait a few more minutes, I guess, Sammy."

The two approached the couple, who were sitting on either side of the booth's table. Each wore a Citizen brand watch. *Haven't had your ship come in, just yet,* thought Jane. She slid next to the woman and Sammy, the man.

Mrs. Ginsberg's hair was so tightly tied in a bun that, unlike Thomas, she'd never require Botox for forehead wrinkles. Her husband's appearance was remarkable for being unremarkable—except that throughout the conversation, Jane thought his face seemed permanently set to *dour*. Neither knew Vivino, except by sight, and certainly did not know the detective. They had yet to receive their food and were both playing with their phones.

Jane presented her badge and announced she was investigating the death of Melinda-Ann. Jill Ginsburg let out a gasp and Jack's face turned dourer. *Not used to talking to cops, it would seem,* the detective surmised. *Probably not very good poker players, either.*

Jane immediately got to the point about suspecting murder and both, yet again, repeated the now burned-into-her-brain line about the NYPD's determination of suicide. Jane then mentioned the file contents and Jack and Jill, it seemed, were ready to admit to masterminding the Kennedy assassination, anything to avoid having the IRS sicced on them. They were so busy laying the blame concerning the financial dealings on the others they forgot they were suspects in a murder investigation. After Jane allayed their fears about the money, they profusely thanked her, but now concentrating on MAQ's death, had nothing to add except they were, of course, together all night, watching Netflix. Jane asked them each to write the name of the movie on a napkin, unseen by the other; they successfully complied.

Shit was all the detective could manage to think as her blood sugar continued to drop rapidly. After a few more minutes, it seemed clear the couple was too inept and petrified of jail to ever consider murdering anyone, unless they were the best acting family since the Barrymores. They apparently were so upset with the line of questioning that, once dismissed by Jane, they got up and exited. *Even his ass looks dour*, the detective thought as she viewed the creases in the man's pants from behind.

She and Sammy remained seated, and within a few seconds, the waiter appeared with two platefuls of food. He seemed confused. "What have you got there?" Jane asked.

"A cheese omelet and—"

"I'll take it. Put it here," she barked, pointing to the table in front of her.

"And" the waiter continued, "a turkey on whole-wheat."

Sammy considered the non-kosher meat. *I haven't converted yet*, he reasoned. "I prefer club, but okay, let me have it. And bring me a Diet Coke."

"Yeah," Jane added. "Me too."

And they both ate without speaking for the next fifteen minutes.

When they had finished their meals, Jane felt she should deliver the bad news and get it over with. Her companion was not surprised.

"I'm sorry Sammy, I know you and Joe wanted justice here, but with no actual evidence, nothing said today really changes anything. Worse, I think we may be barking up an entirely wrong tree."

"What do you mean, Jane?"

"Well, with each suspect, I made a point of mentioning that *deleted* file of MAQ's."

"Yes, I noticed. Why?"

"Because if we're right, whoever killed her deleted the file, assuming it would never see the light of day. Probably didn't know it could be retrieved or figured no one would bother to look. I mentioned it to see the reaction. I watched extremely closely as I said the words, looking for a *tell*, any hint of surprise. Trouble is, I saw none, from any of them. Sure, whoever the murderer is may be a very slick, cool customer, like B.B.—or that bitch Thomas. But the fact is, no one seemed surprised Melinda's computer still had that file with her claims on it. It's possible we're wrong, either about the murder, which I doubt, or there is yet an unknown player, totally unrelated to the board business. Maybe a jilted lover, who knows?

"In any event, I'm sorry, but I think the thing to do now is move on. We've got a joyous wedding coming up to finish planning, and you've got your Judaica studies to deal with. And who knows? Maybe another wedding to plan, in about a year or so, no? What do you think?"

Sammy smiled and took a last sip from his glass. "You're right Jane. I'll speak to Joe. Like you said, it's time to make plans for the future. It pains me, though. I deeply cared for that woman and the thought of her, helpless, in the hands of some monster it... it..." The man started to tear up and used his napkin to wipe his eyes. "But you're right. You know what? My studies have led me to believe there *is* a life after this. We will all be judged. Hopefully, when the time comes for whoever did this, they will finally face justice. My only wish, and please don't tell Helen, is that whenever the one who did this finally dies—he dies, *screaming*."

Jane nodded, and Sammy took her hand. "Thank you, Jane, for at least trying. I hope you don't get into any trouble. I don't trust that lawyer; but then again, I don't trust *any* lawyers." Jane laughed. "You are a true friend, and, as I've said before, what you did for my Angelica will never be forgotten." He kissed her hand and Jane then took his and reciprocated.

Sammy left forty dollars on the table. "Let's go home, my friend."

And they left, content they had done their best, both looking forward to planning, as Jane had said, for a bright future.

Man plans...

Chapter 33

February 18
Garden City High School
1:00 AM

The three teens met, as planned, at the exterior door that led to the gymnasium. Tommy Blake, the leader, had earlier taped the door bolt so it would not engage the strike-plate hole. They had chipped in fifty dollars each to bribe Chris, the custodian (a past student to whom the teens often provided weed), to ignore this little detail during his evening rounds before leaving for home at midnight. They already knew from Chris the sign on the door warning an alarm would sound if opened was, in the man's words, "pure bullshit." Chris had accepted the payoff and needed the steady supply of marijuana; he could be counted on to keep his mouth shut.

On October 1, 2019, the age at which a teen could be tried as an adult in New York State was raised to eighteen. Given each student was seventeen, the boys knew the worst that could happen in the aftermath of what they were planning would be a trip to Family Court—thank you, New York State Legislature!

They weren't into mass murder, thankfully—just seniors, high school misanthropes, none with over a C-minus average. Their ninth-grade algebra teacher had once joked to a colleague that whenever the three entered his classroom, he would imagine *The Three Stooges* theme music playing in the background. They'd all be headed to community college if not for their wealthy Garden City parents' ability to pay the huge tuition costs an out-of-town, mediocre four-year school would charge to accept their sons despite poor academic performances. Except Tommy. His father, who owned a chain of dry-cleaners in Nassau and Suffolk counties, felt if his son couldn't even get into a state school, with its minimal tuition, then, "Fuck it." Tommy Blake was headed to work in one of dad's hot, smelling-of-chemicals stores, "to learn the business," the chances similar to Lenny Schwartz ever learning Mel's. Well, if *that hell,* Tommy thought, was where he was headed, the teen figured it was time to have at least one last hurrah. So, along with his other friends, miscreants all, he'd planned tomorrow's big event. They all hated their schoolmates, teachers, parents, and the cops—everyone who had showered all manner of real or imagined indignities upon their heads. Well, in twelve hours, they'd have some measure of revenge, they believed.

Each carried two compact, yet powerful, battery-operated WiFi enabled speakers and carefully maneuvered the halls, evading the few surveillance cameras the school had long ago installed. The cameras' blind spots were quickly learned by the students years ago and passed along, year after year, senior to freshman, like religious lore. Many loved to test the system now and then and make out or smoke a joint in one of the spots. No one had yet to be caught, so the three knew they would not be seen when the footage was reviewed over the coming days. But, not total morons, they wore hoodies, just in case. They also knew the four dome-shaped cameras installed by the Garden City Police were kept off—*privacy issues*, the parents of the wealthy town had protested. The only time those cameras were activated was in case of emergency. The teens knew the devices would come alive tomorrow—they were counting on it.

Each student knew his assignment—place his speakers atop a bank of lockers on each floor of the school in a centralized area where any sounds emanating would be carried to most of the classrooms and administrative offices. With diligence never applied to their studies, they had spent hours scouring the internet for MP3 files of sub-machine gun and handgun-fire reports. They also included sounds of people screaming.

It was going to be a glorious prank! At exactly 1:17 PM—seventeen was Tommy's lucky number—he would, from the comfort and obscurity of his seat in English class, trigger his pair of speakers to play one of the MP3 files via an app on his iPhone. Then, at fifteen second intervals, guaranteed precisely by each of their Apple Watches, his pals would, in turn, do the same with the files set to play on their devices, scattered throughout the school.

By 1:18 PM, there'd be absolute chaos. The sounds of bullets firing and people screaming would quickly lead to lockdown procedures. Tommy and his friends would fuel the fire with hysterical speculations about multiple shooters. The students would stay in their rooms, gathered into multiple groups to avoid large targets for a shooter to aim at. The principal would dial 9-1-1 and every cruiser the Garden City Police owned, along with every officer of the town's own dedicated police force, would converge on the high school. Ambulances would come from NYU/Winthrop Medical Center. More than likely, Nassau County Police would be requested to assist with their Emergency Services Unit. Students and teachers alike, in their panic, would flood 9-1-1 with calls, as would their parents, once alerted. The system would quickly be overloaded. "I sure hope no old geezer has a heart attack walking his fuckin' dog during all this," Tommy had joked to his friends as they discussed their plan. "*NO 9-1-1 FOR YOU!*" he said in a tone reminiscent of *Seinfeld's* "Soup Nazi." They had all collapsed in laughter.

Future leaders of America.

Yes, it would be *glorious*—Tommy's favorite word—fun. The teens, showing just a hint of intelligence, decided to *remotely*, thus anonymously, set the chaos in motion. They did not want to deal with the police and jail, even if they were minors destined for just a slap on the wrist. No, it was enough for them to know they had pulled the prank of the century and maybe, after a suitable period, they'd get together for one of those Infotainment TV shows and announce to the world they were the ones behind "The Glorious Garden City Con," as Tommy decided it would be referred to. Maybe make a few bucks and get laid out of the experience, too.

By 2 AM, they had completed their work and returned home to their beds. None could sleep, however—each imagining the pandemonium that was to ensue in less than twelve hours. Tommy was especially psyched and repeated the same word, over and over—

"Glorious!"

Chapter 34

Nassau County Police Headquarters
Garden City
12 Noon

Detective Jane Rieger-Franklin sat at her desk—and smiled. Her team had just returned from a huge collar—a gangbanger who'd shot and killed an innocent, twenty-four-year-old female bystander. The tragedy had occurred two days earlier during an exchange of gunfire with a rival gang member in Hempstead. Jane's team had surprised and arrested the twenty-year-old suspect, still asleep in his bed at 11 AM—without firing a shot. Over the past four months, attrition, including the retirement of her sergeant, had by default promoted her to senior detective on the team.

Jane had recently taken the sergeant's exam, and the results would be announced shortly. The test was a snap for the detective, but the expected passing grade would be bittersweet. Promotion to sergeant meant returning to uniform ("back in the bag," it's called), to wait once again for promotion to Detective Sergeant, which would be at the whim of the Police Commissioner. But for now, she could bask in the joy of the arrest and relax while Dan Mason, the lowest-ranking detective, dutifully wrote up the official arrest report.

The commissioner was still evaluating candidates for a new detective sergeant and supposedly was down to one from Plainview and another from Manhasset. Jane knew both, and would be happy with either for the rest of her time on the team. Meanwhile, she was the boss and way proud of her crew's performance. The after-shift beers would be on her.

"Jane, *Betty* on line two," said team member Steve Wilson, stressing the latter's name.

Shit, Jane thought, interrupted from her reverie. *Just when I was thinking this was going to be a perfect day.*

All the members of the team stopped what they were doing and stared at their leader. A call from Betty, Detective Captain John Hall's secretary, meant only one thing—the man wanted to speak with Jane. On what was a personal day off.

It was common knowledge the man never, NEVER, wanted to be disturbed on his days off. An alarm that *The Four Horsemen of the Apocalypse* were seen galloping down Franklin Avenue, lopping off the heads of the English nannies as each pushed their employer's *Dior* strollers?—don't even think about bothering Captain Hall on his day off! Call Lieutenant Charles.

Taking time out from whatever personal stuff he was doing to call in and ask for Jane meant only one thing—

"I sense a disturbance in *The Force*, Jane. You're fucked." Those words of wisdom were from Dave, the next detective in seniority, and a huge Star Wars fan. Jane had to agree, but still, smirking, gave the man the finger. *What could Hall want that's so important? To congratulate me on the bust? Nah, that would wait till tomorrow. What did I... uh, oh. Shit.*

She picked up the phone and punched in the extension. "Yes, Betty, I'm here. Yeah, I'll hold... Captain! Good after—"

"Rieger! Do you know where I am?" Captain Hall began.

"Er, no sir."

"Well, I'll tell you. I'm at home. Up until about three minutes ago, I was relaxing, doing a crossword puzzle. You know what the twenty-letter answer to the clue, 'The person Captain Hall least wants to hear from while relaxing at home doing the crossword puzzle,' is Rieger?"

Jane wasn't sure if technically that was considered a rhetorical question, since such questions, by definition, were asked without expecting a response. Ace detective that she was, Jane figured her captain wanted her to at least say, as she did, "No sir, I don't."

"*Commissioner of Police.* I didn't even have to check with Rex Parker on that one."

"Rex P—?"

"Google him!

"Yes, sir."

"Actually, Commissioner of Police, Janet Masefield, to be precise."

Jane knew who the Commissioner of Police was, but hearing the name still sent a shiver through her body.

Double shit. There goes Detective Sergeant anytime this century.

"It seems," continued Hall, "Commissioner Masefield just got off the phone with some shyster lawyer who just happens to live in Garden City and, can you imagine the odds, amazingly belongs to the same country club as she. Plays golf with her fucking husband during the season! What are the chances? I'm so lucky today, I should buy a Lotto ticket."

Fuck me.

"It seems this shyster lawyer, and I know he's a shyster because they all are, is the attorney for the QueensGate Towers cooperative—in the BOROUGH OF QUEENS, in case you're geographically challenged. Yet somehow, this officer of the court gets a visit from a Nassau County Detective who, according to him, attempted extortion, accused the man of financial impropriety and, here's the kicker—all but charged him with premeditated murder!"

263

"I did *not* accuse him of murder, sir. He is, however, probably guilty of multiple shady, almost certainly illegal monetary—"

"You're missing the point, Rieger! I don't care if the SOB robs banks when he's not overcharging his clients. If he does it in Queens, it's none of your business. Even if he's a 21st Century Jack the Ripper, as long as he confines his cutting west of the Nassau County line, it's also, none—of—your—business."

"But my investigation has been during my off hours, sir, and—"

"Are you going to argue the fine point of just where you're allowed to flash your badge and assert your authority, on or off duty—especially in a case already closed by the NYPD, Detective Rieger-Franklin?"

"No, sir... I am not."

"Good! Now the fact this shyster is a friend of Masefield is not surprising"—FYI, Captain Hall and Commissioner Masefield were not the best of friends—"but I still had to sit on the phone and take her abuse and promise to make it up to her husband's golf buddy! So, this is what *you're* going to do. This prick is going to be home today until four, I'm told. His address is One Whisper Lane and, aren't you lucky—it's just a hop, skip and a jump from where your ass is planted right now. So, drop whatever you're doing, and I mean whatever. I don't care if you just got a tip and were on your way to dig up the remains of Jimmy Hoffa on the grounds of Hofstra. You get on over to his, I'm sure, *way*-too-ostentatious home, given the address, bend down, kiss his ass until it's beet red and apologize. You understand?"

Jane had a lot she still wanted to say, but she enjoyed being the temporary boss of her squad and would not risk demotion. So, she answered, "Yes, sir," and looked at her team members. Her face must have told the whole story because each had that forlorn, 'there but for the grace of God, go I,' look on their own.

Hall sighed deeply. Calmly, he added, "Look, Jane. I know you probably had a good reason for doing what you did, and tomorrow you can tell me all about it. But Masefield is looking for any reason to kick me sideways, out of 1490"—that's 1490 Franklin Avenue, headquarters of the NCPD—"and bring in one of her pals. So go over there and try to make nice. Okay?"

Captain Hall was, in fact, a good guy, Jane knew. She felt terrible he had been put in this position by her off-the-books investigation. "Don't worry, Captain, I'll make it right. I'll get on it as soon as I find my Chapstick."

The man sighed. Jane's attempt at humor had fallen flat, she realized. "Thank you, Jane. See you tomorrow." And he hung up.

The rest of Jane's team had resumed their busy work, not willing to even ask what the discussion was about. They knew their boss had screwed something up, at least in the eyes of the higher-ups. If she needed them to have her back, they would, to a man. And she knew it, too. But this was her mess, and Jane would have to face the consequences alone. But she was furious at *that fucking son-of-a-bitch Crowe*! She looked into her desk and found the slip of paper she had written on two days ago. She was going to throw it into the garbage this morning, but the call came in on her perp and she and the team had rushed out. Now, she decided, hope against hope, to give this Queen thing one last try. If she succeeded, it would go a long way to appease Hall and even Masefield. If Crowe turned out to be the murderer, by chance, so much the better.

If ifs and buts were candy and nuts, what a lovely Christmas this would be, she thought. That adage, often quoted by Martin Rieger, always brought a smile to his daughter's face, as it briefly did now.

Anyway, there's no risk in doing this, right? she mused. *Yeah, famous last words.* Jane rose from her chair.

"As you've surmised, gentlemen. I've got some crow to eat..." she shook her head and spat—"... literally!"

Jane stormed out of the room, her colleagues puzzled by that last remark, and headed straight for the Intel Group.

<hr>

Thomas had taken a few days off, leading into the weekend to celebrate his engagement with his fiancée. So, he was in Montauk and Harold was at lunch. That meant Tony was alone. *Just as well*, Jane thought. *No need to get anyone else involved in my problems.* She entered the room and Tony saw her immediately. "Hi Jane."

The detective closed the door.

"Oh, shit," the man said, frowning.

"Yeah, I know Tony. I have one more, off-the-books-favor." She handed him the slip of paper. "On this sheet are two lists of names. On the left are my suspects"—she had written Abraham Crowe, Tina Thomas, William Brown, Peter Plick and Jack and Jill Ginsburg, along with their addresses—"and on the right are six suicides. Maybe." There she had written everyone, even those not on the board of directors, such as the murder/suicide cop. *Might as well throw the kitchen sink in and see what happens*, she thought. This was, after all, her *Hail Mary pass*.

"You know that movie, or was it a show, *Six Degrees of Separation*, right?"

"It was a movie."

"Right. Anyway, you know the premise. Given six random names, there will be a connection between at least two of them. Well, here are twelve. What I'd like, is for you to put these into your computer and run the left side against the right, through every fucking database you can think of—court records, police reports, college rosters, whatever, and see if anyone on the left-hand column is found in the same document or report with anyone on the right. Any connection at all. Can it be done, Tony?"

"Sure, Jane. It's pretty quiet, so not a problem. It will take a while, though."

"What do you think?"

"Figure an hour."

Jane smiled. "That long, huh? Actually, I thought you were going to say days. An hour is fine. Just call me on my *cell*—not the radio, when you're done, okay?"

Her friend nodded. He understood Jane didn't want any official communication regarding her request—for both their sakes.

"Thanks, Tony. You're the best. Speak to you soon."

Jane proceeded out of the building onto Franklin Avenue. She had time. First, lunch. *Pizza.* That thought slightly lightened her mood. Then she'd make her way to One Whisper Lane.

She went into her purse, took out her phone and began to call Anna, to let her know where she'd be. It was their routine to always inform the other what was going on. She did it this morning before the bust and immediately after, knowing her wife would be on pins-and-needles. But she stopped. *Not now. Too embarrassing. Tonight,* she thought. *Tonight, I'll tell her all about it. After some wine and TLC.*

She put the phone back in her purse.

It was 12:30 PM.

Chapter 35

One Whisper Lane
Garden City
1:15:03 PM

Jane pulled up to the stately, center-hall colonial on Whisper Lane. There was a circular driveway, and she drove to its middle, parking right in front of the door. Dreading the encounter, she slowly exited the car and rang the doorbell. Almost immediately, as if the occupants were given advance notice—*wouldn't put it past that bitch Masefield,* Jane thought—Celine Crowe appeared.

"Detective Rieger-Franklin. How nice to see you again."

So, she did know in advance. "Yes, Mrs. Crowe. I'm here to see your husband, if you don't mind."

"Certainly, Detective. I'm sure he'll be *just thrilled* to hear what you have to say." And with that, the woman turned as if dismissing the visitor, and Jane followed, shutting the door behind her. Their paths led them past the upstairs staircase, and they approached two closed doors—pocket doors, which Crowe now spread apart. She bade Jane enter and, without closing the doors, retreated into the sizable house as the detective continued.

Jane appeared to be in the den, a large area with a fireplace as the central ornament against the far wall, opposite the doors. The largeness of the room was made to appear even more so by that wall being paneled, not with wood, but mirrors. To her right, as she entered, was a pedestal with a large, about eighteen-inch sized, solid glass pyramid. It was exquisite, with swirls of many colors throughout. The light, streaming in from multiple windows, made the whirls appear alive, creating ever-changing hues as the rays hit the multiple glass sides and were, as in any prism, diffracted within. The entire room, in fact, was decorated beautifully with many antique pieces, not the least being the large mahogany desk at which the lawyer sat, on the right side of the expanse. He didn't rise to meet his guest. Instead, looking down at some papers, he said, "So, Detective. The Commissioner tells me you have something to say. Out with it and then go."

Prick. Easy Jane, just get this over with. For no particular reason, she glanced at her Apple Watch—

It was 1:16:50 PM.

Garden City High School

Tommy Blake sat in his seat in English class and waited. All the preparations were made. The speakers were in place, and last night he and his friends had coated all the cameras that would be activated by the GCPD, once the alarm was sounded, with Vaseline. Sightless, the police would be convinced something was indeed amiss at the school.

He looked at his phone. The screen was open. All he had to do was hit the play button. He watched the time in the upper-left corner as it changed to exactly 1:17:00 PM.

Showtime.

One Whisper Lane
1:17:01 PM

"Well," began Jane, "I just wanted to tell you my investigation is complete. You'll be happy to know there is no evidence anyone at QueensGate Towers was involved in Melinda-Ann Queen's death. It appears... as was determined earlier by the NYPD, the woman committed suicide."

Crowe hadn't looked up from his work all this time. Now he did. "And..."

Jane swallowed hard. "And I want to apologize for any insinuations I might have made otherwise. And,"—*might as well grovel all the way*—"thank you for speeding up my friends' application and approving their dog." Jane felt like crawling into a hole somewhere to die. *Just shoot me now.*

The man smiled. "There, that wasn't so difficult, now was it?" Jane decided that *was* a rhetorical question and didn't bother to answer. Antsy, she strolled over to the fireplace and there noticed some photos on the mantelpiece. They interested her. As Crowe continued to drone on about young people today being so headstrong and disrespectful of their elders—"... blah, blah, blah..." was all Jane heard—she examined three photos. At one end was a picture of the Crowes, again in front of the Eiffel Tower. At the other end was one taken in China, at the Great Wall. The center photo seemed out of place. It was of the husband and wife in the man's QGT office, though the seat was taken by another, older gentleman—*that's the guy from the portrait,* Jane realized—the younger couple standing at each side of him, all smiling for the camera. The central man was clearly the boss. The one in charge.

I thought Crowe was the co-op's lawyer from the beginning? The detective asked herself.

Then, interrupting the man's soliloquy, she said, "You do a lot of traveling, Mr. Crowe? My wife and I would love to travel more."

The lawyer was taken aback by the interruption. But he liked to brag about how well-traveled he and his wife were, so, "Yes, we do. We go to Paris at least twice a year—Celine's mother is still alive

270

and lives there. Celine left for college in the States and decided to stay. Once or twice, at other times in the year, we go elsewhere."

"Ever been to Singapore, counselor?"

Crowe, to his credit, did not show any surprise. He just stared, and then, without missing a beat, "As a matter of fact, yes. Wonderful place. We've encouraged everyone we know to try to get there, if possible."

Yeah, I'll bet.

"Now, if you're finished with the fawning, I've got work to do."

"Sorry. Just curious, though. Who's this guy?" She pointed to the man in the center picture. "I remember him from another photo in your office."

"Oh," he began, smiling. "That was Doug McCallan. He was the first attorney for the co-op. Eight years. Sort of a mentor to me. Gave me work right after law school, when I really needed it, helping him out with closings and such at QueensGate. Introduced me to my wife, in fact. She was his legal secretary. He died way too young. Only sixty."

Jane's head tried to process this new information, and it was intoxicating as well as bewildering. Pieces were fitting into places she hadn't known even existed. "Really? How did he die?"

The lawyer was now in a reminiscing mood, not seeing Jane as an adversary—after all, she'd just groveled before him—but someone whose questions were evoking happy memories. "Anaphylactic shock." Jane was stunned, remembering her own experience with Don Fortuna. "He was allergic to shellfish. Kept a needle filled with some medicine in his drawer, just in case. Each day, he ordered out for lunch from a local deli. He didn't like the one on premises. They knew him well and had *strict* instructions no shellfish come anywhere near his food. Well, one day, Celine brought back a tuna sandwich, and—"

"Your wife got his lunches?"

"Yes, every day. Anyway, it seems some of the deli's shrimp salad found its way into his tuna. Died before he could get to his

271

medicine. Celine even tried mouth-to-mouth, to no avail." The man stopped for a few beats, remembering. Then, the lawyer in him kicked into high gear. "Sued the deli bastards and settled for a small fortune from their insurance company." He smiled. "Anyway, since I was already working with him on a good many co-op contracts, Ms. Thomas and the board appointed me immediately to take his place and I've been there ever since."

"And your wife stayed on as your legal secretary."

"Well, we weren't married yet. That came six months later. Now if you'll excuse me, I've—"

Jane's iPhone exploded with the ringtone of *Star Wars*—the Intel Group. To her Homicide office she'd assigned Darth Vader's Theme.

"Sorry, Mr. Crowe, I'll just be a second and then I'll be on my way."

The detective picked up the phone, noticed the time was 1:19, and answered. "Tony?"

"Yeah, Jane. Look, gotta make this quick. Things are getting a little hectic over here. There's a report of a shooter at GC High. 9-1-1 is swamped. ESU has been requested. Anyway, I ran those names and came up pretty empty." Jane's heart sank. "Just one hit, and not one I would think will be useful, but anyway, here it is. The only match I got was between Abraham Crowe and one of the suicides, Harriet Gold. Seems in 2001, Crowe's wife sued for divorce..." *Yes*, Jane thought, *Agatha Monroe had mentioned something like that...* "and, turns out, the woman named as the co-defendant was Harriet Gold, for 'alienation of affection.'" Jane's heart instantaneously doubled its rate. "Then, just two weeks later, the complaint was dropped by the wife. Crazy."

Jane's mind was racing. "What was the exact date the complaint was dropped, Tony?"

"Hmm, let's see. Here it is—February 1, 2001."

Two days after Gold's supposed suicide.

Jane's mind raced: *'Asshole-Abe and his frog wife—been here from the beginning,' Agatha Monroe had said. 'Frog,' not in appearance, but as in the outdated reference to being French! She didn't mean Crowe had been at QGT from the beginning. That's what I assumed. That's where I made my mistake. There had been a pause after 'Abe,' before the 'And.' The lawyer wasn't even around at the time of Finberg's death—that guy McCallan was. Agatha meant just the wife;* she'd *been here from the beginning, not just the twenty years since she married. Shit, she's been around for* all *the 'suicides!' I discounted Harriet Gold because she wasn't a board member. But she wasn't killed for any co-op related reason. She was killed for the oldest reason in the book—'Hell hath no fury like a woman scorned!' It ain't Shakespeare, but it should be.*

"Thanks, Tony." Jane ended the call.

The detective knew she was right. She also knew there was no proof, nothing that would stand up in court. Still... *Fuck the Commissioner. Time to rattle a cage.*

"Mr. Crowe. Does the name Harriet Gold ring a bell?"

The man's face turned red, and he started to stammer. Jane was so engrossed in anticipation of his response she didn't hear the approaching footsteps. She was first dazzled by a colorful beam of reflected sunlight appearing to her right. Then the glass pyramid entered her peripheral vision. Finally, there was sharp pain—

And everything went black as Jane crashed to the marble floor. It was 1:20:00 PM.

Lake Success
1:20:41 PM

Anna had just finished lunch when the text came in. She looked at her phone—and froze:

Jane Rieger-Franklin's Apple Watch has detected a hard fall. Emergency Services Have Been Notified.

Longitude and latitude coordinates followed, which Anna pressed. Apple Maps then opened and zeroed in on a satellite image of a house. Anna long-pressed and an address appeared - **1 Whisper Lane, Garden City NY**.

Anna, though startled, knew Jane's watch often suffered false alarms due to its fall-detection app. These usually occurred when they were playing tennis or doing their weekly self-defense training Jane had established with her wife. Anna knew the watch would first alert the wearer it had detected a fall. It would not alert emergency contacts and 9-1-1 unless the user did not respond within forty seconds. The fact she was getting this alert meant Jane had not responded in time.

There are many reasons, Anna thought, *this could be: Jane might be involved in a serious altercation and had no time to respond. Or...* Try as she might, the woman could not come up with another explanation. *Jane would never want me to worry. She would have called or texted she was okay!* Anna quickly dialed her wife's number, but after five rings, it went to voicemail. She ended the call and pulled up the 'Find My' app and searched for Jane's iPhone. The app showed the last location, again 1 Whisper Lane in Garden City, but after fifteen seconds of attempting to reload, a message appeared telling Anna that Jane's phone could not be located at this moment in time.

Okay, calm down, she pleaded with herself. *There's got to be a simple explanation. Anyway 9-1-1 was called and cops and an ambulance are on their way, right?* But as her heart rate accelerated, the woman could not relax. She grabbed her car keys and raced to the door but then stopped—*Angelica and the kids are at the mall! That's right by Garden City*. Anna reached again for the phone and dialed.

––––––––––––––––––––

1:21:30

"Okay, ladies. Buckle up."

274

Angelica, Felicity, Khaleesi and Maverick had just entered the Mercedes to head back to home base. They had a wonderful time window-shopping, getting their nails done and browsing through multiple stores, including the Comic Book shop. There, they purchased some Manga the two kids loved so much. Then, after visiting the Apple Store and playing with the MacBooks and iPads, they ended up at the Food Court where they all, including Maverick, enjoyed ice-cream. Jane had a friend at Animal Control who provided her, as a favor, with a Service Animal jacket for Maverick to wear in circumstances such as at the Roosevelt Field Mall, where only such pets were allowed. A service license was also delivered. It was skirting the law, but Jane was no stranger to pushing legal boundaries.

Right after she pressed the ignition button, a call came in on Angelica's phone, which was immediately routed to the car's communication system, its speakers taking over for the phone's. The ring tone notified all that it was Anna calling. Angelica pushed the answer button on the car's large LCD display. "Hi, Anna, we're just—"

"Angelica! I need your help!" The girls, who had been petting Maverick in the back seat, stopped and looked at each other with concern.

"What is it?"

"I just got an alert on my phone that Jane's watch detected a fall. The thing is, we get those false alarms all the time and Jane just cancels them. But this time, no. I think she would have had about forty seconds to respond. So, for whatever reason, she didn't. Couldn't. I'm worried and the watch tells me her last known location was One Whisper Lane in Garden City. I remembered you were close by—"

"I'm way ahead of you, Anna. Already inputting the address into the NAV system. Just give me a second... there. Yes, that address is just two miles away, maybe four minutes tops. I'll drive by and see what's up, though hopefully 9-1-1 was notified and cops and an ambulance are already there."

"Yeah, I know, but I just saw a notification on my phone that there's an active shooter at the local High School. So who knows if the police have the ability at the moment to answer a call from *a fucking watch! Who knows if 9-1-1 is even still working!*"

She's losing it, thought Angelica. "Okay, Anna. I'm on my way!"

"Me too. See you there!" And the call ended.

Felicity had taken Khaleesi's hand during the conversation. "Do you think Mama's all right?" the older girl asked, sounding, for once, as young as her age—the nightmares intruding into reality.

"Sure, babe. Your kick-ass mama can handle herself as well as anybody. But no harm in checking it out." Angelica, her thoughts at odds with her words, put the car in Drive. "Hang on, everyone." *Let's see what this baby can do when pushed to the limit!*

It was 1:22:20 PM.

One Whisper Lane
Two minutes, fifteen seconds earlier
1:20:05 PM

"WHAT THE FUCK DID YOU DO!?" Abe Crowe screamed.

Celine looked at the glass pyramid. It was partially covered in blood. The detective's body lay at her feet, more of the blood pooling around the head where the globe had struck. The cop lay still, but her chest continued to move with each labored breath. Mrs. Crowe, wearing latex gloves, placed the figurine on the floor.

Man and wife looked at each other. No words for about half a minute. Suddenly, there came a beeping noise near the fallen woman. Celine walked over and realized the sound was emanating from the cop's watch. She was unaware of the workings of the Apple Watch, but decided not to take any chances. She first found

276

the detective's phone and smashed it with the pyramid. Then, grabbing Jane's left hand, Crowe repeatedly slammed the watch-face to the floor until the beeping stopped.

Abe Crowe had sufficiently recovered to speak again. "Celine, do you know what you've done?"

The woman looked at the man with disdain. "Of course I know, you idiot. You were about to tell her all about that Jezebel, Gold, weren't you? You'd already said much too much. Don't you see the bitch had already figured it all out?"

The man was incredulous. "Figured out what?"

The woman shook her head and stood up, though not before grasping Jane's gun from her side holster. "You've always been so clueless, haven't you, Abe? Your brain can figure out all the intricate schemes for making shitloads of money, but when it comes to seeing what's in front of your face... fucking clueless. I know you didn't come on the QueensGate scene until after Ted Finberg's death. But you were there for Jerry's. Don't you think it's just too coincidental that Jerry and Melinda-Ann both decided to jump off their balconies after confronting the board with evidence of abuse? And you must have heard Ted had also been troubled about the goings on at the Towers. I couldn't let anyone get in the way of our schemes. Or let anyone go to the IRS.

"Doug was giving me a nice monthly stipend to keep my mouth shut back in the day. But once *we* got engaged, I knew my share would sky-rocket with marriage: so, I got rid of poor, old Doug—"

"Wait! Are you telling me you—"

"Of course! *I* mixed in the shrimp salad with his tuna, you schmuck. I knew the board would replace him with you given your involvement already with co-op matters. Doug tried to get to his injection, but instead of performing mouth to mouth, I forcibly held his hands back until he expired.

"Everything was going so well—then you decided to dip your wick into Harriet Gold! At first, I was furious and contacted a

277

lawyer, deciding to sue your ass for divorce. This you know. But then I thought, why should I get a pittance in a divorce settlement when you'd just finalized the antenna deal? There were millions in future payments to be made. I wasn't going to let that cunt be the one to share those payments with you. So, I threw her off her balcony too, just like Melinda-Ann. Then I *tearfully* forgave you, remember? And stopped the divorce proceedings. We've had a pretty good life since, no? Fucking you is a small price to pay for all the trips, cars, antiques and all."

Abe Crowe just stared, a look of stunned, abject defeat on his face. Then, in a soft voice said, "So just how do you expect to get away with attacking this police-woman?"

The wife smiled. "It's simple, really. She came here because her boss forced her to apologize. But she was seething with rage and accused you again of having something to do with MAQ's murder. Then she blamed you for the rebuke from her superiors. Accused you of sabotaging her career. You feared for your life and were about to run away but she took out her gun and fired, missing you and hitting the fireplace." One of Celine's old boyfriends was a real *gun-nut*, as she called him. But he taught her well, and she knew enough about how to rack the slide, load a round into the chamber of an automatic weapon and check the safety was off, which is what she just did. Then she fired to the man's right, hitting the brick of the hearth. The man recoiled in fear. "Jesus, Celine. What the fuck?"

"Then," she continued, "having heard the gunshot from outside the doors, I raced in and saw, to my *horror*," the woman giggled, "the cop raise the gun again and shoot, this time hitting you in the chest." Abe Crowe looked at his wife with a puzzling expression. At which point she aimed at the man, center mass, and fired. The look of bewilderment remained as he fell, face first, onto the floor.

"I was stunned," she continued, speaking aloud to no one but herself and a semi-conscious Jane, "and grabbed the heavy glass pyramid from the pedestal, took a running start and jumped up, bringing it down on the detective's head. I was quite the athlete in college. *Strong as bull.* Then,"—a low grunt came from Jane. She had sustained a concussion and was now teetering on the thin line separating consciousness from nothingness—"I rushed over to my *dear* husband, but soon realized he was dead. Overcome with grief, I realized *le objet d'art* was still in my hand, and came at the detective in a mad fury, striking her *again and again*, making sure she was dead. Speaking of which..."

Celine started to move toward the glass pyramid on the floor, removed her gloves, but stopped in mid-stoop as her phone beeped. She knew the sound. It represented her Ring camera at the front door, notifying her a car had approached within its wide-angle coverage. She stood, looked at the screen and saw a live view. A vehicle was pulling up. The murderer watched as it just came into view behind the detective's car. A few moments passed, and a woman exited and approached the door. As she came closer, Celine thought, *Shit, I know her. She's Sammy's daughter. The one buying the apartment with the doctor. And a friend of the fucking cop!* She pondered for a moment and decided. Finishing off the detective would have to wait. Crowe left the glass object on the floor, put the gloves in her pocket, and walked out of the room. She closed the pocket doors behind her, placing Jane's gun under her shirt, between her pants and the small of her back, and approached the door.

Time for another fly to enter the web.

Thirty seconds earlier
1:24:20 PM

Angelica stopped behind Jane's car. She had driven like a Formula One racer and ignored all the red lights to arrive as quickly as she did. She turned to the kids.

"Listen, guys. I'm gonna go have a looksee. You wait here. Felicity, when you see me enter the house, use your watch and time for sixty seconds. If I'm not back by then, or if I don't at least appear at the door and signal all is okay," she gave a thumbs-up sign, "You call 9-1-1 and tell them, and this is important, 'OFFICER DOWN, OFFICER DOWN! That'll get them here fast. Then you give the address, One Whisper Lane, Garden City. You got that?"

Felicity nodded. "Office down, officer down, One Whisper Lane Garden City." She looked at Khaleesi who repeated, "Officer down, One Whisper Lane, Garden City."

"Good girls," Angelica added. Then she opened the door and approached the house. Looking back one last time at the car, she rang the doorbell as she reached down to her right ankle—and came up empty.

Shit! Fucking New York gun laws, she thought, realizing there was no Sig to grab. All she had was Needle. *Just you and me, babe.*

Suddenly, the door opened, and Celine Crowe appeared, seemingly out of breath. Angelica didn't want her to see the children in the car, so she immediately entered to be at the interior side of the doorway.

"Thank God, you're here. You're the detective's friend, right?"

"Yes, what's going on?"

"There's been a terrible accident. In there." She walked toward the den and Angelica followed, leaving the front door open. Halfway, Crowe stopped and pointed to the closed pocket doors. Angelica, thinking only of her friend's condition, ran to the doors and spread them open—to find, in horror, Jane sprawled on the floor, her legs pointing in toward the fireplace. Her head was near the doors, blood pooling around it. Then Angelica saw the blood-smeared glass pyramid. *This is no fucking accident,* she thought and turned—just in time to see Celine Crowe raise Jane's gun. Angelica made an initial move but was too slow as the bullet tore into her left shoulder, forcing her down to the floor. She fell with her legs pointing out of the room, her head within inches and to the right of her friend's. Angelica was in agonizing pain and noticed bubbling

280

bright red blood oozing from her arm. She was trained by *Il Pugnale* well in anatomy and knew the location of every vital vessel that could be reached by an assassin's blade. She was sure her brachial artery was nicked by the bullet as it broke through her upper arm bone.

Shit, I'm going to bleed to death soon if I don't get to a hospital.

But the pain and concern for her own life were suddenly superseded by the terror she felt looking at her friend's face. Jane's eyes were open—

Unblinking—

Cloudy—

Dead.

1:25:31 PM

"Shit, a gun-shot!" Felicity screamed, her nightmares come fully alive. "I've got to go help. Mama's in there!" She turned to Khaleesi. "Call 9-1-1. You know what to say. I've got to go." She turned, but the younger girl grabbed her hand.

"Felicity, I'm scared. Don't leave me."

The older of the two gently but firmly released the younger's hand. "Look, Khal. Angelica, Mama, they need our help. I'm counting on you to do your part. You're smart. You know what to do. I've got to go." She grabbed the other by the shoulders. "I believe in you, *sister.*" And she kissed her quickly on the forehead and opened the door.

"Maverick, come!"

The dog quickly followed out the door, and the two approached the house. The door was luckily ajar, and they disappeared. Khaleesi took out her new iPhone, a gift from her soon-to-be parents, and opened the phone app. She pressed 9-1-1—and received a busy signal almost immediately.

"SHIT!" she shrieked. She tried again, same result. Five more times, the girl unsuccessfully attempted to reach the 9-1-1 operator.

"Shit, shit, shit—what do I do? Felicity, what do I do *now*?" She started to cry, but her sister's words echoed: *You're smart. You know what to do.*

"Mama's office!" the child said aloud—the first time she referred to Jane as such. The women had programmed the girl's iPhone with all the important numbers she'd need. One was Jane's work number. Khaleesi quickly opened the *Favorites* choice under the keypad and pressed *Jane's Office*. It rang.

Come on, come on, the girl pleaded. Then—"Nassau County Police, Homicide. Detective Mason. How can I help you?"

Khaleesi froze. The words just wouldn't come out. She was terrified. "Can I help you?" the man repeated.

The young child recalled Felicity's words: *I believe in you, sister.* And she responded—

"OFFICER DOWN OFFICER DOWN ONE WHISPER LANE GARDEN CITY! OFFICER JANE RIEGER DOWN!"

Sixty-one Seconds Earlier
1:26:00 PM

Jane blinked!

In her concussed state, her blink rate had diminished, thus leaving her corneas exposed to the air for longer periods, causing them to cloud up. It was probably painful, but at least she was still alive.

Celine Crowe walked to the fireplace, turned, and spoke.

"Well, this is indeed a complication." She paused, thinking. Then, "No problem. I'll just say you came to help your friend with her investigation, found her on the floor, and went berserk. Attacked me. We struggled, and I picked up the detective's gun and

282

shot you. Not perfect, I agree, but it's my word against two dead women, one who was reprimanded by her own commissioner. Yeah, it'll work and then..."

She continued to talk, but I wasn't listening. I knew I had only one chance. I was bleeding to death, tiring rapidly. This fucking madwoman was about to finish me off. I had one shot at this— *Needle*.

Amazing what can be remembered in mere milliseconds as I recalled *Il Pugnale's* training. The man could be brutal at times, none more so than when he'd take me to the local high school track and set up paper targets to throw at. Ten throws, aimed at center mass. By the time I had graduated from his schooling, I could, at first attempt, get ten out of ten. Then, he'd make me run around the quarter-mile track and throw once more. He'd repeat this procedure again and again until I was totally exhausted and could hardly lift the blades. At that last sequence, if I'd manage fifty percent, he considered it acceptable. Anything less, we'd continue with this exercise the next day until that magic fifty percent level was reached.

So, I knew I maybe had a fifty-fifty chance of hitting center mass, though I had never practiced throwing from the exact position I now found myself in. I lay on my left side, thus adding to the already excruciating pain in my left arm. I had, with my right hand, been applying pressure to stem the flow of blood, so the grip would be slippery at best. My legs were splayed behind me, the right leg bent at the knee, Needle nestled in her new sheath at my calf. As the woman spoke, I removed my right hand from the wound and slowly rolled up my pant leg to expose the sheath. Since it faced toward the door, Crowe did not see the blade—she was still babbling on.

I put my lips to Jane's ear. "Jane, I need a diversion. When you hear me cough, grunt as loud as you can. I need this bitch to look your way for a second. Okay?"

All Jane could do was blink twice in rapid succession. I took that as a positive response, her not wanting to speak and waste any energy. At least, that's what I told myself.

I saw my blood continue to pour from my shoulder and my vision was becoming blurry. It had to be now. I coughed.

The eyes. Always watch the eyes, I was taught. Jane let out a grunt, and though far from loud, it was enough to draw the attention of our adversary and I saw her eyes shift ever so slightly from me to my friend. *Center mass,* I repeated to myself. *Center mass. Hit the heart, a great vessel, anything.* I drew Needle from her sheath and flipped, with as much force as I could muster, underhanded, at my target—

And missed.

Carle Place, NY
1:27:33 PM

Detective Captain John Hall tossed the Frisbee to his golden retriever, Lucy, in the backyard of his home. He had taken the day off, a personal day. The last two weeks had taken a heavy toll. Two of his detectives were involved in gunplay. Both had not been injured, but in those moments between hearing of the incident and finding out all was well, the thoughts, the memories brought to the fore were almost unbearable. Especially the memories. He was also pissed-off at the Commissioner for using him as her errand boy to tell Jane she had to go and apologize to Masefield's shyster friend.

Lucy happily returned the thrown Frisbee, which she'd caught between her teeth. "Good girl," the man said as he reached into his pocket, retrieving a treat which he presented to his pet. She eagerly gobbled it down and awaited another toss. But just as Hall was about to oblige, his phone rang. It was his office. His secretary. The woman knew better than to call her boss on a day off unless there was no alternative. The man's chest tightened as he answered.

"Yes, Betty, what's wrong?"

"Captain, we have... we have a 10-78. Officer down... in Garden City!" The woman's words were getting caught up in her throat. She was close to sobbing.

Hall knew it was more than just any officer. Betty would not have called unless it was one of his own. Before he had a chance to ask, the secretary added, "It's Jane!"

Hall could not speak for a moment. Then, "Where's the location?"

"One Whisper Lane."

The man's knees buckled, and he was forced to sit on the grass. Not only was one of his detectives down, but she had been sent to her assailant by his own order! He couldn't get the words out, but his secretary knew the drill.

"I've alerted everyone, and all available units are on their way. Winthrop's ER has been notified and a trauma team is standing by. They're having one of their ambulances already at the high school divert to the address. ETA is five minutes."

Call it adrenaline, call it a sense of duty, but Hall suddenly rose. The fear, the terror, would have to be put aside for the moment. He had to get to his officer. "I'll be there in four!"

One Minute Earlier
1:26:33 PM

"YOU FUCKING BITCH!"

Celine Crowe was not happy.

When I said I'd missed, I wasn't being entirely accurate. I had missed my target, for sure. But, for what it was worth, the blade ended up partially embedded in the woman's right biceps muscle. It had penetrated deep enough for it to remain there, but not enough to hit any major arteries. Painful, I was sure, but not life threatening. The shock had caused her to involuntarily throw her gun about eight feet away. If this were Hollywood, and not Garden City, the gun would have landed near my right hand, I would have picked it up, and shot the fiend. But this wasn't a movie, and the gun was thrown to *her* right side, thus even further away from me. There was no way I could crawl to it in time. I placed my right hand over my wound to again try to stem the blood loss. I didn't have much time left. My assailant, though obviously in pain, was actually grinning.

"You stupid cunt. You can go suck my dick! Do you realize you've just given me the perfect alibi? Or should I say, a perfect excuse for my shooting you. You attacked me! You threw your knife at me! I had to shoot!" She laughed. "It's perfect. No one will doubt me now." And then she went on to rant some more.

I was no longer listening. I couldn't believe it. I had faced so many deadly foes, *Il Fucile* and *Il Boa* just the last in a long line. Yet this godforsaken troll was going to be my undoing. *I'm so sorry Joe, Papà, Mamma. I love you all. Please forgive my failure. And please God, keep the girls safe from this monster.* Then I looked at Jane. There were tears in her eyes now. I leaned toward her, our lips met, and we kissed. A farewell to my friend. My sister.

Out of the corner of my eye, I saw Crowe start walking toward the gun. It would soon be over. I shut my eyes.

Then, I heard the woman stop, suddenly, as a voice came from the doorway—

"You're going to owe a shitload of money to the swear-jar, bitch!"

My eyes opened. I couldn't turn around, but I knew it was Felicity. I could only look ahead and in the wall of mirrors I saw the child partially in the entrance with the rest of her body hidden by a slightly closed pocket door.

Crowe was incensed. "What is this, Grand Central Station? Who the fuck are?... Wait, I remember you now. You're the brat with that mangy mutt who——"

286

Suddenly, there was the low rumble of a growl, and Felicity stepped to her right, away from the door to reveal Maverick at her side. "Now look what you've done. You've upset my dog. He doesn't like to be called names, though 'mangy mutt' is not quite how you referred to him in your office. I think your words were, and I quote, 'my worst, *fucking*, nightmare!'—unquote. Well," she giggled, "I may have thrown in an extra word of my own, there."

The expression of sheer terror that spread across Celine Crowe's face was unlike any I'd ever seen. Felicity, who had been staring at the murderer, now smiled. My *stare-smile*.

If I survive this somehow, we're going to have another long talk. I could not allow her to follow my path into darkness. She needed to live the normal life of a child. She needed what was denied to me. Yet, at this moment in time, paradoxically, what I and Jane needed was for Felicity to harness not her inner child, but her inner Lover Girl...

Or, make that... Lover *Child*.

I saw the woman start to run toward the gun. I calculated it would take her a second-and-a-half. It would be a half-second too long.

And as I calmly slipped into oblivion, I knew no matter what happened to me or Jane, Felicity and Khaleesi would be safe. They, at least, would survive.

For the last sight I could make out was the child pointing with her index and middle finger at Celine Crowe.

And the last words I heard were—

"Maverick—*FASS!*

Chapter 36

Henderson, Nevada
2 PM, Pacific Standard Time

Julie was in the storage room, restocking supplies, when the call came. She picked up her phone and looked at the Caller ID— **Lovelock, Nevada**.

Who the hell is?... she began to think—then realized. *The Lovelock Correctional Center!* The prison, in Pershing County, Nevada, was where her ex-boyfriend, Brett, had been residing for the past two years—and still should be, at least for another three months. Julie had had no contact with him since testifying against the abusive, alcoholic man in court. He'd received a two-to-five-year sentence for armed robbery. A liquor store, naturally. The sentence would have probably been less, but the facts relating to the beatings she had received by his hand were allowed into testimony, despite strong objections from the abuser's court-appointed attorney. That was all the jury needed to justify a conviction on all, including the more severe charges and for the judge to come down with the maximum allowable sentence.

The earliest chance for parole was supposed to be in three months' time. Julie had decided she would not be around, in

Henderson or anywhere nearby by then, just as Angelica had always suggested.

The woman had found a job in Temecula, California. She was to be a check-out girl at a local Home Depot and was planning the move sometime next month. Then she would be free of Henderson and Brett, once and for all. As she stared at the phone, Julie was of a mind to switch it off. But... *what if... no, I have to know for sure.*

"Yes?" she answered, trembling.

"Hey babe! It's your lovin' boyfriend. Miss me?"

Shit. Her next-to-worst fear confirmed. "Guess what? I'm on my way home!" *Oh, God.* Her worst fear, also realized.

"Turns out there's a bed shortage here and, given my two years of *good behavior*, they're letting me out a little early. Can you imagine that—me, good behavior?" He started to cackle. Julie did not respond. She didn't think she could muster enough air to form words, her heart beating furiously in her chest.

"Two fucking years, Julie. That's what your testimony bought me. Two—fucking—years! But hey, no hard feelings, right? I got this buddy who's also bein' released with me. His brother just picked us up and is giving me a lift to Henderson on their way to Phoenix. He's done this haul before and figures in about nine-to-ten short hours, I'll be at your doorstep. Then they're off to Vegas for some fun. But don't worry, *girl*, we're going to have our own fun! I haven't had a woman for two long years, babe, so get ready for some serious fucking! Then, you and me will have a little talk about what you said at the trial. Yeah, you remember our little talks, right?" The tone of the monster's words was as menacing as she'd remembered—*he's got more than talk on his mind.* "See you soon, babe." The call ended.

Julie was still frozen in place. *Fuck, I should have left months ago!* she berated herself. *I should have listened to Angelica right away.* Tears flowed. *Shit, shit, shit. What am I going to do? He's going to beat the hell out of me after he gets his rocks off. Maybe even kill me and bury me in some hole in the desert. I'm not packed, haven't even settled on an apartment yet, let alone the moving van. Even if I could, he'd find me. He'll never let me go.* She drew her sleeve across her eyes to wipe away the tears. Then she remembered:

Call me whenever you need to. Any time, day or night. Promise me.

Those were the words her friend had left her with on New Year's Eve. Now, close to two months later, Julie knew she, alone, couldn't think straight. Any decision made would be out of fear, not logic. She needed to talk to someone. She needed guidance.

She needed Angelica.

Chapter 37

Twenty Minutes Earlier
Surgical Waiting Room—NYU/Winthrop Medical Center
4:40 PM, Eastern Standard Time

Anna sat, her right hand holding Joe's left. Sammy was there as well, all sitting in the brightly lit waiting room. There were only two other families with them, the elective surgeries all completed and now only emergencies occupying the ORs. Jane and Angelica were in two of those and had been for over two hours. In her mind, Anna re-lived the last hours.

She had arrived at the Crowe home in Garden City about forty minutes after hanging up with Angelica. It should have been a twenty-minute ride, but there had been a few detours precipitated by the goings on at the high school, which turned out, she learned, to be a prank.

Stupid fucking kids, she fumed as she heard the report on the radio, turning into the cul-de-sac. As soon as she'd completed the turn, the scene she faced seemed more out of *Die Hard* than that of a normally tranquil, Garden City reality. Instead of Nakatomi Plaza, the towering skyscraper in the Bruce Willis film, there stood the two-story, white-shingled, One Whisper Lane—surrounded by at least twelve cars, many of them police cruisers with their red flashers pulsing. For the first of what would be multiple times in the next few hours, Anna's heart caught in her mouth as she saw, prominently stationed in front of Jane's car, a black van with the words "Medical Examiner of Nassau County" written across the left side-doors. Anna knew enough to know that meant there was a dead body inside the house—maybe more than one. Then she realized she had not heard from either Felicity or Khaleesi for forty minutes. Anna had considered calling as she drove. But fear and the *no news is good news syndrome* had taken hold. Now, the woman realized, *no news* might mean tragedy. She'd later learn her children had their own emotional reason for not calling their mother—they feared upsetting her while driving.

Not allowing herself to be paralyzed by her fears, however, Anna parked at the first open spot and ran to the front door where she was stopped by a uniformed policeman. He would not let her pass, even after explaining her detective wife and their two daughters might be in there. Her voice was shrill, loud, and carried into the hallway.

"Anna, is that you?"

"Captain Hall! Yes. It's me!" The two had met on many police department occasions, the last being at the Christmas party.

The man had been in the foyer, having his own argument with two other men with 'Animal Control' printed over their white coats. He lifted one finger to Anna, indicating he'd be with her in a moment, and finished his conversation with, "Listen, I'm taking full responsibility for the dog. You can have your boss call my boss and we'll straighten it out later, but for now, get the *fuck* away from my crime scene or I'll have you arrested." And with that, he turned and walked toward the front door. He and Anna embraced.

"Where's Jane? Where are my children?" Anna's voice hovered just below the level of hysterical. Just.

Hall had not been surprised with the plural "children," having just completed his first of many-to-come interviews with the two. He was informed of the impending adoption plus the recent chain of events as Felicity had calmly recounted Anna's phone call, Angelica's entry, the gunshot, and Maverick's response to the girl's command. The child had arrived just in time to witness Angelica's desperate throw of her blade.

"The girls are doing fine, Anna. Felicity and... yes, the younger one, Khaleesi, are in there," he pointed to the den. "Jane is at the hospital with the other woman, Angelica. Jane will also be fine, though probably has a concussion and will need some plastic surgery to her scalp. Your friend, I'm afraid... well, I don't know if she's going to make it." He looked down. Anna now vacillated between joy at hearing her family was safe, and horror upon learning about Angelica. "She was shot in the shoulder," he continued. "Hit an artery and lost a ton of blood." Hall was about to take the woman into the den, but Anna quickly found her phone, dived into the contacts and pressed the one for the private number of Tom Smith, the CEO of Winthrop. Within a few seconds, the man was on speaker: "Yes, Anna, what—"

"Tom, listen up." Her frantic yet determined tone of voice quickly told the man this was *not* a social call. "There are two ambulances headed your way. One has my wife, Jane. She probably has a concussion and is also going to need stitching to her scalp. Get your best neurologist, neurosurgeon and plastics man to the ER stat, and get them working on her."

"Yes, right away," the man said.

"Wait! More importantly, is the other woman; she's *very* badly injured. She's in her early thirties. Her name's Angelica Foster. She's my *best friend* and direly needs a vascular surgeon and orthopedics. Shot in the shoulder, arterial bleeding. Lost a *lot* of blood. I don't care if you've got to fuckin' helicopter someone in—she needs the best vascular surgeon you can get hold of, STAT!"

"Okay, Anna, right," the man answered. "In a way, the shit that went down at the high school will turn out to be a plus. We had multiple trauma teams prepared and waiting in the ER for casualties. They're all still there. I'll get in touch immediately. Don't worry, your wife and friend will get the very best care."

"Thank you, Tom." Anna replaced her phone in her back pocket. She saw the admiring but bewildered look on Hall's face and felt she had to explain. "I donate $10 million a year to that freakin' hospital! If I can't call in a favor, now and then..." She let the thought hang. The policeman smiled and admiringly said, "Jesus, if there were ever two badasses who were made for each other, it's you and Jane." He then took her hand and led her into the den. "Don't let the blood frighten you, Anna."

Anna Franklin, RN, a retired ER-nurse herself, was not afraid of blood and was pretty sure the policeman knew this. So, she was surprised by his warning—until she saw her children. Again, her heart leaped upward, and her hand went to her mouth.

Both Felicity's and Khaleesi's jeans were soaked in blood, as was the latter's T-shirt. *Incarnadine* immediately came to Anna's mind, the gore as red as the stains poetically described on Macbeth's hands. She then noticed that Felicity's tee was missing. *Where the hell is your shirt, girl?* the mother screamed inwardly. Felicity wore Khaleesi's light jacket, though, being too small for the older child, it couldn't be fully buttoned. From the waist up, all the older girl had on was the training-bra mother and daughter had both shopped for two weeks earlier. Amazing now, even amid this horror, Anna inwardly smiled as she recalled how excited her daughter had been with the new purchase and how she couldn't wait to get home and *show Mama.*

"Mommy!" both girls cried out when they saw her. They and Anna ran to each other and embraced, Maverick following, rubbing up against Felicity's leg, whining. The three cried and kissed each other. Khaleesi, Jane realized, had also used the title *Mommy.* The woman, now equally embracing both, fully appreciated, maybe for the first time since her and Jane's decision, her new role as mother to another precious child. Anna looked down and saw Maverick's muzzle, also covered in blood, as was much of his fur. She released the girls and removed her long coat, placing it over Felicity. The woman then turned three-hundred-sixty degrees, taking in the entire scene.

A man lay face down, dead, the back of his crisp, white shirt covered in blood; there was an obvious exit wound in the center. Near him was a sight Anna would take to her grave—a woman with a look of absolute terror on her face and... no neck to speak of. Just a tangle of sinew, raw flesh and cruor. She lay face up in a lake of blood, as if her entire body were drained. Later, Anna would learn that both of the woman's carotid arteries were severed by Maverick's sharp teeth. There were also two smaller, but not insignificant, crimson pools where the girls had been standing. Anna shivered when she realized those probably belonged to Jane and Angelica. Amid everything were men and women milling about, taking photos, marking evidence, and yelling orders. Choreographed chaos.

To Anna, she felt she had been thrown into a lost, unknown painting by Hieronymus Bosch: *Three Franklins and Their Dog—in Hell*.

Over the next half hour, Anna learned the basic facts of the story. So many emotions—horror, pride, joy and terror, just being a few. Captain Hall gave them leave to return home, telling the girls they would have to make an official statement sometime tomorrow. Right now, as senior officer at the scene, he had to supervise. There were a dozen detectives milling about, including all from Jane's team and the CSI group (known as FIU in Nassau, The Forensic Investigative Unit). There was also the M.E. to deal with and, to end his *day off*, Hall would call Commissioner Masefield. He'd let her in on the fact her husband's golfing buddy was, along with his wife, dead, and a detective was in the hospital all because Masefield had to *stick her fucking nose in where it didn't belong*, he screamed, inwardly. He was going to enjoy rubbing that nose in all of this. Jane had almost gotten herself killed, and he didn't *give a shit* anymore about pissing his boss off. He'd take the consequences.

When Anna, Felicity, Khaleesi and Maverick returned home, they all ditched their clothes. The girls' had been bloodied by sitting in both Angelica and Jane's blood as they comforted them and, in Felicity's case, as all would learn, helped save her *sister's* life. Maverick joined the three as they stepped into the huge shower in the woman's master bedroom. Anna had first asked if the children were okay with them all being naked together. The two sisters looked at each other and shrugged. "Hey, we're all women here, right?" said Khaleesi.

Anna smiled. *Yes,* she thought, her heart bursting with pride— *my two little women.*

It took a while to get all the blood out of the dog's fur and the kids' hair. But once done, the girls retreated to Felicity's room to change, taking the dog with them. Anna quickly donned a sweater and some jeans, just in time to hear the doorbell ring.

On the way home, the woman had called Joe's office and explained the situation to Helen. Anna was, frankly, glad to leave the notification of Joe and Sammy concerning Angelica's condition to the religious office-manager. Anna couldn't see how she could break the news herself and was frightened almost as much of that than of anything else that had occurred. Helen would tell both men, and, it was decided, she would come to Lake Success and baby-sit the girls while Anna went to the hospital. True, there was the nurse upstairs taking care of Martin Rieger, but that was a full-time job. Helen had agreed to her role immediately and Jane was surprised to see not just her, but Sammy as well, as she opened the door.

"I came to take you to the hospital, Anna. I didn't think you'd be in a safe frame-of-mind to drive. I hope you're not insulted."

The woman smiled. "Of course not, Sammy. Thank you. In fact, I can now take that glass of wine I've been craving and not worry.

I'll be right back, and we'll go. Thank you again, Helen." The two hugged.

As Anna retreated into the living room, Helen removed from her purse a small prayer book, which she kept at the office. She quickly turned to the page marked with a paperclip. Within a few moments, Anna reappeared. She seemingly had just taken a long swig from a bottle of wine and was ready to leave. She noticed the book.

"I brought this, Anna. You remember from last time, the prayers I said, over and over until Felicity was brought home?"

Anna nodded. "Well, there are others; for the sick and infirm. I thought, and I know you're not Jewish but you've told me of your belief in God, you might want, before you left, to join me and Sammy."

Anna was touched. "Yes, Helen. Thank you. I would like that."

Helen smiled and said, "Which way is East?"

Anna pointed, and they stood facing that direction. Sammy reached into his pocket and retrieved a head covering known as a *yarmulka*. "Just repeat after me," said Helen. "I'll go nice and slow." The woman then began the short prayer:

"*Mi Sheberakh...*"

"Mrs. Franklin?"

The man in surgical scrubs had just appeared. Anna stood as he approached. They shook hands.

"I'm Dr. Shear, the plastic surgeon. We're all done, and your wife is headed to the recovery room. Let me first review what was done before surgery to make sure you're up to speed.

"In the ER, Dr. Linderman, our chief of neurology, examined Jane and concurred with the ongoing opinion that she'd suffered a moderate concussion. She was alert, but still not quite totally with it. They rushed your wife to MRI, and the scan showed just a small intracranial bleed on the right side, where she was struck. Linderman, the neuroradiologist and Dr. Small, our chief of neurosurgery, all reviewed the films and agreed—leave it alone and monitor. They'll re-scan before she leaves the hospital, which should be the day after tomorrow. Good chance it will be gone by then or reduced even further. There should be no consequences except for some headaches. She should do just fine. Dr. Linderman was called to another emergency, but he said he'll find you tonight to go over everything.

"Now, to the scalp. As you probably know—I hear you're an RN—the scalp, when cut, bleeds like a sonuvabitch. We had to give her a unit of blood. Your wife had two injured areas."

Anna was surprised. This was the first she had heard of this.

"The first one was where she was struck—I was told it was with a pyramidal, glass object, quite solid. This was the major injury, on the right side of her skull. However, when she fell, she landed on the left, and her head hit something, probably a table or some such on the way down to the floor, also causing a scalp laceration. That was relatively minor and just required twelve stitches. The other, however, was much more involved. Oh, and before you're shocked at her appearance, we had to shave her head, completely, to get to the areas in question." Anna had not thought of this and was saddened. *Oh, my poor Janie*, she thought. *Don't worry, we'll get a new wig*. As if reading her mind, Dr. Shear said, "It will all grow back, though it will take months. In the meantime, a wig can be fitted over the head once the bulky dressing is removed, which should be next week. Anyway, the wound on the right was complex and required not just some fancy stitching but grafting from the left scalp, which, as I said, was minimally injured. It all went beautifully. Though I'm sure she'll want to go with a wig, if she decides on a goth, bald look, in six months you'll never know she had surgery." Both the doctor and Anna chuckled.

"I'll see her tomorrow morning and change the dressing, and then we'll make an appointment for next week to remove the stitches. Any questions?"

Anna was relieved that all seemed to have turned out well. She was somewhat anxious about the concussion and would speak about those worries with the neurologist later.

"No, doctor, I'm truly grateful. Can you tell me anything about my friend, Angelica Foster?"

"The other woman brought in with your wife? No, sorry, I don't know anything except, and this is good news, she's being taken care of by Dr. Edsel, chief of vascular surgery. He's a legend—worked in Iraq and Afghanistan, so he knows a thing or two about gunshot wounds. The orthopod is Charlie Post, best shoulder man around. He did my rotator cuff." Joe's head lifted as he heard the last name. "Oh, I know Charlie." He now stood.

"This is Dr. Joseph Peck, ophthalmologist," Anna introduced.

The men shook hands. Then Shear looked over their shoulders and said, "Oh, there's Dr. Edsel now. I'll leave you to him. See you tomorrow."

And with that, the plastic surgeon left, pointing Edsel at Anna and Joe. Sammy also now stood.

The surgeon, average height, dressed in scrubs, seemed about sixty with mostly gray hair still partially covered by the hair-net surgeons wear. His mask hung from his neck, his expression neutral. He was carrying an opaque plastic bag, its contents unviewable. He looked at the three and said, "Hi, I'm Dr. Edsel, the vascular surgeon. Is there a husband, or," he looked at the elderly Sammy, "a father here for Angelica Foster?"

Joe went first. "I'm her fiancé. Dr. Joe Peck, ophthalmology." They shook hands. "This is her father," he pointed to Sammy, "And this is our good friend, Anna Franklin." Edsel stood for a beat, clearly shocked at the beauty of the woman, but quickly recovered. "Ah, so it's you I have to thank for Tom Smith pulling me out of that boring lecture to the residents. I'm very grateful," he said, now smiling, shaking her hand. Then, "Please, let's all sit down." And the three took a seat along the wall and the physician pulled up a chair to face them. Then he said the magic words: "Well, it was touch and go for a while..."

Everyone breathed a simultaneous sigh of relief. Joe had informed them all, on more than one occasion, that surgeons love to say those words—it makes what they do, though already difficult, sound even more so—but they would only say it if things went well. Still, the man's expression remained neutral, maybe because, they soon learned, his words were all too accurate.

"First," he took the plastic bag and handed it to Anna. "I have a feeling this belongs to your daughter. It's a bloody T-shirt, and I mean real blood, not British-speak." Anna nodded.

"Your daughter saved your friend's life, Mrs. Franklin. Can't say it plainer than that." Joe and Anna looked at each other. "EMS guys told the ER docs your daughter had taken off her shirt, twirled it around a few times, forming a tight, rope-like band of fabric, and used it as a tourniquet. She told them she'd learned how to do it from watching a video in health class. Amazing. I'll have to reconsider my opinion of letting kids watch videos in school.

"Given how much blood Angelica lost, if not for the tourniquet stemming the tide, you'd be planning your friend's funeral. In the ambulance, they infused her with enough IV fluid to float a battleship, and, in the ER, after a second IV was placed, two units of blood were given before I even saw her. We added another two in the OR. Yes, that little girl deserves a medal of honor. As does, I hear, your other daughter."

Anna was surprised. As far as she knew, Khaleesi had just provided Felicity with moral support—important, but not lifesaving.

"You know the chaos those idiots who pulled that stunt at the high school caused, right?" Everyone nodded. "Well, it totally took down the 9-1-1 system. I can tell you this now. A few minutes after Angelica was wheeled into the ER, she went into cardiac arrest. The team did a great job, quickly shocking her back to life. She was only gone for a moment or two. But, if the ambulance hadn't gotten to her so quickly, she would have coded in the house and died right there on the floor. Even with the tourniquet, if she hadn't gotten to the hospital as quickly as she did, she would have bled to death before any ambulance finally arrived.

"The EMS people tell me it was because of your other daughter's quick thinking that they and the police were dispatched so soon. It seems, after not getting through to 9-1-1 she had the intelligence and fortitude to call police headquarters directly and speak with a detective on Angelica's team. Incredible—what resourceful kids. Anyway, the cops called Winthrop immediately and got the ambulance right on its way. If she hadn't thought to make that call, well..." And the man just let the thought hang. Everyone there now knew what both children, mere babes, had accomplished. Khaleesi hadn't even mentioned the call to Anna.

Now I'm really *ashamed of what I used to call her*, thought Joe of Felicity.

"When I first saw Ms. Foster in the OR, I wasn't optimistic. The two units in the ER had helped, and her vitals were stable, but she was still losing blood and her hand was an ugly bluish gray. Cold as ice. I thought we might have to amputate it, maybe the arm as well." No one spoke. They all held their breath. "Luckily, the artery, though nicked, was cut by bone and not directly hit by the bullet. A bullet would have destroyed the vessel and made the procedure much more likely to fail. A bone cut was just that, a clean cut; I was able to easily and, much more importantly, *quickly* repair it. Almost immediately I could see the hand take up some color and now, as I left the OR to come speak with you, I would say the color is almost 90% normal. Better still, the Doppler ultrasound shows excellent blood-flow restored. We're not totally out of the woods, but I would say with luck and a lot of physical therapy, Angelica should have, if not full, *mostly* full use of the left arm and hand. There was a contusion to the median nerve, but they tend to resolve well. We'll see. Tonight, my PA will take Dopplers every hour and will inform me of any problems. I'll see her in the morning and if all is going well, I think she can go home the day after.

"One caveat, though. Once Dr. Post gets done with repairing the bone—he tells me external fixation will be the safest method—Angelica will be taken to MRI. And before you ask, Dr. Peck, yes, Dr. Post tells me with today's orthopedic hardware and MRI technology, it's perfectly safe to use the machine's magnets on your fiancé." Joe nodded. "With all the blood loss, the worry is brain damage. No way to know yet until the scan. The two things she has going for her are her age and the fact she's in extraordinary physical shape." He looked directly at Joe. "She's putting out plenty of urine, and the latest BUN, Creatinine, hemoglobin and hematocrit are fine." He again looked at them all. "The human body, especially one as fit as hers, has excellent ways of protecting its most vital areas. Let's keep our fingers crossed. I expect her to sleep until about 6-7AM. Maybe later. Questions?"

It had all been quite overwhelming, especially for the non-physicians, so Joe spoke for them all. "Not yet, Dr. Edsel. I can't tell you how thankful we all are. I'm sure by tomorrow when we see you in her room, we'll have come up with some. But for now, no. We're just going to sit and wait for Dr. Post to come talk with us."

The man stood, shook all the hands, and left.

The three friends stood and surrounded each other in a hug. After a few moments, Anna said, "I'm going to call the kids, and tell them the good news, then—"

Here comes the sun, do, do, do, do... There was the sound of an obvious ringtone. All three checked their phones and came up empty. "Where the hell?..." Joe began, and then they understood. When Sammy and Anna had showed up in the ER, all of Angelica's possessions, which had been placed in a bag, were given to her father, as next of kin. It was her phone ringing. Sammy removed the phone and looked at the display. "Henderson, Nevada?" he said. The three looked at one another, confused. "I'll go out in the hall," Sammy said, which is what he did, and then answered. "Hello?"

"Oh, sorry. Maybe I have the wrong number," came the female voice at the other end. "I'm looking for Angelica Foster."

Sammy realized who it must be. "Is this Julie?"

"Yes, is this Mr. Foster?"

Sammy realized the woman would certainly think his last name and her friend's were the same. "You can call me Sammy, my dear. Let me say right off a word of thanks. Angelica says you were a great friend to her when she needed it most. I am most grateful."

"You're very welcome, Mr... er, Sammy. Is Angelica around?"

"No, my dear. I'm afraid there's been a terrible accident. I'm actually at the hospital and Angelica is in surgery. Can I help you with something?"

There was a pause at the other end, then, "Oh, my. Will she be all right?"

"Yes, it seems so, but won't be able to talk for quite a while. What can I do for you?"

Julie hesitated. "Please, Julie. Maybe I can help. Tell me."

The man's voice, Julie thought, was kind. A lot like Angelica's during their heart-to-hearts. "Okay, Sammy. I'll tell you everything."

And so, she did.

The man let the woman talk, uninterrupted, and for a few moments, his worry about his daughter was supplanted by his fury at this Brett, another *figlio di puttana* who abused women. At the end, he had to agree with the girl's assessment of the situation. After two years in jail, for which this *animale* blamed her, and given his history, Julie was in mortal danger. She needed a way out—and a way so she would never have to worry again.

She helped save his daughter's sanity. She was there for Angelica.

Lover Boy silently vowed he'd be there for her.

303

"Julie, I think I can help you. I need to speak to a friend and make some arrangements. I will call you back in thirty minutes. No more."

The woman, at first, thought the man at the other end was blowing her off. That once disconnected, she'd never hear from him again. Unfortunately, Julie was all too well experienced with men such as that. Sammy seemed to sense her hesitation. "Listen, my dear, I'm sure Angelica told you about the phone call I promised I'd make, New Year's Eve, right?"

"Yes."

"Well, as you now know, I kept my word. I *always* keep my word, Julie. I will call you back. You should have no doubt."

The young woman thought for a moment. It was not as if she had any great alternatives. Might as well trust in this stranger whose voice she found soothing and trustworthy. *Must be the accent,* she thought. "Okay, Sammy. I'll be waiting." And she hung up.

Sammy returned to the waiting room. Anna was finishing up with the girls who were on speaker.

"Helen will stay with you tonight and bring you and Maverick first thing in the morning. Love you."

"Love you, Mommy," came the response from both.

Anna turned and saw Sammy standing in the doorway. She could see by his face he was troubled.

"What is it, Sammy?"

He approached and took her hand. "Anna, I need a favor."

Julie sat by her phone in the kitchen. It was approaching twenty-eight minutes since the conversation, and she was worrying. Suddenly, the iPhone came alive.

"Hello."

"Julie, it's Sammy. I have two questions for you. One, are you wedded to staying in Henderson for the rest of your life?"

304

Julie laughed. "Henderson? I was about to move to California, so a definite *no* to that. And before you ask, I'm not *wedded* to freakin' Temecula, either.

"Good. I assume you're not particularly looking forward to working at 7-Eleven or Home Depot forever either, right?"

"Right. Why?"

"Okay, Julie. I want you to pack as many bags as you need. If you require more, tell me. In about seven hours, I will be at your home, and we will take a jet to New York, where I have an excellent job waiting, plus free lodging. Also, I guarantee you will never have to worry about that *bastardo*, ever again."

Julie was stunned. "Seven hours? It takes six hours just in the air. You've got to go to the airport, find a flight, wait around, get from the Vegas airport, there's no way—"

"Julie. When I tell you I'll be there in seven hours, you can, as they say in Vegas, 'bet on it.' Just be ready to leave. Okay? You need more suitcases?"

Julie was beginning to believe in this stranger. "No, Sammy. I don't own much. What I have will be plenty. Please, hurry. I'll be waiting."

Sammy returned one last time to the waiting room.

"Okay," said Anna. "Frankie will be here in ten minutes. By the way, he insists on going with you to Nevada."

"He's a good friend. It will be nice having him along."

"The jet will be ready in an hour." She looked at her watch. "It's now six—3 PM her time. Figure five hours flight time or so with this jet. That'll get you there, including an hour drive-time, by 9 PM. Plenty of time to spare, from what you said. The jet will wait for you at Henderson—all night if it must. They'll love it—tens of thousands of dollars an hour of wait time. We'll see you tomorrow when you get back. I'll text you with all the room info later and what the orthopedist had to say. I'm going to be camping out in the hospital all night. Jane should wake up in a couple of hours and by midnight will be transferred to the room I've reserved in the

Penthouse. That's a collection of suites for VIPs. Angelica will probably come a few hours later. If needed, they have ICU capabilities there too.

"But no matter when she wakes, my face, Jane's or Joe's will be the first thing Angelica sees. Once she's in the Penthouse, both of us will be there until that time. You have my word—we won't leave her side."

Sammy, not a man prone to emotion, spontaneously wept. It had been a roller-coaster of a day, to be sure, and Anna, seeing her friend as she'd never had, took him in her arms and they remained as such, for a few moments. Joe watched and was also having a difficult time holding back his own tears. Sammy and Anna separated. "Kiss your wife for me when she awakens," he said.

Anna smiled. "I will, Sammy. I will. Now—

"Go save our girl's friend!"

Chapter 38

The Long Island Expressway
6:15 PM

Sammy had just ended his conversation with Helen. He brought her up to speed on Angelica's and Jane's conditions, though her little charges had already done so after their talk with Anna. Then came the story of Julie. Helen listened attentively, and when Sammy was done, had only one question.

"So, Samuel,"—*Uh oh*, Sammy thought, s*he's entering super-serious mode*—"just how are you going to make sure this, admittedly loathsome excuse for a human being, will never bother Julie again?"

Sammy knew that question would be coming. He had gotten to know Helen well enough to believe, though she wanted an answer, it didn't have to be an exquisitely detailed one. She was willing to accept some ambiguity.

"I'll make him an offer he can't refuse."

Helen laughed. Her favorite movie was *The Godfather*, Sammy knew. She often used that line herself, usually regarding Joe. Then, "Promise me you won't kill him. Please."

Lover Boy knew that request would be coming, too. He answered it, truthfully—"Don't worry, my love. I won't kill him. See you tomorrow. I love you."

"As I you, *meyn lib*."

The call over, Sammy dialed again. It was his past associate's last known phone number—a Brooklyn, 718 area code. Lover Boy knew *Il Garrote,* as the man was called, had moved to Las Vegas in 2012, two years after Lover Boy had retired. If the number had changed, Sammy had other contacts in Vegas he could call upon to

307

provide it. That is, of course, if *Il Garrote* still lived. If he did not, Sammy Vivino had alternate plans. He always did.

Most, when they think of a garrote, think of a cord or wire, maybe a belt that, in the movies, is wrapped around the victim's throat to cut off air and suffocate. A famous example being Clemenza's garroting of Carlo in the car at the end of *The Godfather*. It's impossible to tell from that brief scene, but the ends of the wire or cord are always secured to a few inches of wooden dowel. These dowels, called *garrotes* in Spanish (from which the name of the entire weapon comes), are used to give a secure handhold for the wire. Also, by the crossing of the assassin's hands behind the neck, the dowels could be interlocked and twisted to tighten the wire to a much higher degree than without them. Using the wire without the dowels could cause serious harm to the assassin's hands—not good form.

Il Garrote, whose real name was Mario Baroni, was second only to Lover Boy among the pantheon of assassins in the Esposito Family. Where Sammy was the one the Don called upon for the subtle, made to look accidental, deaths, Mario was used when a statement needed to be made. For *Il Garrote's* favorite material to use was fine, razor-sharp, barbed wire. Within two seconds of its tightening around the victim's neck, the wire would have already sliced through skin and muscle, leaving the carotid arteries exposed and easily severed. Within another ten seconds, enough blood would have been lost to render the victim unconscious; and within yet another twenty—exsanguinated. Depending upon just how long the heart continued to pump after the carotids were opened, the amount of blood found at the scene could amount to a full gallon. Quite a splash, and a scene that anyone happening upon would always remember. Tonight, however, Sammy had something less bloody in mind.

The phone rang and was picked up almost immediately.

"What?!" came the brusque greeting. Sammy had found his man.

"A man of few words, as always. Some things never change, my friend."

"Sammy! As I live and breathe. Long time, *mio amico*. I hate to put you off, but can I call you back in a bit? I'm down *two large* here at the craps table and I feel a winning streak coming on."

Always the gambler, Sammy thought. *And losing. Truly, some things never change.*

"Mario, if I can pry you out of retirement and away from your beloved craps-table for a few hours, I can guarantee *fifty* large for your time."

There was a short pause, and Sammy could hear, "Seven out. New shooter up."

"Shit!" came the loud response over the phone. "Mother-fucker! So much for that winning streak. You'd think God would take pity on me for once."

Sammy chuckled. "Well, my friend, given the Almighty has to keep the Earth spinning and the planets in their orbits, I doubt he really has time to worry about Mario Baroni making his point." *Or, that He has time to worry whether Helen eats some lobster now and then, either*—a theological point he decided not to bring up with her or with the rabbi.

Il Garrote laughed heartily, then seemed to remember an important detail: "You did say *fifty* large, Lover Boy, right?"

"*Si.*"

Baroni took his mouth away from his phone for a moment and was heard saying, "Dominic, get my chips." Then, returning to the receiver, the man added—

"Talk to me, Sammy."

Executive Airport, Henderson, Nevada
8:30 PM, PST

Sammy and Frankie exited their jet and walked the short distance to the Lincoln Continental, standing just off the runway. The door opened and, looking no different from he did when last seen, ten years earlier, at Sammy's retirement dinner, Mario Baroni emerged. As imposing as ever, the ex-prize fighter turned assassin was six-foot-two, and, though slightly over his fighting-trim weight, appeared in excellent shape. Turns out the man still spent an hour with the heavy-bag each day. The other twenty-three, it seemed, were spent at the casinos. No one who knew him ever had seen him sleep.

Behind him was a younger man, also impressive in physique. *Could be another fighter. Or a bar-bouncer,* Sammy thought.

The older men looked at each other and embraced. After a few words, Baroni then similarly greeted Frankie. "Nice to see you again, Larry."

During their cross-country trip, the two friends had discussed the obsolete moniker and decided it wasn't worth explaining the change. So, for the next few hours, Frankie was again, Limo Larry.

Il Garotte then introduced the other man. "This is my son, Dominic."

The man approached Sammy. "Mr. Vivino. It's an honor to meet you, sir. I can't believe it—the legend, himself. Dad talks about you all the time." The men shook hands and then Dominic moved on to Frankie. "And you too, Larry. Dad has many fond memories of sharing car rides with you during the day." Frankie laughed. "As do I, Dominic. Nice to meet you."

"Okay," Mario said. "My younger son, Luca, is already on the girl's block, at the end, just in case the *figlio di puttana* shows early. If he does, Sammy, Luca's orders are to put a bullet in the back of the head before he gets to the door. From what you said, we can't allow him to enter, right? Too dangerous for the girl." It now seemed to Lover Boy that *Il Garrote,* and he, for that matter, might be better described as *semi*-retired. Baroni's sons, though, seemed fully immersed in the Las Vegas crime scene.

Sammy reluctantly nodded in response, and then they all entered the Lincoln. The jet would refuel and be waiting when they returned.

Baroni handed Sammy the gun. "A Glock 26. Couldn't get a suppressed model. Not enough time."

"That's fine, Mario. It's only for show anyway, I hope. You have what *you* need?"

Il Garrote nodded, then gave Sammy a slip of paper. "Here are my bank routing and account numbers."

"Good. I'll text the info to my employer on the jet-ride back. She will have already wired the fifty thousand in the morning by the time your bank opens. You should find it in your account then. If not, give it to noon, your time. She tells me it can take a few hours. If it's not there by then, call me and she will have her banker's balls in her hands within minutes, squeezing so hard you'll hear the screams at the craps table."

Baroni laughed. "I'd like to get a look at this woman who can command so much cash *and* not hesitate to grab a man by his *coglioni* when need be."

Now Sammy laughed. "My friend, she is indeed a sight to behold."

Julie went to her door and opened it. The man looked exactly as she'd envisioned him from her friend's description. "Sammy," she said, with relief. Brett had not yet arrived.

"Yes, Julie. This is my friend, Frankie." He pointed to his companion.

311

"Nice to meet you, miss."

"You too, Frankie. Come on in, both of you."

The men entered. It was a small basement apartment, the upstairs belonging to an elderly couple. Julie felt bad about up-and-leaving, but she had written a check for a month's rent and placed it in their mailbox with a note thanking them for their kindness over the years. She didn't bother telling her new boss at the 7-Eleven— *fuck 'im* was her thought on that.

Her ex-boyfriend was due in one-two hours, based on his approximation. Julie offered the men some wine, which they refused. They wanted their wits about them, even if the heavy lifting was being done by others. The young woman was packed and ready; four suitcases in her bedroom contained all her worldly possessions. When she had finished packing, the sadness of that fact was almost overwhelming to her.

Now Julie, Sammy, and Frankie sat around a small living room table. They left the front door ajar for Brett to enter. Mario and Dominic waited across the street in the Lincoln, the black car being inconspicuous on the dark, minimally illuminated street. Luca remained at the far end of the block in a small moving van which contained only a large wardrobe.

Since they had time to kill, Sammy decided, given Julie would soon become a member of his extended family, the woman should be made aware of the Vivino/Fortuna history. It was only right. So, over the next seventy minutes, Lover Boy told his, Angelica's, Frankie's, Joe's and the Franklin's stories. The entire time, Julie sat, transfixed. When it was over, Sammy stressed the necessity of keeping what she had just learned within this small circle of friends. She understood.

"I would die before I'd put Angelica's life in danger," she said.

And Sammy believed her.

————————————

A few minutes after Julie had reassured Sammy, they heard a car pull up to the front of the house.

Looks like he's here, came the text from Mario.

"Okay, Julie. First, let me have your car keys, please." The girl complied. Then, "I want you to go to your bedroom and stay there. Do not come out until I get you. Understand?"

Still reeling from what she'd recently learned, the woman nodded and made her way to her room. Sammy found a more comfortable chair to sit on and removed the Glock from his pocket. He placed the weapon on his lap and covered it with a People Magazine found nearby. Frankie stood unseen behind a pillar in the kitchen. Mario and his son would wait until Brett had entered and then approach from the rear.

There were sounds of men talking. A car-door slammed, footsteps were heard and then a young, bearded man entered after pushing the already partially opened door wide. Brett was tall and muscular.

Two years using the prison's weight room, Sammy surmised. *He'll be a challenge.*

"Honey... I'm hooome," he mockingly cried—and then saw the elderly man sitting before him. He moved slowly into the room. "Who the fuck are you, grandpa?"

"A friend of Julie's."

"A friend?" Brett snorted. "Is that what they're calling it these days? I knew money was tight, but I never pictured Julie with a Sugar Daddy. Well, can't say I blame you, old man. She's sure a fine piece of ass. But the good times are over, so beat it before I make you wish you never met the bitch."

Sammy had placed another chair in the middle of the room. He pointed to it and said, "Sit down, Brett."

The man was immediately incensed at being spoken to in such a manner. He was about to advance when Sammy pulled the magazine off his lap and pointed the Glock at his target.

"Whoa, pops. Relax! No need for that. Why don't we—"

"Sit! I won't ask again."

Brett sat. Beads of sweat began forming on his forehead.

"So," began Sammy. "You're what passes for a man these days. You get your kicks by beating on women, Brett?"

The man, though wary of the gun, still seemed unable to grasp the situation he was in. His acceptance letter to MENSA would be a long time in coming. "Only when they deserve it," he laughingly answered. "Which is often, in my experience." Sammy, proud of his own vocabulary's growth after years spent perusing *Reader's Digest* Word Power sections, was surprised the man's lexicon included a term longer than two syllables.

Mario and Dominic entered, making enough noise for Brett to turn and notice. Finally, the man understood that maybe, just maybe, a change in attitude might be prudent.

"These are my friends, Mario and Dominic. They too find creatures such as you an insult to our sex. Yes, men such as you don't deserve to live."

That last phrase was the clincher for Brett. Now, terrified, he began his plea.

"Look, mister. I'm sorry I hit Julie, okay? Really. I swear I'll never do it again. On my mother's grave. In fact, just let me leave and I'll get out of town, way out. Julie will never see me again. I SWEAR! PLEASE DON'T KILL ME!"

Sammy was all-too-familiar with the lies of desperate men. He looked at the pathetic abuser and smiled. Then he lowered the gun, and his eyes.

"Oh, don't worry, Brett—I made a promise. I'm not going to kill you."

The young man smiled and gave a nervous laugh.

Sammy looked up. "*Mario* is."

Almost simultaneously, Brett's smile disappeared, and he began to turn. Before the head could rotate ten degrees, *Il Garrote*, the years in semi-retirement not diminishing his skill, looped a thin, steel chain around the victim's neck. He simultaneously kicked the chair out from under Brett and, as he fell, the chain immediately tightened. Mario twisted the thick dowels attached at the ends, but the younger man fought tenaciously, kicking with his legs, now untangled after his fall. Dominic came from behind and grabbed the left leg, but the right escaped him. Frankie quickly emerged and took hold of the free one. Mario continued to tighten the chain until a "Crack" was heard—Brett's larynx, crushed. The abuser still fought but was tiring quickly as air was no longer entering his lungs. That, plus the pain of the cracked bone and the realization he was going to die, together, triggered a surrender response and within a few more seconds, the body went limp. Unconscious, it took Brett three more minutes to die.

"Jesus!" said Mario as he removed the garrote. "He was a tough one. Quite a workout, eh, boys? I think I can skip the bag tonight."

One more hour at the tables, Sammy thought, smiling.

Mario went to his phone and texted his younger son. Within seconds, the boy, all six-feet-four of him, was at the door with a large wardrobe and hand truck. He introduced himself to Lover Boy and Limo Larry and expressed his honor and delight in meeting them. The brothers then lifted the body into the box, righted it and placed it on the dolly. Sammy handed Julie's car keys to Dominic, and the two brothers quickly wheeled the makeshift coffin out and into the van. Anyone who happened to look out their window would see a team of movers merely transporting a standard wardrobe to its destination. The older son would take Julie's car and the younger would drive the van.

Sammy handed the Glock to Baroni. "So, it's a *Goldfinger* for Brett, correct?"

Mario smiled. *Goldfinger* was one of his favorite movies and it had introduced him to what would become his preferred method of body disposal. The corpse would be taken to a local wreckage/salvage dump, placed in Julie's (once Angelica's) car, and run through an industrial car-crusher. The small, one-ton cube that emerged would be placed on a flat-bed truck and driven to the desert. Already, a hole was being dug by two other associates of Baroni. By the time the brothers arrived, the task would be completed, and they'd dump the cube into the freshly prepared grave and replace the dirt.

Julie's abuser would bake in the desert heat, encased in, and fused with steel—along with countless others—for all eternity. Or, until being unearthed by some centuries-in-the-future archeologist, after which Brett and his cube might make a fine museum attraction.

Even the worms probably couldn't get to all those potential meals, Mario had often thought.

Sammy knocked on Julie's bedroom door. "Julie, it's Sammy. Time to go."

The girl opened the door. Sammy introduced Mario and the three men each took one of her bags. She saw no blood, or any evidence of a disturbance, Sammy having righted the chair on which Brett sat. There'd be no signs any crime had been committed to follow Julie on her journey.

"Is he gone?"

"Yes, Julie. He'll never bother you again."

Considering the story Sammy had recently told, Julie didn't ask for any details. She went to Sammy and hugged him. "Thank you, Sammy," she said, tearing up. She kissed him on the forehead and repeated the sequence with Frankie and Mario.

"Let's get the hell out of here," she said.

And that's just what they did.

It was 12:05 AM and, as three hours before, in New York, Wednesday the 19th had arrived—

A new day.

Chapter 39

February 19
NYU/Winthrop Medical Center—The Penthouse
8:00 AM

I'm still alive.

At least, I thought I was. Given that what presented itself to my eyes (after the few seconds it took for my vision to clear) was so contradictory, I couldn't be sure. On one hand, it seemed like I was in a hospital room. I heard beeping machines, could feel small objects stuck to my chest, and my right arm attached to an intravenous line. My left arm appeared to be encased in something metallic out of a science-fiction movie. Yet, on the other hand, not only did the room seem part of a larger suite, as decorated and spacious as one might find at a Four Seasons Hotel, but Maverick (in his Service Animal jacket) lay at my feet in Felicity's lap—on my bed! What kind of hospital has rooms that look like this—and allows pets? Was I in Heaven?

Then I remembered what hospital was nearest to Garden City, and who its major benefactor was. So, I guessed I was in a heavenly hospital suite—being friends with billionaires has its privileges.

As my wits further emerged from the haze of unconsciousness, I realized my right hand was being held by another who sat in a similar bed to my right. I slowly turned my head to see.

Jane! She was alive as well. That, more than realizing my own survival, caused my heart to soar. I *was* curious, though, as to what was up with what looked like a mini turban on her head.

"She's awake!" I heard Khaleesi cry, and then Maverick started barking. Felicity moved him off the bed, handing the leash to Anna

317

and both she and her sister rushed to either side and gently hugged me, which wasn't easy given my left arm's enclosure and the IV and Jane's hand in my right. I kissed them both on the cheek, over and over.

The two girls reluctantly gave up their spots at my side as they saw Joe enter. He had been in the kitchen—yep, you heard me right—preparing coffee for the others and had heard the commotion. He bent over me and we kissed for a long, long time. I could hear the children giggling. Then he gingerly stepped back, carefully avoiding my bionic left-arm.

"I look like the Borg Queen," I said, referring to the leader of the part-human, part-machine enemies of later-day Star Trek fame. Joe smiled and said, "Actually, I prefer to think of you as *Seven-of-Nine*"—the most famous and beautiful member of the Borg Collective. He bent down to whisper in my ear. "I always fantasized about fucking *Seven-of-Nine*, you know."

"I heard that!" screamed Felicity. Khaleesi, who hadn't, grabbed her sister's hand. "What did he say, what did he say?" she breathlessly asked. Felicity cupped her hand over the younger girl's ear and whispered. Khaleesi jumped back, eyes widened, and smiled. Then the two broke out in hysterical laughter.

"Okay, girls, enough of that. Joe's got some swear-jar donations ahead of him." It was Jane, on my right, still holding firmly to my hand, and smiling as widely as I'd ever witnessed. "Welcome back to the land of the living, Angelica," she said. We stared at each other for a few moments, and then were joined by Anna, who had passed the dog off to Felicity. She took her wife's hand in her left and mine in her right, then bent down and kissed me lovingly on my mouth, followed with the same for Jane.

And then we all began to cry.

After Helen had given me a hug and plenty of kisses, I realized someone was missing. For a moment, not believing he'd not be at my side, I was frightened.

"Where's *Papà*? Is he okay?"

"Don't worry, Angelica," said Helen. "He's on a bit of an errand. He just texted me from the airport and should be here shortly."

"Airport?"

"You'll see," said Anna. "It's a surprise."

Despite the strong mien I tried to present to my friends, I was still too exhausted to argue, so I instead asked the woman to give me a rundown of all that had occurred. I remembered entering the house on Whisper Lane and seeing Jane on the ground in a pool of blood; but the rest was a bit hazy.

Anna complied with my request and by the time she was through, about thirty minutes later, one thing had been made crystal clear to me—if it weren't for Felicity and Khaleesi, both I and Jane would be dead. I motioned with my right hand for the girls to approach and gingerly lifted my Borg arm and my right to allow for them to rest on my breasts, after which both arms came down, surrounding them. I kissed them both on their foreheads and, some of the ESP Anna and Jane shared must have rubbed off on us as we looked each other in the eye, and then simultaneously voiced the one word which bonded us now, and would continue, for the rest of our lives—"Sisters."

"Knock, knock." I knew that voice. "*Papà!*" My father stood at the door to the room, partially blocked by its frame. "I have a visitor, *mia cara*," he said with a twinkle in his eye. Then he entered, his hand holding another's.

"Julie!" The word came out with difficulty, wrapped in a sob of joy. Maverick barked and ran to my friend, getting up on his hind legs, placing the front paws on her chest as he began licking her face, just like he had with Felicity in Boca. I saw the just mentioned girl and Khaleesi look at each other. They nodded, smiling, and then moved away to join Anna.

"Hey, buddy," Julie happily greeted my dog. "You miss me?" And for a few seconds, she massaged his neck while *Papà* and I greeted each other with kisses. Then, finally getting Maverick down, Julie approached, made an exaggerated move to avoid hitting my left arm, and we hugged. "Damn, girl. You look like the Borg Queen!"

Is it any wonder she and I got along so well?

"Actually, Joe prefers *Seven-of-Nine*." And I pointed to my love. Julie turned, and realizing she was looking at my fiancé, approached and embraced him.

"You're a lucky guy, Joe. Angie's a lot hotter than *Seven*. Just so you know, Doc, if you do anything to hurt my girl here, you'll have to deal with me—and it won't be pretty. She may be Queen Borg, but I'm Lady Terminator."

Everyone laughed. I asked Julie how this was all brought about, and she re-created the entire story, from Brett's phone call to *Papà's* and Frankie's intervention. *Papà* turned to Helen. "Have no worries, my love. I didn't kill him." *Hmm*, I thought. *He lingered ever so slightly on the "I" word. We'll talk later, in private.* Quickly changing the subject, my father said, "Julie, let me introduce you to your new employers."

Employers?

Papà first pointed to Anna. "This is Anna Franklin, and," he turned, pointing to the bed beside me, "that's Jane Rieger-Franklin." Julie first approached Jane. "I'm so happy to hear you're doing so well, Mrs. Franklin."

"*Jane* is fine, Julie. Welcome to the family. I wish I could get up to give you a big hug, but I hear that's not allowed quite yet. I'm sure Anna will make up for it."

Julie turned as Anna approached and she did, indeed, hug the girl. Tightly. "Welcome, Julie. I never would have considered someone to replace Marta while she's away. But knowing how close you were to Angelica, I was sure you'd be perfect. Now, after meeting you, I *know* you'll be."

"Thank you, Mrs.—"

"*Anna*, please."

"Thank you, Anna. I really can't thank you enough," she turned, "and Jane," she turned back, "for this opportunity. I promise I'll do my best for your children."

Anna smiled and looked toward the aforementioned duo. They approached. Julie figured the older one would set the tone for the other, so she outstretched her hand. "I assume you're Felicity. It's so nice to meet you."

Knowing she would be the toughest one to woo, everyone in the room seemed to stiffen in anticipation of Felicity's response. And then relaxed, as the girl reached out her hand, saying, "Any friend of Angelica, and Maverick, is a friend of mine." She melodramatically shook Julie's hand. Khaleesi didn't bother with shaking hands. She just approached and gave Julie a warm hug. "Nice to meet you too, Khaleesi. You, me, and Felicity are going to have so much fun together. We may even let Angelica tag along now and then, too."

Anna, to put it mildly, was greatly relieved. "As you know, Julie, this is just temporary, for, we think, about six months, until Marta returns. We've moved her belongings into storage, so you can fix her room up as you wish. We thought a reasonable starting salary would be $2,000 a week. Is that satisfactory?"

Julie's mouth opened in shock, and quickly closed. "Oh, gee, I don't know. That would be a yearly rate of about... over four times what I was making at 7-Eleven. In Henderson. Instead of here, within spitting distance of The Big–Freakin'–Apple!" My friend smiled. "Yeah, I think it will be satisfactory." Julie and I—two sarcastic, yet loveable, peas in a pod.

"By the way, I'm Helen," the one remaining un-introduced person in the room began. She took Julie's hand. "Oh, yes, Helen. Sammy told me you and he were a couple. You must really be quite a woman for him to go through the conversion he told me about. Especially considering the... you know." She smiled.

Helen turned to my *padre*. "Can we adopt her once we're married, Sammy?"

Everyone laughed, but Helen was not finished. "And have no worries, Julie. Joe and I have been talking. I've *repeatedly*," she gave her employer one of her Medusa-like stares, "asked about getting me some help in the office. So, when Marta returns, you can, if you wish, join us. *No* decrease in salary, *right* Joe?"

I could see my man, though he agreed with the job proposal, felt meeting Anna's salary offer was a bit much for an office-worker. He looked at me and our own ESP went into overdrive. He turned to Julie. "Of course, Julie. Of course." He silently mouthed to Anna—*Thanks a lot!*

Just then, another knock on the door.

"Captain Hall!" Jane exclaimed. She tried to sit up in the bed.

"At ease, Rieger. For Christ's sake, at ease."

He approached Anna, and they hugged. "Well, it looks like the gang's all here. What a suite of rooms this is. I may decide to retire here." Everyone had a chuckle at that and for the first time, I noticed the man carried two manilla envelopes.

"Felicity Franklin and Khaleesi Fell, please step forward!"

The two girls looked at each other, then, holding hands, tentatively approached the captain. He reached into one of the envelopes and withdrew two diploma sized pieces of yellowish-green parchment. I could see elaborate, printed lettering on them plus a red, white, and blue ribbon attached at the bottom of each.

"As Captain in the Nassau County Police Department, I have been authorized to present Felicity Franklin and Khaleesi Fell our department's highest civilian honor—the Certificate of Valor—presented to those who," he now read from one parchment, 'showed extreme courage and valor in the face of grave danger, aiding and assisting an officer of the Nassau County Police Department.'"

He presented the awards to the girls, then saluted. Despite their precociousness and, at times, wisdom beyond their years, I was

322

reminded that deep down, my "sisters" were mere children and, as such, responded to the captain's presentation as most children would—they returned his salute. Then they ran to Anna to show off their precious mementos, then to Jane and me, beaming as much as I'd ever seen them.

"Wait until I show Mommy!" Khaleesi exclaimed. We all knew which Mommy she meant, and we were all, Anna especially, happy for her. Joyful that Khal felt she could bring her dying mother some happiness in her final days.

I could see Jane give Captain Hall a knowing look and an almost imperceptible nod. She knew no such award existed. It turns out, the captain was first in line at Staples when it opened at 7 AM in Garden City Park. There, he purchased the proper paper. He had spoken to Tony the night before, and the two men met at 7:15 in the office of the *Intel Group* where the tech-expert printed the certificates and affixed them with the ribbons the captain supplied from a stash he had in his office.

Maverick sauntered over to Captain Hall once the man was alone. "Hey, boy." Hall reached into his pocket and came up with one of his own dog's treats. He presented it to my pet who proceeded to gobble it down.

"Let me first allay any fears about Maverick here. I've just come from a meeting with Commissioner of Police Masefield and the Superintendent of the Animal Control Unit, a man older than Methuselah who should have been put out to pasture years ago. He was livid I had summarily dismissed his representatives, who appeared at that house of horrors to take Maverick away. I explained to him my reasoning—

"When I arrived at the scene, my first course of action was getting to Jane to see how badly she was hurt. Once ascertaining she was alive and, despite the blood loss, conscious and fairly lucid, I examined the other survivor." He glanced my way. "I saw the tourniquet had stopped much of the bleeding and figured all I could do was more harm than good, so I waited until the ambulance came, which was within a minute—and directed them to take you first after having called in another for Jane." I nodded—his decision also was likely lifesaving. "I then quickly took in the surroundings, saw the dead woman and the dog. It didn't take a genius to see what had occurred. Yet, here sat that dog, in a young girl's lap, as calm as could be. I recognized Felicity and could see she recognized me from the various police department parties we'd both attended. She said, 'Maverick,' then pointed to me, then to her heart, and said, 'Friend.' The dog approached and started sniffing at my pocket. I realized I had Sally's, that's my golden retriever, treats still on me. I handed Maverick one, who took it greedily and then started to lick my hand.

"With two tours in the army, the last in Iraq, 2003, with a canine patrol, I know a well-trained dog when I see one. There was no way Maverick would have attacked the woman unless ordered to. I saw Jane's gun just inches from the woman, a dagger sticking out of her arm and a knife sheath attached to," he turned again to me, "your calf, and put two and two together, realizing little Felicity here had ordered Maverick to attack. She later confirmed everything. When those dolts from Animal Control came, I explained the situation, but they had their rules and were sticking by them, insisting the dog come with them. After *dissuading* them, they left, obviously running to their *daddy* to complain. Thus, the meeting first thing this morning in Commissioner Masefield's office. Jane, you'll be surprised to learn that Masefield backed me to the hilt and essentially told the Superintendent to *go fuck himself,* er, sorry Anna, Jane," he contritely added, nodding at the girls.

"Don't worry, Captain," Anna said. "Jane and I have given up trying to shield the kids from profanity. They could probably even teach *you* a few choice words."

Hall smiled. "So, Maverick is officially exonerated, and no one will take your dog away from you, Angelica," he said, again looking my way.

"Thank you, Captain," I said. "I'm most appreciative."

"Yes, well, I'm also appreciative. That was quite a throw of yours."

Uh-oh. "Well, I *was* aiming for the bitch's heart."

"So I would have thought. Still, given the loss of blood, the pain and your position on the floor, it was a miracle you could even hit her and, fortunately, knock the gun from her hand. Yes, quite skillful... as I would expect from one as trained as Angelica Fortuna."

Shit. The room became quiet as the grave. Even Maverick lay down on the floor, making no sound.

"When I first arrived and saw Jane, the girls and you, Angelica, I asked them if they knew who you were. Felicity, though putting up a brave façade, I could see was, as Khaleesi, terrified—of losing her mother, and you. Not thinking, she blurted out the name Angelica Fortuna, then quickly caught herself and changed it to Foster. But the cat was out of the bag."

I looked over at Felicity. Tears began to stream from her eyes. "I'm so sorry, Angelica," she said, now sobbing uncontrollably. "I didn't mean to." And she ran to Anna and buried her head between the woman's breasts."

I knew, from my own childhood, the most cathartic place to cry was within a mother's embrace.

"Don't cry, sweetie," I immediately said. "I know you didn't mean to. It's no problem. I could never be mad at you." Felicity continued to sob, though more quietly.

"Anyway," Captain Hall continued, "the name was unfamiliar but after some Googling and with the help of the FBI's organized crime database, I learned quite a lot about the daughter of Don Vito Fortuna, not the least being that she was supposed to be dead. Her date of death was clearly listed at about seven months ago, just a month or so before a remarkable crack-down began on the Philadelphia Mafia. Assuming the news of your death was incorrect, after all, here you were in Garden City, I could only assume you had entered WITSEC, as payment for information used to come down on the Philly Mob. I know a bit about the program, and they never relocate anyone within a thousand miles of where they lived before. So, if you were in New York, it was probably because you no longer requested protection. Then I found out about the death of your father, just shy of New Year's Day. If you don't mind my saying so, the world is a better place for it."

I stared at the policeman. "Don Vito Fortuna was *not* my real father, Captain. I'm as glad he's been sent to Hell as anyone."

Finally, I seemed to have produced the tidbit of information Captain Hall lacked. I saw him nod, then look at *Papà,* the only one close to the age of a possible parent. He approached Hall and offered his hand. "Sammy Vivino, Captain. I'm Angelica's true father. Nice to make your acquaintance." They shook.

"Sammy Vivino. Now *that's* a name I *have* come across—I started my career in Brooklyn." He paused, then, "Remarkable. Well, I can see where your daughter's skills come from."

The room continued to hold, what it seemed, its collective breath. What was this man going to do with this information? I had acted in self-defense, true, but I was a civilian now, as Agent Simons had warned. I no longer had government protection and *could* see how a case could be made against me, if so desired by an ambitious prosecutor. Also, Hall could easily blow my cover if he wished.

The cop went to the other envelope, opened it and removed its contents, placing them in my right hand. A lump quickly formed in my throat—*Needle!* She was in the sheath *Papà* had gifted me. I looked, bewilderingly, I'm sure, at the Captain of Detectives.

"I signed out your dagger. After the official inquiry, I'm sure it would be returned, anyway, though to be official, an ADA Release form will have to be submitted. I can't really get into any trouble from signing it out, unless you decide to take off with it and disappear. I'm hoping you won't."

"Have no fear, Captain. I'm here to stay. Getting married in a couple of weeks, in fact."

"Well, congratulations." He looked around the room and, since Joe was the only other male, he smiled at him and nodded, seemingly as much in admiration as anything else. *Men!* "I knew your having a knife on you was one thing. It alone could be explained away, though it being a combat dagger will be a bit of a problem; but I could finesse it. *But,* with such a professionally made sheath, form-fitted to your calf, well, that could be problematic. Questions might be asked, ones I could not deflect. Too risky. So, I removed it and placed it in my pocket before anyone else could notice it. As far as the official report, it never existed."

I was having a problem controlling my emotions. Tears were forming as I asked, "Why?"

"Yes, Captain," added Jane, also seeming to suppress tears. "Why?" She had never known her captain to do anything, if not *by the book.*

The man, now looking older than when he first entered, sat on the edge of Jane's bed, and continued.

"When I was in Iraq, I saw my share of death. Much too much. Men in my squad, as well as others. While it was occurring, you said to yourself, 'this is what war is.' And you dealt with it. But when I returned home, call it Post Traumatic Stress Disorder, whatever, but I was in a bad way. I had been a police officer when I enlisted and returned to my post, here in Nassau County, and hid my PTSD as best I could. For years, I succeeded. I moved up the ladder, and, just four years ago, made captain. But just one year after, disaster struck. Two of my detectives, during an arrest, were killed. Even though it was before you joined us, Jane, I'm sure you've heard of it."

Jane nodded.

"That was, as they say, the camel that broke the back of my PTSD. I went into a severe depression, took four months of disability leave, and even though the psychiatrist reported me fit to resume duty, I seriously considered resigning. Just couldn't take the thought of losing another under my command. After my divorce, they were the only family I had." He paused for a few long moments. Then, "But I was persuaded to return, by none other than Commissioner Masefield."

I could see Jane was surprised at this revelation. "Janet and I have had our clashes over the years, as you know, Jane. But she herself has not been untouched by tragedy in her life. Her son, a uniformed cop in the NYPD, was killed in action seven years ago. She, too, fought the same inner battles. So, she understood where I was coming from—and would not hear of me giving up, as she had not. I've been forever grateful to her for that, which is why, despite my seeming hostility toward her now and then, I have a soft spot for the woman. I know, despite at times acting in ways seeming to the contrary, Janet has the best interests of the men and women of the force at heart.

"Anyway, two weeks ago, when some of my men came under fire and, for a few moments, I was unaware of their condition, the old feelings, the old fears started to creep to the surface. Yesterday, when I heard *you* were down, and that *I* had possibly, *unnecessarily*, sent you to your death, I fell to the ground outside my house. Don't know where I found the strength to get up and get myself over to Whisper Lane. But I did, and learned the details from these two brave girls here."

Captain Hall now stood and approached me. "If it weren't for you, Angelica, selflessly and fearlessly, at your own peril, entering the fray for your friend and finding the strength to act even being almost mortally wounded, I would have lost another of my officers... another of my family. I have no doubt it would have finished me. Who knows what I would have done? Resign, certainly. Drink myself to death, probably. I've been in AA since the war. Slit my wrists?... He just let that hang. Then, "I don't care what you've done in the past, Angelica *Foster*. When my officer needed a guardian angel, you were there. You saved her—and, in so doing, you saved me, as well." He wiped his now wet eyes with the back of his hand. "Maybe Jane, Anna, one day you'll tell me how all your paths crossed in the first place."

Maybe, I thought. *When you're retired, though.*

"Anyway, considering your prowess with the knife, and I'm sure with the gun, as well, if you ever want to consider doing some more good with your life, Angelica, the head of the police academy is a friend of mine. Just say the word, and a spot will be opened for you. I'll even, upon graduation, make sure you're placed in our building, where Jane and I can *both* keep an eye on you." He chuckled.

"Thank you, Captain," I said. "I will consider it." And I would.

Hall now turned to Anna. "Anna, please have Felicity and Khaleesi come to 1490 at noon. One, I need to take their official statements. And two, I hear Jane's team has some more awards and presents for them."

I saw the two smile, Felicity no longer in despair over revealing my past identity.

"Speaking of the team, they'll all be here later, Jane, after shift." And with that, he started to leave, but then stopped and turned.

"By the way, I spoke to your neurologist this morning. Assuming tomorrow's MRI is good, he's given you the green light to return to work on Monday—desk duty. Two weeks there and then you're good to go. It'll give you time to fix up your office."

"Office?"

"Oh, yeah, guess I forgot. After the Superintendent left, Masefield and I had a long talk. She was devastated that she had let her personal feelings almost get you killed. You can expect a visit later and, I'm sure, a departmental commendation with TV cameras, news crews, the works. So, as a firm believer in never letting the commissioner's guilty conscience go to waste, I asked her to first call the Civil Service Chief who confidentially confirmed what we already figured—you'd passed the sergeant's exam. But, I'm not in the mood to see you go back to the bag, so I strongly suggested that Masefield use her vast discretionary powers to assuage her guilt. And she readily agreed."

Captain Hall reached into his pocket, brought out a blue and gold shield, and tossed it on Jane's lap. She picked it up. On top was printed, "Nassau County Police Department," and on the bottom: "Detective Sergeant." For once, since I've known her, my friend Jane was speechless.

Hall, despite being of higher rank, saluted. "Congratulations, *Detective Sergeant* Jane Rieger-Franklin."

Felicity and Khaleesi looked at each other and joined the captain at their Mama's bed. And saluted.

The room erupted in applause as tears came to Jane's eyes. Anna was first with a kiss, then Joe, Helen, and *Papà*. I grabbed her hand and squeezed as tightly as I could.

Hall turned and was on his way out when Felicity said, "Captain Hall. You should stay a while. You're almost family, after all. I know you're on duty and all that shit—er, stuff, but..." she went to a chair upon which sat her backpack. She opened it and withdrew what appeared to be a cooling sleeve. I learned later it contained a gel in its lining which, when frozen, kept whatever bottle of liquid you placed within it ice cold for hours.

"I took the liberty of preparing this last night once I heard all was well." Felicity unzipped the sleeve and removed a bottle of Dom Perignon 2010. She held it up for all to see, and smiled—

"Champagne, anyone?"

Epilogue

"Motherhood: all love begins and ends there."

~Robert Browning

Friday, February 28, 2020
NYU/Winthrop Medical Center
9 AM

Two days before my wedding and here I was, sitting in my neurologist's waiting room. After Dr. Linderman, there would be a trip to the lab for blood and urine to check all sorts of shit, including liver and kidney function, plus blood counts. Finally, another MRI of the brain to wrap up the ideal way to spend the second to last day before one's wedding.

A spa day would have been nicer, don't you think?

Anyway, my first scan, as an unconscious inpatient, was normal. But now, if there were any subtle brain damage, some evidence would show. I *felt* fine but was occasionally having brief bouts of nausea. Google found it could be a symptom of post-concussion syndrome and, though it wasn't on my list of official diagnoses, no one could be sure. I did fall and hit my head after being shot, after all. Brain damage or late bleeding could, depending upon where situated, lead to queasiness. I was anxious, especially this last week; COVID, and the threatened lockdowns, might interfere with the wedding. It would be just my luck, right?

Joe, who'd be taking a week off after the wedding, was having quite a busy time in the office. All the women, and everyone else in my circle, were also having a hectic day with final preparations. So Frankie had driven me to the hospital and would pick me up when I was done. Waiting here gave me a chance to reflect on the past week.

About twenty minutes after Joe had opened the champagne bottle—Captain Hall, still in AA, politely passed on drinking—Frankie, Linda, Tony, and Morris arrived. Anna had called the latter three the night before to fill them in, after learning that Jane and I were out of immediate danger. She had arranged for a jet to fly them out at 6 AM, but it was delayed by a typical deluge of South Florida thunderstorms. Frankie had picked them up at the airport.

After discharge, the next days were a whirlwind of pre-wedding preparation. Morris stayed with Joe and me. Tony and Linda, with the Franklins. The childless visiting couple doted on the kids, especially Khaleesi, who they had just met. Linda took them on multiple shopping jaunts at the mall. It was too late for Julie to get a custom-made dress, so Anna arranged for one off the rack. Of course, what you and I might consider *off the rack* differed greatly from what my billionaire friend contemplated. She took Julie to the most chic and expensive bridal store on Long Island and the latter tried on many pre-made gowns before deciding. Then, it was just a matter of two days for the minor alterations to be made. My bridal gown was altered a bit, too. The left sleeve was removed at the shoulder and replaced with one that ended just above my external fixation hardware. The seamstress could have extended it over my Borg arm, but Julie thought the whole sci-fi/Tim Burton-movie-bride look would be a sight to remember. And it was.

An official inquest exonerated me of any faults regarding my actions at One Whisper Lane—the testimonies of *Sergeant* Rieger-Franklin (I really like saying that), Captain Hall, Khaleesi and Felicity all dispositive to the final verdict. The latter, young participant in the deadly doings in Garden City, was also cleared of any misconduct in unleashing Maverick—clearly, self-defense. Even Commissioner Masefield testified as a character witness on my behalf after a meeting at the hospital where she greeted me as Jane's savior, tears in her eyes. She asked no questions regarding my past—and I proffered no insight. Don't ask, don't tell, right?

"Angelica?" It was Dr. Linderman. He accompanied me to his exam room and, after thirty minutes of poking and prodding, I was pronounced "remarkably, neurologically sound." He inquired about the arm, and I related that, at my most recent visit, Dr. Edsel was very encouraging. As was the orthopedist, though, this damn contraption on my arm would be with me for at least three months.

The neurologist was optimistic the labs and the MRI results would agree with his conclusions. As he sat behind his desk, he checked off some entries on a pre-printed list of blood and urine tests. I asked about the queasiness, informing him of my Internet searches.

"Google—the bane of my existence! Here's some advice, my dear. Spend the next week in bed with your new husband and don't even think of turning on your computer or searching your phone for any medical advice." We both laughed, though I saw him check off another box on his list as he did. "I've got a while until my next patient. I'll walk you to the lab and after, just ask the technician to point you to MRI. I'll call you if there is anything to be concerned about. Else, I'll get in touch on Monday—later in the day. You'll probably want to sleep-in for a while." And he smiled again. I liked Dr. Linderman—he had a dirty mind, just like me.

I left the hospital after depositing my blood and urine and laying, conscious this time, in that God-awful, claustrophobic MRI machine. These things have been around for decades—you'd think someone would have come up with a way of taking these pictures without putting you into a freezing coffin for an hour.

I know, I'm ranting. But I'm getting married in two days and am freaking out!

Frankie picked me up and I took his arm. He's a good friend. It was about noon, and I asked, "You hungry, Frankie? Lunch is on me."

"I could eat."

I smiled. *Frankie could eat—all's well with the world.*

By Sunday afternoon I'd be Mrs. Angelica Peck. No hyphenations for me—I'm an old-fashioned girl. Angelica Foster, as Angelica Fortuna was my past. I planned for a long and happy future with Joe. Just the two of us, so much in love.

Man plans...

Sunday, March 1, 2020
Lake Success
1 PM

Angelica, her flower-girls and bridesmaids, were ready to go. They had spent the day in Julie's room at the Franklin home, getting their makeup and hair done. Anna had hired her stylist, who came with *seven* assistants. Getting the bride into her dress was a challenge with the added hardware surrounding the left arm but, in the end, looking into the full-length mirror, she'd almost broke down in tears. In her gown, makeup and hair, turning slightly sideways to hide the bionic arm, Angelica looked as she'd always dreamed, since she was a child, of looking on her wedding day.

The weather had cooperated—no snow or rain and the temperature stood at forty-three degrees; not really a problem. The Franklin's had erected two heated tents in their huge backyard, one small one for the service and a larger one with a wooden floor for the reception and dancing. For Morris's sake, a rabbi would perform the ceremony and for him, Morris, Helen and, yes indeed, Sammy, the food would be strictly kosher. The Franklins suggested and everyone agreed to invite Agatha Monroe to the festivities. Jane had quickly developed a soft spot in her heart for the lonely woman who, unfortunately, was born too soon and had to hide her and her lover's relationship through the decades. She also hoped having a grandmother figure in her children's lives might be of benefit. Her own father was rapidly deteriorating and couldn't even be brought down to the wedding of her friends.

There was a knock at the door and Joe entered. The girls started throwing excess flower-girl mini bouquets at him. "Get out of here," Julie said. "Bad luck to see the bride right before the wedding!" The rest of the friends started berating him as well.

Joe held up his hands. "Okay, okay. Just letting you know. Five minutes to showtime." And then he quickly left.

"Okay, ladies. Time to go." Julie was getting into the spirit of being the maid of honor. Just then, Angelica's phone, which she'd silenced and placed on a night-table, started buzzing. She was going to ignore it, but something in the back of her mind prompted the bride to say, "You guys go ahead. I'll just get this and be there in five."

The others all thought she was crazy, taking a call minutes before her wedding, but gave in and departed. "Five... fucking... minutes, girl," Julie admonished.

Angelica looked at the display—Dr. Linderman. He had given his patient his cell number, and it was added to the phone's contacts. His words on parting came back to her: *I'll call you if there is anything to be concerned about.*

Please God, not now. Not this day, she thought. She answered the call.

"Hello... Yes, Dr. Linderman... No, it's okay, we haven't started yet. I didn't think you'd call unless... Oh, I see. Blood test?... Are you sure?... You repeated it... All right, I'm glad you called. I understand not wanting to wait... You have the name of someone I can use?... All right, I'll check your text and call tomorrow to set up an appointment... Yeah, in five minutes, actually... Thank you... Okay, thanks again for calling... Bye."

Angelica slowly put the phone down.

Shocked and temporarily paralyzed by a tsunami of emotions, she sat on Julie's bed—and cried.

I dried my eyes, quickly fixed my makeup and joined my friends, only three minutes late. If I'd waited any longer, Julie would probably have thought I had last-minute cold feet and would have come to slap some sense into me. All the guests were seated, and the string quartet started to play. First came Khaleesi and Felicity, the flower girls—Maverick walking between them. They were so beautiful, throwing small bouquets of flowers along the path. Marlene Fell had been able to attend and, seated in her wheelchair, beamed as her treasured daughter made her way down the aisle. Khaleesi threw the woman a kiss as she passed.

Then came Linda, a bridesmaid, with Tony, the best man. They were followed by bridesmaids Jane and Anna. All the women were radiantly dressed, courtesy of the Franklins, and the men were GQ handsome. The detective sported the long, black wig she had worn on two other important occasions—Felicity's rescue and Don Fortuna's demise. She was superstitious and felt changing her *coiffure* for another special occasion would be unlucky. Finally came Julie, arm-in-arm (in a last-minute decision), with Harold. He and the rest of the Intel Group had already been invited, so my friends and I asked him if he'd accompany the maid of honor down the aisle. Jane, Anna and my ulterior motives were obvious, I would think. So far, so good. I'd noticed them talking during the rehearsal and they seemed to be getting along just fine. Both were nerds, which also was a plus. I *so* hoped they would hit it off.

Next came Joe and his father. They walked together and then waited at the altar, er, *chuppah* as it is called in the Jewish religion— a canopy under which the couple stands composed of cloth stretched and supported by four poles.

The musicians switched to *Here Comes the Bride* and I and *Papà* walked halfway down the aisle. He lifted my veil.

"*La mia bellissima angioletta.* I love you with all my heart and wish only the best."

"And I love you too, *Papà.* You have no idea how much." We both were tearing up

He kissed me on each cheek and lowered the veil. Then he walked on to unite with the others. Joe moved to join me, but his father stopped him and whispered in his ear. Joe looked stunned, then grinned. Later, during the reception, I asked Tony what Morris had said. The answer: "This time, don't fuck it up!" I love that old man so much.

Joe met me, and I took his arm. We walked together to the *chuppah*, and upon arriving, Julie straightened my train.

Tony produced the rings with no frivolities—I had warned him beforehand a fate worse than death awaited if he fucked around. The ceremony went smoothly, the rabbi speaking and singing. We had memorized our lines the night before—the clergyman granting us dispensation to say them in English rather than Hebrew. Joe started with, "Behold, with this ring you are consecrated unto me, according to the Law of Moses and Israel." Then, it was my turn: "I am my beloved's, and my beloved is mine"—from Solomon's *Song of Songs*.

Finally, the rabbi took a small glass, wrapped it in a cloth napkin and placed it on the floor between Joe and me. Then, with one quick and forceful move (it would be more than a little embarrassing if he botched this), Joe stomped down, breaking the glass. This end to all Jewish weddings is to remember the destruction of the two Jewish temples a couple of thousand years ago. To allow a moment of sad reflection, even amid a joyous occasion. Talk about a mood-killer!

It seems most modern-day Jews don't have a clue to that explanation. It's just become a tradition. Don't know if that's a good or bad thing, but for me, I just wanted this all to be over. I needed to talk to Joe. Alone.

So, with the successful smashing, the room erupted with the established response—"*Mazel Tov!*" It means *good luck* but it is often, as now, used as *congratulations*. Joe and I kissed and, to the applause of all, walked briskly back up the aisle to Julie's room, now referred to as the Seclusion Room, again, as per tradition.

Joe closed the door behind us and grinned.

"You know, way, way back, I'm pretty sure the new bride and groom were supposed to consummate the marriage in this *room of seclusion*. Almost sounds like a *Harry Potter* title."

338

"In your dreams, Dr. Voldemort," I said, grinning. "It took me almost an hour to get into this gown, so unless you have some magic spell for removing and replacing it, it's on for the duration."

Joe took me in his arms, and we kissed, oh, so passionately. "Hello, Mrs. Peck. Has a nice ring to it, no?"

"Just as long as Ace never refers to me as Mrs. *Pecker*, we're fine."

Joe laughed and said, "Well, if we're not going to do *the nasty*, we might as well greet our guests." And then he took my hand and turned to the door. I stood fast.

"Wait, Joe. I have to talk to you about something." I led him to Julie's bed, still holding his hand, and we sat. He could tell something important was coming and said, "What is it, Angie?"

I took a deep breath. "Right before I came out, I got a call from Dr. Linderman, the neurologist." I paused.

"Yeaaah," he said, drawing out the word for an extra moment.

"He said the MRI was fine, and that all the other tests were negative, too. Except, that is, for one result from my bloodwork. He felt it was important enough to call me on my wedding day."

Joe stared. Then, grabbing my other hand, as well, he said, "Angie, whatever it is, we'll get through it together. I know tons of specialists. We'll fight this and win..."

He continued to speak rapidly, and I realized, *Shit, I'm such an asshole.*

"No! No, Joe," I interrupted. "I'm so sorry, so, so sorry."

Joe looked at me, now completely befuddled. I brought both his hands up and kissed them. Then, I told my new husband, who I loved with all my heart, what Dr. Linderman thought was so important I had to be told, even on this, of all days. "Joe," I began...

:

:

:

:

"I'm pregnant!"

339

Acknowledgments

First, let me repeat: Lover Child is a work of fiction. Although some of the named places, such as cities and states, obviously exist, the events described that occur in each of those places are the imaginings of the author and any event that might coincide with actual events are purely coincidental. Any structures or buildings mentioned may, by chance, resemble true structures or buildings at or near the locations cited, but again, the structures and buildings in this novel, as well as the story itself, are totally fictitious and imaginary.

And finally, any resemblance of the characters in Lover Child to real persons, living or dead, is purely coincidental.

Now that we've gotten all that out of the way, let's get to it. As mentioned in past acknowledgments, when writing a novel, an author creates a fictional story, parts of which may involve stretching the truth to fit the story. For example, there is no Penthouse Wing at any hospital that I know of on Long Island. However, the idea was based upon a real VIP patient floor I encountered during my medical training when rotating through a hospital on Miami Beach. So I moved that wing about fifteen-hundred miles north. Also, those sharp ones among you who have read the previous entries in the *Lover Boy* series, and have done the math, may have noticed that a year has been added to the ages of Felicity and Khaleesi. Though I've met many intelligent pre-teens in my career, I felt making both girls slightly older would make their precociousness a bit more plausible.

As far as *thank-yous* go, the first, as always, goes to my very patient wife who had the thankless job of reading and re-reading the manuscript, correcting my grammar and spelling while providing story improvements and catching logic flaws along the way.

For legal advice, I thank my cousins Michael Shapiro and Steven Chase. For educating me about Marlene's cancer, I thank Ear Nose and Throat specialist, Phillip Perlman, M.D. And for insights into orthodox conversion, I again thank Stacey Teich, my office-manager throughout my entire medical practice.

As in the previous Lover Boy novels, thanks go to Dr. Leonard Marino for aiding with Italian grammar and word selection.

I'm pleased I can finally thank retired New York State Police Captain, Jose Febo. His contributions to making the organized crime and police procedures in each of my novels as accurate as possible have been invaluable. He is now head of *Advanced Proactive Solutions* in Manorville, NY, a firm specializing in investigations, and litigation/conflict strategies consultations. I know of no one more professional and honest than that man.

For *Lover Child*, with much of the action occurring within the boundaries of New York City, I was also very lucky to call upon the expertise of retired, NYPD Detective 2nd Grade Todd Heiman for all my questions regarding homicide investigation in NYC. One of New York's Finest.

As for those police procedures, sometimes I had to stretch the truth regarding them to better fit the dramatic narrative. Any minor inaccuracies are on me, not my consultants.

By the way, for those of you who think there's a French error in Chapter 32, where B.B. says "*mon cher*" to Tina Thomas, you're correct. This was done purposely, and meant to be a clue (among others, sprinkled throughout the story) that eliminates B.B. from suspicion. The murderer proved knowledgeable of the correctly gendered "*ma cherie*" when addressing Melinda-Ann in her apartment—B.B. showed he was not.

So for those who realized this discrepancy and scratched B.B. off your list of suspects, nice catch. For those interested in some of the other, admittedly, subtle clues, you can e-mail me at the address that appears at the end of the page after next.

Also by Stephen Kronwith, M.D.

Lover Boy (2020)
Lover Girl (2121)

About the Author

Stephen Kronwith, M.D., Ph.D. lives in Floral Park, N.Y. Born in Brooklyn, he's had an unusual career, including working as a university professor of mathematics, a programmer for IBM and, for 31 years, as a private/university-based pediatric-ophthalmologist. He had wanted to write a novel for many years but just couldn't find the time until recently. He started writing *"Lover Boy"* six months before retiring and, though complicated and slowed by being among the many healthcare professionals working in the hospital and office during the early, hectic months of the COVID crises, he completed the manuscript about eight months later. Writing *"Lover Girl"* went a lot faster, with retirement and COVID restrictions allowing little else to do, as did *"Lover Child,"* this third entry in the *Lover Boy* series.

If you wish to get in contact with the author, he can be reached at:

LoverBoyBook@gmail.com

Made in United States
North Haven, CT
19 February 2022

16278922R00189